RABBIT'S EROTIC
FANTASY

OMA PUBLISHING COMPANY
Seguin, Texas

Printed by CreateSpace - An Amazon.com Company

Library of Congress Cataloging–in–Publications Data
De Georgio, Gina
Rabbit's Erotic Fantasy / Gina De Georgio

ISBN 978-0-9747175-1-7

Erotic Romance – Mature Audience

RABBIT'S EROTIC FANTASY

GINA DE GEORGIO

ONE

Upon awakening I instinctively reach over to touch him. The bed is warm but Pep is gone. Turning, I spy him through the open bathroom door in the shower. Even through the cloudy glass door his naked silhouette sends a shiver of desire through me.

"Damn, why didn't I wake before him?" I mutter to myself. What's the point? It would be the same evasive reaction: "Shit, I'm late. Got to move it," he would say and hop out of bed without as much as a gentle good morning cuddle. What the hell is going on this last few months? *Make that a year or more*, my conscience pipes in.

I release a breath of tension as my continuing frustration is already reaching the boiling point. This is going to be another glorious day in the life of sex-deprived Gina as she weathers . . . *Oh, give it up, Gina*, my inner voice demands. I sit up in bed. Pulling my knees to my chest I feel the nipples of my bare breasts harden against my thighs as he steps out of the shower.

In spite of being married to Giuseppe Wabbit for over fourteen years, he still looks as young as ever. His wet hair loops around his ears framing chiseled cheekbones, dark piercing eyes and an Italian nose that he is not particularly fond of. A recently grown beard and mustache add a roughness to his sexiness and his smile silently demands attention—like nibbling his lower lip.

My heartbeat quickens and desire floods my belly as I watch him dry himself with a large bath towel. Jeez, it would be great to be that towel, rubbing over every inch of his body. It's as if his every movement is coordinated solely to spring within me a need to touch him, to feel him.

Naked, he leaves the bathroom with a nonchalant grace that emphasizes the firmness of his thighs and the slimness of his hips and abs. Preoccupied in thought he is unaware I am awake.

He opens the top drawer of the chest, takes a pair of black bikini underwear and slips them on. A strange shiver runs down my spine and settles as a knot in my stomach as I bite my lower lip. Wow, I'd love taking them off with my teeth.

He retrieves a white dress shirt from the closet and slips it on without bothering to button. He chooses a conservative blue tie, drapes it over his shoulder and grabs a pair of black slacks off the hanger. Stepping into them he loses his balance, takes a couple of hops–steps and crashes into the wall with a thud. He chuckles and looks over to see if he woke me.

Upon seeing me watching a wry smile crosses his lips. "Graceful, huh?" he says absently as he buttons the shirt and tucks it in his pants.

"But intriguing to be sure," I offer coyly, arching a mischievous brow. Shit, I have to get him back into bed before I explode with frustration. I plant both feet on the bed, spread my knees slightly and lean back demurely on my elbows. "You know you could easily have stumbled into bed. I would've provided an interesting landing."

For an instant he studies me, looking down into my eyes, his face unreadable. My heart sinks when he turns away as if I hadn't spoken. Gazing in the mirror he knots his tie without as much as a glance at me.

The knot in my belly leaps into high gear and I feel as if my body is turning in on itself, imploding—white clouds rolling and turning gray as they engulf me, wrapping my body in a chill. *Damn, Pep. Stop it! Don't do this to me! Don't do this to us!* I scream inside. I quickly slide beneath the covers pulling them over my head, trying to ignore the latest rejection and quell the sexual desire engulfing me.

I momentarily hear Pep leave without comment. Damn, damn, damn. I can't take this any longer. Something's got to give and soon. I've felt that our problems would pass but we're drifting further and further apart each day.

Sex has become almost nonexistent. It's dwindled down to maybe once a month and there is no spontaneity or excitement. It's as if we're just checking it off lately to get it out of sight. It's to the point that I have to beg or badger him for that basic check in the square fuck. Why do I bother? I feel like I'm slowly withering away inside.

I had originally blamed our problem on the increased stress that both of us are under. I know we've had our priorities mixed up, putting our relationship on hold to deal with other so–called pressing things. But, I wonder if there are other issues involved? I've tried to discuss it but he refuses saying that things will work out in time. They've become progressively worse.

The whole scene is really getting bad when I find masturbation is more gratifying than sex. At least my fantasy lover is definitely into it and always available. I can reach an immediate physical release. However, the relief is usually short lived and the pleasure is vastly tempered by the lack of emotional calmness only achieved by the clash and ultimate release of sexual energy by two mating opposites.

That's my source of continuing frustration. Will I ever experience that blissful, overwhelming, orgasmic high again? I run a lone finger up my inner thigh until I reach my fantasy place.

> *I wake in the middle of the night by the light teasing touch of his hand on my breast as I lay on my side with my back to him. My heart leaps as I feel his warm breath against my neck and his building erection pressing against me. I take his hand and guide it down over my belly as I turn on my back and spread my legs.*
>
> *He briefly runs his fingers through my soft pubic hair before gently thrusting two fingers into my warm wetness that awaits him. The sensation spirals with the light massaging pressure of his fingers increasing in tempo, quickly bringing me to that point of no return. I run my hand over his hip and firmly grab his upper leg, urging him over on top of me. I raise*

*my legs and with both hands guide his welcome
hardness into me. Moving my hands to his hips,
I pull him deeper, then relax my hands, allowing him to slightly withdraw, only to repeat,
orchestrating each increasingly harder thrust
as our bodies melt together in growing ecstasy.
Shit, this is unbelievable. Unable to hold back
any longer as we lose control, we explode together in a flood of fiery sensations. I cry out in
a burst of pleasure as I completely lose myself
in a downpour of relief and complete content-
ment.*

"Mom, are you sick?" a cheery voice wakes me.
Temporarily satisfied by my fantasy lover, I fell asleep,
forgetting I have two kids that need to be roused out, fed
breakfast and sent to the school bus.

I peer out from under the covers to find my eight–
year–old daughter Donna eyeing me with a stern quizzical
brow as if she is the mother and I'm the wayward child.

She is dressed for school in yellow jeans and a
blue cotton shirt with a picture of a multicolored rabbit on
the front, and her usual pink Chuck Taylor canvas shoes
and orange socks. She has her dark hair braided into pig-
tails tied off with red ribbons. Nothing ever matches with
this child but that's the way she wants it.

She has a heavy, dark brow over gorgeous brown
eyes with long lashes and a decent size nose unlike mine
and Pep's. She did get my mouth which has a natural
pouty look and she uses it wisely, especially on her father.
By the way, the family and her friends call her Bunny.

I throw the covers off, gearing for my supermom
role and she, as usual, is fascinated by my nakedness.

"Yes, Bunny Wabbit," I answer before she asks,
"for the hundredth time, I like sleeping nude because I like
the way the sheets and covers feel, and no, I will not catch
a cold without pajamas."

Also, it's none of your business but it's easier to
get a little in the morning if I'm naked and ready when the
opportunity arises. Which it hasn't lately. *So, what else is
new?*

Donna flashes a knowing grin as if she read my thoughts. "We're late," she says dryly.

"Is Don up?" I hop out of bed and slip on my robe.

"Yes, he's eating cereal. I've already had mine."

"Great. Sorry I overslept. I don't want you to miss your bus."

"That's alright. You can take us," she nods with tight determined lips, "since it's your fault."

Yes, mother dear. "No, that won't work. I'm going to be late getting to the office as it is. So get your butt in gear and get out to the bus stop."

"Oh, I forgot, today is Monday."

"I have my usual pow–wow with John and the other brains at ten o'clock, so I have to get going as soon as I can," I answer as we head for the kitchen.

"Mr. John. He's cool. He likes you, I can tell by the way he looks at you."

Where is this heading? "He's my friend. Of course he likes me. We've known each other a long time, since college before you were even born."

"Okay," she shrugs indifferently as we enter the kitchen, just like her father on occasion when he acts like he knows what's going on but doesn't have a clue.

Given a nickname of Jack—as in Jack Wabbit—by his friends when he started school at age six, Don, my ten–year–old son is sitting at the breakfast table. He has long dark hair that he annoyingly refuses to keep brushed and we on occasion call him our mountain man.

Otherwise he is his father's son as he has many of his dad's characteristics, mainly Italian with the dark eyes, sculptured face, large nose and very sensual mouth, even as a child. He is tall for his age and seems a bit awkward at times keeping his legs untangled. Like his sister the way he dresses does not register very high on his priority list, so it's not unusual for him to be completely uncoordinated in what he wears.

As both Don and Donna are miniature copies of their dad with the same characteristics and mannerisms, most of the time I know what to expect from all three.

"Sorry I overslept, Jack."

He nods, but doesn't look up from his cereal and the magazine he's thumbing through. Donna swings her pack over her shoulder, forces a heavy sigh and makes a production of rolling her eyes for my benefit. And, of course, there's the pouty mouth. I nod at her, reach over and close the magazine.

"Move it. You're going to miss the bus."

"Gotcha, Mom." He grabs a piece of yesterday's cold toast and flashes his dad's smile as he stands and reaches for his book pack. "Go, Bunny girl," he says as he motions toward the door.

He pats me lightly on the butt as he passes. "Bye, pretty lady."

"Bye, I think," I mumble, my mouth agape. What was that all about? He's ten. What are they teaching . . . ?

As the shower warms up I slip off my robe and intently gaze at myself in the mirror. Umm, not too shabby. Thirty—six—years old and I've still got it. I put most of the local bikini laden college babes here on the lake to shame in spite of birthing two kids. I've maintained the same weight and curvy figure that tapers into legs that I've always thought were a tad too long. Pep disagrees. He says my legs are the exclamation point to the rest of my sexy bod, and he loves to have them wrapped around him when we get it on. *Umm, how long as it been since that's happened?*

I ruffle my straight dark hair and let it drop back into place. I'm glad I cut it short several years ago. It's so much easier to manage. Pep finds it much more sexy short and likes to grab a handful during sex. *But, not lately. Why not?*

Nice breasts, though not as large as I would like. Pep calls them my champagne glass boobs and likes to lick that last drop. *Damn, go for it.*

My heavy Italian brow and dark eyes I like a lot, but that slightly large nose, like Pep's, I could do without. According to Pep I have a mouth that appears to be set in a permanent pout that he finds incredibly sexy. How long has it been since he's mentioned anything about me being sexy? *Shit. Why the hell not?*

6

"Yeah, why the hell not, Pep?" I shout as I enter the shower and close the door. As the warm water engulfs me I quickly lather my body with a shower sponge soaked with my favorite body wash. This is exquisite and if I weren't already pressed to get to the office on time, I would spend a few more glorious minutes at that fantasy place. Wouldn't it be great to have some guy do this for me, to me? Well, shit, I guess I do have it bad.

My inner voice pipes in: *Some guy?*

Yes, some hunk of a guy. I can't take this any longer. If Pep doesn't desire me there's got to be someone out there that does—that wants to touch me, to feel me, to screw me, and everything else me. I want someone, now, that will do whatever it takes to satisfy me. Because it's apparent that you don't care to, Pep.

My conscience is working overtime: *What about the vows, Gina? Isn't this called infidelity, disloyalty, betrayal or just plain old cheating?*

Yes, and fucking yes. But what about me? How long should I have to wait before I have my needs taken care of—to get laid when I want and in the way I desire?

This is going to be guilt city, the inner voice is pressing on. I'll handle that later. Right now, it's all about me and what my needs are. I want to fuck and be gloriously fucked again and again. *Wow, you've got it bad.*

As I step out of the shower and dry myself, I suddenly feel elated about my decision to take charge and be proactive in finally getting some relief from this incredible sexual tension that seems like has been going on forever.

So, Miss I–can't–take–this–any–longer, how are you going to get laid?

Well, since I've been out of circulation forever, I know that the right guy isn't going to just show up because I'm ready and willing. And how will I know when any guy is the right one for that matter? I guess I need a plan. *A plan? This is ridiculous.*

Finally leaving the burg of McQueeney at nine o'clock, I make my way to Interstate 10 for my weekly forty–five minute trek west to San Antonio to meet with Jonathan Bales and his executive board. At this time of day traffic is light on 10, so it is usually a good time for me to turn off the technology, tune out the world and focus on me and mine.

This morning is no different because of the crazy decision I have made to go against all my past beliefs about love, honor, respect, and of course, sex in the marriage relationship.

Maybe I can get some input from Jonathan. God knows we've cussed, discussed, or shared everything we've experienced about love and sex except actually having sex with each other.

But you must not attempt to make him part of the solution. In doing so you could destroy your friendship and your job.

Yeah, thanks, but bug off.

What a history Jonathan and I have. We met early in our freshman year at Texas Christian University in Fort Worth. Both having decided on journalism as our major, we volunteered to work on the university newspaper. Four years we worked alongside each other, laughing, crying, doting, partying and occasionally feuding.

We were good friends and still are today, despite two ill–fated times we hit on each other, both ending in absolute rejection and embarrassment. Needless to say since the last fiasco we are strictly hands off. There is still, however, a latent desire for each other as even my eight–year–old has observed.

After graduating from TCU I moved to San Antonio and stayed in my old room at my parent's until I found a job with a commercial realty company. My boss Pep Wabbit and I hit it off immediately.

He, being full-blooded Italian, is the grandson of Alfonse Lunetta, who fled for his life from Italy in the late thirties or early forties because he spoke out against Benito Mussolini's National Fascist Party. Upon reaching the United States he was told by family left in Italy that the assassins were still determined to find and kill him, even in the United States.

He decided for his safety he should change his name. On a lark, after seeing a movie theatre Looney Tunes cartoon featuring Elmer Fudd and Bugs Bunny, he changed his name from Alfonse Lunetta to Alfonse Wabbit as in pesky wabbit. Really brilliant, Alfonse.

Pep and I married after six months of courtship. I switched from my beautiful Italian name Gina De Georgio to Gina Wabbit. Thanks, Alfonse. That was brilliant.

Now, fourteen years later, college buddy Jonathan is my boss and my employer as owner of Bales Publishing, the company I work for. He moved to San Antonio after conning his family to finance his buyout of a local publishing company.

A few years later, his business thriving, he, his wife Link and a one–year–old child moved their residence to Lake McQueeney from which he commutes daily to his business in San Antonio. Shortly after their move and at the Bales' urging Pep, I and our one kid moved to the lake, as luck would have it, next door to the Bales.

The kids and adults of the two families thoroughly enjoy spending time together both on and off the lake and often share vacations. Jonathan's wife, Link, and Pep have insisted from the early days of the two families' relationship that there be no boring shoptalk during our outings and gatherings. Jonathan and I agreed and have stuck pretty much to that agreement.

Jonathan's a great guy to work for since we seldom see each other at work except for our weekly executive board meeting and an occasional lunch to discuss my work or whatever madness we want to share. I have no regular supervisor other than Jonathan because of the nature of my job as liaison with our offices which are now located globally.

My duty is to monitor glitches in ongoing projects and referee feuds and disagreements between employees, supervisors and departments in the different offices worldwide.

Jonathan says my main job is to troubleshoot and do the dirty work so he doesn't have to. He has a chain of command which I am, to the consternation of the other four board members, number one behind Jonathan.

When Jonathan is out of pocket or on vacation, it is my duty to take over in his place. I have done so several times, but I feel uncomfortable in that position because I get no support from the other execs who feel they are better qualified. Experience wise, they have a point, but it is what it is. I am, by Jonathan's choice, their superior in the company. All in all I enjoy my work although I have to travel on occasion when I'm unable to solve the problems by use of modern technology.

Along with other unrelated projects, BP owns and publishes sixteen different magazines in several different languages. The weekly and monthly publications cover a range of subjects including health, men and women's issues, sex, lovelorn, the music industry, fashion, Hollywood, the gay and lesbian world, and auto mechanics among others.

I've worked for BP for twelve years except for time off to birth two kids. Even though I have an office on the fifth floor of our headquarters, I work my own hours and I do most of my work at home. I like my job and Jonathan says I do excellent work.

I am certainly aware that many of the other sixty–four local employees are jealous of my position with the company. Too bad. I deserve everything the company offers because I work hard. Also, I know the boss well and he likes me—so says my daughter.

It's always a bit nostalgic when I arrive at the intersection of Broadway and Austin Highway in the San Antonio suburb of Alamo Heights as it was my old stomping ground as a youngster. I graduated from high school there before leaving for college in Fort Worth. However, I no longer have any close ties left in the area as my friends have all moved on as well as my parents who relocated to the hill country northwest of San Antonio.

Arriving at the large parking lot at Bales Publishing headquarters on Austin Highway I park my Mercedes in my reserved parking space close to Jonathan's. This perk does not go unnoticed and is also cause for consternation from employees, especially since I seldom use it.

The two story foyer of BP's seven story building provides a nice welcome to visitors and employees alike. Windows from floor to ceiling on two sides shower adequate light to the jungle of trees and plants scattered throughout the large reception area. The receptionist's mahogany desk and work area, and two elevators occupy the west wall. Elaborate leather sofas and chairs are spread out among the forest.

When I walk through the front door, an old friend and longtime receptionist rises from her desk. Behind her a uniformed security guard, Clement, is leaning against the wall drinking coffee out of a Styrofoam cup. As I approach both nod and the elderly receptionist, Jo Beth, or JB as she prefers to be called, smiles a genuine welcome, unlike what I'm used to by most of the other employees.

"Gina, good to see you. Missed you last week," she exclaims, looking over her wire rim glasses as she extends a fragile, vein streaked hand. "Mr. Bales just called to announce that he has canceled the executive meeting and that you should come on up when you arrive. He doesn't have any other appointments today."

Great. I need his undivided attention. I nod as I release her hand. "You're looking good. How's Chester?"

JB shakes her head and twists her lips in mock disgust. "The old fart's cantankerous as ever. But, he's all I got, so I put up with his bullshit." She suddenly grins, "And Pep?"

"I tend to lean toward asshole these days, but that's another story," I retort, bringing a chuckle from JB and the guard. "Anything exciting happen here lately?"

JB releases an exaggerated sigh. "Nothing down here worthwhile. Upstairs, though, who knows? I'm sure there's something juicy going on in a closet or storeroom that's worth watching. I'll be the last one invited to witness that though. Everybody else has all the fun."

"You're impossible, JB," I laugh along with Clement. "I don't think if I'm getting a little in the closet that I'd be inclined to invite you or anyone else to witness the deed. You have to participate if you want in on the action."

Her gray brow draws together in a forced agonized expression. "Well, that's not going to happen. Nobody would want to noodle this old woman."

Clement chuckles and rolls his eyes. I can't help but laugh. "Noodle? Interesting. 'Say, big fella, how about you and I go noodle in the closet?' Sounds pretty erotic."

JB retorts quickly: "Actually, it's not noodle. It's canoodle. You know, your daily canoodle."

The guard walks away, scratching the top of his head. We overhear him say, "Canoodle?"

I figure that's a good enough response for both of us and don't offer additional comment. Turning serious, JB says, "I'll call the man to let him know you're on your way up."

"Good. Tell him I'll have a jigger of Jameson in my coffee, please. That should make him wonder what the hell I'm up to."

I watch her cock a wary brow and raise a hesitant finger of caution before apparently deciding she best not go there.

"Bye, JB," I follow with a wink before heading for the elevator. I press the button and the elevator door pings and opens immediately. Before entering I wave at JB and call out, "Send me an invitation to the next, uh, canoodle. This I've got to see."

When the elevator door opens on the seventh floor, I step out into the familiar spacious waiting area manned by Jonathan's secretary, Pat. She is a very attractive woman, perhaps in her late twenties or early thirties, with dark long straight hair, large brown eyes and a well-rounded face with beautiful skin made up with care. She has a full sensuous mouth, however I've never seen her project a genuine open smile. Still, even as a woman I find her sexy as all get-out.

Always impeccably dressed in very expensive stylish clothes, she looks up from her computer screen and nods her acknowledgement of my presence with her usual pasted-on smile and indifferent stare. I've noticed in the past that she doesn't wear a wedding ring. I muse to myself that it's probably because she treats everyone like she treats me and no one will have her.

"Hello, Mrs. Wabbit," she finally says dryly.

Well, screw you too. "Hey, Pat," I bubble. "It's good to see you. I trust you're doing well."

Pat nods, but she's obviously uncomfortable with my effort to be openly friendly. "Yes, I'm doing good," she forces. "Uh, Mr. Bales. Just go, uh, just go on in." She gestures toward his office and immediately turns her gaze back to her computer screen.

"Hey, Thanks, Pat." Bitch. I resist the urge to walk over and give her a well–deserved slap because that would give all the disgruntled employees more cannon fodder. And I'm sure Pat would enjoy calling out the sheriff. No additional comment forthcoming I guess I'm dismissed. I turn and head for Jonathan's office.

The door is open and he is at his circular birch desk, his attention buried in one of the company's more risqué magazines. I raise an arm to prop myself in the doorway and quickly survey the familiar office. It is a large room, well furnished with a conference table surrounded by eight leather chairs and a brown leather sofa against a wall to the right of his desk which faces the door.

The left wall is covered with photographs and framed covers of past magazines and publications, and shelves of memorabilia and classic books he has collected over the years. Directly behind his desk there are floor to ceiling windows looking out over the San Antonio skyline and Austin Highway.

"Hey, sailor, can you spare a destitute woman a small saucer of milk?" I coo, bringing him out of his concentration.

He looks up and offers a wary smile as he folds the magazine and builds a steeple with his hands, elbows on the desk and fingers touching his bearded chin. He purses his lips and lowers a quizzical brow. "Why do I feel there's a crisis brewing?" he asks flatly.

"And just why do you think that?" I smile as I close the door, cross the room and sit on one of the overstuffed leather chairs across from him. I cross a leg, not bothering to cover my knee, glad that I wore one of my more seductive outfits—plunging beige camisole top, light green knee length pencil skirt with taupe heels. *What the hell are you doing, Gina? Don't even think of going there.*

He notices and shakes his head. "Probably Jameson in your coffee is a good sign." Without standing he swings his chair around, collects two waiting cups of coffee from an étagère and places one in front of me. "As you requested, one jigger." He leans back in his chair and takes a sip of his coffee while studying me seriously. "So, what's up?" he asks. Another sip.

I take a long sip with the cup cradled in both hands, nod my approval of the taste and set the cup on his desk in front of me. Forcing a thin smile, I cross my arms protectively and murmur dryly, "Slow boat to China." In the past we have used that term when it was time to run away and hide from a situation or problem.

"Uh-oh . . . well, that's bad . . . I guess," he nods with a tight smile and gathered brow.

I am now confident that I have come to the right place to talk about my dilemma. He exudes his usual inherent strength with gentle understanding brown eyes framed by a handsome square face. His lips are firm and sensual, over teeth, even and white, surrounded by a short dark beard and mustache. In contrast to his well–groomed beard, his hair is also dark, but moderately long and unruly. And sexy. He never fails to send a delightful shiver of desire throughout my being.

"So, what's up?" he repeats when I don't comment.

"Sex," I mumble softly with a wary smile.

Jonathan waits for more but I don't follow up. He releases a short puff of tension and clicks his tongue. "Well, well . . ." he finally replies, but pauses, cocking his brow and contorting his lips in thought.

"Sixteen years ago I would certainly understand. It seemed like your whole existence was wrapped around your never–ending drama about sex. If it wasn't one thing it was another. If it wasn't one guy it was another. I'm sure it was monumentally important to you at the time, but I always thought it was kind of comical. Much ado about nothing."

He gazes at me curiously as he strokes his bearded chin in thought. "You know, I have felt, particularly since I hit on you at that party two years ago, that you have a good sex life and everything is, uh, cool."

He pauses and again builds the steeple with his fingers. My eyes caress his hands and I fleetingly wonder how they would feel touching my face—shit, touching me anywhere.

My heart skips as my thought drifts back to that New Year's Eve. Pep was involved in what was sure to be an all–night high stakes poker game, and Link and the kids were visiting her parents in Georgia for a week.

Both Jonathan and I had gone a bit overboard on booze and somehow we ended up alone in the party giver's boathouse. What happened next is a blur but I do know that we got hot and heavy. I finally came to my senses—or nonsenses—broke away and actually ran back to the party.

Later we apologized to each other and had a good laugh over the whole ordeal. In moments of desire and weakness I have since regretted breaking it off that night. We might have started a long term affair despite our both being married. Living next door to each other would be convenient. *Would you be sitting across the desk from Jonathan right now if you had gone through with it?*

"So tell me more," Jonathan brings me back to the present with what appears to be a sensuous gleam in his eyes. Or perhaps not.

I squirm a bit, searching for the right words to keep me from sounding like a complete idiot. I sigh and stare down at my hands to escape his gaze and say softly, "I'm not getting any." Silence fills the room and I am forced to look up for his reaction. His expression is stoic.

After forever he answers, genuinely curious, "I don't . . . think, uh, I don't believe this. You, the sex machine of my college years are high and dry some fifteen years later. Tell me it isn't so, Gina."

I watch him as he grins, cocking his head to the side, waiting for me to comment. I conjure a picture of myself as this sex machine of yesteryear and I am engulfed by the same sudden wave of desire for him that I had during spring of our senior year. Working late at the newspaper, we were alone and in a moment of passion, or madness, I hit on him royally. Taken aback, he hastily retreated.

I was crushed and embarrassed by the rejection, but weeks later he told me that his wife of one year, my good friend, was momentarily due to pick him up that fateful evening and there was no other option than to reject me. He didn't say what would have happened if his wife Link hadn't been on the way, or shall I say, in the way. I didn't ask but I have wished I had ever since. I've always wondered.

Nonetheless, bringing myself back to the present, I am again lusting over the man sitting in front of me. I can feel my heart and pulse pounding as I try to throttle the dizzying current racing throughout my body. *Watch out, now. This can't happen, Gina.* I push the feeling back and smile wryly as I shake my head, attempting to control my runaway thoughts.

His eyes show some confusion at my smile but he silently waits.

Petulantly I murmur softly, "No sex, Johnny. That's my life lately." His silence is deafening. I raise my tone a notch: "I'm going fucking crazy. There's one big sexual monkey on my back." God, I wish I could throw him on the sofa and devour him right here and now. *Get a grip, Gina. You are not going there.*

My heart leaps as Jonathan slowly stands and moves around the desk toward me, his eyes softly fixed on mine. My heartbeat escalates in anticipation and I feel my cheeks flush as my blood heats to feverous heights. He is so hot. Damn, here it comes. He gently touches the top of my head with a single finger—a spark that will surely ignite and explode all that pent up sexual energy. *Settle down, Gina.*

Oh, no. Please, no. I feel my whole body imploding, disintegrating into a numbing mass as he strolls past me toward the window. I am completely devastated. How can he not feel the energy that just passed between us? How can he ignore my feelings—our feelings?

Leaning against a central horizontal brace of the window with one hand, he looks down toward Austin Highway. I refuse to give up until I have him. I push on, attempting to gather my unraveled feelings as I soak up his tempting, attractive male physique.

For a middle aged man his body is still beautifully proportioned as I remember it in college. Now, however, there is a much higher sexual attractiveness that I haven't realized before. I want to feel his touch. I want to smell his body. I want him. Now.

> *In an instant I'm behind him and rest a hand on his shoulder. He turns and I offer up the same hand for him to take. He's puzzled but takes my hand and I pull him over to the sofa. I push him down to the sofa on his back with his feet still on the floor.*
>
> *He attempts to say something but I put a finger on his lips to silence him. I am in control and I intend to take every advantage while I have the chance. He warily watches, his mouth agape as I loosen his belt, unhook his pants and unzip them. Yes, I am in complete control. I place my hands under both of his hips and pull up gently, urging him to lift his hips, which he does. I deftly pull his pants and gray bikini underwear down to his knees, exposing him to whatever I desire.*
>
> *Oh, my. He is absolutely exquisite. My blood boils with yearning as I reach out to take what is finally mine. He reaches up and—*

I silently scream in protest as Jonathan suddenly jerks me out of my fantasy by clearing his throat. My senses are in complete disarray.

Facing me, he is leaning back on the window brace. His head is cocked to the side and his brow furrowed in confusion about my loss of composure and my heavy breathing.

He studies me curiously before spreading his arms and flashing a thin smile: "Gina, I want to hear your whole tantalizing story but right now, let's get out of here and have an early lunch. Then perhaps an early happy hour."

"Excellent idea," I exclaim with a smile of mixed relief. My inner voice cheers: *Saved by the lunch bell, Gina. You were getting ready to make a fool of yourself.*

Gina De Georgio

TWO

The El Cabrito Mexican Restaurant is our frequent lunch spot on Austin Highway and you had better come early to avoid waiting for a table. Not today. It is eleven–thirty and we're the only customers sitting at the bar, peering silently at each other in the mirror behind the liquor display. The bartender is absently mixing our Bloody Marys nearby.

With a faint shrug Jonathan's face melts into a buttery smile. How much of this guy can I take without coaxing him to bed? That would certainly make my day—and probably his one way or the other. This is crazy. Why am I heating up over him when I have so much husband stuff to deal with?

Gina, why do you even have the hots for this guy or any guy for that matter? You are married. Remember? Act like it.

He winks at me in the mirror. "Nice day so far, huh?"

"I guess it's how you look at it. If it ends with my getting laid, that would be a great day." I answer jokingly—or is it suggestively. Jeez, just say the word and I'll follow you anywhere.

Give it up, Gina. I push back at my nagging helper. Just bug off, will you?

He studies me curiously in the mirror before replying softly, "Damn, you do have it bad. Does Pep have any idea what's going on with you?"

I scowl my frustration in the mirror. "I wonder? I wonder if he gives a rat's ass about what's going on with me. We're . . . I'm a disaster but he's oblivious to me and what my needs or wants are. I don't know how much more of this I can take." I shake my head dejectedly and I'm sure Jonathan notices the tears welling up in my eyes.

The bartender appears with two Bloody Marys, sets them on a napkin in front of us and quickly disappears, probably because he doesn't want to deal with a bawling woman. Isn't that what bartenders are for?

Picking up my Mary, I hold it up in salute to Jonathan. "What's that Willie Nelson song? 'It's a Bloody Mary morning. My baby left me without warning, somewhere in the night.'"

Jonathan chuckles and salutes me back, "I don't think your, uh, baby has left. At least not yet."

"Might as well of," I reply grimly.

"Umm . . . that's bad. Why do you think that?"

I stir my drink with the plastic straw as I consider all the reasons I think Pep is looking for a way out. "Well, first, we no longer have any type of sexual relationship. We're married for God's sake. We sleep, but only sleep, in the same bed. We used to crave each other. Now, nothing. At least nothing worth the time. He doesn't want me to even touch him. Shit." I slowly shake my head despondently, my eyes still rimmed in tears.

Jonathan delays his response as he pushes the ice around in his drink with the straw. He glances sideways at me and raises a quirky brow. "Mates mate," he says softly. With tight lips and a quick nod he repeats, "Mates do mate and it is an integral part of what makes a couple a couple.

"I've always wondered why couples even stay together if they don't mate and mate often. The union becomes a partnership of convenience or some kind of business deal. I just don't get it."

"Tell me about it." I nod, pause and then continue: "Pep likes sex. In fact, he used to be a real sexual animal." I force a wry grin. "I loved every second of it."

Jonathan studies his drink, his brow furrowed. "Sounds like he's getting some on the side."

I eye him in the mirror and release a long sigh of resignation. "I hate to admit it but yeah, he's found someone else to screw. I guess I've messed up our marriage somehow."

He runs a hand through his disheveled hair as he gazes at me in the mirror in thought. "Not good. Don't blame yourself for what he's up to," he replies firmly. "As far as I've observed, you've been a model wife. I'm sure you have some stuff that's undesirable in a relationship. We all do, but not enough to chase Pep into someone else's bed."

I struggle to stave off completely breaking down in a massive embarrassing cry. "But, why? After all these great, really great years has he decided that he needs someone else to satisfy his . . . his what? What is she providing that I can't . . . or didn't? This makes no sense to me."

I pause for his reply but none forthcoming I wince and carry on fervently: "Dammit, Pep, you have a family that loves you—a wife and two kids, and you're going to chuck it all. Just give me a reason."

I finally lose it as the tears flow freely down my cheeks. I retrieve a tissue from my purse and wipe my eyes as Jonathan compassionately looks on. I take a deep breath in an effort to get my shit together. "I can't be all that bad a wife . . . or lover. What the hell is going on, John?"

When he still doesn't reply, I add miserably, "John, I'm sorry I brought you into this. You don't need to deal with my grief." Or my lust. *Stop it, Gina.*

He eyes me sympathetically as he lightly strokes his beard in thought. "You know, several months ago I found it strange that Pep started growing a beard and mustache. I've read several articles about this behavior.

"A middle aged male that makes a sudden unusual change in his lifestyle or appearance usually has a problem with his self–esteem for whatever reason. Perhaps it's a loss of confidence in his maleness or sexual capabilities.

"So this person buys a new red Corvette, gets a tattoo, loses weight, buys fancy clothes . . . uh . . . changes his grooming habits, grows a beard or even finds a willing neighbor to shack up with. Then he gets caught up in a whirlwind of contradictions or downright craziness that could destroy him as well as those around him."

I take a tentative sip of my Mary and dab at the remaining tears. "So, what do those around him do, or what do I do? This has been going on for months. I haven't been able to—to what?—get him to go back to being the person I married. I'm completely perplexed . . . and totally frustrated."

He shrugs his shoulders. "Beats me. I'm only trying to give some insight into what the guy might be doing."

"Thanks a lot, Johnny, for the great explanation, whether right or wrong," I answer somewhat sarcastically. I grin and cock a single brow. "Now, that brings up a big question; what about you?"

"Me? What about me?"

A change in direction allows my hormones to click back in. Damn, he's hot. I want to nibble that sugary lip. "You have a beard. Do you have the same stuff as Pep? Are you screwing your neighbor?"

Jonathan chuckles. "Touché. Excellent question, me lady. But I think I'm a different case. As you remember I started my beard in college. It's part of my whole persona—the way I dress, the way I don't comb my hair, the car or boat I drive. Of course what other people think of the way I present myself is important, but I didn't just suddenly change when I turned thirty five because of . . . because I lost confidence in myself as a viral, magnificent woman killer lover."

He pauses holding up his index finger, then smiles and adds, "As to your last question, not too long ago as surely you recall, I did attempt to screw my next door neighbor."

The very mention of that night brings a jolt to my heart and tingling welling up in the pit of my stomach. I am surprised that he even brought it up. I can't deny that I am caught between my desire for the man sitting beside me and the pressing need to solve the problems with my marriage. Caught in this awful dilemma, I would welcome any distraction even though only temporary. *Don't even go there, Gina.*

I flash my best flirty smile. "So, John boy, that night you attempted to . . . uh, screw your neighbor, what could you have been thinking to do such a dastardly deed?" Damn, can I touch you—just a little? *Cut it out, Gina.*

He throws his head back and lets out a loud peal of laughter as I watch, wondering where this conversation is headed. He suddenly replaces the laugh with a smile, his eyes crinkling in amusement.

"As soon as I said that I knew I was in trouble. That situation should not be revisited. It was one of those times I wish I could go back and do over again—and get it right this time. But I can't, so it is what it is."

I turn on my bar stool to face him and cross my legs, making sure my skirt rides well above my knee. I bow my head slightly and raise my eyes, studying him as I lightly bite at my lower lip. I lean toward him and conveniently bump my leg against his. The current is revved once again, traveling through me as if I stuck my finger in a light socket.

In my most seductive voice, hardly above a whisper I say, "Okay, Jonathan Bales, old friend, old pal, old buddy, failed lover, sexy boss man, now that you've opened this can of worms, tell me something." *You shouldn't be doing this, Gina. You've got enough problems without adding more.*

Of course I ignore that persistent caution. I reach up and touch Jonathan's beard lightly beside his chin with one finger. It feels soft, yet prickly and my heart skips a beat when I imagine what it would feel like if I kissed him. I am tempted to find out but hold back because I'm still not sure how he would react.

"Okay, you wish you could go back and do it over again so you can get it right." I lightly trail the finger over to the middle of his chin. He eyes me warily but otherwise doesn't react. I sense he is enjoying this. I know I am.

"That brings up the question, what was wrong the first time other than I scampered off? And of course, depending on your answer, the second question is, what would you change if you could do it over?"

I wish I could touch his face forever but I drop the finger, raise my brow and spread my hands anticipating his reply.

Gina De Georgio

At a most unwelcome time, Manuel, the owner of the restaurant, suddenly shows up and pats Jonathan on the back.

"Senor Bales," he bellows. "I have saved you a private table in the garden as you requested but the cafe is filling up. Please come so I don't get molested by two senoritas that have an eye on the table."

Jonathan laughs and expresses his appreciation as we grab our drinks and follow Manuel through the main dining room. The spacious room's walls are covered with murals depicting traditional Mexican social life, revolutions and long–lost Aztec culture. And it is crowded with a noisy and festive mass of people wanting their Monday Mexican food fix.

We enter the tiled courtyard with a tall three-tiered cascading fountain in the center surrounded by numerous exotic plants. Manual escorts us to the only vacant table tucked in a small alcove, hidden from other diners by a jungle of plants and vines.

"Perfect, Manuel," Jonathan says as the owner pulls out my chair for me.

When I am seated he turns to Jonathan and smiles. "Let's see if I remember; it's two Margaritas on the rocks."

Jonathan nods, *"Si Senor. Hecho mucho grande, por favor."*

Manuel bows as he backs out of the jungle.

I present my sexiest smile to Jonathan as my heart flutters. It seems the longer we are together this morning the more I want to jump his bones.

He gazes at me curiously. When I don't comment he spreads his hands. "Alright already. What?"

I answer flatly with a thin smile, "Before we were interrupted by our well–meaning host, I asked two questions—two questions of the century to be exact. And of course they are begging to be answered, Mr. Bales. And you, sir, must understand, I fully expect them to be answered before this lunch is over. *Comprendes*?"

Jonathan eyes crinkle but he remains silent.

Our usual waitress Juanita pops magically at our table. She nods without comment so as not to interrupt

24

our conversation and sets a large margarita in front of me. We pause to watch her usual show.

Middle aged, she is a handsome woman that is slightly overweight or, as Jonathan has said in the past, decidedly plump. Dressed in the traditional red, green and yellow floor length Mexican skirt and blouse, she carries herself confidently. It is obvious that she is on her usual mission to flirt with Jonathan who of course enjoys the attention.

She circles behind him and reaches over his shoulder to place his Margarita in front of him while not accidently pressing one overly large breast against his shoulder. Jonathan grins at me and winks.

"It is a pleasure to see you again, *Juan*," she greets while pointing at our empty Bloody Mary glasses.

"Yes you may take them, Juanita. And it is indeed our pleasure to see you again. We look forward to the sunshine that you bring to our lunch table."

Juanita beams a smile and cocks a stern brow. "Well thank you. But I must tell you," she scolds, wagging a finger at Jonathan, "it is apparent that you people aren't going to get any work done this afternoon. This is your second drink already."

Jonathan grins and flirts away. "Well I'll tell you what, Juanita. We just might spend the rest of the afternoon here swimming in Margaritas and forget work altogether. Why don't you join us and we'll turn it into a party?"

Juanita's face lights up with a full smile. Again, she wags the finger at Jonathan. "Watch out now, *Juan*. I just might do that. Then where will you be?" She gestures toward me. "I can tell *Senora Conejo* doesn't want to share you with me or anyone else."

I nod in agreement and answer for Jonathan's benefit: "You've got that right, Juanita. This is my day good or bad, and no matter where it's headed I'm not sharing." I nod, smile at Juanita and raise a finger for emphasis. "I can tell that Jonathan would like to spend a little time with you too."

Juanita giggles. "That would be *mina mucho amante*, I'm sure." She winks and pats Jonathan on the shoulder before retrieving her order pad from a large pocket in her skirt signaling the banter is over. "So what's it going to be today besides Margaritas?"

Jonathan looks at me to order first. "I'll have the special cheese enchilada plate with *boracho* beans instead of refrieds. And corn instead of flour tortillas please."

Juanita turns her attention to Jonathan, pencil poised over her pad. "Sounds good. I'll have the same," he nods.

"Excellent choice," she says and tucks the pad back into her skirt pocket. "You want me to keep the Margaritas coming?"

Jonathan replies with a quick shake of his head, "Oh, no. I think not. We both have to drive home later. Speaking for myself, I'd just as soon not total me and my car on Interstate Ten."

"Good. You're my best customers. I don't want to lose you." Juanita is suddenly gone.

"She keeps calling me *Canejo*. What does that mean?" I puzzle.

Jonathan smiles. "Rabbit. It means rabbit in Spanish."

Again we lift our glasses to each other. "To today," I toast.

"To us . . . and ours," Jonathan replies.

I take a sip from my straw as Jonathan watches, his gaze as soft as a caress. "Umm, I think I could lose myself in this Margarita very easily," I comment as a highly charged sensuous spark passes between us.

I wonder if it is just me or does he have the same urge to reach out and touch me and even better, lay me. Damn, my body aches for him. Is there no relief? I want to be crushed by his embrace right now. *Get a grip. You're hopeless, Gina.*

I wish I could read what he's feeling or thinking. But I can't so maybe I should just back off. I've made a fool of myself with him more times than I would like and I certainly don't want to add another to the list.

No matter what my needs are I should just let things happen without forcing them. Is it John I desire, or some relief for this unbearable sexual desire overload from someone, anyone, a warm body? *Gina, you need help, not sex.*

I release a long sigh of frustration that doesn't go unnoticed by Jonathan. I force a smile. "Okay . . . Senor Bales, about that fateful New Year's Eve when you hit on your neighbor; you said if you had a chance to do it over again you would get it right.

"That indicates to me that you feel you did something wrong that night. I certainly don't feel you did anything wrong. In fact maybe I got it wrong by running away."

Jonathan nods his understanding and contemplates while softly tugging at his beard. Sexy. "I guess this whole thing goes back to when I was a teenager and just starting to date. I couldn't take being turned down or told no, so I just quit asking girls out altogether unless I was absolutely sure the answer would be yes.

"That carried over into this whole sexual thing. It is devastating for me to hit on a woman and then get turned down. I don't know why I feel that way but the rejection is massive—a threat to my very manhood."

Jonathan pauses and I am intrigued. "Wow, don't turn you down or you might slit your throat, huh?"

"Close." He studies his Margarita momentarily, then continues: "That night was completely demoralizing for me when you broke and ran away from what I felt was a sure thing. Simple as that."

I nod my understanding of what he said but am surprised that any man would be devastated because I didn't agree to have sex with him, particularly Jonathan, who appears so self–assured and confident of himself. The shudders and tightness in the pit of my stomach increase. His vulnerability even turns me on. I'm helpless.

He is pensively watching and waiting for my response. "Okay I think I understand your . . . sensitivity toward being rejected, so what would you do if you could do it over?"

Jonathan shrugs faintly with a thin smile. "Nothing. I wouldn't go there. You can't get turned down if you don't play—if you don't ask. Simple as that."

I bite my lower lip in thought and reply, "If you don't buy a lottery ticket you aren't ever going to win the lottery."

Jonathan contorts his lips and slowly shakes his head. I lift a finger indicating I have more to say. "I'll tell you this; it just makes this whole . . . uh, comedy a bit more tragic. At least for me."

I pause only to have my keeper harangue: *Stop, right now. Don't say another word, Gina,* she orders. As usual I ignore sanity as Jonathan quizzically spreads his hands.

Well here goes. I lower my eyes and gaze at my hands folded in my lap. I say softly as, dammit, the tears again well up, "I've wished a thousand times over the last two years that I hadn't run away from you that night."

I sneak a peek at Jonathan to find him staring at me, his eyes alight with surprise. After what seems forever he releases a long winded sigh and mutters simply, "Shit."

I wipe a lone tear streaking down my cheek with my Margarita napkin, reach across the table and touch the back of his hand with my fingers. "I guess that says it all, Jonathan."

Juanita suddenly pops in carrying a tray with our order. One look at me and she is immediately aware that she needs to be elsewhere. She quickly places the enchiladas and warmer of tortillas in front of us and departs, simply saying, "I'll check back later."

Perfect timing. It was just what we needed. We burst out laughing at her reaction, immediately relieving the tension in our little private dining area. We eat silently, both wondering the ramifications of what I just said. Perhaps my conscience was right: *Stop, right now. Don't say another word, Gina.* Well too late for that.

We silently agree to not discuss or dwell on my statement—at least for now. Jonathan runs his hand through his unruly hair in thought and I watch, wishing I too could run my fingers through his hair.

My keeper is right. I need help—or perhaps a little yin yang emergency sexual energy explosion might do. I smile at the thought and as usual, Jonathan is curiously watching. I offer no explanation.

"So, do you have a plan for how to solve your monumental sexual or, whatever, husband problem?" he asks casually.

I answer flippantly, throwing both hands up: "Yeah, I'm going on a sexual crusade. I'm going to lay everything in my path."

His eyes alight with humor as he slowly shakes his head. He stands and announces it's time for a restroom pause, excuses himself and ducks through the narrow alcove doorway.

I think back over the day and my mind drifts as my desire for Jonathan escalates, coursing throughout my body and reawakening that yearning in my fantasy place.

He appears behind me and motions for me to stand. Surprised, I do as I'm told and he immediately turns me around and takes me into his arms. I wrap my arms around his shoulders and moan softly as I lean into him.

We kiss—first soft and easy but growing in a crescendo of biting lips and tongue twisting around tongue. I love the feel of his beard against my lips and hope our kisses go on forever.

Momentarily we are forced to come up for air, and my heart skips as he slowly runs his fingers down my back to rest on my hips. He clutches my hips and pulls me closer to him. I can feel his breathing in my hair and his smell is intoxicating. With the sensation of his erection pressing against me my knees weaken and I press even closer.

Although wanting a full measure of this opportunity immediately, I gasp in surprise when he pulls away from me and runs both hands down the sides of my legs and deftly lifts my skirt. In the same instant, he grasps the waist band of my panties and slides them down to my knees. Stooping down, he slides them to my ankles and whispers for me to step out of them. I willingly oblige, the blood coursing through my veins nearing the boiling point. Holy shit, I don't know what's next but I'm ready. Go for it.

Jonathan pushes me back against the table and clears the dishes near the edge away with a quick sweep of his hand. Grabbing me by the waist he commands me to sit on the table and lightly assists me by lifting me up. He drops to his knees, grasps my thighs and spreads my legs allowing my knees to fold. My fantasy place is demanding attention and he obliges.

He takes my hands and places them on his shoulders to give me stability. I close my eyes as he runs his fingers up my inner thighs, through my pubic hair and suddenly thrusts a finger in that warm wet place sending shock waves riveting through my body. I want to cry out in sheer pleasure but hold back lest I disturb the whole restaurant.

He magically manipulates his finger in and out, and around my clitoris, bringing me close to that desired explosion but he stops short.

Withdrawing his finger, he is suddenly kissing my inner thigh, slowly working his way up. I groan in ecstasy when he thrusts his tongue into my vagina and does a tongue dance around my clit. It is exquisite but he is not through. He wraps his lips around my clit and sucks, sending shock waves through my whole being.

I've forgotten how this feeling can completely overwhelm me. He takes me higher and higher, my whole body in a whirlpool of sensation, inching closer to that expected and desired explosion.

Jonathan is suddenly on his feet, un-buckling his belt and unzipping his pants. He lets his pants drop to his ankles while slipping down his bikini underwear. I grab the back of my thighs and lift my legs even higher as he teases me by lightly circling his erection around my clit bringing me ever closer to eruption.

He places his hands under my hips, freeing my hands to finally run my fingers through his hair. I moan as I thrust my hips forward in anticipation of his deeper penetration. He pushes forward lightly and pulls back. Forward again, harder and deeper.

I again moan my pleasure as I throw my hips forward, pulling his hair until his head is touching mine. A deep guttural sound comes from his throat as he thrusts deeper into me pushing us both over the edge. Our bodies explode in complete ecstasy as I cry out in pleasure, melting together in complete gratification and serenity.

When I open my eyes I am shocked as I'm suddenly jerked out of my daydream. Well fuck. Jonathan is sitting across the table from me curiously watching me as I breathe heavy and unevenly.

Is this whole scene a dream or is it real? Regardless I feel my face flush in embarrassment. Damn, I've just made a fool of myself. I feel between my legs under the table to make sure that I have my panties on. It's a dream.

Jonathan maintains his gaze and comments softly, "Wow . . . that must have been some trip. What are you on?"

I bow my head and cover my eyes with one hand. I wish I had somewhere to hide. Maybe the floor will swallow me up. I take a long deep calming breath, then reply in a broken husky whisper: "I certainly didn't buy it on the street."

I spread my fingers and peer up at Jonathan through them. "It's not my drug of choice but I think it has me hooked."

His brow furrows as he studies me curiously and spreads his hands. "What in hell are you talking about? What has you hooked?"

"Raging female hormones. They've completely taken me over. Did I cry out? I suppose the whole fucking restaurant heard me?" I remove the hand from my eyes, sigh in frustration and try to compose myself.

He flashes an adorable sugar coated smile. "Yeah, but it was more like a whimper and I don't think anyone heard. When I returned from the restroom you appeared to be having a rather good time . . . uh, experience but I don't think anyone noticed."

I really don't deserve this man but I'm lucky he is my friend and puts up with my craziness. I mumble softly: "Sorry, my madness has gotten to be a pain for you. I certainly don't want that."

He smiles compassionately. "Gina, you're going through some crazy stuff and I'll help if I can. But most of your stuff is indeed your stuff and only you can deal with it. I can certainly see that your sexual issue has become a monster for you, literally taking over your thought process and coloring nearly everything you do. I really hurt for you. You need help but I don't have any idea what kind."

I force a throaty chuckle and smile.

In confusion he tilts his head and lifts a brow. "What . . . ?"

"You aren't the first today to tell me I need help. I didn't listen the first time but now I guess I should."

"You've completely lost me. I haven't the foggiest idea what you're talking about."

"My conscience has been acting like an overprotective mother all day. She told me earlier that I need help before I screw everything up."

Jonathan nods, his eyes projecting compassion— as well as amusement.

I feel the tears welling up. "Maybe I should pay more attention to what I'm trying to tell myself." *Hooray for you, Gina,* the voice cheers while doing a little jig.

"Perhaps," Jonathan follows. For a moment of uneasy silence he watches and waits for me to continue.

I lightly bite at my lower lip. "You know what? I think I have been enjoying my misery too much lately. Sex has become such an obsession with me I can't even concentrate on picayune stuff. And what's worse I don't want to. Sex or the lack of it owns me."

Jonathan doesn't reply but I can see he has something to say. I wait pensively. He scratches his beard in thought. Damn, even though I'm in a shitty situation I'm still sexually obsessed with his every movement. *Cut it out, Gina.* "Yeah, cut it out," I whisper to myself, for once agreeing with my conscience.

"I'm sorry, did you say something?" Jonathan asks tilting an ear toward me.

"Just berating myself. Trying to get my act together."

"So, do you have a plan of some sort for the overall problem?" Jonathan queries to steer the conversation away from the fantasy embarrassment. "And I personally don't think that—what did you say?—'going on a sexual crusade to lay every man in your path,' is a viable solution, do you?"

"I guess not. It might work for a while if I can find anyone interested but it won't work in the long run."

"Seems to me the problem starts and ends with Pep."

I slowly nod my head in affirmation and press my mouth into a hard line. "Yeah, but he won't address the problem. If he is getting some on the side I can't prove it, and why doesn't he just go all in for it if he is?"

"Maybe he wants the fun and games but deep down he doesn't want to disrupt or possibly lose his family and lifestyle—a great wife and two beautiful kids, a high dollar place on the lake, a fancy car and boat, and a great life in general. That's a lot to give up just to shack up with some bimbo, whatever."

I consider what he said before I reply, "Umm . . . you're probably right, but what if he genuinely cares for her but can't make the decision to cut the ties with all the people and stuff he values. I can't do that for him."

"Perhaps you can. Confront him," he replies with tight lips and determined eyes. He holds up a hand and counts off the issues wiggling a different finger for each.

"This is the way it is, Bub: one, I certainly don't approve of what you're doing.

"Two, I'm sick of your pussyfooting around with another woman . . . or women.

"Three, I've had it with your treating me like crap.

"Four, it's time for you to shit or get off the pot.

"Five, if you can't make a decision, I'll do it for you."

He wiggles all five fingers. "Well that's five but who's counting? I'm sure you could come up with a lot more."

My stomach twists and the usual butterflies are suddenly ants boring holes in my belly. And it's not about sex this time. I am already dreading the confrontation that I know is coming. "That's going to be tough."

"Of course it is. No one wants conflict or confrontation, particularly if there is a possibility that the end result or solution may not be what you desire." Jonathan shrugs his shoulders absently and tilts his head, "It's your call, but sooner or later you're going to have to put the whole thing on him and make it stick."

I weigh what Jonathan said and exhale a long deep sigh of apprehension. "There's something else that is really bugging me. What if there is another woman but he decides he wants to give her up and remain with his beautiful, dutiful, lovable, sex-crazed wife? Maybe her pride won't allow her to forgive the infidelity and betrayal?"

Jonathan slowly nods his agreement. "Uh-huh, and maybe she can't live with someone that could, and might run off into the boonies with another fantastic female specimen in the future. This goes on and on. Does she want to have a partnership or, God forbid, a sexual relationship with anyone that considers her his second choice? Try sleeping with that."

I glumly nod my head with lips pressed in determination. "This gets worse by the minute and I don't see it getting resolved anytime soon the way it's going."

I raise my hands defensively toward Jonathan and resign, "Okay, okay, I get your point. It isn't going away until I pressure him. I'll confront Pep as soon as possible. At the least, good or bad, it will get things moving."

He lays a compassionate hand on my arm and smiles. "Good. I wish I could assist you but that isn't going to happen."

I present a bright smile, widen my eyes and lift my brow. "But you can assist me, Johnny. In the meantime you can provide me with fantastic, uninhibited, no holds barred, obligatory sex to help me through this. What do you think?" I spread my hands and comically giggle.

He chuckles and with a quick shake of his head replies, "I think you're incurable. A little not necessarily free sex sounds entertaining, but in your present state it could completely destroy you . . . and possibly me.

"So, no. Get us, meaning you and me, out of your system at least for the time being. If there's something out there for us together, I assure you it'll come later without forcing it. Your priority is to take care of what's going on in your marriage. Put up with your frustrations and fix first things first."

I reluctantly smile and wink. "Well, shit. You're no fun at all but I thought as much—and you're absolutely right."

I widen my smile: "Johnny Bales, thanks for a great day, to-die-for Bloody Marys, good Margaritas, greasy enchiladas, and of course the best and most embarrassing part, an incredible, unbelievable fantasy. Now can I go home to my adorable loving husband?"

Gina De Georgio

THREE

A rriving back at the BP's parking lot, Jonathan pulls into his parking space next to my car. "Well . . ." he resigns cocking his head to one side, genuine compassion in his eyes. He curls his lips as he runs his hand through his hair before continuing: "I guess good luck is the best advice I can give. If you could only fast–forward six months maybe this would all be behind you."

I hope he doesn't see the tears pooling in the corners of my eyes. I release a long tension releasing sigh. "Thanks, John. I don't know what I would do without you to prop me up."

I pause and stare down at my hands folded in my lap. I force a sardonic grin and turn my gaze toward him. "If the lake wasn't so damn cold, I think it would be easier to drown myself than deal with Pep."

He releases a chuckle from deep in his throat and follows it with that buttery smile. "I don't believe you really want to do yourself in if it's just the temperature of the water that is holding you back."

I delay my response and he watches me, his brow furrowed in concern. I resist the urge to break down and bawl, letting it all hang out. I certainly need that but he has already put up with enough of my emotional shit today.

I experience an involuntary shiver that courses through my body leaving my hands cold. I release another sigh of tension. "Oh well, I'm sure I'll survive what's coming but I certainly don't look forward to it."

"Yeah, you'll make it." He lightly touches me on my shoulder with one finger and lets it linger there momentarily. I love it.

My heart speeds up and I feel that knot growing in my belly. Holy shit. Do that some more. Damn it. I'm a complete disaster. Crying one minute, lusting the next. Is there no relief for me from myself.

I grasp the door latch, open the door slightly and look over toward my friend. I force a smile for his benefit. "Thanks, John. You're a life-saver; I'll never get through this without your help."

I open the door completely and step out. I bend over to take one last look at Jonathan. He nods, his brow lifted and his mouth in a tight narrow smile. He flips a wave of goodbye and I close the door.

I settle into my Mercedes, wait and watch as Jonathan enters the building. Despite all the trouble it would probably cause the both of us, I still wish I could have gone along with him. I'm sure that leather sofa would be a fantastic place to devour him piece by piece. My keeper is again shaking her head: *Go home, Gina. Just go home.*

I start the car and glance at the dash clock. Jeez, it's only one o'clock. I should be home by one forty five. I start the car and shift into reverse. Before I push on the accelerator I feel a queasiness in my chest and tightness in my throat as my eyes glass over with tears.

I turn off the engine and take a deep breath. No help. This time there is no holding back the tears—there is no need to. Still gripping the steering wheel, I bow my head until my forehead is resting on it as the tears begin to flow unhindered down my cheeks. The sobs follow—big body shaking sobs and I cry out softly, cursing my husband, cursing myself.

I tell myself, don't hold back. Purge this unbelievable tension out of your system. And it's working. After several minutes I release a long uneven sigh as I wipe the tears, bringing a lightness and calmness spreading from my lungs and washing throughout my body. At last a release from this monster that has been controlling me—if only temporarily.

I release another long shaky breath, trying to gather myself completely before my trek home. I start the car but before shifting my cellphone chimes for attention.

I dig through my purse and check. It's Pep. That's unusual. He seldom calls during the day. I shut off the engine.

"Hello, Pep," I answer cheerfully. "Surprised to hear from you. What's up?"

"Where are you," he answers flatly without discernable emotion.

Umm . . . what's this all about? "I'm just leaving Bales," I answer trying to match his tone.

"When will you get here?"

"Uh, where is here?"

"Home."

"Home? I thought you were going to be late coming in from Austin."

"Decided I needed to cut . . . to cut the day short."

My heart skips a bit and I feel my pulse step up a notch. This doesn't sound good. "Barring traffic problems, probably by two o'clock. Is there a problem?"

"No . . . well, we, uh, we have to talk. There's something I need to . . . to tell you."

"Well, that's a switch," I answer not hiding my sarcasm even though the butterflies have taken over my stomach.

"Uh, I suppose. Well anyway, I'll see you when you get here."

I don't like the sound of this. I hang up without saying anything else.

My head is spinning and my heart is racing as I start the car and back out. Well at least something is going to happen. Good or bad I'm okay with that if we are going to finally address our problems. Now I won't have to tie him up to get the conversation started. I do have a bad feeling about this however. I certainly don't think this crazy day is over. Not by a long shot.

In spite of the purging bawl I just had I've worked myself back into a nervous wreck by the time I turn into our driveway, a foreboding anxiety churning in my stomach; a cold nervous sweat is completely engulfing me. This can't be; I can't meet Pep face to face like this—a quivering mess. I've got to present a strong, cool, businesslike approach. Get a grip. Now.

Turning off the engine I sit for a moment to collect myself. My mind keeps going back to a statement Jonathan made: "Sooner or later you're going to have to put the whole thing on Pep and make it stick." To achieve this, over the forty–five minute drive I have been mulling over a checklist to fortify myself. For the fourth time I repeat the list out loud:

"Keep calm. Don't show my emotions no matter what is said, good or bad.

"Be firm in expressing my opinion, expectations or misgivings.

"Don't be afraid to make reasonable demands.

"Don't give in to any demands he may have that aren't in accord with my own desires, wants or needs.

"This is about me; don't accept anything that is not good for me.

"Don't sacrifice myself and my needs or desires because of the kids—they will survive as long as I am looking out for them with or without Pep.

"Walk away if no agreement can be reached; I can negotiate, demand, or fight another day.

"Above all, keep my dignity."

I attempt to release my tension with a deep exhale, open my car door and walk unsteadily, toward the house. Keep calm I remind myself. Opening the front door I am immediately face to face with Pep, sitting on the sofa still dressed in his suit sans tie. Even now is sexy and desirable as ever. I feel my heart quicken and my face flush. *Get a grip, Gina. You've got business here and it isn't about sex.*

Pep nods without expression and motions for me to set in a chair across from him. I nod with a trace of a pasted on smile, not taking my eyes off of him, happy to sit as I feel my knees about to buckle. *Be strong and don't get emotional.*

He doesn't speak and after a nerve shattering moment I gesture for him to begin. Come on, Pep, damn it. You wanted this meeting, so talk.

No response and the butterflies in my stomach become nauseating. I have the impulse to say, well screw

40

you and walk away, but it may not be easy to reschedule this meeting anytime soon.

For his benefit I twist my lips in disgust and unhappily shake my head while staring daggers at him. It's time to go on the offensive to push this conversation along.

I lower my eyes to my hands tightly clutching the arms of the chair as my anger builds. I speak, my voice shaking and hardly above a whisper. "So, we, uh, see each other every evening without, uh . . . we're oblivious to one another. Now, suddenly, you want to meet me in the middle of Monday afternoon when you should be in Austin closing a multimillion dollar real estate deal. What gives? Surely it's not about earth–shaking sex." I roll my eyes at myself. *Damn, Gina, you didn't need to say that.*

He ignores my comment and deliberates without expression other than stroking his beard. His brow suddenly furrows curiously and our eyes meet devoid of any emotion. My heart pounds and a shiver runs over my neck and shoulders. Will you just say something, anything, I silently scream. How much of his silence can I stand?

"I, uh, wanted to meet in the afternoon," he mumbles, also hardly above a whisper, "because I didn't want the kids to be here when we talk." He pauses and gazes at me stoically.

My heart sinks and my mind is paralyzed. This can go no way but down. My stomach twists as I bite my lower lip. *Don't answer, Gina. Don't make it easy for him*, my inner voice commands. I remain silent.

When he still doesn't continue, I steel myself and take a deep breath. *Hold it together, Gina.* I rise and walk around my chair and grab the back to steady myself while glaring at Pep. Do not lose it in front of him I demand of myself. Be cool.

My mind is reeling as I struggle for something to say. I surprise myself when I blurt out: "So, you've had enough of this fantastic marriage. What's your plan?"

His jaw drops, showing that he is obviously caught off guard by my outburst, but I feel he is also relieved that he didn't have to say it. He studies me intently, his eyes neutral before exhaling and dropping his gaze to the floor.

I urge myself to settle down. Do not speak another word. *Alright bub, out with it*, my inner judge rants.

After forever he nods without expression, "Yeah, I think we need a separation so I can, maybe, get it together." He will not look at me.

My heart hitches a bit but I'm oddly serene as I wait for more. None comes so it's time to push. I speak positively, even taking care to mince my words: "Okay, you want a, uh, separation. What's the deal? What's going on with you? Nobody just up and destroys a relationship, rejects his wife and family just to get away for a while?"

I wait. Nothing. I now know the course is set. I also know I can get through this present ordeal without losing it. *Take command, Gina. Save a little face. Put it on him. Get this confrontation over with*.

"Alright, so you're leaving. Where are you headed? Where are you going to live? I assume you're going to move in with her. I'll bet she's waiting for you right now." *Go, Gina, Go.*

Surprised, he inhales quickly as intense astonishment touches his face. He nervously clears his throat, I assume to buy time to contemplate his response.

Clearly uneasy he says anxiously, "Uh, I don't understand. What makes you think I have . . . I'm going to live with?—" He stops short and stares down at the floor. I have never seen Pep this flustered.

Alright, dude, it's my time to get in a few licks. *Are you actually enjoying this?* "I know because I'm a woman, Pep. Do you think I'm blind? All women know when they're being cheated on. It's built into the system." *It is?* My inner muse chuckles. *Go for the kill, woman.*

I push on: "I don't suppose you want to tell me who she is do you?" No answer. "I assume the sex is fantastic. Is she better than?—No, I'm not going there."

I pause to wait for any comment. None forthcoming, I throw up both hands in a what–the–hell gesture and blurt out: "But on the other hand, apparently she is better than me or you wouldn't be leaving me for her." *Fantastic, Gina. More.*

I pause to catch my breath and give him a chance to respond. He doesn't and suddenly, along with all the other emotions that I'm feeling, I'm pissed. I'm really big–time pissed.

With pressed lips I point an accusing finger at the man in front of me. "You know what, Pep? You are going to find out sooner or later—probably sooner, that she isn't better than me. No woman is better than me in bed."

I again press my lips firmly as I glare at the stranger in front of me. "No, let me rephrase that: You are definitely going to find out that no woman is better than me, period."

He silently stares at the floor while I wait. He appears defeated and I feel bad for him. This must be tough but it's going to be just as hard or harder on me and the kids.

I spread my hands when he still doesn't respond and press on: "Well, is there anything you wish to say?" I can tell this is not going as easy as he thought it would. He is certainly stewing in his own shit, but he can't turn back now. He's done it and it can't be undone without major changes. I'm sure he knows that.

I wait and finally he mumbles, "We need to tell the kids."

I retort taking complete charge of the moment. "No, we, meaning us, don't need to tell the kids anything. I, meaning me, will let the kids know what you are doing to us."

He has no recourse. This is his decision to dump us, but I will be in command when it comes to his wants, needs, and rights in this family. That's how it is and that's how it will stay.

I wait for his reply as he dismally shakes his head, his eyes actually tearing up. *Ignore his misery, Gina.* After a long tense, heavy silence, I walk around the chair and stand in front of him, I speak short and to the point:

"Okay, I have three things to say. First, you're leaving to go shack–up with your new, uh . . . babe." I pause and for his benefit loudly clear my throat. "So be it.

"Second, you've had over a year to play games with Miss Magnificent, whoever, without making a decision on what's really important to you." I shake my head in disgust and, I can't believe it, I actually shake a threatening finger at the man sitting in front of me. "So, you've got about forty five minutes before the kids get home. Get your shit together and get out of here before they arrive."

His eyes widen, his jaw drops slightly and his brow furrows sadly as the finality of my decision is sinking in. He doesn't comment. After all what is left to say? I've certainly made it easy for him.

"Third, and I'm sure this isn't the last thing: this is not just a separation. After a year of your screwing around there is no going back. I will not become your second choice, now or later. This is it, Pep. I want a divorce. And the sooner the better."

His mouth parts slightly as disappointment and defeat cloud his eyes. I know later I am going to be crushed but now I feel elated—and free.

I raise my brow over wide dry eyes and force a confident smile for the sad man sitting in front of me. I spread my hands and positively nod my head. "Now, sir. I'm going to fix me a strong Chivas Royal Salute with just a small splash of water, go down and sit on the—no!—make that my dock and ponder my future. Good luck to you. You're certainly going to need it."

I turn and head for the kitchen. After mixing my drink and having heard no sounds from Pep, I shrug my indifference, open the back door and head down to the lake. I settle into my favorite padded chair on the dock and take a long slug from my scotch and water.

In spite of what has just happened I am relatively relaxed as I look out over the lake, my lake. I never get tired of sitting on the water, particularly in the evening with a glass of wine.

The lake renews me and right now I need big time renewal. It gives me so much energy while relaxing me at the same time, particularly during the winter when the kids don't have as much time to spend making noise on the water.

The pecan, cypress and oak trees seem to be a mile high and provide ample shade even in the middle of the hottest days in August. The lake itself is formed by a dam on the Guadalupe River that flows from springs about a hundred twenty-five miles northwest of here in the hill country and winds to the Texas gulf coast, one hundred sixty miles to the southeast. The dammed portion of the lake is about nine miles long and a quarter of a mile across at it widest point.

About seventy percent of its shore is lined with high–dollar vacation and weekend homes owned by those that live and work in Houston, three hour's drive to the east. The other thirty percent of the homes are owned by those who are retired, work locally or commute to San Antonio on a daily basis.

For years the lake has been a favorite ski and wakeboard destination, and is known as the water ski capitol of Texas—tongue in cheek of course. It is said, during the summer when the Houston crowd is all on site, if they all turn on their outside lights, one can ski at midnight. I haven't seen that however, but I've seen a lot of other unspeakable juicy stuff on the lake, both night and day.

I release a long sigh of relief and review the last ten hours. I feel my heart flutter and my stomach do its usual butterfly thing as I recall this very morning lusting over Pep as he emerged from the shower. Already I'm experiencing withdrawal from him even though lately there has been very little to withdraw from.

Nonetheless as the day progressed it got crazier and crazier. I would have never dreamed that Pep and I would split up today, but deep down I've known it was coming—just not so soon. Well what's done is done. And the day is far from being over. I still have to deal with the kids.

It was no easy task breaking the news to Jack and Bunny but they appeared to take it in stride. Did they not understand what's happening, or did they already sense that something was up because of the coolness Pep and I have shared lately?

Whatever, they took the news without showing very much emotion. It will certainly affect them when it sinks in that this is certainly life changing for all three of us. We've agreed that we can and will support each other and we will survive despite the departure of their dad. We'll see. I haven't any idea what part he will be playing in their lives from here on. It's probably up to him.

Now, here I am; it's six thirty, the kids have been fed and they have headed to their bedrooms for the usual studies and perhaps some television.

I have changed into my grungy shorts and halter top, and now stand at the back window watching Jonathan and Link sitting on their boat dock drinking wine.

Should I join them and break the news or not? As I contemplate my action I open a bottle of merlot and pour myself a glass. How much have I had to drink today? Surely not enough. I grab the bottle and head down to join the Bales.

Link spies me and immediately hops to her feet and holds up her empty wine glass. "Perfect timing, Gina. I hope you're sharing. I hate to go back to the house for more wine."

"Well, I wasn't planning on it," I laugh, nodding a hello at Jonathan as I fill her glass. Jonathan declines when I point the bottle at him. "But, I can't turn down any woman that is desperate for vino."

Link gestures for me to sit but I prefer to stand. She is a fantastic woman to be around, always with a kind remark or hearty laugh. She has often remarked when anyone compliments her on her kind demeanor: "I'm just trying to get along." And she does just that. I have never heard her say an unkind word or criticize anyone.

Born in the same bedroom that her mom was born in on a four hundred acre farm in south central Georgia, she is truly a farm girl in every sense in contrast to her city boy husband.

She probably weighs every bit of one hundred and five pounds, as Jonathan says, soaking wet. However she has a fantastic figure that she is constantly striving to maintain—except for consuming a large amount of high caloric wine every night.

46

Today for her usual cool off plunge in the lake she is dressed, or I should say undressed in a black string bikini with matching string halter that is bordering on too small to corral her more than ample boobs.

Although I'm proud of my figure she is a much better proportioned miniature me. She reminds me of those pixy gymnasts in the Olympics. And she is not only sexy, she is as Jonathan points out, to die for sexy.

Since moving to the lake she has kept her natural curly red hair cut short because she spends so much time on or in the lake. She has to be careful as her freckled skin burns easily if she spends too long in the mid–day sun. When she knows she's going to be in the sun for very long she covers her pouty little face and lips with that white zinc goop to keep from frying. With this makeup, Jonathan calls her the lake clown.

She is very athletic and is continually challenging her two kids and other teens on the lake to match her water skiing skills. She seldom loses a contest and most, even the boys, usually decline to take her on. However the teenage boys are smitten by her and often make a fool of themselves trying to impress her. This of course does not make their immature girlfriends happy. Jonathan laughs and kids about her testosterone army always sniffing around.

Even though I have hit on Link's husband on occasion, I consider her my best friend. Am I crazy?

Jonathan, shirtless and barefooted, is dressed in a worn baggy red swim suit. He is warily studying me as I ogle over him and wish I could run my fingers through the hair on his chest. My hormones never rest.

Usually he can read my emotions and after this morning he's going to be acutely observant. He raises a perfectly arched brow when he catches my eye. I'm sure Link is also aware of a difference in me. I probably look like I've been through a wringer. I know that I feel like it.

I hold up my glass in toast. How many times have we toasted today? They hold up their glasses, watching curiously to see what I have to say.

I force a thin smile and speak, my voice calm and soft, "Here's to the different, or shall I say, new family next door." I sip my wine, set the glass on the table and watch for their reaction.

Link is befuddled but Jonathan raises a questioning brow over firm lips. Link looks to Jonathan for explanation.

He doesn't take his eyes off of me as he takes the last sip of wine from his glass. He picks up my merlot bottle and half fills his glass.

He asks in his calm buttery voice, "You talked to Pep didn't you?"

I nod and Link is completely confused, looking back and forth at us for explanation.

Jonathan stares at me curiously. "And . . . ?"

I twist my lips and shrug, "He's gone."

His eyes express surprise if only briefly. "Well crap."

Link throws up her hands and looks first to me then Jonathan for explanation.

We both ignore her as Jonathan asks, "Did he just leave or did you throw him out?"

Link is beside herself waiting for explanation: "Pep left? What the hell is going on, Gina?"

Jonathan turns his focus to his wife and says as a matter of fact, "Gina and Pep have split up."

Link calmly sets her glass down and looks first to Jonathan, then me. She narrows her eyes and asks softly, "You're kidding, right?"

I slowly shake my head as I feel the tears well up. "He got a better deal, Link. He left."

Link is completely blown away. She waits for further explanation. When I offer none, she turns to Jonathan. "Did you know this was going to happen?"

"Not until this morning."

Link squints her eyes and presses her lips in thought. Jonathan and I watch to see what her reaction is going to be.

She slowly shakes her head. "Shit, I didn't have a clue." She stands and drapes her arms around me and says, "I'm so sorry, Gina."

As I wrap my arms around her shoulders with my hands on her bare back, I suddenly feel her energy tugging

48

me closer. She feels good pressing her small body against mine and I am perplexed as I feel a curious, shimmering spark zinging down my spine. My knees weaken and I press even closer.

What is this? Does Link feel what I'm feeling? Why do I want to feel more, to hold onto her, to feel her touching me? This has got to be wrong. What is the matter with me? *Go for it, Gina. Link can save you from yourself.*

That was definitely unexpected from my keeper and all I need for me to come unglued. When Link releases me I feel my face flush and I'm in full bawl mode, my shoulders shaking and tears flowing freely down my cheeks.

Jonathan, silently aware of the drama unfolding between the two women standing before him, just happens to be ready with a tissue. As I take it from him with blurry eyes I fleetingly wonder if he knew I was going to need a tissue this evening. I also cringe at the possibility that he might have actually seen sparks flying between Link and me. *Very funny, Gina.*

I sit down, grasp my wine glass and try to calm myself while Link, her lips flashing a sympathetic half smile, and Jonathan wait and watch quietly. I again wipe my tears and take a long gulp of wine.

Damn, I've already hit on Jonathan today more than once and now I have this crazy urge to hit on his wife. In my whole life I have never had the desire or even an impulse to get sexually involved with another woman. I definitely need help. *Weird lady,* my keeper chimes in. I smile sadly.

Jonathan and Link exchange curious glances at my smile. "Insanity," I answer their thought. As Jonathan peers out on the lake, I sneak a peek at Link. I raise a quizzical brow and lightly bite my lower lip. She sends back a tight little smile and nods. What does that mean? What the hell is going on?

Link and I join Jonathan in surveying the lake and I attempt to gather myself because I know they'll want additional explanation of my ordeal. Link says something about wine, jumps up and hurries off. For a nanosecond I find myself distracted by her hips as she scurries up the walkway.

Jonathan is watching me closely. He momentarily reaches over and squeezes my bare thigh just above my knee. He allows his hand to linger there and I smile my appreciation as my heart revs up and I feel that knot develop down low. *Come on. Get a life, Gina.*

Just before Link returns with two bottles of chardonnay Jonathan releases my leg.

I smile at Link and gesture toward the wine. "Looking to celebrate, Link?"

She grins as she sets the bottles on the table and winks at her husband. "It may not be a celebration but it's sure as hell going to be a rousing, drunken orgy . . . uh-oh," she giggles, covering her mouth with both hands. "I mean party."

Jonathan and I laugh as she grasps one of the bottles and fills our glasses. Having more or less collected myself I smile at Link and lightly touch her arm with a lone finger. I ignore another zap of strange energy. "Do you guys want to hear the gory details?"

Before they can answer we hear the familiar rumble of a ski boat as it comes around the bend with a skier in tow. It reaches us in a few seconds and the skier releases the rope and glides up to the dock, turning just in time to end up sitting on the edge. He turns and gleams at Link. Not Jonathan. Not me.

"Hi, Link, Mr. Bales, Mrs. Wabbit," he greets with a big grin. The kid must be all of fourteen years old, with long blonde, wet hair and a bronzed body from spending too many hours hanging onto a ski rope. He's a bit skinny because he hasn't reached the age for his muscles to bulk.

He slips off the skis and stands, waiting for the boat to turn and come back to the dock. There is another boy driving and a couple of babes sitting in the back. After tying the boat to the dock, both girls stand so, I'm sure, Jonathan can get a good look at them in their skimpy bikinis.

"Still wet behind the ears," Link mutters softly to us. She calls out to the skier, "Neat landing, Justin, but not in the same league as me."

He frowns his disappointment. It appears he is certainly full of himself as he tries to charm Link. He shakes his head dejectedly, "Dang, what do I have to do to show you I need to be appreciated."

Link laughs, "You might try putting on about ten years. Then I'll probably appreciate you more."

One of the gals on the boat doesn't care for the banter between her guy and this Link woman, and she won't have it.

"Come on, Justin, let's go," she squeaks, drawn brow, squinty eyes, pouty lips and all.

Justin grins and takes the offered ski rope as the other guy unties the boat and starts up. After donning his skis he is off with a quick wave at Link. Not Jonathan. Not me.

We watch as he unsuccessfully attempts to gain some air and make his skis pop as he crosses the boat's wake, just to impress Link. She chuckles and shakes her head. "Justin is such a baby. He's just been weaned from his mom's tit; now he wants to suck mine."

Gina De Georgio

FOUR

It has been three days since the great Wabbit split up. I must say I have done better than I thought I would, mainly because I have plunged into my work. The day after the split I requested that Jonathan find more work for me to do even if was stuffing envelopes. I impressed upon him that I didn't want to come to the big city every day for the additional duties.

He complied and I have been doing some long-needed employee record updates which mainly can be done on my home computer. It's boring and below my job description, whatever that is, but better than my sitting around stewing over my predicament. And thinking about sex that I'm not getting. However I'm getting about the same as before the split—none. And I miss my wayward husband in spite of his being a flaming asshole.

The kids appear to be doing well and haven't even asked about their dad and what he's up to. I think they have things pretty well figured out as several of their friends have had their parents split. I'm sure that sharing these experiences is part of the kid network. They realize that they are caught up in this drama and there's not much they can do about it other than support their mom. They have done that, even to the point I wish they would back off; but I definitely can't tell them to.

This thing with Link is really bothering me. I tell myself to not add anything to what happened and just let it pass. So far it hasn't and I'm beginning to wonder if it will. I still cannot believe I had the hots for Jonathan and Link on the same frigging day. And why Link, anyway? I have never considered nor desired any type of sexual relationship with a woman and don't intend to start now. That is not me; I desire men. And that's the way it is going to stay. Of course it would help and be nice to take at least a bite out of some hunk now and then.

Because of school functions two nights running I haven't had evening wine with the Bales since that fateful Monday night. I talked to Jonathan on the phone Tuesday but not to Link. I have this nagging thought that perhaps I should just talk to Link about the dock incident just to get my head straight.

I don't want to talk to her in Jonathan's presence, but she doesn't like to be disturbed while she is painting during the day. Her studio is separate from the house and she keeps the door locked and won't open it if anyone knocks. Even Jonathan. He says she won't even answer the phone but does eventually return calls if the caller leaves a message.

I understand because she is in a pressure cooker situation right now. She has a one person gallery show coming up in late April in Houston and she has promised thirty paintings. She mentioned that there's no way for her to get them done but she's going to give it her best shot.

I think that just this one time she wouldn't mind the interruption since we've become pretty tight over the years. And like she says, "I am just trying to get along."

What would I say to her? Hey, Link, I'm sorry I got the hots for you down on the dock the other day. . . . Oh, really. You too? . . . So, what do you think we should do about it? *Yeah, right*, my inner voice is laughing.

I know; I'll leave her a text message. Pulling the phone out of my back pocket, I open contacts and scroll down to Link, quickly type and send:

Gina Wabbit   *10:29 AM*

Can we talk? Maybe at lunch on my dock at 12. I have tuna salad over lettuce, fruit, and a pitcher of iced tea. Won't keep you long. If you can't break away, no problem. We'll do it another time.
Gina

Butterflies take over my stomach, my heart skips, and I feel my face flush. Damn, what's with me? *Just cool it, Gina.*

Suddenly my phone beckons with a text:

Link Bales   10:33AM

Great!!! Be there at noon sharp.
Link

Wow, that was fast. Now what? Do I really want to do this? No but I have to sooner or later. May as well be now. Okay, I've got an hour and a half. I have to get moving—make tea, choose fruit, panic. My heart is still pounding and the butterflies have turned into nausea. What should I wear? *What? You're just having lunch with a friend*, the voice chimes in. *Those baggy shorts and halter top are just fine.*

I resisted the urge to change out of the shorts and halter but I did put on a dash of perfume. Why? I arrange two plates of tuna and a mutual bowl of fruit on the dock table. The tea is poured into glasses, and napkins and forks are laid out. It's five minutes until twelve and I'm a quivering mess as I look out over the water.

"Hey," Link says, having come up behind me without my hearing her. She lightly lays a hand on my shoulder and I melt. That same spark zings down my spine exploding down low and I feel my mind in a tizzy, completely paralyzed with apprehension. *Cool it, Gina*, the voice advises.

"Hi, Link." I reach and cover her hand with mine and squeeze softly before turning toward her. She is barefooted and wearing a white loosely fitting pullover smock, a garment that is usually worn over other clothes to protect them. It is made of some type of gauzy material and I can't resist the urge to feel the texture.

She grins. "Neat, huh? I usually paint naked but if it's cold or whatever I wear this. It's so light and frilly, and doesn't hinder my movement." She does a little comical pirouette and the smock twirls loosely around with her.

When she stops I can tell that she is not wearing a bra as her nipples are making little dark buds protruding against the material.

"And sexy," I nod. "I want one." I reach out and feel the material again, resisting the urge to touch her breast. What's the matter with me? I clear my throat reminding myself to be cool. Why do I feel the need to touch her? *Go, girl.*

She stoops and grabs the smock at the lower hem and lifts it up above mid-thigh. "Here, take mine," she jokes then smiles. She releases the smock and we both laugh—me nervously.

I gesture toward the table and we both sit. "Wow, this looks great. Thanks for inviting me," She says with her lips arching in a cute smile and her eyes dancing as they settle on me.

I am drawn to her mouth and I find myself biting at my lower lip in curious anticipation. Like Monday evening I can feel that pull, that fantastic electricity arcing between us—pure palpable energy about to combust at any second. *Whoopee.*

As she spoons some fruit on her plate she eyes me curiously, amusement in her eyes. We sit in silence as we nibble on our food. Where is this headed I wonder? My senses in disarray are spewing delightful shivers throughout my body drowning me in—in what? Desire? That's not possible.

She lays down her fork and takes a sip of tea, smiles and cocks her head to one side. "So, Gina Wabbit, you said we need to talk. And I agree. I know what I want to talk about and assume you want to talk about the same thing."

She pauses for me to answer and I again bite my lower lip in apprehension. I sigh wishing I had her poise. Taking a deep breath to calm my nerves I ask softly, looking into her eyes: "What happened between us the other night?"

She nods her understanding of the question and reaches over and lays her hand on mine. "Desire," she answers simply causing my heart to hitch. "We desired each other. We still do." She pauses and watches for my reaction.

I can't take my eyes off of her eyes but the view blurs because of the tears welling up in my eyes. Dammit, do I have to cry about everything lately? "That's what I was afraid of," I mumble. *Just hang in there*, the voice encourages.

Link slowly shakes her head compassionately. "Don't be afraid. It is what it is. We turn each other on. You are one hot lady and you've been turning me on for years."

"But why now?" I plead. "I've always thought you are sexy but that doesn't mean I want some sort of . . . of a sexual thing or fling or whatever with you."

She replies quickly, "Because in the past you've had someone that satisfied your sexual needs and you also met his. Now you have a void and new doors are opening for you."

My heartbeat accelerates and I feel blood pounding like a pulse in my ears. My whole system seems to be coming alive. "And maybe that door opening has Link standing there?"

Link tilts her head to one side and smiles while shrugging. "Perhaps but you don't have to walk through that door. It's like any other potential sexual relationship; you go for it or you don't. You fill your needs with what is presented or you forget it and move on. Simple as that."

She pauses but when I don't respond she asks, "I assume you haven't ever, uh, been with a woman."

Why are my eyes tearing up again? "No," I answer hardly above a whisper. "What about you?"

She answers with a nod of the head and a sigh of resignation. "Yeah but not since I starting dating John. Before I met him I thought all men were jerks. Because I thought women were real and sincere I was attracted to them, even to the point of organizing women only orgies. I was one cunt sucking lady. I'll bet you had no idea that was going on at TCU."

I shake my head. "I must have been wearing blinders." I wipe a lone tear trickling down my cheek with the back of my hand as I study her momentarily. I ask soft and flat, trying to restrain my emotion: "Do you want to, you know . . . with me?"

She nods and presses her lips together while looking me in the eye. "The last two days I have thought of nothing else. I want you. I want you a lot. The energy between us was, is, incredible."

"Shit!" I exclaim under my breath. I feel my body about to explode as hot blood curses through me fueling my desire.

She chuckles as she lightly squeezes my hand. "So where do we go from here?"

Crap, don't just squeeze my hand. Embrace all of me. "Uh, I'm confused. I have a thousand questions about what is happening to me and why I'm attracted to you."

"Okay, fire away."

"You said that you haven't been with a woman since you started dating John. What changed? Does he no longer give you the same, uh, pleasure he used to?"

Link nods and stares down at her hand caressing mine. "I thought you'd ask that. John still turns me on as always. It's just that the last few months I've felt like something was missing. I didn't know what it was until the other night when you put your arms around me pressing up against me. The electricity, your energy blew me away and I can't get it or you out of my system."

Oh wow. This is insane. I can feel my heart beating in my throat. "Umm . . . I still don't . . . whenever you first met John, what was it that made you want him and no longer women?"

Link gazes into my eyes sending sparks down my spine stirring up my belly. "First off he wasn't a jerk like most of the guys I had dated. Then there's the man to woman thing—the two opposite poles of energy clashing, exploding and eventually dissipating during orgasm that brings that elation or euphoria and a long lasting calmness. The orgasm between two women has an emotional climax but no energy explosion because they have the same charge."

"I understand the yin yang deal so why me? I'm the same charge as you."

She shrugs indifferently. "Desire. Fun and games. Change. Emotional uplift. Did I say desire? All those things. And don't get me wrong; sex with another woman can be fantastic. It's just not as great as with the right man."

"Oh."

"It's also about you, Gina. You need sex. John says you're about to come unglued. I would love giving you at the very least some release from your sexual frustration."

I nod surprised at the honesty between us. If this is confession time I should let it all hang out. "Did John tell you I hit on him Monday morning, the same day that we, uh, hugged?"

"He did," Link nods positively. "He also was acutely aware when we hugged it was more than your or-dinary friendly hug. He definitely picked up on the desire and emotion involved."

"Does that bother you that I hit on your hus-band?" I wonder where this could possibly be headed.

Link nods. "I should be saying, 'Hey bitch, why are you hitting on my man?' because it's kind of like be-trayal by my best friend."

She squeezes my hand, smiles thinly and tilts her head in a what–the–hell shrug. But in certain situations you have to keep a level head. It's human nature to copu-late and not necessarily with only one person. That's the way we're programed or wired.

"There will be times that this programming leads us to someone that perhaps we shouldn't be messing with like a friend's mate. I hope I'm open–minded enough to see that. You are not necessarily intruding in my territory. You're just heeding the programming."

I start to reply but she holds up a hand indicating there is more. "However these situations in my opinion have to have rules. One, this isn't a free for all. No one should be out trying to get laid continuously or spraying sperm all over the countryside with any and every one. That is betrayal for sure.

"Two, you don't get so wrapped up in your passion that you decide to run off with this person or destroy your marriage."

59

I nod, "Amen to that."

She smiles compassionately. "Three, there has to be something between the couple pairing up. What I'm trying to say is they need to care about each other.

"And four, be sure to take care of your sexual business with your permanent partner. They have their sexual needs also."

I chuckle, "I don't have that problem but you do."

Link merely smiles and I study her before asking, "Does John feel the same way you do about sex with another?"

"He does and we try to respect what is going on with each other when either of us carries through with actually having sex with another. I personally don't want to know about it if he does."

I nod and say hardly above a whisper, "Wow."

"There's more. John and I are upfront about our emotional or sexual thoughts concerning someone else. He not only told me about hitting on you on that New Year's Eve, he mentioned that you had hit on him in college. And he had no problem in pointing out to me that he was aware of what was going on between you and me on Monday."

"Are you alright with John's hitting on me?"

"Let me just say I understand and leave it at that." Link flashes her quirky little smile. "But it goes both ways and this also concerns you even though you were unaware at the time."

Concerns me? She pauses and I nod for her to continue.

"For several years I have had the hots for Pep. Of course you didn't know but John was well–aware. I never hit on Pep however and I don't have any idea if he had any feelings for me."

I sigh deeply as I pull my hand from under hers and place it on top of hers. The tears pool in the corners of my eyes. "Damn, I have been so naïve. All this sexual stuff going on with me and I'm hardly aware that others are having their own drama."

Link nods and searches my eyes. "What now?"

Well crap; here goes. I lower my eyes and focus on my hand covering hers. I squeeze lightly then look up into her eyes. Softly I plea, "Link, I want you. Right now. Can we go somewhere?" *Yes, Yes, Yes,* comes the voice.

Link smiles and slowly stands. She offers her hand to me and assists me in getting up. I lean into her and she softly grasps my lower back sending that familiar current cascading down my spinal cord and splashing into my fantasy place.

"The dishes?" she asks.

"No," I force an uneasy smile. "I'll take care of them later. Right now I can't wait to nibble on your toes."

Link raises a brow and laughs heartily. "Something tells me this is going to be fantastic." She takes my hand and we silently walk across the lawn to her studio, my body quivering in anticipation.

Link opens the door and ushers me in. I am greeted with the smell of brush cleaner and paint. Because this is her private little world she doesn't invite guests and discourages even her husband from entering. I toured it one time five years ago when it was first built but not since.

The thought enters my mind that this must really be a special event for her to bring anyone here. It is certainly special for me. I want to speed it along but I also want to slow it down and savior it.

While she quietly watches me I stand in the middle of her cluttered studio and marvel at the surroundings. I didn't ask to intrude in her world but it's a treat because very few are privy to what she actually does here although her finished product is prevalent in many galleries in San Antonio, Austin, Dallas and Houston.

I can't suppress the urge to walk among the paintings, most unfinished but many finished and waiting to be framed for her upcoming show in Houston. Her work is breathtaking and it jumps off the canvas, the vibrant colors demanding that you pay close attention to the detail. I don't comment but I am aware that she is watching for my reaction. I raise a brow and smile my approval and she nods.

Gina De Georgio

Suddenly I am mesmerized by this large finished painting of what appears to be a celebration, a party or a carnival. The colors are magical and I take a closer look while she watches. How can people look this happy?

"Fantastic," I gush. "This is beautiful."

She smiles. "It's certainly my favorite of all the works I have ever done. I'm going to hate to see it sold."

"What have you named it?"

"I call the painting *Carnival*."

"That fits."

Moving on I note the whole studio is lined with shelves in every available space to provide ample storage for her supplies. There is a small kitchen in one corner of the room with a door that leads to what appears to be a bathroom.

Then there's the bed. How inviting. It is located next to the kitchen and its very presence suggests that a person could actually live in this studio in comfort. My attention riveted on the bed I sneak a glance at Link.

She smiles with encouragement and nods.

I smile back and cock a lone brow, my heart rate picking up and my face flushing. I point at the bed. "Has it been christened yet?"

She flashes an amusing wide grin. "No but I think this is the day. What do you think?"

I keep my gaze on her as I walk over to her. It enters my mind, who takes the lead here? I push it aside assuming she knows exactly what she's doing and will be a more than adequate guide for my complete lack of experience.

She watches as I reach out and touch her temple lightly with one finger. I hear her breath hitch as I run the finger up into her hairline and spread my fingers to run them through her curly red hair. *Is this really happening?* My keeper is cheering.

I run my hand back behind her ear to her neck. Her mouth opens slightly as I bend down and gently kiss the side of her face next to her mouth. I softly kiss her lips and bite at her lower lip. I trace her upper lip with my tongue tip and she groans, pushing her body against mine as I place my lips on hers and explore her open mouth with my tongue.

I have her full attention as she is content to let me take this moment wherever it goes. I can't believe I'm doing this. I feel like I'm going to explode as my blood pounds through my head and my heart begins to race. My senses are completely out of control and spurts of energy are spewing up and down my spine.

I drop my hand down to the small of her back and gather her smock in a fist of gauze, pulling it up her spine. Reaching over her shoulder with my other arm I grab the hem on both sides, lift the smock over her head and drop it to puddle on the floor. I step back and look at her naked body as she returns an amused stare.

"Pretty nifty move, Wabbit," she smiles. "Have you been practicing disrobing a defenseless woman?"

Without taking her eyes off of me she reaches over my shoulder and unties my halter, removing it in one swift motion and holds it up for me to observe. "Ah–ha." She grins and forces a sinister smile. "Madam, I can play this game also." She flips it on the floor.

"You are putty in my hands and I shall have my way with you," she adds evilly rubbing her hands together. Her hands are now on my breasts circling around with her fingers lightly pinching and pressing my nipples. My knees weaken as she guides me over to the bed. Facing me she grips my baggy shorts on each side of the waist band and deftly pulls them down and I step out of them.

She gazes at my body before smiling and easily pushing me back on the bed. She lifts and shifts my legs over toward the center of the bed, puts one knee on the bed and is suddenly on her knees next to me.

She runs the back of her hand around my navel and down over my bikini panties to my upper thighs. She turns her hand over and runs the fingers up my inner thighs and caresses my clitoris through my panties. It is exquisite and I find myself melting under her touch as she runs the fingers of both hands under the waist band of my panties before sliding them down to my knees. She bends my knees and slips the panties off.

She again runs two fingers up my thighs and thrusts them gently into my vagina. I groan in sheer ecstasy but suddenly they are gone. "No, please don't stop." I cry out but she moves on.

Link giggles, "Not in a hurry are you?"

She trails her fingers up my abdomen and with both hands pinches and rolls my now swollen nipples. Taking one nipple in her mouth she bites teasingly then sucks bringing a renewed electric current washing over my whole being.

"Oh shit," I moan as she abandons my breasts. She moves her fingers up to my chin and encircles my lips with the tip of one finger.

She parts my lips with the same finger and softly runs it into my mouth. "Suck, Gina." she whispers. "Suck my finger."

I obey and it is strangely erotic. Is this penis related stuff supposed to be in sex between women?

Withdrawing the finger she places nibbling biting kisses on my lips, then her tongue darts into my mouth twisting in and out before tangling and twirling with my tongue. I feel my heart beating in my throat and I think I'm going to suffocate because my breathing has stopped. I push her away gasping for breath and she grins.

Now her lips are back on mine nibbling and teasing. They feel incredibly soft and smooth unlike a male's that are usually rough and demanding. The feeling is so exquisite.

I raise my arms and place both hands on her head and finger comb her hair. She smiles down at me as I drop one hand to find a breast. She groans as I squeeze and knead her nipple until it is as hard as a pebble.

Still on her knees I place my hand above one knee and the other hand on her opposite hip. I push the knee until the leg straightens and pull the hip back with the other hand gently laying her on her back. I kneel beside her on both knees.

She watches as I run a finger around her navel. I smile down at her. "You have to remember this is new to me so you are about to experience amateur hour. If you enjoy it tips are expected. Do you understand?"

Link giggles like a teenager. "Go for it, lady. Is screaming allowed?"

"Not only allowed but expected," I reply shifting my gaze down to my hand as I trail it down to her red pubic hair. It is soft like corn silk and erotic to my exploring fingers."

I run my hand lower and cover her vagina. I nudge her legs apart with the other hand and as I slowly slide a finger down with a slight pressure it becomes moist and warm as it finds her clitoris.

She groans and lifts her hips while she grabs my hand to assist in putting more pressure. I take her hand and place it on the bed beside her.

"Watch out there. Not in a hurry are you?" I grin.

"Touché," she whispers while again raising her hips to get closer to my touch. "Just hurry will you?"

I chuckle. "Remember I'm just learning so I have to go slow to get it right."

"You're doing it right, Gina. Now go for it," she demands with a short giggle.

I bite at my lower lip as I watch her expression. I add a second finger and step up the pressure on her clit as I circle it and squeeze it between my fingers. I circle again and squeeze harder, then harder.

"Oh . . . please!" she cries out pumping her hips in unison with my fingers. Her labored breathing quickens as she closes her eyes and throws her head back. "Damn, you're killing me, Gina. Please harder."

Just watching her enjoyment has a profound effect on me. I feel my blood boiling in my veins as my heart spikes. My body flushes and my skin gleams with sweat as my desire for this woman peaks. I want what Link is experiencing. And I want it now. *Crap, cool it, Gina. Your time is coming*.

I sense she is about to come. Not yet I tell myself. The best part is approaching I think if I can figure out what to do. I grasp both thighs and spread her legs completely apart and bend her knees. I move over between them on my knees.

"Oh, yes, Gina," she moans. "I want you. Fuck me. Fuck me hard, now."

I have a fleeting thought about what a man feels about now when he is in this position. I certainly feel all powerful and completely in control of Link's feelings. My muse is having a ball, laughing and dancing in a circle. *Don't screw this up, Gina. I'm counting on you.*

I lean in close and her smell is intoxicating. I wonder if I smell that good. I spread open her vagina with fingers of both hands and gently touch that wet, warm nest with my tongue. The taste is sweet and inviting. I gently run my tongue over her clitoris.

She groans and pushes her hips to apply more pressure. "Oh, yes, Gina. That's what I want. Go harder."

I must be doing something right. This is easy. My tongue circles her clit then I draw it back and take her clit between my lips. I suck lightly then hold tight with my lips and twist my head slightly from side to side.

"Oh!" Link gasps. "You are frigging fantastic. You said you didn't know what to do. You can do this forever."

I'm certainly proud of myself as I pull back and kiss the inside of her thigh as my body quivers in its own yearning for relief.

"No, don't stop. Not yet," Link pleads. "Please, I want more."

I chuckle breathlessly. "Quiet down, woman. I promise you are going to beg me to stop before I'm through. Just relax and take it as it comes."

Link commands, "No, I want it all right now."

I run my tongue up and down one thigh then switch to the other. All the while she has her hands grabbing my hair tugging me upward.

I giggle at her antics but she doesn't stop, tugging even harder. I burst out laughing and roll over on the bed stretched out beside her.

"No fair. What are you doing? You can't stop now," she laughs. "There's no recess during sex."

"So how long have you been wanting me?" I ask with a smile. I am loving every second of this and I hope it lasts well into the evening.

"Too long," she answers poking a finger in my chest between my breasts while grinning.

"Then you shouldn't have a problem waiting a little longer then."

"Umm, I think I'm losing interest. You might have to start over."

"That isn't going to happen," I chuckle. I spread her legs and position myself between them. I bend one knee and kiss the inside then I run my tongue up her thigh pausing every few inches to mix kisses before tonguing my way ever higher.

"Is this where I left off," I say looking up and smiling when I reach the top of her thigh.

"Well crap, will you quit talking and get back to fucking me please."

"Damn, you're no fun at all." I spread her legs wider and instantly my tongue has found her clitoris.

Her breath hitches and she exclaims softly, "Oh yes!"

I circle her clit with my tongue and suck again harder. Then I grasp her clit tightly with my lips, rotating my head back and forth. I feel the muscles tense up in her legs and hear a muffled groan above her heavy breathing. She suddenly grasps my hair and pulls me closer.

I reach up with both hands and grasp her breasts, squeezing her nipples while increasing the pressure on her clit. It has swollen larger and I know that Link is ready to come and will not be able to hold off much longer.

I withdraw from her vagina and she moans in complaint. "No Gina, I want to come now. Don't make me wait," she begs.

I drop her legs to the bed and slide up on top of her. I kiss her lightly on the neck and she throws her head back and grasps me behind my head. With one move of her hand she turns my head so that our lips meet. She bites lightly at my lips before forcing her tongue into my mouth. She puts her hands on my cheeks and presses our mouths tightly together as she bites and sucks on my tongue. I hear a groan coming from deep in her throat before she pulls away.

Her chest is rising and falling with each breath and her face is flushed as she looks at me with a trace of a smile on a partially open mouth.

"Enough Gina," she breathes. "I want you. Take care of me now." She pushes me down as she bends her knees and raises her hips.

I grin and work my way down trailing my fingers and kissing breasts, a flat stomach, a cute navel, even silky red pubic hair. Link is impatiently looking down watching me with a look of anguish on her face.

I again search for her clitoris. Wrapping my lips around it I'm surprised at how much it has swollen in the last few minutes. I suck lightly and sneak a look at Link.

She has thrown her head back, closed her eyes and is breathing heavily. Her hips and knees begin to move in rhythm as she pushes toward me gradually picking up speed. I suck then pull the clit slightly with my lips and let up, then suck and pull again harder and quicker this time. Then again harder and quicker as her hips keep up their tireless flailing, pushing forward and back with her knees keeping time.

"Oh, Gina," she groans. "Yes, please," she pleads as a soft whine comes from deep in her throat with each breath. "Oh, harder, Gina." Her breathing is more labored, nearly panting and her body writhes as if being fueled by the pumping of her hips.

I press on sucking and pulling her clitoris thoroughly caught up in the pleasure Link is experiencing. How long can she go on?

My hands on her breasts I can feel her muscles tensing up and the deep throaty sounds increasing as it appears she gasps for every breath. Her hips suddenly stop pumping as she thrusts them against me one last time and cries out a beautiful sound of release—of relief.

I pull back just as she drops her knees and her legs lay flat, still spread on the bed with me kneeling between them. I stretch out and lay between them with my head resting on her stomach. I listen as her pulse pounds in my ear. The warmness of her stomach reminds me of my own unquenched desire which I had temporarily put aside in my quest to make sure she was completely satisfied.

I feel her hand on my head as she twirls my hair around her fingers. She says softly, "Damn, where have you been?"

Umm, I guess that was a compliment.

We lay quietly as her breathing settles. We have turned on our sides facing each other. She reaches up and trails a lone finger around my lips.

"Wow, Gina," she says softly. "You are one fantastic lover. Have you been practicing?"

"I wish. It's been a long dry spell for me. I haven't had a real orgasm since, well, over a month unless you call masturbation . . . uh, you know what I mean."

She smiles and kisses me lightly on the lips then lightly bites my lips, bringing that yeaning deep in the pit of my stomach. "I guess that's about to end," she says as she pushes me over on my back. She is suddenly on top of me sitting on my pelvis with her knees bent pressing against my sides beneath my arms.

"Are you up to this? We don't have to do this now," she teases rubbing her tongue along her bottom lip.

I take her hands and place them on my breasts. "I want it now and you can start here." I command with a smile. "And would you please speed things up. I want you and I want you now."

"Yes ma'am," she answers wide–eyed with an open–mouthed grin. She bends over and lightly twirls her tongue around one nipple and then the other. "Your breasts are beautiful, Gina. I love the way they look. I love the way they feel when I touch them. I love the way they feel in my mouth."

My heartbeat kicks up a notch and I feel my face flush. I am immediately thrust back into the mode I was in just minutes ago. I groan as Link nibbles and sucks one nipple and then the other. I close my eyes and throw my head back, my body beginning a slow burn. I am thoroughly relishing the moment yet anticipating what is sure to come.

Now she has moved up and is lightly kissing my neck, then my ear lobe before tracing her lips down my cheek to my mouth.

"Oh," I murmur from deep in my throat as I open my mouth to accept hers. Our lips clash as we lightly bite and suck before our tongues meet in a tangling, sucking, groaning feast of pure pleasure.

I grasp her hair and pull her head back. Her eyes are burning with desire and her mouth is slightly open with a hint of a smile.

I reach up and grasp her checks with both hands. "Link, I can't take this any longer. I have to have you now." I drop my hands to her shoulders and push down. As she gets off of me I lift my legs and bend my knees.

She sits back on her bent knees and places her hands on my thighs. She slowly slides her fingers up to find my clitoris.

I gasp as I feel my blood approaching a boil, my heart racing and that queasy knotting in my belly.

She lightly kneads my clit before pressing it firmly against my pubic bone with her thumb. She rotates her thumb while slowly increasing the pressure against the bone. Suddenly my senses are facing that borderline between outright pain and sensual euphoria.

"Oh, please, Link," I cry out grasping her wrist, caught between pulling her hand back and begging for more. "Damn, that hurts . . . so fucking good. Please stop." I force a half groan, half laugh. "No dammit, don't stop."

Link laughs smugly as she withdraws her thumb. She lies down on her stomach between my legs and places her hands under my hips repositioning them on the bed for easier access to my vagina. She lightly kisses and trails her tongue on one inner thigh then switches to the other.

Shifting her attention she withdraws her hands from my hips, parts and lightly cups my clitoris with her lips. She clamps my clit harder with her lips and holds tightly as she waits for the reaction from me that she seems to know is coming.

My senses already in disarray I gasp at the sensual intensity this continual pressure causes. "Augh," I gasp. "Shit, Link. What are you doing to me?" I grasp her curly hair with both hands and pull as I throw my head back.

"Hey, easy!" She reaches up with both hands, and pinches and twists my nipples. "Pain begets pain, woman."

"Okay, okay. No more hair pulling. No more tit pulling," I laugh letting go of her hair and pulling her hands off my nipples. "Can you get back to the job at hand?"

Link grins and dives in. Her mouth settles around my clitoris and her tongue trails around it pausing only for her to suck. Then the tongue again. I feel my blood boiling and my heartbeat racing as the energy between us builds, the intensity reverberating throughout my body flooding me with delightful anticipation.

How much more of this can I take? I grasp Link's shoulders as I draw my hips back and lightly thrust forward while pulling against her shoulders.

"Oh, Link! Go harder. I want you now," I cry out.

She groans and sucks my clit harder. "Go for it, babe," she mumbles without missing a beat.

The room is spinning as my body pulsates from my accelerating heartbeat and I feel as if I'm about to explode, completely coming apart internally. I can't hold back any longer.

"Harder! Please Link, fuck me hard! Faster! I'm coming!"

I feel Link sucking my clit harder as she grasps my nipples squeezing and twisting them. Energy is shooting down my spine splashing wildly in my vagina.

I thrust my hips forward trying to get even closer to Link when finally I lose it—every muscle in my body seems to contract in one massive spasm before my whole being down to its very core explodes in a frenzied ecstasy.

For several minutes we hold onto each other in silence watching our breathing ebb and savoring every moment of this fantastic union.

"Hey," Link whispers.

"Hey," I answer. "Nice, huh?"

Link pushes me on the shoulder and stares at me. "What do you mean nice? That was fantastic. It was better than fantastic."

I laugh. "Whoa. Sorry, if you remember I have no reference point having never screwed a woman before. But in all my years of great sex—and I've had a lot of years of great sex—that had to surely be in my top ten."

Link frowns, tilts her head to the side, looking at me askew. "Top ten, huh? Well I guess that's about the same with me. Considering all those great male escapades we've both had I guess that's saying a lot." She shrugs and grins. "But you've got to be my number one woman."

I smile and nod my head. "Well then, that is saying a lot especially since I'm a beginner."

Link grins, "Yeah, I guess that makes you rookie of the year. But if I get a vote you're the most valuable player."

"I suppose that means you want to play me again?"

"Damn right."

"Right now?"

"Damn right," she nods with a thin smile. "Want to play?"

Without answering, I move closer to her, wrap my arms around her and wedge a knee between her legs. I kiss her softly and lightly nibble at her upper lip. I whisper, "Link, I promise I won't screw it up this time. Now I have a lot of experience."

FIVE

Well it's Friday and I feel fantastic for the first time in—how many months now?—about eight or ten, possibly more. I've experienced very little sexual need. My only thoughts about sex today have been a recurring fantasy about getting Link back into the sack—which I hope is soon. She saved me from myself, if only temporarily, and I can't wait to tell her. I'm sure I'll get the chance during wine time later after dinner.

All in all it's been a great day except for the forty–five minutes I spent this morning with my lawyer, Bill Jenkins, mapping out a strategy for the divorce. I can tell already this whole divorce thing is going to be one big mess. Bill is going to file on Monday and Pep will be served shortly thereafter at his real estate office since I don't have any idea where he lives.

It has been five days since we split and things still seem to be going relatively well with the kids. However, since they've said very little about it I really don't know what they are thinking. They are certainly being support-ive of me, actually asking me on occasion if I need any-thing. Are these really my kids? Maybe there's hope for them.

As for myself I do miss Pep a lot. Even though our sexual relationship was shitty I was used to having him in bed next to me and having him seated at the dinner table. His leaving has left a gaping hole in our whole living mode. But I guess we'll adjust. We have to.

After dinner Jack, Bunny and I head for the dock for my Friday night wine time. Although the water is too cold for me we are all dressed for swimming—me in my most skimpy yellow bikini. Before long the Bales kids join us.

Johnny Bales, eleven years old, is smaller than Jack but definitely on the front row of any activity on our portion of the lake. His voice can always be heard over the rest of his cronies even when they are congregated four houses down. He has his dad's looks to be sure—dark skin, determined jaw, piercing eyes and even the unruly dark hair. He is definitely the ring leader of the immediate neighborhood kids of which there are eight total—four girls and four boys, all aged within three years of each other.

Year round, even when the weather is in the forties they are demanding that the adults take them skiing. There are four families involved so we all try to take our turn in driving the boat. Of course we haven't discussed who is going to take Pep's turn now that he is gone. I guess that will fall to me. Great. Double duty.

The other Bales kid, Jody, is eight, three months younger than Bunny. She, being the youngest of the eight, is also the quietest. She hardly ever enters the constant kid's squabbles, content to hang back and follow the group. She is a 3-D print of her mom—very petite with the curly red hair and more than her share of freckles. Like her mom she has to protect herself from the sun or pay the consequences. She has one area in which she surpasses the other seven kids; she is by far the best skier and the four boys have a problem accepting that.

The kids are summoned by their other four friends yelling at them from several houses down the way. They dive in the water and swim down the shoreline toward their friends, constantly chattering, with Jody bringing up the rear.

I pour my third glass of merlot. Gazing out across the lake I think back to my talk with my attorney this morning and wonder if I'm going to lose my lake home because of the divorce.

"Hey," comes the familiar voice behind me.

I turn to see Link joining me on the dock. I flash my best smile. "Hey to you too. Seems like someone said that to me during a special time yesterday." I motion for her to sit.

Her lips curl into that funky smile. "She did and that lucky someone was me."

She is dressed in one of her usual skimpy bikinis and my heart skips a beat. I want to take a bite out of her but settle for touching her on the thigh with one finger. Wow, the electricity between us is the same as yesterday.

"So how was your day? I suppose you had to put in extra hours to catch up for, uh, literally screwing around so much yesterday afternoon."

She nods and lays her hand on my thigh and I want to jump her bones.

Cocking her head slightly to one side she clicks her tongue as her brow furrows. "It was my intent to put in more hours but I'm afraid I wasn't very productive. I wanted to call to see if you would come for a little visit but instead I trudged on valiantly."

I squint my eyes, curl my lips and project my most disappointed frown. "Oh, Link, hurt me, hurt me. I would've been there in about twelve seconds. I've been having fantasies all day about repeating yesterday."

Link chuckles, "They'll be other days and next time like yesterday screw painting; I'd rather screw you." She raises a hesitant finger. "Contrary to my standing rule about no interruptions when I'm at work I want you to call anytime. Okay?"

Some crazy muscles in my stomach clench unexpectedly as I smile. "Damn, I can't wait. Am I drooling? With that attitude and my craving for you you're liable to never get any work done."

She squeezes my thigh and withdraws her hand as we spy Jonathan approaching barefooted and bare–chested, walking across the lawn dressed in his favorite grungy red swim suit, wine in hand.

Right before Jonathan gets to the dock, I whisper, "By the way you were a lifesaver yesterday.

"Hey, John boy, we thought you would never show up," I greet with a smile and point to a chair. "You're about three glasses behind."

"Jerry Boyd called from London and I couldn't get him off the phone. Sometimes I think that guy doesn't know shit but he always comes up with the greatest ideas. So I'm glad he's on our team. I just wish he would quit calling at these crazy hours."

"I thought that it's my job to deal with the likes of him."

Jonathan grins and strokes his beard as if in deliberation. "Yes, my dear, it is your job and every time he calls I tell him he should be talking to you. And he keeps forgetting."

He rubs his hands together indicating a change of direction. "Did you talk to Bill Jenkins?"

"Yeah," I nod with tight curled lips and a tilt of my head. "He's going to file Monday and Pep will be served a day or two after."

I watch as Jonathan again strokes his beard, waking my hormones from a long day's rest. Damn, you are sexy. Can I run my fingers through your beard also?

He wrests me from my erotic mini–fantasy. "Well, it looks like the whole pile of it is going to hit the fan, huh?"

"I'm not looking forward to this for sure," I reply while glumly shaking my head. "This certainly isn't in my life's plan but it is definitely a happening thing."

We quietly sit with our private thoughts as we look out over the water. There's the never ending screeching of the kids down the way but there isn't any of the usual Friday noisy boat activity.

"How is this going to play out? Surely Bill has a plan to protect you and the kids?"

I release a long sigh. "First, he'll have the judge set up some type of financial agreement that Pep will have to abide by until the divorce is final. The same for visitation rights for him and the kids."

"Did you talk about a property settlement?"

I clear my throat in an attempt to steady my nerves. "This is kind of scary for me. I certainly don't want to give up this property but it is so valuable that I may not be able to buy his half.

"He can't buy my share unless I agree to sell because the kids will be living with me. The judge isn't about to have the kids thrown out of their own house.

"If I am unable to buy him out and I don't agree to sell to him we would have to sell it and divide the money."

Link looks puzzled and I nod for her to speak. "What if he gets custody of the kids? Doesn't that give him the advantage to buy your half?"

"He won't get custody because he ran off with some babe. Even if he didn't this is Texas and men have shitty rights when it comes to custody."

Jonathan nods, his eyes showing concern. "I assume the property is paid for so to buy him out you would have to come up with a little over five hundred grand."

I nod. "Yes, there's some cash stashed away that we'll split and a great deal of stock, but I don't have any idea what it's worth."

I shake my head sadly. "I don't think that half the proceeds would be enough to buy him out."

Jonathan looks to Link. "You're awfully quiet. Got any ideas?"

Link shakes her head with a trace of a smile. "No ideas but I have a couple of temporary distractions."

"Alright, I'll bite. What's the first?"

Link grins, "Pass the bottle."

We chuckle and Jonathan nods, "That's time-honored. Now, what's the second?"

Link opens her eyes wide and presses into a broad smile. "I think we need to have a threesome."

We all laugh and I wink at Link. That would be great for me because I will finally get Jonathan into bed. I wait for Jonathan to reply but he merely shakes his head at Link.

After a short moment I smile. "Link, surely you aren't serious but if you are I think you'll have a hard time convincing John and me to participate. What do you think, John boy?"

Jonathan smiles wryly at his wife and slowly shakes his head. "Ma'am, you never cease to amaze me. You are continually coming up with something I didn't know about you. Now you're suggesting a threesome. Whether you're serious or not I can't see myself participating. I'm having a difficult time satisfying one woman and it would be a total disaster for me to try to satisfy two."

Link laughs and pats Jonathan on his bare knee. "You do alright. You just need more practice."

Jonathan rolls his eyes for his wife's benefit then turns back toward me. "Alright, let's get back to your possible financial crisis, Gina. Maybe it's time for you to reinvent yourself and use your degree in journalism."

I gaze at him warily but don't respond.

He continues: "I've been kicking this idea around for a long time but I thought that you wouldn't be interested since you have this rich husband, cushy job and push–over boss."

He pauses and studies me. I like it when he studies me. It brings out his sexiness and makes me feel sexy.

"This is what I propose: you become a syndicated columnist. We have enough magazines to pull this off initially then you can expand to other rags that we don't own. Just this morning I talked to five of our editors and they are on board. There's probably five others—maybe more if auto mechanics is an option."

Auto mechanics? I raise a doubtful brow and tilt my head while eying him suspiciously. "And . . . what is it I'm writing about in my syndicated column?"

Jonathan grins and spreads his arms, his eyes projecting a kid's enthusiasm. "Sex." He looks at me, then Link, then back at me. "What do you think?"

I pause and notice that Link is stifling her amusement with us. I shake my head while feigning dismay. "John, I think you have a screw loose—maybe two. Like I'm some kind of authority on sex. All I know is, you put it in, have a little joy ride, then take it out when it won't work anymore."

Of course Link nearly falls off her chair with her usual hearty laughter and Jonathan chuckles.

"You've got to be kidding, Johnny. I can't even get laid with any regularity. How can I guide somebody else if I can't even get my own act together?"

I sneak a look at Link and she is grinning. Did I see her lick her upper lip? Did Jonathan see that? Apparently not. He's also grinning at me. Shit, your turn Jonathan.

"Gina, you don't have to be an authority. It's all bullshit anyway. You just have to be better at bullshitting than the next guy. It's a matter of selling yourself and we certainly have the clout to do that."

"I don't know, John. Sounds too far–fetched to me."

"Alright, there's more. Hear me out." Jonathan scratches his beard and it again triggers my slow melt twisted hormone thing. "Another angle: along with your column you include a website with a blog, Face Book, email, the whole package.

"You can have your fans send in their questions via these social media. Then print the questions you choose in your column and ask others to send in their opinions or advice via the same media. You print the advice in the next column. This is plain old blog stuff. Everybody has an opinion. You'll just be the brilliant middle man."

I see where he is coming from but wonder if it can be pulled off. "And this is all about sex?"

"Oh, no. It's about anything people want to ask or talk about—sex, lesbianism, gay life, bisexuality, cooking," Jonathan grins, "hell, the price of football tickets, best cabbage recipes, everything. Just think, you'll have the whole world coming to you, to your column for answers to the unanswerable. You'll become famous and rich as all get out."

Jonathan folds his arms and grins smugly. "It's a piece of cake, Gina. You've got to do it."

Link claps. "Fantastic, John. Gina, go for it. I'll send you a question about a recent experience I had. And I'll bet you'll have a ready answer." She rubs her hands together and grins mischievously as Jonathan looks on and nods his agreement.

I aim a lifted brow at Link and shake my head with a smirk on my lips. Jonathan feigns innocence.

I study Jonathan, attracted to his shirtless chest and wishing I could run my fingers through the hair. Or the hair on his head for that matter. Or his beard; I'm not choosy. He's so fucking hot.

Damn, how can I be lusting over these two people sitting before me? I'm the idiot that should be writing for advice. My inner voice wakes up. *Good idea, Gina. You can write the first letter to yourself. Then you answer it.*

I release a long–winded breath of tension as I look first to Link, then Jonathan. Shit, maybe a threesome would be nice after all. *Gina, just get your head straight.*

I resign: "Alright, Johnny, let's do it. I assume I still have my day job, right?" *Alright, Gina. Go for it. You need this. It's going to be great.*

Jonathan jumps up from his chair, claps his hands together then offers a high–five, first to Link then to me. "Great decision, Gina. You won't regret it."

He raises a finger of caution and cocks a perfect brow. "Of course you still have a job because it'll be a while before you have any real bucks coming in. Also for your information, when you're rich and famous you are not al-lowed to quit your cushy job and push–over boss. Under-stood?"

"Fair enough. Now, what's next?"

"First you'll need a catchy name for yourself and the column. Then you'll have to get the social media set up through BP; Bob Couser can help you with that. After all that the Project Department can design the column for-mat and you're off and running."

I smile curiously at Jonathan. "Why are you doing all this for me?"

Jonathan gestures toward Link. She smiles, "Be-cause he's madly in love with you, Gina." Jonathan nods his agreement.

The tears well up in my eyes and I trap one with a finger just as it starts to trail down my cheek. Link briefly puts a comforting hand on my knee. Of course her touch sends a delicious shiver traipsing down my spine to ex-plode in that hot spot. *Damn, Gina, you're turned on to everybody.*

After waiting a moment for me to collect myself, Jonathan continues: "One more thing, Gina. Link and I want to help you get through this divorce any way we can. If push comes to shove and it looks like you won't be able to rake up enough bucks to buy Pep's half of this property BP will loan you the money to do so."

Link nods her affirmation. "We don't really like you but we don't want to have to break in a new neighbor if you leave."

Tears again, dammit. This time the wiping is more involved. They wait.

"I don't know how I'll ever repay you for what you're doing for me," I mumble softly.

"We'll think of something," Jonathan says.

"You've already made a down payment," Link grins and Jonathan studies her curiously.

The Lake McQueeney Country Club and Water Ski Resort is basically the only game in town when it comes to dining on the lake. It is a year round hang–out for the kids especially during the summer and the adults join them on the weekends. It is easily accessible by boat or car and many of the younger kids ride their bikes when their parents are not able to ferry them.

The club has all the amenities of your usual coun-try club—golf, tennis, gym and pool. Of course the biggest attraction is water skiing and there are several ski teams for different skill levels; many of the kids enter competi-tions worldwide. It is definitely an advantage when you have parents that have the means to fund these trips.

It is Saturday evening and we have gathered for our usual dinner at the club. Our large group of regulars include a countless number of kids, the Bales and several other couples, a divorcee, a widower and me, out for the first time without Pep.

The group has been kind enough to ignore my sit-uation as nothing has been mentioned and no questions asked. It does seem a bit strange to be here without Pep but I will survive. However it has been six days since the split and I do miss him—a lot.

Gina De Georgio

After dinner the kids disappear to the game room. Jonathan, Link and I have found our way to the deck of the bar on the second floor of the restaurant overlooking the lake.

Being supported by them this last week has been a real lifesaver for me in several interesting ways. Jeez, I can't believe the week I've had. And here I am sitting across from them drinking my Martini—yes, Martini—because that's what you drink on Saturday night at the country club. I'll switch to merlot later—or maybe some high–dollar Chivas. I don't get drunk cheaply.

Speaking of drunk, my hormones are on active duty making me tipsy with pure sexual energy sparking and pin–balling throughout my system. I am again lusting over Jonathan and Link—both at the same time. I believe that Link's suggestion that we have a threesome has more merit than I have given it. But I can't imagine what or how we would do it. It certainly would add another dimension to the whole sexual experience. I suppose I could wing it like I did with Link. That certainly turned out well.

It was difficult deciding what to wear this evening. Is there a difference in how you project your sexiness to a man than it is to a woman? Because it is still a bit chilly in the evening I finally decided on white slacks, a black long–sleeved cotton top with a plunging neckline, and a light beige silk sweater. For shoes I have chosen my black Steve Madden Brrit Platform Sandals. I don't know if I am projecting sexy but I certainly feel sexy.

As we sip our Martinis we are content to sit quietly and watch the docking of the fancy boats bringing families to the conclusive activity of this long spring Saturday. I glance at Link and find her studying me while lightly biting at her lower lip. She winks at me bringing my yearning for her back to full throttle. I make sure Jonathan isn't watching and stick my tongue out at her. She answers by jutting out her lower lip in that full pout only she can do.

She is wearing a floor length, pleated skirt with a multicolored floral design, and a yellow long–sleeved, tightly fitted top that barely keeps her breasts from breaking free. Her top and yellow plastic banana earrings contrast with her red curly hair, and her size four feet are incased in yellow canvas Kenzo Espadrilles. And she is oh so hot this evening.

The three of us return our attention to the boat dock. I am suddenly aware of a toe, a foot, rubbing against my calf. I look first at Link, then Jonathan but there is no indication of who is toying with me. My heart hitches and I have the urge to ask which one is the guilty party but I don't think that would go over too well with the non–player.

So I wait and of course here it goes again. I straighten my leg a bit so that the culprit can have a more exposed leg to play with and I watch both for reaction. Nothing. If it is Link she would at least acknowledge but I'm just guessing. It would be nice if it was Jonathan. No, that's wrong; it is nice whoever it is.

Suddenly the little teenage game is over when Jonathan speaks while scratching his beard, his voice full of enthusiasm:

"Gina, have you thought anymore about the fantastic column you're going to write—your column of worldwide fame?"

"Funny you bring that up, Mr. Bales," I nod positively. "I have spent a large portion of this day trying to come up with a handle for the column. I would like to bounce my favorite off of you and Link.

"First off, the name of the column could be: *The Italian Rabbit*. This main title Rabbit would be spelled with an R."

I pause and hold up both hands as if to orchestrate. "Now, I think it needs a subtitle and I have come up with, *Straight Talk with Gina De Georgio Wabbit*. This Wabbit spelled with a W."

Jonathan nods positively with pressed lips. Link merely smiles as she touches my lower leg with her toe and winks. I kick back at her under the table and she merely bites her lower lip letting me know that she was the original foot molester.

Jonathan hesitates in his answer and I switch my attention to him. He is wearing tight blue jeans and a dark blue turtleneck, blue and red striped athletic shoes with blue socks to match the shirt. He is his usual sexy.

He broadens his smile. "Both are catchy and could supply an original hook to get the reader's attention. I'll tell you what: get all your ideas together and we'll get the experts together at BP and have a brainstorming session. Maybe they can come up with something else or make some minor tweaks of your idea."

I nod but don't comment. Jonathan continues:

"I told you yesterday that we could put your column under the BP domain for social media purposes but I think I have a better idea for the long run. It would probably serve you better if you get your own domain so your email, website and other media will be attached to whatever you name your domain."

Link briefly lifts a finger for clarification. "You mean, if she names her domain ItalianRabbit, her email address would be Gina@ItalianRabbit?"

Jonathan affirms, "Same for the website; instead of having BP attached to your social media you would have Italian Rabbit. If you end up massively successful the media would be under your own roof instead of under BP's."

"I'm afraid I don't understand much about domains. This is beginning to sound a bit overwhelming," I comment wondering if I even want to go there.

"Domains are really quite simple. It's like if you get an email address through Google, your address would be gina@gmail.com. Through BP's domain, you already have an email address by that name—gina@bp.com. Most domains come with unlimited email accounts; BP's domain has five hundred so all our employees worldwide have an email address through the company they work for. Ditto for their kids."

"The cost?"

"It depends on all the services your domain provides. Yours will probably cost about ten dollars a month, give or take. I think that would give you about thirty email addresses. Your kids and all their friends could have an email account through Italian Rabbit."

"It's still scary. Can I still have Bob Couser's help in setting everything up?"

"Of course and I'm sure he would love doing it for you. He's a geek in every sense of the word. And as I said yesterday, all of BP's muscle and brain power will back you to get the word out and to get the column on line."

Studying my empty Martini glass I slowly shake my head and offer a hesitant smile. I ask softly as I look up and grin at Link, "And all this is going to make my name a household word?"

Jonathan and Link laugh and Jonathan motions for the bar lady.

She returns with wine for the Bales and a Chivas Royal Salute and water for me. I take an immediate slug but caution myself to slow down. Link and Jonathan head for the dance floor and I watch wishing I could dance with Jonathan. At least I could legally press my body against his. The mere thought brings that bolt of energy coursing through my being and landing with a thump in my belly.

As they return the DJ is already playing a slow oldie and Jonathan offers his hand for an obligatory dance. Call it what you want, I get to press against him if only for a couple of minutes.

Whoa, I wasn't prepared for this. As I lean into him his scent is breathtaking while the energy between us is even more electric than with Link on Monday. I melt against him with energy coursing down my spine and splashing somewhere deep down there. I wonder if I am affecting him the same way.

I snuggle my chin next to his beard and catch a sideways glance at Link. She smiles and nods for my benefit. This is totally weird; I'm practically dry–fucking her husband right in front of her and wishing the song would go on forever.

I can't resist telling him what I'm feeling: "Well, Johnny, I finally get to feel you close to me even if it's for a dance."

With his hand on my low back he gently pulls me closer. "Yeah, it appears after all these years we are be-coming an odd couple."

I chuckle softly, "Or an odd threesome."

"That's what I'm afraid of. We shouldn't even think of going there. Link gives it some lip service but I don't think any of us can handle that."

The music ends too soon and Jonathan leads me by the hand back to our table. Link projects that funky grin as I sit down and take a sip of my scotch. "You guys look pretty tight. Known each other long?"

Jonathan is noncommittal so I answer while patting Link on the knee under the table. "A little too long I think."

There is commotion on the stairway and all eight of the neighborhood gang of kids suddenly appear. Tonight is the night for their periodic all night movie party at the Bedford's home. They bring their sleeping bags and pillows and crash on the living room floor when they can't take it anymore. And sometimes sleep until noon on Sunday.

The spokesman, Johnny, informs his dad, "Time to go. We'll ride on the Bedford's boat. That way you won't have to leave here early to drop us off."

Jonathan exaggerates a frown at his son. "It's not even eight yet. What's your hurry?"

Johnny grins at his dad. "We have five movies to watch."

Jonathan, Link and I laugh at the thought of watching five movies in one night. Our attention is turned to the dance floor where Jody has left the group and is uncharacteristically dancing to the Beatle's *Eleanor Rigby*, swaying back and forth and adding a chicken dance move occasionally with her arms. She knows she has caught the eye of others in the bar and is milking the moment.

Jonathan arches a lone quizzical brow and says to Link, "That's definitely not my shy daughter out there. She's trying to imitate you."

"Wow, maybe there's hope for her." That was Link.

Applause follows the song and Jonathan's attention returns to Johnny. "What movies are you guys going to watch?

"I only know the first one."

"And that would be?"

86

Without expression Johnny answers, *"Fifty Shades of Grey."* The other kids commence to giggle.

Link and I don't buy it but we sit and silently wait for Jonathan's reply.

"Yeah, right," Jonathan says while sticking a tongue in his cheek and slowly shaking his head for his son's benefit. "Who might I ask chose this movie for you guys to watch?"

Johnny grins and answers while spreading his arms, "Mrs. Bedford. She said it's a cool movie and we need to see it."

The kids try to suppress a giggle but are not successful.

Jonathan nods his head at his son. "So tell me, do you have any idea what this film is about?"

"Yes, sir."

Jonathan waits for further explanation but when none comes he motions for his son to continue.

Johnny looks at his cronies who are grinning at him. "It's about you and mom."

The kids, Link and I laugh.

Jonathan is stoic as he studies his son. "Very funny, and Mrs. Bedford chose the film? No, don't answer that." Jonathan turns toward the kids. "Monica, did your mom choose this film for you guys to watch?"

Monica giggles, "No, Sir. We're playing a trick on you."

Jonathan points a threatening finger at his son. "Will you take your little band of misfits and get out of our sight? And make sure everyone gets their sleeping stuff out of our boat so we don't have to stop and deliver it."

Johnny shoots a grin at his dad. "We'll try." He turns to the others and commands, "All right, let's move it, guys. We've got movies to watch." He and the other kids wave their goodbyes and suddenly are gone, clomping down the stairs while chattering up a storm.

"Jeez, I'm glad Barbara always hosts this party. I think I would go freaking mad if I had to put up with those crazy preteens every two or three weeks."

I chuckle, "She's definitely supermom."

Gina De Georgio

A welcome and familiar face approaches and smiles his greeting. "Looks like your kids are on a mission. The nearly ran over me on the stairs."

We chuckle as Jonathan stands, extending his hand. "Hello, Preacher. Looks like you have your usual rambunctious crowd this evening."

"Yeah, ain't it great," he bubbles with a warm smile. "Are you people being taken care of in the way you deserve?"

"Service and food excellent," Link replies. "We certainly appreciate it."

William Elliot Carmichael, better known as Preacher is the owner and head straw boss of the country club. He not only keeps the place operating smoothly, he is not below the most menial of jobs including dishwasher.

He is a friend, confident and advisor to kids and adults alike. Preacher is someone always ready to lend a helping hand or even a discrete buck or two if someone is down on their luck.

Although he is reluctant to talk about his past, searches on the Internet and other bits and pieces suggest he is an ordained minister that was relieved of his duties at a church in Alabama—a church that he formed and financed with his own inheritance.

The church under his guidance grew to the point that a board was formed to oversee church operation. The board eventually voted to pay him back the money he originally invested. For unknown reasons sometime later he was relieved of his position.

He ended up on Lake McQueeney and about ten years ago paid cash for the bankrupt restaurant and ski club. He and the club have prospered and he has become a valued member of Lake McQueeney society and silent benefactor of individuals and organizations in need. He has affectionately earned the moniker Preacher by those that know him.

The kids tell a story of seeing Preacher one morning pick up a homeless man and woman on the road near the club. Later they observed Preacher personally serving the same couple a hearty meal in the club restaurant.

Everyone who knows Preacher has their own personal story of one of his low key attempts to help someone who is in dire need. The kids even maintain, tongue in cheek perhaps, that he glows in the dark. Interesting.

He is in his late forties or early fifties with a blond crew haircut and a square jaw framing an angelic face with wide blue eyes. His mouth and dimples are such that he appears to be smiling even when his expression is in neutral. His lithe muscular build suggests he works out at the gym on a regular basis. He is not married but how could he not be attached to someone, male or female? To me he is sexy as it gets. Always the hormones.

He sits at John's gesture and beams at Link: "I got some good news today. That Garcia guy who runs the operation at TexMex Foods suggested a trade off on your Thanksgiving feed."

Preacher came up with the idea several years ago to feed the homeless and others who don't have the means to have Thanksgiving dinner. On that day the country club closes the restaurant to the regulars and provides a non-traditional Mexican Thanksgiving meal free of charge.

In four hours the club members and other volunteers serve upwards of a thousand meals. To finance this meal donations of food and money are sought and anyone can purchase tickets at four dollars each to give to those they personally know who are in need. Only one thousand tickets are allotted and no one is served without a ticket. Tickets are usually in short supply. Preacher has been known to fudge on this requirement. "We'll do anything possible to feed those in need."

Link has served as head honcho and organizer for this dinner for four years and is usually under pressure to find enough funds or donations of food to feed this many people. She certainly listens when anyone or company wants to help out even if a deal has to be made.

Gaining Link's attention Preacher continues: "Garcia said they are in need of tickets to feed upwards of forty people that they know who need assistance.

"They are willing to donate over one thousand tamales for these forty tickets."

Link's eyes widen with a surprised smile. "That's huge. Tamales are our highest priced item. If they are willing to foot that bill, forty tickets is definitely a doable deal. We can't go wrong. They donate us close to seven hundred dollars–worth of tamales and we give them less than two hundred dollars–worth of tickets for them to pass on."

Preacher adds to his permanent smile. "Thought you would like that." He stands and says, "Gotta go. Give me a call and I'll pass along his name and contact info."

He gives a quick wave and before we can say good-bye he is gone practically leaping down the stairs.

Jonathan shakes his head with a grin. "Amazing human being." He stops short when he sees two older kids approaching.

"Hey, here they are: God's gift to the human race." He rises and pulls out two chairs for the newcomers and shakes hands with the male.

Judging by their attentiveness to each other, Cory Voltz and Griffin Fritz are obviously lovers as well as friends. They sit and enthusiastically greet the three of us.

"I see you guys are gearing up into the summer mode since both of our lawns have recently gotten a workover," Jonathan nods.

From Dime Box, Texas, Cory is a muscular tanned farm boy with a square jaw, high cheek bones and light brown eyes. He is a junior at the local Texas Lutheran University and is paying his way through school as neighborhood yard and handyman.

"Yes sir," he nods, "Griffin is helping me out until I can hire someone later on." He grins and touches her lightly on her forearm with a single finger and a wink. "She works harder than I do. I don't know if I can find anyone to take her place."

"Well find somebody because we aren't going to give her up to do manual labor," Link replies smiling. "We can't replace her."

Griffin, also a junior at TLU is the Bales and Wabbit's house cleaner, house sitter, kid keeper and nanny during the summer—and anything else we need. She is a local girl from a well–respected McQueeney family. A striking long–haired blonde, very tan with light blue eyes below a heavy brow, a slightly turned up nose and deeply dimpled cheeks when she smiles. Nearly as tall as Cory she has a fantastic figure and turns a head or two at the club when she strolls by. And most important our kids love her.

In fact, they are so valuable to us we have finagled with Preacher to add them as a rider on our family membership at the club, hence their presence here this evening. They have all the privileges that our kids have including running a tab on food and drink which we pay out of their earnings.

Since late in their freshman year they have lived together in a small apartment just off campus sharing a bed and expenses. It is apparent they are smitten with each other.

Griffin bites nervously at her lower lip and makes eye contact with me. "We just heard, Gina, about Pep . . . his, uh, going, leaving. I'm sorry. I've done laundry and cleaned the house since he left and didn't even realize that I wasn't washing his, you know, stuff. Anyway, we're sorry and if there is anything we can do to help please ask. Both your families are very important to us."

The tears, dammit. I nod but before I can answer Cory adds:

"You people help us survive without our parent's help and we'll do anything to keep on helping in any way we can. We'll never forget that."

"Thanks, Cory," I nod wiping a lone tear. "I think I might need your help—actually both of you—soon in a job that might be a bit more fun. Since Pep left I need someone to take some of the pressure off of me in towing the kids skiing if you guys want."

"You kidding? Of course we will," Cory booms. "We'd love to. Since ferrying the kids back and forth to the club last summer Griffin says your boat is a dream to drive. I can't wait."

Jonathan nods, "Yeah, we need skiing help too. Come summer it is probably time for Griffin to take on ski towing as part of her nanny job with both families—with your help of course."

Cory looks toward Griffin for confirmation. "Wow, this is great. What do you think, babe?"

91

Griffin slowly shakes her head: "No, I don't think so, Cory. You don't have the experience I do in driving the boat. Won't happen." She grins, "Unless you pay the price."

Cory plays along. "And the price is...?"

She opens her mouth in a sexy smile. "I'll tell you later."

We all chuckle and Link says. "This I would like to see."

"I don't think so," Griffin replies with a grin.

"Well, people, we have to move on." It's Cory. "Nice to see you when it's not work." He stands and pulls Griffin's chair back as she stands.

"Again," Griffin says to me, "sorry about, uh, stuff."

"Thanks guys. I appreciate your concern."

Following a few more goodbyes they are off and down the stairs.

Jonathan rubs his hands together indicating a change of direction: "Alright, folks. What do you say we vacate this place? It's a good night to open a little wine, sit and watch the moon from our boat dock."

I smile but despondently shake my head. "Yeah, Johnny boy, I'm ready but after living through this past week I think I'll get scotch drunk and howl a little at the moon if it's okay with you."

"You've had an interesting week for sure."

I glance at Link before replying, "John, if you only knew the half of it."

Jonathan winks at Link. "I'll bet. Okay, drink up and let's hit the water."

Minutes later we are on our way downstairs when Jonathan suddenly disappears. We shrug it off and head for the boat and settle in.

Jonathan momentarily appears with three Margaritas on the rocks in Styrofoam cups. He hands one to me and the other two to Link before stepping into the boat. "One for the road," he grins.

He's so sexy. Hold me back. *Give it up, Gina.*

Link and I untie the boat while Jonathan starts up. He backs out and we're on a Margarita run to home.

The trip seems to take forever because Jonathan feels with so much traffic on the lake on Saturday night he must drive slowly. About the time the Margaritas have been consumed we dock at the Bales'. Link and I work the boat lift while Jonathan runs up to the house for libations.

He returns with an armload of goodies. Of course, two bottles of wine, a bowl of cheese and crackers and, not only a large scotch and water, but the bottle, extra water and ice in case I need a refill. This is not good.

I grasp a pinch of his pants and tug. "Hey waiter, do you hire out? Or perhaps do you want another wife? I certainly could use some old fashioned waiting–on for a change."

Jonathan chuckles. "No offense woman, but you've got too much baggage for me to take you in at this time."

I stick my tongue out at him before we relax with our drinks and peer out over the lake. All of Houston must have arrived last night as nearly every home is lit up. I hear their music and children screeching up and down the shoreline.

Link lays a hand on my knee and squeezes. "Rough week. What are you thinking?"

I cover her hand with mine as the tears return. "Thank you for asking. I need to unload and soon. I haven't really begun dealing with the issues."

I look out over the lake and slowly, gloomily shake my head as they wait patiently. "John, Link, thank you for listening to me. I need to get this out. If you weren't here for me right now I would probably be talking to the wall, slowly coming unglued.

"It hit me late this afternoon. I suddenly felt my life shattering right before my eyes. I've got to get a grip because I know I'm losing it, stewing in my own shit."

I pause and wipe my eyes with the tissue offered by Jonathan. Does he always carry a tissue for me? "Please don't feel that you have to comment but any advice is welcome."

"Dammit, Pep," I blurt out, "how can you do this to me? How can you do this to us? I'm so angry with you. Right now, if I were to see you, I would consider killing you with my bare hands. But it's a frigging, crazy dilemma. I also love you and miss you so much. It's just too much to handle."

I again pause and look up into the cypress trees swaying in the light breeze. I notice out of the corner of my vision that Jonathan is offering Link a tissue. Woman cry for themselves and each other. That reminds me.

"I have really cried very little over losing him and what he has done to me and the kids. I need to do that. I've got to cry more and deal with all that's going on. I can't ignore it."

I pause and force a chuckle and they look at me curiously. "I'm rambling. Sorry. This is not me talking but thanks again for listening. Other than Jack and Bunny you guys are all I have."

Thankfully they don't respond. I take a long gulp of scotch and I know I'm going to soon crash and burn in an alcohol fueled disaster. I smile openly at my friends or whatever they should be called after the events of this week.

"So, this has been another week in the saga of one Gina De Georgio Wabbit, royal fuck-up, world famous syndicated columnist, and sex deprived—or should I say, depraved?—single mother of two preteens. Oh, and let's don't forget, sexual pervert. Wait, did I mention, world famous syndicated columnist? Tune in tomorrow to get an update on her whimsical, however intriguing trek through life's pitfalls—and shit. Lots of it." *Nice speech, Gina.*

They look at me oddly. I think I see a trace of amusement in their eyes but they make no comment. That's okay because they listened and that will hopefully help make me be okay. I stand up and take a long slug of my expensive scotch that was free, and hold it up in toast to the two people sitting in front of me, both probably wondering what to make of this total idiot. All this evening's alcohol is beginning to click in and I'm like the trees, swaying a bit in the breeze.

"Now people, please know that you are special—probably too special for your own good. I am about to leave you sitting by your beautiful lake and go to my bed chamber for a good hearty body shaking bawl. I now know a good periodic purgative cry will have to be a part of my healing and moving on from one character, meaning Pep—or should I say, phase?—to the next."

I salute them with my last swallow and gulp it down. "So again, thanks for your . . . uh . . . hospitality. I will now call it a long day and of course a very long week."

Link jumps to her feet in objection. "No, Gina, you can't leave. We're going to sit in the hot tub. You have to come with us. It's too early for you to go to bed."

"If you had asked two hours ago I would have loved it, but now I'm too far gone. I would probably drown and then where would you be? And anyway, I don't have my swimsuit."

"No, you don't need a swimsuit," she retorts and Jonathan dismally shakes his head.

Although I'm soused I know what Link's up to and I can't resist a bit of fun. I wish I was sober enough to take her up on the offer. The way I've been guzzling I know from experience I'm going to be unconscious shortly and won't be able to enjoy it anyway.

"Uh-huh, Link," I slur as I sway a bit more. "Johnny boy and I can see what you're up too. You're working on the old threesome angle again. And I want you to know we refuse to have a threesome with you in the hot tub. The only way we'll have a threesome is in bed and it has to be a big bed at that. So, get off the hot tub stuff. That's really, really kinky, Link—Kinky, Linky."

Both Jonathan and Link laugh heartily and it echoes up and down the lake as it bounces off the houses.

I hand Jonathan the bottle of scotch. "Thanks for the cheap whisky, sir. I'll finish this tomorrow. Okay?" I linger a long kiss on his bearded cheek.

I take Link into my arms and whisper softly so that Jonathan can't hear: "The hot tub would be fantastic." I kiss her softly on her cheek. "I love you, woman."

I step back and force a sloppy smile while wondering if I'm going to be able to get off the dock without falling in the water. "Well, shit. I think you guys are going to have to walk me to my door. Even if I don't end up in the lake I might get lost." *Really cool, Gina.*

Jonathan grins, his eyes dancing in amusement. "Hey, this takes me back. I haven't had to carry you home since college."

"Come on, Johnny. You've never had to carry me home. That must have been one of your lovers."

"No, my dear. It was not a lover. It was you, and I probably carried you home at least ten times. Maybe more."

"Oh," I whisper, pointing a shaky drunken finger at Jonathan. "I guess you're right, sir. Maybe it was me."

He and Link each grasp an elbow to steady me and we're off, stumbling and laughing the whole way. I am near the point that they will need to carry me and I wonder if they are going to have to pour me into bed.

I laugh into the night and slur, "Is this the yellow brick road? I could use one of those wizard guys."

Reaching my back door I'm forced to keep my balance by holding onto the doorframe. "Hey, people, my lovely friends," I slur, "could you please help me to my bed? I don't wanna crash in the hall and have to spend the night on the floor."

Jonathan chuckles, "Glad to, Gina dear. Just hold onto us. We'll put you to bed."

"You owe us big time," Link giggles while grasping my elbow. "Come on, little one. Let's get your teddy bear so you can go beddy–bye."

When we reach the bed I sit on the edge and shake my head to clear it. No help. "Well, thank you for saving me. I think I'll just sit right here the rest of my life."

Link grins in amusement. "Your pajamas?"

"Oh, no," I rebut. "Never use them."

"You sleep naked, then?"

"Yeah, yes, ma'am. Gotta be ready in case I have a chance to get a little."

"Not likely you'll get any sleeping alone," Link follows, winking at her husband.

"Well, I just want you to know," I slur on, holding up a finger for emphasis, "I still have my fantasies. Just ask old John boy. He knows."

"Sure, I've heard. Perhaps we should get you undressed so you can be ready just in case."

I stand hesitantly to assist them. "Undress me, woman," I command, holding out my arms.

Steadying me, they commence to remove my blouse with John looking quizzically at Link, I'm sure he's wondering what his part is in this charade.

She grins at him. "Isn't this fun?"

"A laugh a minute," he answers sarcastically. "Perhaps I should leave you two to get this done. I'll just wait outside."

Link chuckles, "Oh no. You stay right here. I need all the help I can get."

"Yeah, John boy. And you'll finally get to see one of the most beautiful bodies you will ever see."

"Of course, the most beautiful naked drunk I've ever seen for sure."

"Yes sir, and you'll never forget what you see. I'll be in your dreams." *Yeah, dream on, Gina.*

Link is busily unbuttoning and unzipping my pants. She slides my pants and panties down to my knees and pushes me back on the bed in a sitting position. Jonathan watches while feigning disinterest.

"What do you think, John?" I giggle.

"Can we just get this job done? I need a drink."

Link unhooks my bra, slips the shoulder straps down my arms, flips it on a chair and instructs me to get under the sheets.

"No," I giggle. "I don't want to. I want to have a threesome. I'm undressed and ready. All you guys have to do is get naked and join me." *No, Gina.*

Link giggles as Jonathan dejectedly shakes his head and drops his chin to his chest. "What's with you, Gina?" he asks. "You can't even walk and you want to have a threesome."

"I don't need to walk. I'm going to be lying down I think. You don't have a threesome standing up do you?"

Link cannot stop laughing and Jonathan merely stares at me with a cocked brow.

He answers casually, "Go to bed, Gina. There isn't going to be a threesome."

"Then how about a twosome?"

Link grins and looks to Jonathan to see what his answer is. He shakes his head in mock disgust.

"Okay, maybe a foursome?"

Jonathan stares at me quizzically. "A foursome? There is no such thing as a foursome. That would be mate swapping or an orgy, whatever. Anyway, we're only three. Who would be the fourth?"

"How about Pep?"

"Pep? You want Pep to join us in a, uh, mate swap or orgy?"

"No, but we could pretend he's here like I do in my fantasies." My keeper shakes her head: *Idiot.*

"You're drunk and impossible. Just get under the covers."

"Okay" I announce, holding up a single finger and nodding hesitantly. "I guess I'll have to have a onesome if you won't join me in a threesome."

"Shit," Jonathan chuckles, "I wish we had made a video of this. It would go viral in minutes. Link, pull down the covers so we can get this crazy woman to sleep."

"Someday, Mr. John, you are going to regret not having an orgy or whatever tonight."

Link is assisting me to stretch my beautiful necked body out so she can cover me.

"One last chance, John." I slur.

"Go to sleep, Gina."

"Chicken shit. Link, your cold hearted husband is a chicken shit. What man . . . or woman would pass up a chance to hop into bed with me?"

SIX

I can't move. I can't breathe. The weight on top of me is unbearable. Am I being attacked? I have to fight back. I flail my arms trying to free myself but it is impossible. I'm being overpowered. "No, no!" I cry out. "Leave me alone! Stop it!"

"Gina, Gina. It's me. Wake up."

I waken from this terrible dream to realize I'm in my own bed and Link dressed in her usual bikini is sitting on me grinning.

"Oh, shit, what? What are you doing here, Link?" I ask grasping her hands.

"I'm here to save you, woman," she giggles, "And it looks like I got here just in time. You appeared to be in a hell of a fix."

"Damn, I'm a mess. What time is it?"

"After eleven. We thought you had overdosed on scotch and died so I came to check," she answers with a faint shrug. She leans down and kisses me on the neck. "Damn, you smell good."

"I'll bet, probably like the local lush. Is it really eleven o'clock?"

"Yeah, John has already taken our four kids skiing."

"I must have been really looped. I've been dead to the world for about twelve hours." I pause and touch Link's cheek with a lone finger. "Want to fuck?"

She pouts those lips. "Aw, you know I do but the kids are due here any minute. I'm sure that would be an education for them."

"Then how about a quickie? Something to tie us over until we can do the big one."

99

"Guess what, Gina. Women don't do quickies. That's cookie cutter sex and women don't have a cookie-cutter—in this case a penis to pull it off."

"Oh . . . uh . . . why is a penis necessary?"

"Because since neither of us has a penis we've got to improvise, be creative and that takes time. There are no shortcuts, no cookie cutter sex." She lightly kisses my right breast then my left and I feel that familiar surge coursing down my spine and splashing into that intimate place.

"Umm . . . then why are you sitting on me, getting me all worked up, if you aren't going to take care of me?"

She flashes that open mouthed smile, raises a lone brow over her dreamy eyes and answers softly: "That's easy: I want to keep you, uh, as you say, worked up so when we do screw you'll be primed and ready." She leans down and kisses me softly on my lips, disregarding my morning–mouth.

"When?"

"When, what?"

I giggle. "Where and when are we going to fuck again?"

She raises a quirky brow and points a lone finger against her check. "Let's see now . . . tomorrow at about three o'clock you will have been single for one whole week. How about we meet at the usual place at twelve for a pre–celebration of your week's survival?"

"I'll be there—oops, I hear the kids. Get off of me, woman."

Link laughs and we both hop out of bed. I slip on my robe just in time.

It's day eight at eleven thirty in the morning. I've just talked to Bill Jenkins and he has filed the divorce suit. Next, Pep will be served, then hopefully we'll hear from his attorney. I'm sure he is going to be upset when he learns that I have already hired his favorite lawyer. I guess that's one small preliminary win for me.

Bill laughed when I told him about Pep being pissed. He said, "I'm sure he'll get over it. He has no choice."

I have about twenty five minutes before heading over to the studio. That's just enough time to have a light snack. I texted Link earlier to see if she wanted me to bring her something to eat. She immediately texted that she planned on eating me. My whole body is gearing up for round two of Gina and Link's great escapade.

Well, I made myself a sandwich but I'm flying so high I can't eat it. I undress completely and don a moo–moo house dress without panties or bra for ease of undressing and I'm just sitting here counting the minutes. I really think I'm going to explode. It seems like every cell in my being is dancing with energy waiting to be unleashed.

Ten minutes more. Well, screw it; I can't wait any longer. I actually run to the studio. I scratch on the door and hear link giggle. She yells to come in.

I open the door to find her naked sitting cross–legged on the bed with her lips slightly parted in that buttery smile. Without taking my eyes off her I walk across the studio. By the time I reach her I have slipped the moo–moo over my head and I pitch it on a chair next to the bed. I join her on the bed on my knees in front of her.

I put a finger to her lips and whisper softly, "Don't say a word; just enjoy what is about to happen to you."

She quickly runs a finger and thumb across her mouth to zip it up.

"Good, we understand each other. You look like a rare red lotus flower perched up here waiting to be picked. I intend to do just that."

With my hands I grasp both her cheeks, softly nibble at her lower lip and hear a soft groan coming deep in her throat. "I am going to eat you one petal at a time. And when I'm through I'll live to love and make love every day for a hundred years."

I run my tongue along her upper lip and again nibble her lower lip. "Since Friday I've been wanting you every second of the day," I whisper between nibbles, "and now you are going to pay the price for making me wait so long." My helper is doing a little dance. *Wow, she's got to like this. Pour it on.*

I run the fingers of one hand over her breasts, pinching her nipples ever so lightly while I grasp her curly red hair with the other to turn her head. I run my lips across her cheek to her neck behind her ear, then run my tongue around the rim of her ear renewing that low groan in her throat.

Leaving her breast I trail my hand down over her soft belly and twirl her pubic hair between my fingers. Sensing my next move, she uncrosses and spreads her legs with bent knees and feet flat on the bed.

With one hand I gently push her back on the bed while running the other down to that sweet spot. With the heel of my hand I put a mashing pressure on her vagina and rotate with increasing intensity as she repositions her hips to better enjoy the feeling.

I caress the clitoris increasing her deep moan. I feel my own body heat increasing along with that familiar jump in my heart beat and bubbly current traipsing down to my belly. I want her to touch me so badly but she gets the first turn and my attention must be undivided.

I slowly increase the pressure on her clit as I circle it with my fingers lightly pinching and pulling while listening to her heavy breathing.

"Oh shit, Gina," she cries out, "please suck me. Suck me now." She grasps both of my shoulders and pulls me down. I oblige.

Her scent is exquisite. I remove my fingers from her vagina and replace them quickly with my tongue. I circle my tongue around her clit and then grasp it with my lips and pull. She gasps in pleasure as she runs her fingers through my hair.

"Harder, Gina! Fuck me harder! Jeez, you feel so good!"

I let up lightly then gradually increase the sucking pressure. Her breathing increases as she begins to pump her hips against me and lowers her hands to my shoulders for leverage. "Yes, go hard! I want to come now! Hurry!" she exclaims breathlessly. "Please, faster!"

I speed up the tempo waiting until the perfect second right before she comes. She is pumping her legs to better thrust her hips against my pressure, her chest rising and falling with each gasp of breath.

I can feel she is at the peak and grasp her clit tightly with my lips and hold constant pressure. It sends her over the edge in a body convulsing explosion as she cries out, "Aggh! Gina, stop! Enough, already!"

Her knees relax and she straightens her legs. I raise my legs over them and sit on her pelvis, bend over and lightly suck one breast then the other before kissing her lightly on the lips. I sit back up and wait for her to comment.

She studies me as her breathing begins to ease. She smiles softly and it mirrors in her eyes. "Shit, Gina. Did you eat all the lotus petals?"

I giggle. "Most and the taste was exquisite. I saved one for dessert."

I wait a moment for her to come down completely from her orgasm. Still atop her I lightly bite at my lower lip. "So . . . when do you think it's my turn?"

She grins with her eyes dancing in amusement. "Sorry, I'm worn out. You don't get a turn."

I gather my brow, squint my eyes menacingly and press my lips. "Hey, bitch. That's not the way the game is played. You get a little; you give a little."

Still grinning Link tilts her head looking at me askew. "And if I don't?"

"It's curtains for you, woman. You'll regret ever knowing me. They'll have to bring a basket to put your pieces in when I get through with you."

"Oh, mercy. I'm scared. I guess I'd better get with the system lest you maim me. Alright, I guess I have no choice. Get off of me and lie on your back. You are going to get laid and I promise it'll be something you'll want to write home about."

I grin as I roll off of her into a sitting position. "Promises, promises." I grasp her arm and pull her up to sit in front of me. "You talk a big story, lady. Now let's see if you can back it up." I lay back and wait.

She stares down at me while lightly nibbling her lower lip, then moves over to one side of me on her knees. She runs a hand behind my ear and twists my hair with her fingers, then leans over and places little nip–kisses over my eyes.

"Are you ready for this?" she whispers as she runs the kisses down past my nose to the side of my mouth. She lightly bites my lips as she places her hand on one breast and softly pinches my nipple.

My body is quickly waking up as I feel my skin tingle and my stomach go queasy in anticipation. A shiver of energy engulfs my chest and explodes radiating throughout my body.

Her lips press against mine hungrily biting and teasing and I return her kiss with an aggression of my own, nipping her lips and darting my tongue into her mouth. Our tongues tangle together, each trying to outdo the other, each trying to devour each other. My hands are clawing at her back and she moans as she presses her body against mine.

Now our mouths are separated and she moves her kisses down under my chin and slowly down to my breasts, lingering long enough to bite and suck the nipples into hardness. Then she moves south and finds my pubic hair with her mouth, biting and twisting the silk until I am about to complain of the pain, then she moves on.

She raises her leg and throws it over my legs and is now sitting on my thighs facing my feet. Leaning down toward my feet I feel her breast press against my knees while I wonder what is coming next. Caressing one foot with both hands, she takes my big toe into her mouth and sucks rhythmically for a few seconds. The feeling is eerily erotic. She moves to the next toe, then the next, each toe feeling more erotic than the previous. Moving to the other foot she repeats the process starting with the little toe and progressing up to the biggest. It is fantastic but I'm ready for her to move on.

She gets off of my legs, spreads them apart and gets between them on her knees. Gently she bends one knee and lifts the thigh. She kisses my inner thigh and tongues her way up my leg. I can feel my heart rate kick up a notch and my face flush. Now she repeats with the other thigh and I am gearing for heavier action.

Her fingers are suddenly thrust into my vagina and I take a quick breath of elation and surprise. She bypasses the clitoris and lightly massages behind my pelvic bone bringing a bit of pain tempered by a fantastic exotic feeling as I heat up.

The pain causes me to squirm and she backs off slightly only to renew with more pressure. Again she backs off and returns with even more pressure than before. I am caught between unbelievable pleasure and unbearable pain.

"Uncle!" I shout. "Enough, please, Link!"

Link giggles and withdraws the finger. Her lips are suddenly surrounding my clit. I moan my pleasure.

She increases the pressure on my clit, sucking and tonguing with ever increasing pressure. I feel my body moving into high gear nearing that expected explosion that I seem to never get enough of. I feel my blood boiling as it courses through my system firing off waves of energy into all spaces of my body. I feel my breathing quicken, yet I can't get enough air into my system. It is taking me higher and higher.

"Go for it! Gina. Go baby!" Link encourages as she steps up the pressure on my clitoris.

"Oh shit! Yes! Yes! Harder!" I cry out as I reach the very summit, exploding, then crashing and burning in pure ecstasy. My body is suddenly bereft of all energy and I am left in a mass of simmering ashes. I shiver in exhilaration.

When I come down to earth and my breathing has leveled out I find Link sitting on my pelvis grinning, obviously proud of her performance in bringing me pure sexual pleasure.

I look into her eyes and grin. "More, more, more."

She giggles. "I've got all you can take, sweet lady. Just say the word." She rolls off of me and snuggles up next to me.

"So, what is the word?" I turn on my side and lightly kiss her on the mouth.

Link smirks, "Can't tell you. That's one of those things that just comes to you when you're ready for it."

"Dang, you mean I'm not ready?" I croak.

"I guess not." She smiles as she sits up and hugs her knees to her chest. "So what now? What's next?"

I sit up and copy how she is sitting. "I would like some Q and A time."

"Alright, shoot," she answers cocking her head to one side.

I decide to jump right in: "Are you serious about a threesome between you, me and John?"

Her quirky lips project a thin half smile. "What do you think?"

I slowly shake my head and look in her dreamy eyes. "I don't know. I am perplexed yet intrigued about it. I can't understand your even wanting to go there. It seems like only bad can come from this for you."

"Oh, yeah?" she smiles. "How's that?"

I exhale a quick puff of tension while looking directly into Link's eyes. "I fully understand what you said about having an affair occasionally but this seems to be taking it a step further."

"So tell me what that would be?"

"I don't quite know how to say this but you seem to be recruiting me for your husband."

She spreads her arms and widens her eyes. "How's that?"

"Well . . . this is so weird. If I get into bed with your husband as a part of a threesome, what's to say we won't enjoy each other so much that we'll want to continue as a twosome later on?" I pause for comment but she remains silent, her sugary lips parted slightly.

What is she thinking? I slowly shake my head. "Jeez, I can't believe we're having this conversation. But we are, so here we go. As you know Jonathan and I have hit on each other in the past, me as recently as one week ago. So we must have the hots for each other.

"If you throw us together intentionally there is liable to be a cosmic explosion between us. You said if John was having a fling with someone else you'd just as soon not know about it, but here you are promoting it."

Link twists her lips as she studies me; the silence is unnerving. Finally she exhales a long winded sigh. "You're right, Gina. It's crazy, and I feel like I'm getting

106

caught up in my own web sometimes, but it won't leave me alone.

"The only good solution is for me to shut up and quit talking about it. But it keeps jumping out there. Fortunately you and John are against it so that saves me from myself."

She pauses for my response.

I sadly shake my head. "Problem, Link. Now I am thinking about it. And to be very honest with you my motivation has more to do with my desire for John than with curiosity about the threesome. It's about your husband, Link. I want to get him into bed with me."

"I'm not blind, Gina. I know the feeling you guys have for each other. As I told you the other day, John and I are candid with each other about our sexual thoughts and acts with others as long as we follow those rules that I mentioned. About six months ago it would have indeed bothered me if you two got in the sack together."

Link pauses in thought and I wait. I draw my brow together quizzically when she doesn't continue and spread my hands. "What happened six months ago to make you change your attitude about John and me?"

She bites at her lower lip and gazes into my eyes. I can see tears welling up in her eyes. Whatever it is, it certainly is heavy for her emotionally.

"I don't really know how to tell you this without sounding like a complete idiot but it's continually eating on me; it won't go away. I definitely can't tell John, but under the circumstances I need to talk to you about it because in a way it concerns you."

She pauses and I am like, wow, what is going on with you? I wait for her to continue at her own pace.

"Something strange has happened to me and it's ongoing. I really don't know what to make of it but I'm beginning to think I need to take heed although I don't have any idea of what to do. It has definitely changed my thinking about your and John's relationship."

Take heed? My relationship with Jonathan? I wait as I look at her puzzled, not trying to hide my curiosity.

Link puts her hands in the prayer position and lightly taps the fingers against her lips as she slowly shakes her head in dismay. "Shit, Gina, I'm having this re-curring dream that I'm going to die soon. I'm having some variation of it two or three times a week. At first it scared me but now I just observe and ask myself, what's the point? What am I supposed to do? Is this ever going to stop?"

She forces a sad smile for my benefit as she searches my eyes. "Crazy, huh?"

I lay my hand on her knee and look into her eyes. "Can you tell me more about the dreams? I can under-stand someone having recurring dreams about death, but how does that concern me? And for that matter me and John?"

Her eyes study me for a while before she nods as if agreeing with herself. "I want you to know it all but right now I'll just give you a summary—just hit the highlights.

"First off, the original dream was of my funeral. John was actually crying and he never cries. That was pretty powerful. Also at the funeral were our four kids and you all sitting together. There were others but I didn't rec-ognize anyone."

I hold up a finger and she acknowledges for me to speak with a nod. "Pep?"

"No Pep. In fact Pep is never in these dreams. I have wondered all along why not? Then last week when Pep left it hit me square between my eyes. You think I ha-ven't thought about this all week. Pep isn't in the dreams because he is gone before I die."

I stare at Link and shake my head in disbelief. "Crap, Link, I can see how this has gotten to you. It must be driving you up the wall."

"Yeah you've got that right," she answers with a faint nod and a forced thin smile. Tears are banking in the corners of her eyes. "Now, your part. In several of the dreams I'm given the impression that I should look out for John by getting you two together—the perfect match set up by none other than me.

"At the time of my death John is so distraught that he refuses to go on. I am given the task while I'm still alive of getting you two together to make his transition smoother after I die."

"Well, shit." I stare grimly at my neighbor, my friend, my new lover. "You are going to die. So your job is to arrange a relationship between your widowed husband and your lover to take over where you left off."

Link sighs sadly, "You make it sound simple."

"I assume there's more . . . uh, dream stuff."

"Yeah, and I want you to hear it all."

My teary eyes are locked on her teary eyes. "Link, this whole thing is blowing me away as it must be blowing you away. I don't even know what to say to you. I do know that if you haven't already we need to research death dreams. You need all the information you can get for your sanity if for nothing else."

Her sad eyes lock on mine. "Yes, I need to know everything and I certainly need your support."

"Link, I feel terrible about your having to play matchmaker. But can we put all this threesome stuff on the back burner while we try to sort out what's going on?"

She releases a drawn out sigh without comment.

"Shit, shit, shit. This is crazy. We shouldn't even be having this conversation about dreams, pending death, threesomes and sleeping with a lover's husband. It's as if we're talking about three people we don't even know—not us."

She replies with a hint of humor. "I guess we can't go back eight days and relive this week differently?"

I touch her lightly on the knee with a lone finger. "Part of the week has been great and I don't want to lose that. I don't want to lose you as my lover. And I definitely don't want you to die."

Link smiles. "My week with you was fantastic."

"In that case, since we still have an hour left before I celebrate my one week's separation from my husband, maybe we should lose ourselves in each other's arms."

"Umm, does that mean you want to play again?"

Wow, I'm excited. This is noon, Wednesday, day ten after the split. I have just left a pow–wow with Jonathan and Bales' creative team. They have given their enthusiastic help supporting my original ideas and suggesting changes they feel will enhance the whole column project. And—surprise of the year—most of these people are the very ones that have been on my case at Bales since day one. This column is going to be a success; I just feel it.

Jonathan, equally enthused has already pulled geek Bob Couser and his Project Development Department off all other projects to design the column and supporting social media.

I tried to coax Jonathan to El Cabrito Mexican Restaurant but he already had a lunch meeting scheduled with a business associate. He suggested I come along and I turned him down. That wouldn't be any fun if I couldn't hit on him, no matter how fruitless it seems.

So I'm headed home. My desire to go forward with the column is tempered by Link's death dream problem. I have got to help her find an answer to her dilemma if there is one.

Even if these dreams are unimportant or meaningless she needs to know that so they don't grate on her, particularly when she has enough on her plate with the up–coming gallery show. I will get caught up in the Web today as I know she will later to see if there are any magic answers to the reason for her dreams.

It would probably be best if we search together but we would surely end up in bed and accomplish nothing. Well, second thought it would accomplish a lot. At least for me. But that wouldn't move her any closer to her gallery goal and wouldn't give us any answers to the dreams. So, hey, I'll just stay home and make love to the computer. Or not.

Dreams, dreams, crap. Everyone seems to have an answer to what they mean. There are so many sites, all with varied answers to the why and why not of every kind of dream you can imagine—or dream. Oh well, I've made copious notes to compare with Link's. Maybe we can review them in bed? I hope. I wish. I'm a mess.

So here we are in the studio sitting across from each other at Link's small work desk. There are sparks flying between us but we've put off playtime until we compare notes on what we've discovered on the dream thing.

I lead: "Unconscious stuff seems to be the common thread—a message with some deep meaning that is important to you."

"Yeah, I got that. It's as if the dream is like a sign that a part of yourself or your life has become destructive and is no longer useful to you. The dream is an effort to purge this part of you to remove it from your life. By removing this burden perhaps you can have renewal or an emotional change of scenery."

I nod in agreement. "All my research seems to stress that you should not fret too much about these death dreams being a message of your pending death. Instead, think of your dreams as an effort of your subconscious to work out a pending change in your life. That is good news and I hope that you deal with your dreams with that in mind. At least you won't be allowing your dreams to drive you crazy."

Link lightly nibbles at her lower lip in thought. "Okay, I'll approach these dreams as if they are not related to actual death. Maybe there is something in my life that is about to change—that is coming to an end."

I laugh. "Fun. Now you can spend every spare moment wondering what is about to end or change."

"Thanks, Gina, for that little tidbit of insight. I do feel better now and will carry on not worrying if I'm about to die." Her eyes crinkle with that funky smile and she grabs my knee under the desk. "Now, can we move on to the main event?"

"And . . . that would be?"

"Come on; I'll show you."

By the time we reach the bed we have shed our clothes and pitched them on the floor. She urges me to lie on my side and she lies facing me but with her head toward my feet. She gently spreads my legs and inserts two fingers into my vagina, then caresses my clit. I do likewise.

The feeling is exquisite and the smell is sublime. I feel my body reeving up as my heartrate ups a notch and desire smolders deep down in my fantasy place.

In unison we remove our fingers and find the clit with our tongues. A jolt of energy courses through me and I moan with delight as she giggles.

"Damn, you're fantastic," she mumbles as she lightly sucks my clit. I am continuing my slow meltdown while trying to match her every move. She squirms in delight. "Suck harder," she demands.

I can do that. The race is on to bring us to the brink together. Higher and higher we fly with hips thrusting against lips. It's getting difficult to breathe and I feel her gasping for breath likewise. Suddenly she pulls my hips forward and I follow sensing that I am going to drown in her moist nest.

"Yes, Gina," she screams as she thrusts her hips even harder.

I feel my whole body on the verge of going up in flames as she explodes before coming up for air completely satiated. Likewise myself a nanosecond behind.

"Damn, Link," I moan momentarily as I slowly flutter back to earth. "Surely it can't get any better?"

"I guess we'll find out," she giggles.

When I return home the kids have already arrived from school and I go to their rooms to greet them. It has been nine days since Pep left and I feel it is long overdue for the kids to vent their thoughts and feelings.

The time has come. I find Donna lying on her bed crying into her pillow. I sit down beside her and softly rest a hand on her back. "Bunny, are you okay?" I ask. *That's certainly a stupid question. She's obviously hurting.*

"I miss Daddy," she sobs. "How come he hasn't called?" She rolls into a sitting position and drapes her arms around me crying hot tears onto my chest. "I don't think he even cares about us and how we miss him."

I'm at a loss how to answer. "Well, I think he's got some . . . he's got some stuff he has to work out. Then he'll come get you guys to stay with him for a weekend or at least visit with you."

"Jack says he isn't ever going to come back. That lady won't let him," she sniffs while wiping tears with her fingers.

"That lady?" I ask wondering how much of this whole charade they have figured out.

"Monica says he has a girl . . . a girlfriend."

Well, I definitely can't sidestep this issue since they are fully aware of the circumstances of his exit. "Yes, he has a friend and I think he is living at her house. I don't believe she will keep him from seeing you guys but it might take time for him to realize that he needs you and you need him. Then he will come."

The crying has ended and she studies my eyes while wiping the last tear trailing down her cheek. "Why does he want to live with her? Did we make him mad at us? Doesn't he love us anymore?"

Shit. My mind is racing. "I don't know why he wants to live with her." *The hell you don't. He wants to shack up with her*, my inner voice chimes in. "He isn't angry with you and he does love you very much. Right now he's just confused about what is really important to him."

Donna presses her lips tightly together, squints her eyes and grimly shakes her head. "Well, I don't think I love him anymore and he can stay away forever. I don't care. Me and Jack will do okay without him because we have you. I know you love us."

Suddenly she is off the bed and out the door before I can respond. *Well, we'll see how long that lasts before we have the next episode*. I suppose I should approach Don and see if he wants to talk. Then again maybe I should wait until he indicates he's ready.

Bob Couser is a piece of work. He is a computer nerd of the highest order. In his early thirties, he is probably about five foot five, a tad over weight and beginning to show some baldness which he accentuates with a really bad comb–over. He wears thick glasses with wide black frames giving him the appearance of a ringtail raccoon.

He usually looks like he sleeps in an alley somewhere and I'm told he often wears the same clothes several days in a row, shirt half tucked in and occasionally even neglecting to zip up after doing his thing. His colleagues, most dressed in standard casual office attire, often good naturedly razz him about his appearance. He seems to enjoy their harassment, often smiling and silently flipping them the bird.

Jonathan used to take issue with Bob's dress but because he does fantastic work eventually backed off. He even raised his pay high enough to keep him from absconding to the Silicon Valley or, God forbid, an hour north to Austin.

According to the scuttlebutt at Bales, Bob is unmarried and unattached to another human being male or female. Jonathan says several years ago he and a girlfriend were engaged but right before the wedding she ran off with some jock never to be seen or heard from since. After that he soured on any type of close relationship. But in spite of the usual banter about his clothes he gets along well with everyone although he holds in check anything about his personal life.

Bob Couser is also fast. It's Friday, day twelve, and he is excited, practically hopping around his cubicle of an office gesturing wildly with his hands. "This is going to be really cool," he gushes. "We are going to plaster you all over the fucking Internet. You'll be a superstar. I guarantee it. I've always wanted to do this. It's going to be fantastic."

Bob's enthusiasm is contagious and I am rolling with him, anxious to get the program in gear. "I'm with you Bob. What do we do next?"

He laughs and grabs my wrist with a grubby hand. "Just hang on, Gina, and enjoy the ride. This is going to be fun."

Alright already, Bob. Shit, I wish I had his enthusiasm. But right now I'll follow him anywhere, unkempt clothes and all. I'm glad I have him on my side. He's even sexy. *Get a grip,* my keeper points out.

"Okay, this is what we've put together. First, your domain is registered. As you requested it is named *The Italian Rabbit.* Your website will handle up to thirty email addresses, your blob, and it will serve as your operational base for Twitter, Facebook, and whatever other social media you choose."

I grin and slowly shake my head. "I'm glad you are guiding me. This stuff scares me. Other than email I haven't any idea how social media works."

"Piece of cake, Gina," he smirks. "I'll turn you into a geek in no time."

He turns and sits at his computer and gestures for me to sit in a chair next to him. I try to keep some distance between us and hold my breath to avoid the stench. *See you later, Gina*, my keeper mumbles, holding her nose and retreating into the far corner of the cubicle.

Bob taps a couple of keys and a large rabbit appears on the screen. Orbiting above the rabbit's head in a half circle is written, WELCOME TO THE HOME OF THE ITALIAN RABBIT. Below the rabbit in smaller print, YOUR HOST: GINA DE GEORGIO WABBIT.

"You've got to be kidding," I gush. "This is fantastic—no—it's more than that. How did you do this in two days?"

He grins as he touches his temple with an index finger. "Modern computer magic, Gina." He flippantly waves one hand across the screen. "Probably took me all of thirty minutes." He holds up one finger and nods as he curls his lips. "But you have to remember I'm good at what I do. People around here won't admit it though; they think I'm weird."

I don't know how to answer that so with pressed lips I slowly shake my head awkwardly projecting dismay.

He laughs, "But hey, I am weird and I go to great lengths to reinforce it." He places the curser on a button in the lower right hand corner of the screen and clicks. The rabbit is replaced with the beginning of my home page.

"This is going to take some time because I don't know exactly where you're headed. But we'll start filling in the blank areas as soon as you can spend a little time getting me up to speed on what you'll need."

I draw in a full breath and let it out slowly as he waits. "I know where I want to go but it all came down so fast I have no idea what steps I have to take to get there.

"I'll have something for you in two or three days—every-thing from social media to website content."

I flash my best smile at Bob and pat him lightly on the arm. "In the meantime if you have any advice I would appreciate your help."

"Understand, Rabbit," he grins. "I'm sure I can come up with something crazy to help you make this whole project a success." He continues with sincere deter-mination, "Because if you're a success maybe I can claim to be part of the reason."

"Well, shit. This surely will screw up a relatively good day," I mumble to myself after checking the caller ID of my ringing phone. I pull over on the shoulder of Inter-state 10 and stop as I push the answer button.

"Hello," I answer as if I don't know who is calling.

"Gina, Pep here. I thought it was time for me to check in with you to see how things are going, you know, the kids and all."

"As good as can be expected I guess," I answer flatly. "Why don't you call and ask them how they're do-ing? They don't share their feelings with me too much and I'll bet they would like to hear from you."

"Umm..." is his answer after a long moment.

Cool, Pep, my keeper pipes in. *What do you really want*?

I don't feel a response is needed for "Umm" so I remain silent. In your court, dude.

He stammers on: "Well, I guess, you know, it seems like you didn't waste any time filing for the divorce and using my personal lawyer at that. It kind of surprised me that you're in such, you know, such a hurry to get things moving."

I can't let this comment go by without an answer. I reply calmly but with a definite bite to my words: "Let's see now, you've been shacking up with miss magnificent for over a year that I know of. So, yeah, I guess you're right; taking a year to divorce your lily white ass is kind of in a hurry on my part isn't it?"

An uneasy moment of silence. "I just don't understand why you're in such a hurry? You didn't need to file the next day after I left."

"Pep, give me a break," I snap back. "You wanted out. I made it easy for you. Now, you're saying I'm in too much of a hurry. Well, big fucking deal. I certainly didn't want this—you did.

"Now you've got it. I suggest you take the ball and run with it because this divorce is a happening thing, and the sooner it's over with the better it will be for me. It'll also be better for the kids. And you know what? Maybe, just maybe, if you're extremely lucky it'll be what you want. For several reasons I just don't see that happening."

I wait for his reply but when nothing comes I quietly end the call and turn off my phone. "Good day to you, asshole."

My helper is dancing a jig and throwing confetti in the air. *Go, Gina, go!*

I feel relieved to get this first communication after the split over with as I pull back on the highway for the remainder of my trek home. I am also angry. And sad.

"That's a hard one," I smile and take a sip of my chardonnay as I contemplate an answer to the question put forth by Link.

"Let's see . . . how was my day? First off, I really didn't want to get out of bed this morning but I did. I even got to the office on time—at least for lunch with my sexy boss."

I pat Jonathan on the knee and smile at Link. "You know, I have a great job. I get to work in time for free lunch, then I have a short meeting with the company genius and go home."

Link giggles and Jonathan cheerlessly shakes his head. "Tell me about it. My day was similar but go ahead, finish your day."

"Well, on the way home I get a call from the man of the year. I basically told him to go fuck himself and hung up on him. Afterward I felt good, and bad, and relieved . . . angry, uh, depressed and what else? Yeah, very sad and definitely unhappy." I shrug, "I guess that's about it. The whole enchilada."

I widen my smile and draw my brow together as if in contemplation for Jonathan's benefit. "You know, dock time is always my best part of the day but it would be even better if we can follow up with a threesome. The hot tub would be perfect."

Link howls in laughter and claps her hands. Jonathan stoically replies, "Sorry, it isn't happening."

Link peers at her husband with an evil grin while rubbing her hands together: "Kind sir, I suggest you don't get totally soused on wine some night or you will certainly get overwhelmed and waylaid by a couple of horny and conniving women."

Well, shit, I guess I shouldn't even joke about a threesome if Link is going to jump right back on that wagon. I can only manage to shrug a what–can–you–do smile and a wink at Jonathan.

SEVEN

Wow, five days and Bob Couser has me up and running. The website and all the media tools are functioning, and my introductory column is ready and waiting for publication in two weeks.

This is basically what the first column is going to look like:

HUTCH TALK WITH THE ITALIAN RABBIT
by Gina De Georgio Wabbit

Hey out there, Gina here. I'm so glad you're reading my new column. This, my first issue, is being published in eleven different magazines, four of them in languages other than English, all under the banner of Bales Publishing headquartered in San Antonio, Texas. Depending on the magazine the column will be published weekly or monthly.

So what's happening? What am I or should I say are we up to? I say we because we all have an important question that we want answered and we all seem to have an answer to someone else's important question.

How many times have you read questions asked in advice columns and yelled out your answer at the publication: "Come on, get a grip. Dump the idiot. He's a loser and you don't deserve this."

Well I hope to give you that opportunity with this column. It's going to be somewhat like a blog. One week I will publish the question you send to me in the WHAT'S YOUR QUESTION? section and you'll get your answer from the masses out there in the WE HAVE AN ANSWER section of a later edition. In fact, it will be our job to drown you with our advice, like it or not. Of course you can refute it or clap back in a later issue if you don't like the advice.

Does that sound like fun? It'll be like, let it all hang out while we have a war of words.

What's the subject? Are your questions limited to certain areas? This is the great part. Anything you want to ask about, go for it. Ask what you will—be it lovelorn advice, movies, sports, politics, food recipes or personal hygiene for that matter. The subject of your question is wide open.

My publishers, however, have one rule or limitation; their gross meter may rule out certain questions that are certainly, shall I say, uncouth. But, whatever, who knows what is couth—is couth really a word?—these days. So, send your question and we'll see.

One more thing: speaking of being couth, political correctness is not an issue as long as your query is accompanied by your first name and city for rebuttal—or castigation and a bit of clap back if justified.

So much for your limitless questions. The second part of each edition of the column will be the WE HAVE AN ANSWER section to the questions submitted in previous columns. Again, let it all hang out and tell it like it is—or the way you think it is—or should be.

The last part of each column will be the SPEAK OUT section where you can comment about previous questions or answers, or even subject matter we haven't mentioned before but you want to let off some steam over. This will be the fun part and discussion or clap back may go on for weeks about some picayune nothing or worldwide terrorism.

One last thing: as there will not be room in my column to answer all your questions, I will include most of them in my blog. That way you can ask and answer questions as fast as digital technology will allow.

Now, a note about me. I was born and raised in Alamo Heights, a suburb of San Antonio, Texas. I earned a B.S. in journalism from Texas Christian University in

RABBIT'S EROTIC FANTASY

Fort Worth, moved back to the San Antonio area and have worked for Bales Publications for close to fifteen years.

I have just published a novel called Rabbit's Erotic Fantasy. Recently divorced I have a preteen boy and girl. We live on Lake McQueeney. My married name was Wabbit. My maiden name is De Georgio. I am considering changing my last name to Rabbit or maybe even back to my maiden name.

Along with the eleven publications I mentioned previously, there are others considering running this column. My column will be published on some of my social media sites that I have listed below. I can also be contacted at most of them with your questions, answers or comments.

I hope you join me in the next publication of this magazine. I promise with your help to liven up your week. Send me your earth–shaking questions posthaste. And please mention the publication where you read this column.

Gina

MY SOCIAL MEDIA
Website and Blog: italianrabbit.com
Email: gina@italianrabbit.com
Facebook: Gina De Georgio

There you have it. We'll see where Jonathan's big idea takes me. I feel good about it. I don't feel particularly enthusiastic with what has been going on personally the last five days however. Pep is still badgering me about my immediate action on, as he calls it, Gina's quickie divorce.

On both of his calls I lambasted him about his complaining about my quick action when it was he who wanted this whole shakeup in our marriage. I told him I didn't want to discuss it further. And what's the big deal anyway? He acts like he's having second thoughts and wants to go back to where we were. No thanks. I will not be second choice. Or his third choice until he can find someone better?

Gina De Georgio

Link's and my young hot relationship or affair, whatever, has cooled a bit in the last week as we are both being dragged in different directions—her preparation for her upcoming show, which our fucking around has obviously slowed, and me with the new column along with my usual job duties.

In fact, we've only been on her studio bed one time. I think about her constantly. Of course I would still like to get laid by some dude, namely Jonathan, but it is what it is so far—no yin yang sex. That has got to change. I'm going freaking mad.

The kids don't say much but I can tell they are on a downer over the absence of their dad. Between yelling at him during our two phone conversations this week, I encouraged him to contact them but he hasn't. That's not the Pep I know but what can I do? It's his deal one way or the other. It still is a rapidly developing problem with Bunny and Jack.

So here I am, Wednesday night, nine o'clock. The kids, ragged out, have gone to bed and I'm alone with myself wondering just where I'm headed with my life and why. I just don't see the point. It seems I'm on a perpetual roller coaster.

This morning I was riding high with my first column ready for publication. Then by midafternoon I was down on myself because Link had an artist association meeting in the big city all day. It even extended into wine time with Jonathan absent doing kid activities at the club. So, again no sex, not that Jonathan is a candidate. That leaves me to finish off this day depressed as all get out.

A tall Chivas and a long lingering bubble bath sounds like a relaxing picker upper. As I fill the tub I am sitting on the commode feeling sorry for myself and gulping my scotch. Finally as I test the water temperature with a cautious toe the phone beckons.

Well who can that be? I wonder as I cross over to the lavatory counter to retrieve my phone.

Shit, what do you want at this hour? I answer curtly, "Hello, Pep. What's up? . . . I suppose. . . . Yes, they are asleep but I'll ask them first thing in the morning and get back to you. I'm sure they will want to. They have been concerned that they haven't heard from you. . . . Yes, they would be home from school shortly after three thirty. . . . That would be great, and you'll return? . . . That sounds good. . . . Yes, I'm sure they would like to visit their grandparents. It's been awhile. . . . Yes, I'll tell them. . . . Yes, that's good. . . . Alright. . . . That's great, Pep. I'll call as soon as I talk to them in the morning. . . . Sure, okay. Bye."

Well that's good I guess. A nice long weekend visit with their dad and the grandparents close by to buffer their visit should work.

Now me. I must try to not drown myself in my bubble bath. Turning off the light, I slip off my robe and step gingerly into the bath, slowly lowering myself up to my chin, the bubbles tickling my neck.

"Well I could certainly get used to doing this every day," I mutter to myself. I lightly caress my breasts, waking up that longing to be touched by a male again. How long has it been now? Too long for sure.

I slowly run my hand down to my belly, then let my fingers lightly tangle my soft pubic hair. Shit, wouldn't it be nice to experience that blissful orgasmic high again, to smell and feel that male presence engulfing, overwhelming me, fucking me. I run a finger down to that welcome spot and lightly thrust it into the softness.

It is Friday, two thirty in the afternoon when the doorbell rings. Who could that be? I wonder as I open the door. My heart hitches on seeing Pep standing on the porch, one hour earlier than his announced time of arrival to pick up the kids.

I smile as I reach out for his hand. He takes my hand and follows me as I lead him to the bedroom. I face him and run a hand through his beard while laying the other on his chest.

He raises a hand of objection and I pull it down while firmly shaking my head, my lips pressed in determination. I touch two fingers against his lips indicating he must not speak.

Gina De Georgio

His eyes widen and his lips part in surprise but he does not attempt to stop me. And I will not be stopped. I am in charge and he will do as I say and accept what I have to offer gladly—or else.

I fumble with the top button of his shirt as he watches.

"Guess what?" I project an open-mouthed smile. He looks confused.

While biting at my lower lip I release the next button. Then the next.

With the fourth button I announce: "Mister Wabbit, you are fixing to get laid."

The fifth. "To get royally fucked."

His eyes widen and those fantastic lips part slightly.

The last button. "Fucked like never before. And you don't have to do anything but lie here and enjoy it."

I run my hands up and grasp below the collar on both sides of his shirt, pull it back over his shoulders and let it fall to the floor.

Now the belt buckle. Then the button of his trousers. The zipper is next. I project a hint of a sneer as I pull his trousers down in a quick motion. "Do you remember this part? Surely you do. And you know what's coming."

I grasp the waistband of his bikinis with both hands and slide them down to join his pants around his ankles, exposing the magnificent swelling object of my attention. "Step out, kind sir and please lie on your back." I gesture sweepingly at the bed. "I will join you shortly."

He follows my orders and curiously watches me undress. I am fixed on his building erection and I feel a bolt of electricity coursing through me like a projectile, then exploding in my fantasy place.

My breathing is becoming deep and heavy as the desire in me escalates by the second. I project a sexy open mouthed smile as I slowly remove my bra and pitch it beside him on the bed.

"When I get through with you, you might choose to keep that as a souvenir of the time you experienced the best fuck of your life."

His expression tells me I have his complete attention. I grin evilly as I remove my panties. I place a finger under the elastic band and draw them back with the other hand. Upon releasing them they fly through the air, landing perfectly on his face. "Have a smell, sir. You might recognize it from your past."

Suddenly I am on the bed sitting straddled over both of his knees. I grasp his erection and work it slowly between my hands, all the while watching his facial expression melt into enjoyment. This marvelous instrument is so exquisite, soft and pliable, yet firm and strong. I can't get enough of it.

I feel my whole being heating up and my spiraling desire becomes unbearable. I have been here before, many times and each was a different experience. I know this time will be even better because I intend to make it the best ever. I will make him regret ever rejecting me. I will make him miserable for living without me.

I release him and raise up on one knee while urging him to bend his knee to allow me to replace my knee between both of his legs. I repeat with the other knee and spread his legs with me crouched on my knees between them.

"Are you ready for this, mister?" I ask while again grasping his penis with both hands.

When there is no comment, I immediately slide my hands down to the base and take a full measure in my mouth resulting in a gasp from my captive. I release my grip to allow me to take even more in my mouth. There is a guttural groan.

I withdraw about half way and return taking the extent that my mouth will allow. Another groan and a whispered exclamation, "Shit."

Knowing that I have complete control I step up the pace: in . . . out . . . in . . . out, ever faster until I feel that he is going to lose it.

Not yet buster. There is going to be more. A lot more. "What do you think? Are you enjoying what is happening to you? Of course you are."

In one quick motion I release him from my mouth, spread my legs over his and mount him. In an instant he enters me as I slam against him.

I grasp both cheeks and as I bite his lips, my prisoner gasps and I taste blood from his wound. My tongue is now in his mouth dancing and twirling with his tongue as I grasp his hair with both hands and pull.

"Damn, take it easy. You're killing me," he complains as he throws his head back.

"Just shut up and enjoy it," I command. "You are going to remember and relive this moment forever."

I release my hold on his hair and move my hands down his body and slide them under his hips. Immediately I withdraw slightly from him only to slam back against him while pulling his hips up against me. In and out, in and out, harder and faster until he joins in the fun. We become two reckless animals pounding each other trying to get the upper hand.

Suddenly I stop and raise myself to a squat position over him with my feet flat on the bed. I release my full weight and allow my body to clash against his, accepting his full length. I raise my hips up, withdrawing slightly and fall back against him. Again, harder this time. Again and again, harder and harder to his throaty groans.

I plunge again and stop with my full weight pressing against him. "Well, what do you think? Are you ready to for the kill?

"No comment, huh? Well, enjoy because here we go." I raise my hips slightly and fall back against him again and again. I am close to losing it and I know from experience he is too. I feel my blood coursing through me in a boil and the energy sparking between us is on the verge of combustion.

He suddenly cries out like I've never heard him before as we come in our final body slamming heave. Exploding in flames he soars dragging me along with him to forever land.

Well, that was interesting. Why did I go there? I certainly don't need to be fantasizing more torment. I'm a mess.

No. You're a stupid freaking mess, comes my inner voice.

It's Friday and the doorbell rings at precisely three thirty—not an hour earlier as in my fantasy. Well it's just as well I don't have the opportunity to actually live my daydream—not that it would happen anyway. And even if it did there is no way the real deal would play out close to the dream. In the long haul it would surely be tantamount to a massive disaster and definitely not in my best interest—or his.

You've got that right, Gina. Thanks, now go back to your cave. I'll handle this. At least I hope I will.

I open the door to find Pep with his back to the door looking out at the street. At the very sight of him my heart and pulse speed up and I feel that familiar jolt of energy coursing through me, gearing me up for anything remotely sexual with a real live male for a change. Particularly this one. Lots of luck. The kids are due any minute.

He turns at the sound of the door opening and offers a forced smile and meek, "Hi."

"Hey, Pep," Is the best I can offer while considering ravaging him right here on the porch. That would be fun I'm sure. *Just forget it*. "Come on in. The kids should be home soon." I gesture for him to sit on the sofa and he obeys.

"Are the kids, uh, you think they have a problem with my, you know, taking them to Mom and Dad's for the weekend?" he stammers uncomfortably as he scans the room and avoids making eye contact.

Damn, I want him. Now. How crazy is that? I struggle to sidetrack the feeling—to ignore it. Is that possible?

"Can't really tell. They were guarded. I think they want to go but they really don't know what to expect. For instance Bunny asked if I was going along."

I shrug indifferently, "I guess they'll have to learn the new normal before they can relax and enjoy their time with you. "Jack did ask if they had to stay the full two nights, but I think he was searching for an escape hatch if the visit is not working—merely a precaution on his part."

Pep nods, "I understand that. Hell, I don't know what to expect either. But I guess we'll see how it turns out."

"Yeah, I guess." Not wanting the conversation to drift to the divorce, I retreat: "Well look, I have a business call scheduled in about five minutes, but I hope to be through before you leave. If you need a stiff one or something else you know where the kitchen is." I leave the room before he can comment.

I head to my office and watch through the window for the kids and momentarily the bus pulls up and drops off the foursome. Johnny and Jody split and go their own way. I can see the apprehension as Jack and Bunny slowly walk up to the front door talking softly. I'll give them a few minutes alone with their dad before I enter the drama.

Time's up. I close the office door loudly so they will know I'm on my way. I enter a room of heightened tension, stand aside and watch as the kids clam up, answering Pep's questions with monosyllables. I'm sure all three are glad I'm on the scene. Bunny watches me as if wishing for me to get in the conversation.

I oblige. "Okay people. I assume you're packed and ready to go." If course they are. I helped them pack last night. "Go get your stuff so you can get on the road. Houston is a long way to go and you need to get there before dark if you can."

Just what the kids wanted to hear. They are off to their bedrooms to retrieve their packs without comment.

Pep and I have an uneasy silent moment before the kids return and wait for the command to leave.

I smile at them and shrug at Pep. "Well Sunday afternoon then?

"Yeah, hopefully by three. We'll leave at ten and stop somewhere along the way for lunch. Call Mom's number or my cell if you need anything."

I nod without comment and we head toward the front door with Jack and Bunny following behind their dad. At the car I assist them in putting their packs in the truck opened by Pep and give each a long hug. They hop into the car, Jack in the front and Bunny in the back.

As Pep opens his door he draws in a full breath, lets it out and forces a wry smile. "Well, I guess we'll see you Sunday," he says dryly as he shrugs absently and enters the car.

"I guess," I answer, assisting him in closing the door. I step back as he starts his Mercedes and slowly backs down the driveway into the street. As he pulls away I force a wide smile for the kids and wave goodbye.

Well I guess this is the first of many weekend departures. I'm sure I'll get used to it as we all will. Nonetheless I don't have to like it.

Well shit, it's too early for dinner or wine time. I think I'll get a Chivas and head for the boat dock. Perhaps I'll get soused enough to not care about eating or the wine. I wonder if the Bales are going to be around later to rescue me . . . again.

It would really be great to scratch on Link's door but we have agreed that time is running out on her show preparation. Work has to be her highest priority at this time. I have to honor that. Crap.

So here I am sitting on my dock surveying my fragile kingdom and missing my wayward husband who's run off with my kids. Of course I should add feeling massively sorry for myself and wishing the whole mess would end. But then again, if I could get laid by some viral dude that has no baggage or other irritating hang ups, that would surely make everything better . . . I think. *Get over it, Gina.*

"Getting an early start, are you?" comes the familiar voice behind me as Jonathan with wine in hand, and Johnny and Jody join me on the dock.

"Hey, people!" I exclaim. "Yeah, I've been at it for," I shrug indifferently, "about two hours." I grin at Jonathan and motion for him to sit.

I direct my attention to the kids. "I guess you'll have to do without Jack and Bunny this weekend. They've gone with their dad to visit their grandparents."

"Oh," Jody presents her mom's frown. "Bunny went? She said she wasn't going."

"When did she say that?"

"Last night," Johnny answers for his sister. "She said that her dad doesn't love her anymore, so she wasn't going to go with him."

Jody nods her agreement and Jonathan draws his brow together and shakes his head in dejection.

I release a sigh of tension and ask directing my attention to Jody, "Why does she think he doesn't love her anymore."

Jody nods positively—her mom again—"She thinks that girl . . . that lady doesn't want him to . . . to love her anymore."

Johnny nods his agreement.

I glumly shake my head at Jonathan. "Out of the mouth of babes," is the only comment I can come up with.

Suddenly the kids have had enough of this serious talk and ask their father if they can go to Monica's and he nods his approval. They scamper off and Jonathan calls out to them. "Be home by dark."

I've had enough of 'Dad doesn't love me anymore;' I change the subject: "Link working late again?"

"Yeah, she didn't even stop to have dinner. So I fed the kids some leftovers and here we are." He toasts his glass to me. "I guess I'm a little behind, huh?"

"Yeah, John, here we are, just you and me alone together again. What do you want to do Mr. Bales?"

130

Jonathan draws his brow and twists his lips, then grins: "Well there's always the elusive threesome. But we are only two."

I shake my head feigning disgust. "Yeah, right, John, you're all talk and no action . . . as usual." Damn, you're so freaking hot. I wish I could throw you down and jump your bones right here on the dock in front of God and all the neighbors.

Jonathan renews his grin as he crosses his legs and looks out over the water. "I love this lake." He toasts me with his wine glass. I return the gesture with my scotch. "And I love my neighbors," he adds.

Link toasts, "Sixteen days and counting," as we sit at our usual Saturday night deck table in the second floor bar and ballroom of the McQueeney Country Club. "I'll have to complete a painting every three days to make it and that doesn't include framing."

"Can't you hire out the framing? It's nothing fancy anyway," Jonathan quizzes as I watch.

"Probably, but you know me; I have to do everything myself." She takes a sip of her Martini and gazes absently at me. "How about you, Gina. Want to frame with me?" She cocks a brow and winks. It isn't lost on John..

I chuckle, "Well, I can't recall ever framing before, but it sounds really exotic—or even erotic." I grin mischievously at John and rub my hands together in mock anticipation. "Can three people do it together? And do I need my swim suit, sir?"

They both laugh and Jonathan comments, "Always with your head in the gutter, Gina."

I flash my most sexy smile toward Jonathan. "It's easily curable. I just need two or three hours with the right guy." I pause and sneak a look at Link: "Or woman to relieve my dastardly hormone driven misery."

My statement isn't lost on either of them as they glance at each other in silent amusement with nearly matching puzzled expressions.

I shrug when there is no comment and carry on: "I guess there will be no framing tonight—other than paintings. But then I'm confused. What the hell is framing

131

anyway? It must be something you do with your legs. Maybe like wrapping them around your partner's head. Picture that. I think I'm experiencing some kind of comic digression." *Get a life, Gina.*

They laugh and Jonathan scratches his head while studying me. "You're totally amazing, Gina."

I force myself back to sanity. "Really, Link, what can John and I do to help you get the paintings ready?"

Link gloomily shakes her head. "Much as I hate to say it, give me a lot of space and don't expect to see much of me for the next three weeks."

"Doesn't seem like a lot of fun for me or you," Jonathan answers as a matter of fact.

Link nods at John and looks at me for comment.

I send her a mental message without expression other than lightly biting at my lower lip: *Same here, babe.*

Link grimaces. "Wow, it sounds like this is going to be an enjoyable three weeks."

No offence Link but it would be fantastic if Jonathan and I could entertain each other while you are busy. Just kidding. Or maybe not. Shit, Jonathan wouldn't participate anyway. I wonder if Preacher is looking for some free and hearty fun. *Gina, dear. Just give it up. You aren't getting any. Accept it.* Would you just bug off? I can't help it if my hormones are running amuck.

Well this has certainly been an uneventful Saturday night. But what the hell was I expecting? After the long slow Margarita fueled boat ride home, Jonathan, Link and the kids opt for an early bedtime to allow Link an early start Sunday morning in the studio.

I wonder if they are getting any tonight. I know I'm not. So what else is new? I head up to the house to get my scotch and return to the dock alone. I know what I'm going to get tonight. I will certainly remain sane enough to get myself in bed later . . . I hope.

Sneaking a Sunday afternoon nap on the living room sofa I am startled awake by the sound of the front door opening. In walks my kids lugging their packs.

"Hey, girls and boys; you're home. How'd it go?" I look beyond them through the open door. "Your dad?"

"He was in a hurry. He said he would call you later," Jack answers, dropping his pack on the floor.

That's fine with me. The less I see of him the better. He just keeps me upset or aroused—one or the other, or both.

"Well, Bunny, did you have a good time?"

"Uh-huh. Kinda. We went to the zoo and to a movie."

That's nice. How did you get along with your dad? No, I won't ask that. "And you Jack? Are you glad you went?"

"Yeah."

Shit, how about pulling some teeth. "Okay. Do you guys want to go visit with your dad again?"

They both shrug their indifference or is it they are uncomfortable talking about time spent with their dad. Whatever, they both snatch their packs and head to their rooms before I can pry anymore.

Just as well. I can't ask anything simpler than what I've already asked. Maybe later. Maybe not. It least they are home all in one piece. He could have absconded to Brazil with them. Not.

Well Link and I have only been shacking up for a few weeks, but here it is Friday afternoon and it has been—how long now?—over a week since the last time. You'd think we were an old married couple that only have sex once a week or so.

I can't take it anymore. Screw painting, Link. Screw me instead. I don my trusty moo–moo and head for her studio unannounced.

I knock lightly on the door and wait. The door opens a crack and Link peers out. She looks at me questioningly and I say dryly, "We need to fuck. Right now."

Naked, Link flashes a wide buttery smile as she opens the door fully and gestures for me to enter. "What the hell took you so long? I've been thinking about you all week."

Without answering I slam the door closed and pull my moo–moo off over my head. I grab her at the waist and pull her toward me. Our bodies clash in an explosion of energy enveloping and fusing us together.

As if choriographed our hands find each other's butts and we pull each other even closer. We kiss—a long hard, lip biting, tongue sucking collision that eventually demands that we come up for air.

She releases my behind and, holding onto my shoulders, leaves her feet and wraps her legs around my waist, pressing her body against mine. My knees weaken and I lose my balance. We somehow end up on the floor with me on top of her in that glorious missionary position.

We both giggle and she cries out, "Beautiful, Gina. Do that again!"

"I don't think I have two of those in me." I answer as I raise up on my knees to find that warm moist nest waiting for me. I thrust in two fingers, eliciting a low groan from deep in her throat. Finding her clit I encircle it and pinch lightly.

"Enough, Gina," she cries, "Suck me now. I can't wait any longer."

I can do that. "At your service, ma'am," I answer. In an instant I withdraw my fingers, grasp her thighs and bend her knees completely. I dive right into that wet spot with my tongue and lips, searching, licking and sucking.

"Oh my God, Gina. Hurry, please, harder. Fuck me harder," she cries out and I oddly wonder if the neighbors down the way can hear.

She thrusts her hips toward me and I feel a need to back off to get a breath. She suddenly screams out, "Aggh! Enough, Gina, stop!"

She giggles, "Damn, Gina. You're fantastic."

Without allowing her to bask in the after–burn, I lay on my back and, in the same motion, pull her in between my spreaded legs. Grabbing her hand I guide it down to my pleasure spot.

"My turn, woman."

Her fingers slide in quickly and I am instantly primed for the kill. I feel my blood pulse in my chest as it pumps from my heart, gushing throughout my body like sparkling electricity.

I completely fold my knees as her lips replace her fingers and surround my clitoris, sucking, pulling, and squeezing. I feel myself rising in a churning vortex of energy, ready to explode into pure ecstasy.

"Oh, Link, more! Harder! Harder!"

"Go for it, Gina."

"I'm coming Link! Just a little bit . . . yes, there! Suck me hard! Hurry, Link, hurry!" I feel myself soaring higher and higher when suddenly the bottom drops out and I splinter, disappearing into pure white nothingness.

"Whoa, you've been holding out on me Link," I gush breathlessly. "You are fantastic."

"Of course I am."

"And you said woman can't have a quickie together—no cookie cutter sex. That's what you said." I grin and nod positively, "Well that certainly was pretty damn quick . . . and you were definitely sensational."

She grins, "Just doing my job. Now, get your clothes on and get out of my space. I've got work to do."

"Dang," I chuckle. "Screw me, then immediately kick me out. What kind of lover is that?"

"Your kind of lover . . . and I might add, the only lover you have, so take it or leave it."

"Oh . . . in that case, I guess I'll take it." As I open the door I call back, "When can I take it again?"

"We'll see," she calls out as I step out and close the door.

After walking about half the way to my back door, I decide to lend a little humor to Link's lonely life as an artist. I turn and head back to the studio.

I open the door enough to stick my head in. From behind the painting she is working on her head pops up and she studies me curiously without comment.

"Uh, I forget. When did you say we can fuck again?"

"Just leave. Get the hell out . . . and stay out. At least until I'm ready for you to fill my needs. It's all about me." She points her paint brush at me: "Understand, woman?"

I giggle and slowly close the door. Waiting about a minute, I knock loudly on the door and leave.

Because Link is in catchup mode we skipped our usual Saturday night bash at the club as I'm sure we will next week since she only has seventeen days until delivery to Houston.

On Sunday, Jonathan, in his worn red swimsuit and I in my most sexy bikini spent a great deal of the day on the lake as we combined our turns in towing our eight neighborhood kids skiing. At one point when we went by Link was standing outside the studio door waving. I thought of asking Jonathan to drop me off. That certainly wouldn't work.

Later I even asked Jonathan if he would rather be doing something more adult instead of pulling young ski-ers in circles on the lake. Other than a dismal shake of the head I got no answer. No fun at all, this man. Which also meant no fun for me. What else is new? All I achieved Sun-day was a sunburn and more of the usual hormonal im-balance and sexual frustration.

Our Monday morning executive meeting is turn-ing out to be pretty much about me and my first column. The magazines are scheduled to be distributed Monday, April 18, one week from today. Am I excited or what? Jon-athan and the other four execs in our group seated around Jonathan's conference table are not super excited but are surprisingly supportive. This is probably because they had a hand in the original planning.

Josh Butler, Jonathan's second in command after me is usually the most upset when I take over Jonathan's position on occasion but now seems anxious to help.

An overweight balding man in his mid–fifties, with his wire rimmed–reading glasses perched on the end of his nose, Josh often projects a stern look even in this relaxed environment. I always remind myself to take this into account when dealing with him. He is not the bear he appears to be and once I got used to him, I actually like working with him. If I have to.

Of course we seldom cross each other's path at work which is probably good for both of us. I still dread being in charge, particularly if I have to make an important decision. This has not happened in the past because Jonathan has always been just a phone call away. I hope it stays that way in the future. I just don't want to be in charge.

Josh says, "Checked out the website. You and Bob have done a splendid job. I do have a suggestion or two if you like." He actually grins, peering over his glasses.

I smile, "I need all the help I can get. If any of you can give me some solid advice to get this project off and running I would appreciate it."

Jonathan who has been unusually quiet this morning nods his agreement as he sips on his coffee.

Josh folds his hands with his elbows propped on the table and clears his throat. "I think it would be good if you allow all those in this room and any others that would like to help, check out your website before next Monday and stir the pot a little. As soon as people read the column many will check out your social media. If they find others have already contacted you, it will stimulate their also getting involved.

Jesse Ferro, head of publications worldwide, nods his agreement.

"Particularly the blog. If we can get some back and forth going between us this week, it will hopefully encourage readers to get involved over something."

Jonathan smiles as he builds his usual steeple of fingers with his elbows propped on the table. Sexy. "Yeah, we need to make it crazy fun. Something really far out about some useless subject."

Josh nods. "Bring on the idiots. That's what blogs are for. If you can get the crazies to start up a feud about something stupid it could really snowball."

"That will keep your people coming back for more," Chris Hunter of the advertising department adds even though he seems to be directing his attention at Pat who's sitting in on the meeting today.

"It's amusing when I run across a blog and people are getting hyper about nothing. And they appear to be serious." He shrugs while spreading his hands and sneaking a sideways glance at Pat. "Those are the people you want to snare."

"And you will," Josh grins. "And you certainly will."

Jonathan cocks a brow and grins for my benefit as the others look on. "Simple shit. Just keep it simple as you can for simple people."

One of the waitresses didn't show up so Juanita is covering for her and doesn't have time for our usual banter. We quickly order and hustle her out to save the day. In no time she returns with our order.

"Well, what do you think?" Jonathan queries between bites of his usual cheese enchiladas. "Did you get some ideas that will get your column off to a running start?"

I am transfixed by a bit of cheese attached to his beard that he isn't aware of. I have this urge to lick it off.

"Hello in there," he grins waving a hand in front of my eyes.

"Uh, sorry," I giggle as I reach across the table and dab at the cheese with a napkin. "It's really bad when I get hung up over a bit of cheese on your chin."

"Kinky woman," he replies. "Just don't go off on one of your fantasies like last time we ate here. Just one of those is all I care to watch."

I chuckle and take a long drink of my Margarita straight from the glass while peering over the rim at him. Shit, I would screw him right here if I could. Too bad he doesn't want to play. "Oh well," I let slip out.

"Oh well what?"

"Oh crap, oh well," I laugh. "Oh well nothing. That just escaped my mouth. I'm not telling you why."

"I can imagine. I'd just as soon not know. You are really a piece of work. You know that don't you."

I sadly shake my head. "Someday soon I promise to get my act together, John boy and maybe, just maybe, I'll quit harassing you." *Sure you will.*

"Promises, promises," he answers shaking his head, feigning dismay. "You always hear of employees being sexually harassed, abused or discriminated against but never about the boss being sexually whatever. I wonder if there is somewhere I can file a complaint?"

"Wow, go for it. Maybe I'll get my mugshot in the newspaper for being accused of first degree boss sexual harassment."

No comment from him so I change the subject. "Link appears to be a bit stressed about the upcoming show."

John toys with his enchiladas, moving parts around his plate. He carefully lays the fork across his plate and sips his Margarita through a straw before answering: "A bit stressed would be putting it mildly. But yeah, you're right.

"I for one will be glad when this is over and we can get back to . . . to our usual abnormal, if you know what I mean. The kids and I try to avoid her when we can. Fortunately we don't see her that much but that's not good either."

"You think she's going to make the deadline?"

"Probably," he grins, "but I don't think she can transport the paintings if they aren't dry yet."

"Are you going to take off and help her get the paintings to Houston?"

"She said she didn't need any help, but I expected that. I suggested she ask you to go with her but she declined that also."

Damn, I could use three nights in Houston alone with the woman of my choice. Then again I would like even more to be here with the man of my choice for three nights while the woman of my choice is gone for three nights. Well, you get my drift. Craziness. Neither of those scenarios are going to happen. Well, maybe with the woman of my choice. But then again, she has to cooperate. *Yeah, lots of luck.*

"I hope she makes the deadline. It will be nice for the three of us to sit on the dock after next week and have a large flask of wine again. Or a barrel of scotch."

"Yeah, you can say that again."

139

"Are you going back with her to the opening on Saturday?"

"Yeah I have to do that. It's a super big deal for her and although I'll be in the way, she wants me to go so she can impress me . . . and she will for sure."

He presents that adorable grin, reaches over and lightly taps the back of my hand with a finger. "I hope to get a loyal neighbor to keep my kids while we're gone." As usual his touch sends a bolt of electricity coursing through me and thrusting me into orbit. Oh well.

"I can certainly do that," I reply and finish off my Margarita. Dang, keeping their kids while they are having their way with each other is like being a bridesmaid.

EIGHT

My executive cohorts have wasted no time texting and emailing questions. I hope they were correct when they said their questions will prime my social media prior to the publication of my first column Monday. I certainly am glad I don't have to come up with answers for them. I do reserve the right to comment to myself.

> Date: Tuesday April 12 2016 10:22AM
> To: Gina Rabbit
> From: Jesse Ferro
> Subject: mom–in–law
>
> Gina,
> Help. My dingbat emotionally unstable mother–in–law lives in a mobile home on our property. My problem: she brings her lovers home with her when she gets off her job as a bar lady at two in the morning. The neighbors are complaining of the noisy ruckus they make until daylight. The neighbors have threatened to call the sheriff, but my wife is hesitant to confront her mom because it might send her over the edge. What to do?
> Jesse the bewildered

> Very creative, Jesse. Not you for sure. I am well aware you aren't married, hence no mother–in–law. Dingbat?

> Chris Hunter   1:14PM
> I have been working with a certain company for going on ten years now. They only give me eight weeks of vacation a year. What's up with that? Should I quit and find a job with more vacation time?
> Chris

Beautiful, Chris. I'll pass this on to the man. Maybe he'll have an answer for you.

To: Gina Rabbit
Time: Wednesday April 13 2016 2:05PM
From: Josh Butler
Subject: Too much nookie

I have this girlfriend of eleven months. She not only wants, she demands sex at least twice every day. She's killing me. What should I do? I don't want to hurt her feelings or lose her to some oversexed stud.
They call me Josh

Don't know Josh. Damn I personally would be satisfied with half of that—or a fourth. An eighth even. Right now once a week would be great.

Time: Wednesday April 13 2016 3:33PM
To: Gina Rabbit
From: Robert Barclay
Subject: Cheese fraud

Hey, Rabbit,
I read where most of the grated cheese you buy at the supermarket is not one hundred percent cheese as the package says. Most have wood pulp, cellulite and other fillers. What's a person to do if you can't trust the food peddlers?
Lost in the woods

Scary. Don't eat.

Time: Wednesday April 13 2016 4:11PM
To: Gina Rabbit
From: Billy Joe Baker
Subject: Awe, not another blog

Gina girl,
Do we really need another blog? Come on, it had better be good.
Lost on the third floor

Yes, Billy baby. And, with your help it will be great. I guarantee.

Jonathan Bales   4:40PM

RABBIT'S EROTIC FANTASY

What do I do when my wife teams up with my neighbor to coax me to join them in a ménage `a trois? I don't think I want to go there. I have always heard a threesome is kinky. Even if I participated I would have no idea what to do.

A bumpkin

Nice try, Jonathan. But I still don't take no for an answer.

So there you have it. The upper echelon of my coworkers at Bales to the rescue. Josh tells me there are probably more coming from the rank and file. That would be interesting and I think I can come up with some nice ones myself.

Jesse Ferro is right however. I need to get some earth shaking questions on my website blog soon to get some immediate give and take questions and answers started.

I won't have time before the publication deadline of the second column to receive questions asked for in the first column. So I'll also have to use these same questions or make up my own in the WHAT'S YOUR QUESTION section of the second column.

I can then answer them in the WE HAVE AN AN-SWER section of that same second column and ask readers to forward their answers to the same question. By the third column I will be able to depend on both questions and answers from readers. Then I'll be off and running.

Lost in our own silence we observe the noisy group both in the second floor bar and on the dock below. It's the usual Saturday night but special for Link and me because we are celebrating my first column and her gallery opening next week.

My column is going to be published in eleven different magazines on Monday, two days from now. I have over twenty questions from the rank and file of Bales on my website. That should be more than ample for me to choose three for the second column.

Link seems to be more at ease since she will be able to complete the expected number of paintings by Wednesday to allow for basic drying before boxing and crating them up Saturday. We will have to be careful in packing them since some of the paint might still be tacky because of not enough curing time. She has reserved a rental van that we intend to load next Sunday morning for her trip to Houston on Monday.

And lucky me—or us. She has requested alone time with me on Thursday to carry us over until she returns the next Thursday. However I assume she's going to have some quality time with her sexy husband also. I can only assume because I don't ask her about their sexual relationship. Do I really want to know?

I wonder if we can convince what's–his–name to participate in a threesome sometime like next Saturday or Sunday night. Wow, what a send-off that would be. I won't bother holding my breath as I also shouldn't expect any fireworks between Jonathan and me while Link is gone. Aren't I a great friend and lover? Leave town and I try to screw your husband. My keeper's head is gloomily shaking as she covers her eyes with her hands: *Pure insanity*.

John pats my hand sending shivers cascading down my spine. Shit, don't stop. "Well, do you have everything under control for the big day Monday?"

I nod positively with an easy smile. "I'm close. Thanks for getting an extension on my deadline for column two. I didn't plan ahead. It won't happen again."

Jonathan nods and studies me with quizzical eyes. "Close, meaning . . . ?"

"Since I'll be too late for my readers to respond before Monday I have to choose three questions and answers tomorrow so I can forward the second column to the publishers Monday."

"Uh-huh." He pauses and nods while scratching his beard. Sexy. I notice Link also watching her husband closely. I wonder if she is also thinking how sexy he is. I wonder if she realizes how sexy I think she is. Who's on first? I am a disaster.

He continues: "Did you get enough feedback from our people to help you choose your questions?"

"About two dozen including several from the executive group. I've already chosen one suggested question from the head honcho that should go over really well. I just need to reword it for the best impact."

Link cocks a curious brow and grins at her husband. "This I have to hear."

"His question deals with a problem he is having with his wife and her friend ganging up on him to have a threesome. He is looking for answers on how to deal with them—to make them leave him alone."

Link giggles, "I love it. What is your answer?"

I shrug absently then grin, "Don't know yet. But he probably won't like it. Of course he'll also be getting answers from the masses in later columns and on my blog."

Jonathan studies me stoically. His expression turns me on, too. But that's not new. All he has to do is breathe to turn me on.

"I presume you are not going to use my name?" he asks.

I flash a wink at Link. "Of course I am. I'm a trusted syndicated columnist. I have to tell the truth."

"You also need to keep a job."

Link giggles at his response.

"Oh," I grin, "in that case, never mind."

Jonathan nods blandly: "I knew you would agree."

Suddenly Jonathan's eyes light up and he breaks into a wide smile as a friend approaches our table.

"Well what do we have here?" Jonathan exclaims as he stands and extends his hand. "The illustrious Sheriff Charife. Have a seat Jerry. How the hell are you?

"Ladies," he beams. "Good to see you. I am good. Just trying to hang out here incognito in my civilian clothes so I can have a beer without it showing up in the newspaper."

Jerry is a staggering specimen of a man. Standing six foot six with an athletic body and boyish good looks, he sports a deep tan, dark wavy hair and eyes that hide his age which is about the same as ours. Born and raised in neighboring Seguin, he was the hometown hero in football during his four years in high school.

He received a full ride scholarship to quarterback the Horned Frogs of Texas Christian University. We all arrived about the same time as freshmen. He and Jonathan became instant friends when Jonathan interviewed him for an article he was writing about football at TCU. In our senior year, having to leave football due to injury, he joined us on the newspaper.

He came back home to Seguin after graduation and eventually was elected sheriff of Guadalupe County. Although he is well known because of his exploits in high school he felt that he was elected because of his catchy last name that rhymes with sheriff. He has held the job now for over ten years.

"I can't stay long. Geri called and told me to get my butt home," he grins. "I just wanted to stop by to tell Gina how sorry I am about Pep running away."

"Thanks, Jerry. That's very sweet of you."

He squeezes my arm and smiles. "If you like I can arrest him and bring him home."

We laugh at his suggestion as his touch sends a bolt of energy zooming down my spine and splashing in my belly.

"I think not, Jerry. I'm pretty much better off without him."

He stands and nods. "Well folks, I have to go home to momma before she calls the sheriff on me. It certainly is a pleasure to talk with you guys. It always brings back old memories."

"Hold it, hold it," Jonathan objects. "Tell Geri to come on over and have a drink with us. We don't see either of you enough."

"I'm sure she'd love to but her mom is visiting and she's not very mobile. So another time."

"Okay, then tell her we said hi."

"Will do. Now you all be careful out there. Take it from me; it's a jungle. Bye now." We listen to him clomping down the stairs.

We remain silent as we hear the beginning of an old recording by the Eagles being played by the disc jockey:

RABBIT'S EROTIC FANTASY

All alone at the end of the evening.
And the bright lights have faded to blue.

Jonathan grins and touches my shoulder. "Hey Gina, they're playing your song."

Since we've already had too many Martinis, too much scotch and a gallon of wine, our barriers are down, and the three of us break into full voice singing right along with the Eagles:

I was thinking 'bout a woman who might
    have loved me
And I never knew
You know I've always been a dreamer
Spent my life running 'round
And it's so hard to change
Can't seem to settle down

Preacher appears at the top of the stairs and breaks into a wide grin. He is so sexy dressed in baby blue trousers and a tight fitting black T-shirt with white canvas deck shoes.

As if planned, he heads to the middle of the dance floor and gestures with waving arms for everyone in the crowded bar to sing along. They oblige and he orchestrates them as if directing a symphony, the bar erupting in a cacophony of drunks virtually drowning out the Eagles.

But the dreams I've seen lately
Keep on turning out and burning out
And turning out the same
So put me on a highway
And show me a sign
And take it to the limit one more time

Suddenly the stairway is flooded by people coming up to see what the commotion is all about. They join the fun and the singing becomes deafening. Preacher motions for the DJ to jack up the volume and he obliges, the earsplitting sound surely heard by everyone on this end of the lake.

Even the kids get into the act, although most of the younger ones have no idea what the song is or what its message is. They mouth along with the crazy adults and on the front row is shy Jody who has again made the bar dance floor her personal performance stage.

You can spend all your time making money
You can spend all your love making time
If it all falls to pieces tomorrow
Would you still be mine?
And when you're looking for your freedom
Nobody seems to care
And you can't find the door
Can't find it anywhere
When there's nothing to believe in
Still you're coming back
You're running back
Take it to the limit
Take it to the limit
Take it to the limit one more time.

The song ends with a rowdy cheer and clapping from the impromptu crowd of adults and their amazed children, many who have never seen their parents act this crazy.

Link and I watch as Preacher approaches and Link whispers, "Damn, Gina, is he hot or what? Why don't you try to get a little of that. The timing is perfect."

Before I can answer Preacher joins us with a wide grin–splitting face. "You folks responsible for that display?"

Jonathan laughs, "I guess we nearly started a riot. That was fun."

"That was more than fun. I think we should have a singalong every Saturday. You can be the director, John."

Jonathan chuckles, "Afraid not, Preacher. That's a one–time deal for me. Surely I've had too much to drink."

"I'll tell you what, John. We'll ply you with free wine starting about five o'clock on Saturday and by ten you'll be ready to fly."

Jonathan shakes his head. "Just give it up, Preacher. It isn't going to happen."

Preacher jabs a finger lightly into Jonathan's chest. "You'll change your mind. Right ladies?" he says then suddenly he makes his usual quick exit down the stairs three steps at a time.

Jonathan sits down and we follow. "I can't believe we did that. We couldn't have planned anything crazier than that.

"Okay what do you say we round up the kids and head out. I personally could use a little peace and quiet on the dock with two sexy women." He quickly raises a cautionary finger. "Don't get me wrong. There will be not be a threesome tonight. At least not one that I am part of."

"Boo . . . boo," Link and I giggle. She lays a finger against her cheek. "I know, Gina. Let's ask that guy in blue and black if he wants to participate."

Jonathan cocks a quizzical brow and tilts his head. "Guy in blue and black. Who is that?"

Link and I laugh and she shakes her head dismally. "Never mind. You wouldn't understand."

Sunday morning coming down. The questions and answers came easily and I had the second column written by noon. Now it's ski time for Jonathan and the kids. He announced last night that he was going to ski today and suggested that I do the same. Not happening. The water is still too cold. Check back with me in July.

That doesn't keep me from breaking out my favorite bikini—anything to stir up the testosterone of my fellow boat driver. That isn't going to happen; at least he won't admit it or show it even if he's the least bit aroused.

And what's the point of my incurable madness? Even if he is turned on we aren't going to get after it in a boat with four kids. *Get a life, Gina*. I'm trying, I'm trying.

Maybe Jonathan will drop me off at the studio. No, that won't work. Link's got work to do and I would be a massive distraction. Anyway, I have to pull Jonathan skiing. I know; after Jonathan is through with his ski run, maybe I can get him to drop me off at the club.

Preacher would surely like some afternoon company. Yeah, right. He hardly knows me and even if he did I probably wouldn't be on his list of favorite women he would like to shack up with. And what if he's gay? *Give it a break Gina.*

I pull Johnny for about fifteen minutes before he flips the rope indicating he's had enough. Bunny is next up and she immediately plunges into the water before Johnny pulls himself up on the rear ramp.

"Great run, Johnny," I call out and he grins.

"I am pretty good, huh?"

"I wouldn't get too puffed up. Jody is next after Bunny and you know she's going to outshine all of you," Jonathan says, winking at his daughter. She flashes a thumbs up gesture at her dad and a so–there smile at her brother.

Without comment I leave the driver's seat and shrug at Jonathan. "All yours, dude. I need a break."

When he sits down I kiss him lightly on the back of his neck. Damn he smells good. "Thanks, John. I knew I could count on you to take over before your turn."

"That's me. The world's biggest pushover."

"Yeah, when it applies to driving boats."

Since I have work to do that requires staying at the office a while after the executive meeting, I bum a ride with Jonathan upon his promise to take off early if I wanted to leave before his usual time. We ride quietly for several miles down Interstate Ten.

John gives me a sideways glance with a cocked brow. "Kinda quiet, lady. You have something on your mind—something you want to talk about?"

I delay my answer as I bite at my lower lip. "I can't quite figure it out but something is bugging me about Link and has been for several days now."

He steals another sideways look. "I don't . . . I don't follow you. Is she having a particular problem that I don't know about?"

"No. Not really." I respond after a moment of thought.

"My kids are always saying 'not really.' It appears to me not really takes in a lot of wide open territory of fruitful nothingness."

"Yeah, I guess that's not the right answer. It's just that . . . there's something eating at me. Like I'm having a premonition of danger for her."

I pause as he glances curiously at me.

"No, not necessarily danger. I can't grasp it. It's like there's bad energy around her—a black cloud."

Eyes straight ahead on the road, he raises a brow. "You sense a black cloud hanging over her but you can't pinpoint exactly what it is."

"I am really perplexed." I pause as I struggle to find the right words. "I don't know. It's an energy thing. When I'm around her—and it's increasing lately—I feel these bad vibes.

"Not necessarily between her and me. It's her deal. All about her but I can't pin it down. Just what the hell am I feeling? And why? You know what I mean?"

Jonathan shrugs absently and flips a hand as if to blow my feelings off. "I don't know, Gina. I haven't sensed anything unusual about her. She seems like her usual self except for the pressure she has shouldered because of the show. But that has subsided in the last few days. She seems okay to me."

I nod slowly. "Yeah, I guess you're right. My mind is messing with me." *No, Gina. You must be cognizant of what* you *sense. Do not ignore your deep feelings at any time no matter what. Subtle messages can be of major importance. Don't dwell on them but be mindful that these messages or thoughts are there for a purpose.*

"Thanks a lot," I mumble to myself.

Another sideways glance: "Say what?"

"Shit. Sorry, John. Just talking to myself."

"Having one of those fantasies are you?" he grins patting me on the knee.

Shit. Do that some more. I close my eyes as my heart misfires sending an electrical charge spiraling down my spine before exploding in never–never land. Well that's me, never–never getting any.

We've hardly started our executive meeting when gloomy Pat enters with a stack of magazines and without comment places several in front of each of us. The guys take notice of her as she is her usual sexy self and dressed to the nines. Too bad she doesn't ever smile. Chris Hunter in particular gazes at her curiously. I wonder what he's thinking.

Jonathan leans back in his chair and grins at me as he holds up a copy of *Men's Life*. "Lady and gentlemen, it is now time to congratulate one of our own. If you'll turn to page thirty eight you'll see the first edition of our own syndicated columnist, Gina De Georgio Wabbit."

There is momentarily silence other than the ruffling of pages being turned. Then a few wows, a fantastic, a couple of greats and then applause all around.

Don't you dare cry I tell myself as I bite at my lower lip. I'm at a loss for words. Finally, "Damn," is the best I can come up with. I pause: "Damn, damn, damn."

They laugh.

I smile a big one and nod at Jonathan. "Mr. Bales, thanks for your assistance in my pulling this off.

"For the rest of you, thanks for your help and suggestions in getting me to this point. I certainly hope I can approach each of you for advice when I need it in the future—and I will need your guidance for sure."

I pause and look around the table at those that were at one time pushing against me at every opportunity. Now each's smiling and some are nodding. I have somehow won them over.

Suddenly the tears well up. I wipe one escapee and extend my smile. "I don't want to screw this happy time up by bawling so I'll end with this—thank you, each of you for being in my corner when I needed you. Thank you Mr. Jonathan Bales . . . for everything.

I put my hands in the prayer position and bow to their delight.

* * * *

"Wow, I'm certainly glad the first edition is done. Now hopefully I can get into some kind of groove to make each issue easy to produce."

Jonathan nods and takes a sip of his Bloody Mary. "It is going to get easier with each edition. And hopefully you'll have to hire some part time help to handle administrative stuff."

In pops Juanita. "Marys okay, *Conejo*?" she flashes her tantalizing big–lipped smile.

I nod and Jonathan pulls on her sleeve. "Excellent. Why don't you take a break and have one with us?"

She chuckles and pinches Jonathan on the cheek. "Don't tempt me, *Juan*. I just might take you up on that offer. But I don't think Manuel would be too happy about it. I've got orders waiting."

She shrugs and draws out her order pad. "Let me guess: cheese enchiladas."

Jonathan looks to me for confirmation. "All around Juanita."

As she turns to leave Jonathan holds up his Mary glass with one hand and two fingers with the other. "Juanita, *por favor*."

She looks back and nods. She holds up two fingers over her shoulder as she walks away: *"Los doz, senor."*

Jonathan studies me for a moment causing my heart to hitch up a notch and spew energy sparkling throughout my body. *Give it a rest Gina*.

"What are you feeling? Do you feel like a world famous celebrity yet?"

I chuckle and touch a finger to my temple. "What are you feeling? What are you thinking? That's something a woman would ask a man and he just hates it. But I like the question.

"John I feel fantastic and it's all your fault. There's no way I can repay you for what you are doing for me . . . and it's not just the column, it's the support you and Link are giving me. Someday I hope I'll be able to return the favor."

I pause for comment but he merely nods. "And no I don't feel like a world famous celebrity. Right now that is not important. I just want things to settle down in my life and I have this feeling that's not going to happen for a while."

He regards me with a gathered brow over concerned eyes. "That's the second time."

"I don't understand. Second time what?"

"The second time today you've mentioned having strange feelings."

"Yeah but the feeling I just mentioned is related to circumstances in my life. The feeling I've been having about Link is just weird or crazy because it isn't."

He runs a hand through his mussed hair and frowns. "You are really concerned about this Link stuff aren't you?"

I hesitate and reply, "Yes sir. If it was just a one–time deal I don't think it would be a problem but it's beginning to grate on me a little."

"Umm . . . ."

"Yeah, me too. There isn't a hell of a lot I can do about it, but it is there and nagging me."

Juanita returns with the Marys and Jonathan doesn't acknowledge her as she sets the drinks on a napkin. As she collects the empty Mary glasses she is aware of Jonathan's lack of attention. She cocks a brow for my benefit before leaving.

Now I am studying him, wanting him, as he sips on his Mary straw in thought. He looks up at me momentarily and smiles. "Good Bloody Mary, huh?"

"Oh." I take a hurried draw on the straw and nod my approval.

Juanita returns with our lunch and leaves quickly. We eat silently lost in our individual thoughts. Of course my thoughts are wondering what his thoughts are. I wouldn't dare ask him.

The silence is broken: "So how much work do you have to do before you're ready to go home?" he asks softly.

I have to make a couple of calls—one stateside and the other Brazil. If I can track them down without too much hassle I should be through in an hour and a half. Oh, I do want to stop briefly and thank Bob Couser for his help. His tech help was monumental and his art work more than superb."

"The phone calls?"

"Just company shit," I grin. "Handling the side-show. And if you're curious forget it. You don't want to know. It's my job to deal with it so you don't have to even think about it."

He chuckles, "Sounds good to me."

It is Wednesday and questions are already trickling in; that is great. Since I only need three questions per week for the column, surely I can chose the ones most likely to create some interest. The others I can answer on my blog. The blog will also make it easier for those that want to have a go in answering the questions.

I will try to add several questions daily to the blog so that I don't get behind. I also need to deliver each column to the publishers by the deadline each Thursday for the weekly editions, ten days before the actual Monday publication. The monthly editions are the same but only due the second Thursday of each month. Of course this week's Thursday deadline is already covered with questions supplied by the Bales' staff. I chose my three questions yesterday and completed the column for today's delivery.

On the home front Pep has requested visitation with the kids not this weekend but the next. He suggested picking them up again on Friday and bringing them home on Sunday afternoon. He hasn't made plans yet regarding the what and where of the visit.

I have promised Jonathan that I would watch over his kids that weekend as he and Link will be attending the opening of her gallery show in Houston. It would certainly be more convenient if my kids were here over the weekend but it is what it is.

Gina De Georgio

NINE

Yahoo. Today is the day and I'm waiting for my one o'clock play time with Link. How long has it been since we've been in the sack together? Damn gallery show; too long for sure. And it will be a while before the next time because Link doesn't get home from Houston until Thursday afternoon. I'll be a mess by then. Maybe Jonathan will have a change of heart and participate in a special yin yang eruption with me while she's gone.

Give it up, Gina. It isn't going to happen, my muse pipes up.

Thanks a lot. Whose side are you on anyway? It seems like everything I think or do you are somehow against it.

I am your conscience and I know what's best. You should listen. I'll keep you out of trouble.

I chuckle at my subliminal keeper. You are no fun at all and I would just as soon you bug off—as in over and out. With what I'm going through, trouble is definitely another more pleasant option.

And anyway, it's twelve forty–five and I can't wait until one. I practically run over to the studio and scratch on the door.

"Go away," Link calls out from inside. "Whatever you're selling I don't want any."

I giggle and open the door to find her sitting on the bed naked with her legs crossed and it sends a hot flash engulfing me. Damn, she looks yummy.

I close the door and lock it as she watches. As I slowly walk toward her I feel our energies suddenly clashing with bolts of electricity bouncing back and forth, melding and potentially igniting us into one massive uncontrollable explosion. I love this feeling.

I quickly lift my moo–moo over my head and throw it to the side. "What the hell is this?" I ask pointing at the bed where she has spread two beach towels over the top sheet. "If I had known we were going to have a beach party I would have worn my favorite bikini."

"This is a nudist beach. You are already dressed, uh, undressed for this beach. In fact you look pretty appetizing to me. Can I have a bite?"

"Whoa," I reply. "I want you to take more than a bite—take the whole pie. And I suggest you be prepared; before I'm through with you you'll probably want to escape."

"Yeah, right. We'll see who wants to escape and it won't be me." She pulls a serious face and points a threatening finger at me. "I think you should know that I intend to have my way with you. Whatever I desire it is your job to provide it."

I force a glare at her and she laughs.

"Don't laugh at me, bitch," I follow. "I have you under my spell. You'll do what I say when I say."

"Oh really." She flashes that buttery smile that always takes my breath away. "And just what is it that you want me to do?"

"Don't smile at me woman or you will pay the ultimate price."

"Bullshit," she replies with a flip of her hand. "Now get your ass up on this bed, uh, beach and lay belly down. Don't say a word lest you get my full wrath."

I do as she says except for the word part: "Just don't hurt me. I can't stand pain."

"Just shut your mouth before I shut it for you. I promise I'm not going to hurt you . . . much."

I suppress a giggle. "Hurt me, hurt me."

Link leaves the bed and crosses the room, opens the microwave, removes a small bowl of oil and comes back to the beach. She sets the bowl on a small table next to the bed and sticks a finger in it to test the temperature.

"Ma'am, follow my lead. I am systematically going to pamper you. Enjoy it and take notes because after a short spell you will be required to indulge me in a like manner. This is called follow me."

"Umm . . . go for it."

She dips four fingers in the bowl of oil and drips a small amount into her other palm and rubs her hands together. She positions herself next to my feet and folds one knee to apply oil all over that foot. She works the oil between my two smaller toes and lightly massages and pulls each one.

I moan, "Oh my."

There's more. Suddenly she takes both toes into her mouth and sucks ever so lightly.

This is exquisite and I feel the heat again flushing over my body. How can she do this? How can she turn my toes into a sexual organ?

"Shit, Link. More, more."

"Just shut up and enjoy please." She commands as she moves to the third toe and repeats the process. Then the fourth. Now the large toe. Each experience is more sensuous than the last.

Next the bottom of my foot. She massages at the base of each toe, kneading and manipulating the small bones. Now she slowly massages her way toward the heel taking care to provide attention to each area. Now the heel, then to the top of the foot. Holding my ankle stable she twists and massages the foot resulting in a little hurt–so–good pain.

"Oh, that's . . . damn, Link. I hope you don't get tired. I could enjoy this forever."

"Quiet, woman," she commands as she scoots over to the bowl and retrieves more oil. She applies it all over the calf and slowly works her way up to the knee massaging and kneading each muscle.

Again more oil as she repositions herself in front of the other foot. "Still with me?" she asks.

"Damn right. Go for it."

After repeating her performance on the second foot and calf she is suddenly lying beside me. "Okay, lady, follow me. Just do what I've done and I'll be happy."

"Dang, I didn't know I was going to have to do you. I thought this was all about me."

"I'm waiting, Gina."

I get on my knees and dress my hands with the warm massage oil. "Wow, I can't wait until we get to the end part. We'll probably be sliding all over each other."

Link chuckles: "Well get moving. We've got four or five stages to go. Then we'll see just how far we can slide."

I'm intrigued as I commence work on the first two toes. "I don't know if I'm doing this right. How does it feel?"

"The first rule of body massage is time. If you think you're not doing it right, just spend more time and it will turn out perfectly.

"If you spend two minutes on each toe instead of one you're forced into doing more detail. Detail, detail, detail. That's what you're after.

"I want to be touched. The more you touch me the better it gets. Slowly make love to every inch of me. That is what makes a great massage."

I force a pained frown. "Shit, that's a lot to remember. I think this is too hard if you have to think about what and how to do it."

"Gina, just shut up and get with it."

"I can do that." I smile before taking the first two toes in my mouth and suck slowly. Shit, this is exotic. I pause and exclaim, "Yummy!" and dive right back in.

I move on to the other toes, then the foot and the heel just as Link had done. The farther I go the slower I get. The slower I go the better it gets for both of us. I am definitely enjoying giving the massage as much or more than receiving it. I guess that's good.

As I move to the other foot Link smiles. "You appear to be enjoying yourself."

"Hey I like this follow me stuff. How come we haven't done this before?" I ask as I pull each little toe with a slight twist.

"It's only been a few weeks. These things take time. There's a lot more to experience and hopefully someday we're going to do just that. We'll just enjoy the ride as far as it takes us. It can go on forever or end in a day."

Huh? End in a day; what's with that? *Maybe a message*, my advisor says. I disregard the tweet.

Again we change positions and move on. She applies oil to my upper leg and slowly kneads each muscle with her thumbs, starting at the knee and working up.

She massages the inside of my thigh. My pulse kicks up a notch as my desire rises for her to go a little higher between my legs and pay homage to that tender place that always enjoys attention.

She senses my desire and ignores it, choosing to tease me with what's surely to come later.

"Damn, Link, can we put off the massage until later and fuck right now?"

"Nope, can't do it," she giggles while running a quick hand across my vagina bringing a hitch in my pulse. A streak of sparkling energy courses through my being.

"This is all you get right now. Later if you're lucky we'll see."

I protest: "Don't you forget that in a very short time you're going to experience exactly what I'm feeling and I'll be just as mean as you are right now. Then where will you be?"

She smiles and kneads the back of my thigh harder with her thumbs. "You won't find me complaining about anything."

"Ouch. Ease off will you. That hurts," I protest while exaggerating a grimace.

Link giggles as she oils her hands in preparation to begin the other leg "Later maybe you'll appreciate me more if you endure my pain now."

"I think I will enjoy you much more later if there is less pain now if you don't mind."

She doesn't reply as she concentrates on working the oil over my upper leg, then repeats what she did on the other leg. She makes an obvious effort to add a little more time to the ending tease.

"Thanks a whole lot, Link," I comment as I change places with her. "I'll see if I can transfer some of this desire you've brought on back to you. There's no reason I should have all the frustration."

"Bitch, bitch," she chuckles. "Bring it on."

And I do. Oiling up her upper leg I commence with a vengeance. I make every effort to knead to the bone. She appears to squirm a bit but doesn't complain. I double my effort to elicit some type of vocal reaction.

"Enough already," she finally pleads. "I get the message. Now let up will you."

"We'll see." I continue with my muscle work but back off to the point she is no longer uncomfortable. As I near the top of her inner thigh I trail a finger across her vagina eliciting a soft moan.

I rest my hand on her vagina. "You like that, huh. Well you're going to get exactly what I got when I begged—nothing."

I grin. "But maybe not." I lift a hip urging her to turn over face up. I quickly insert two fingers and find her clit. I pinch lightly as I watch for reaction."

"Oh shit, Gina. That . . . damn that feels good. Please, more."

I giggle. "Of course. I won't allow you to suffer the way you did me." I spread her legs and position myself on my knees between them. With my hands on her thighs I push her knees up and back.

"This is what I wanted from you." My mouth finds her clitoris and I squeeze with my lips.

"Crap, Gina," she screams out. "Don't stop. Harder. Oh, I want more."

She presses her hips against my lips as I suck harder. I grasp her breasts and squeeze the nipples until she flinches. Her breathing intensifies as her body wreathes in pleasure.

I feel my own heart kick up a notch as our energies clash. I wonder how long she can last as I step up my pressure, sucking and lip–biting her clit.

"I'm coming, Gina. Please, harder. Hurry. Yes, Yes. Harder." One final push of her hips and she screams out, "Jeez!—"

I giggle as I roll over next to her and straighten her legs. Lying beside her I watch as with her eyes closed and a hint of a smile her breathing starts to calm.

She opens her eyes. "Wow, what did you do to me? I don't think that's listed in the massage manual."

I chuckle as I touch her on the cheek with my finger. "I think I strayed off the schedule a little bit. I assume you're okay with that."

"Are you kidding? That was fantastic." She smiles and places her hand behind my neck. "Do you want to continue with the massage?"

"Yes, and I fully expect to experience what you just did. I get back on my knees and renew the oil on my hands. "Now, if you'll lay back on your stomach I still have one leg to go."

I realize as I work on her leg that I am still flying high and looking for relief. Hopefully it will come quickly.

Soon I find myself back on my stomach as Link oils and begins to massage my behind and back—a large area to cover.

"Your butt is easy to massage," she says absently and she kneads with both hands on both sides at the same time. "It's soft and pliable," she adds as she massages with the heel of he hands.

When I don't answer she stops. "Kind of quiet, you are, Gina. What's up? You have something on your mind?"

I hesitate my answer. "I'm a little concerned about you," I finally reply.

"Well that certainly is a change of direction. And your concern is . . . ?"

"I don't know . . . just something. The last week or so you have been kind of quiet—not your usual bubbly self. It appears to me something is bothering you."

"You're perceptive, woman." She pauses her massage. "I'm a little perplexed—I don't know if that's the right word. I was going to keep it to myself but since you're on to me I guess I'll fess up."

She pauses in thought. I wait.

"Well shit, I guess there's no other way to say it. The dreams have stepped up and I've gone full circle."

I shake my head and frown. "Full circle? I don't understand."

"I'm back to the funeral dreams again. Basically the same old deal. Lots of crying—Jonathan . . . and now you. I try to blow it off but it keeps on eating at me. Maybe there is something there besides changes being made in my life."

"Damn, I'm sorry, Link. You don't need this shit."

She dismally shakes her head. "I just want the dreams to go away—to leave me alone."

I reach back and grasp her calf. "What can I do? How can I help?"

I turn my head back toward her and see a lone tear tracking down her cheek as she replies, "You're doing it. You're listening. I need that. I need someone to share it with—to tell me to give it up and ignore it."

Damn. What can I say? I slowly shake my head. "Link, give it up. It's just a dream," I say comically to lighten the mood.

She laughs, "Thanks, Gina I needed that and I needed someone to talk to."

Link shrugs her shoulders and offers a thin smile. "Well back to the job at hand." She slowly and methodically massages my back haphazardly with her elbows, appearing to have forgotten what we just talked about. Maybe not.

Oh, the elbow treatment is a little uncomfortable but it's a turn—on at the same time. I wonder if I can do that.

Finishing the elbow bit she replenishes the oil on her hands, sits on my butt straddling me and rubs the oil evenly on my back and shoulders. She runs her thumbs along both sides of my spine with a rotation movement from the bottom to the top of the spine, then with a sweeping motion across the top to the shoulder joint.

After a moment kneading both shoulders, she brings both hands over on the left side and works her way down the side of the back over my rib cage. With one hand pulling up and the other pushing down she lightly stretches the rib cage and muscles in the area until she reaches the top of the hip.

She repeats the process on the right side, both hands working together she massages up the back kneading each individual muscle climaxing with the muscles surrounding the shoulder blade.

She repeats on the left side of the back before getting off of me and slapping me on the behind. "Your turn," she grins. "Now me." She lies face down beside me.

"Whoa, No, I can't," I protest. "You've worn me out. I am completely limp—helpless, useless."

She moves next to me and kisses me softly on the lips and touches my check with oily fingers. "Hey, woman, get your butt in gear. My ass wants to be rubbed. I'm waiting. Do me."

Damn her lips taste good. I want to feel them more. I want to feel her licking and sucking all over my body. The energy exchange from just this one little kiss is again fueling my desire and I feel my pulse quicken and my whole body spewing little sparks.

I grin. "No, I don't want to. It's time for you to satisfy me—to fuck me into oblivion. You got yours and now I want mine. No more massaging from me. More screwing from you."

Link giggles and pushes away from me. "You're going to get screwed in due time. Now, get to work on my back."

"Promises, promises. I'll never get laid. All I'll get is a massage," I protest as I oil my hands and begin on her butt the same way she did me.

Midway through the back massage I'm like wow, I didn't realize backs were so sexy. I'll bet a man's back is even sexier. Maybe someday I'll get to find out. Why haven't I massaged anyone before? It's such a small thing to miss out on completely. I'm glad Link is helping me experience this. She's a fantastic teacher about all things sexual. Am I rambling? *Yes, you are rambling.*

Fast forward: Now I am lying on my back with Link on her knees beside me. She oils her hands and commences to work on the fingers of my right hand similar to how she massaged my feet. It feels really fantastic as she pulls each individual finger and works her own fingers between mine.

Now she sucks—does she ever. Each finger gets individual attention as she slides it in and out if her mouth, an unbelievable erogenous experience.

Then the palm of my hand—both of her thumbs kneading until it is painful, then my wrist and forearm, sliding her thumbs up and down the muscles to my elbow. She changes her position and lays my hand on her inner thigh, my fingers touching her silky pubic hair as she prepares to work on the upper arm.

She flashes that creamy smile. "You know it is perfectly okay if you choose to fondle the masseuse while she massages your arm."

I cock a brow and with an open mouthed, hopefully sexy smile I shake my head. "I think not since you have been denying me equal attention. But then again maybe I would enjoy fondling the masseuse." I suddenly thrust two fingers into that moist sweet spot causing her to flinch in surprise.

"Jeez, that feels great!" she exclaims softly as her shoulders droop and she drops her hands from my upper arm. "I think since I'm distracted it's going to take a while to finish your arm. So don't feel like you have to hurry with what you're doing."

I flash a tight-lipped smile. "I fully expect big time payback."

She resumes her massage but with very little enthusiasm as she concentrates on what I'm doing to her. I find the more pressure I put on her the slower she gets. If I let up the pressure she speeds up her job. I make a point of slowing down and speeding up until she realizes what I'm doing.

"Very funny, Gina. Number one rule of being massaged: you don't play games with the masseuse."

"Hey masseuse. Time for the other arm."

She climbs over me, oils up my left hand and continues the ritual. Before long she is working on the upper arm but is slowed considerably by my interference.

As expected Link didn't do me justice as I massaged her arms, so I assume she's saving everything for the finale which is the front of the upper legs—I think. I can't wait.

So here I am lying on my back with Link sitting straddled over my upper legs. Holding the bowl she dips her fingers and drips the oil over my chest, breast and stomach. Setting the bowl on the table, she slowly spreads the oil evenly taking care to lightly pinch my nipples sending the usual quiver of energy traipsing down my spine into that very sensitive area.

"Damn you have fantastic tits," she says as she bends over and takes one nipple in her mouth while pinching the other between her thumb and finger. She stops and smiles while licking her upper lip with her tongue. "More of that later."

I cock a brow while biting at my lower lip. "Good. I want and expect a lot more of that and the sooner the better."

Link smiles but doesn't reply as she takes my right shoulder between both hands and kneads the muscles with her thumbs. It hurts so good.

Soon she completes my left shoulder and focuses on the neck, lightly massaging under the chin.

"Time out," she whispers as she leans over and softly kisses my lips while sticking her tongue in my mouth. Our tongues tangle and it ratchets up my desire to experience even more. I wrap my arms around her shoulders pulling her down closer to me.

Chest to chest my oiled breasts slide against hers creating an eerie sensation and desire to experience her completely oiled body against mine.

"Yeah, me too," she says softly as she ends the kiss.

"Huh, what do you mean, me too?" I whisper.

She grins, pulls my arms from her back and sits up. "I was also thinking how erotic it is going to feel when we get oiled up and slide around this beach."

I laugh. "We think alike. When is this lubricated orgy going to happen?"

"It's getting close. It's getting very close."

She resumes her massage on my upper chest and slowly drifts down to my breasts. After a moment she stops her massage and adds more oil.

She spreads it around my breasts with her palms while occasionally lightly pinching my nipples. I silently wish she would suck my nipples and she readily obliges.

I laugh and she chuckles. As she switches nipples she says, "I'm psychic."

"Then you should know what I want next."

She sits back up and continues the massage. "I do, I do, and it's coming."

"Hurry."

She presents her usual sugary smile. "Patience my dear. Good things come to those who . . . well you know."

"Good things also come to those that are in a hurry . . . don't you think."

Link doesn't reply as she shifts her sitting position down to my thighs, giving her more room to work on my belly. More oil and more gentle massage with the palms before ending just north of the pubic area.

She leaves her spot on my legs and lies down on her back next to me. "You're turn, babe," she smiles.

Knowing we're getting closer to the grand finale, I grasp the bowl and take my position just as she had done earlier. I pretty much follow the same trail that she went down, but not the kissing part. I do a pretty sensational tit suck however and I can tell by the look on her face she thoroughly enjoys it. Down at the other end I consider dropping below the pubic area but decide not to lest I screw up the finale.

It's getting closer still. Link instructs me to lie on my back and she oils my upper legs. She trails one finger from my right knee to the upper inner thigh and traces it back down the other leg to the knee. She looks at me for approval.

"Again," I answer with a nod.

"Absolutely. This part is easy." She runs the finger again from the knee up to the inner thigh. She pauses, then inserts her finger in my fantasy place only long enough for a quick tease.

Of course my pulse picks up and I feel a hot blaze spreading over my body.

She tracks the finger down the other leg. "Okay, the finale," she grins. "There's no turning back now."

"Or waiting," I add as she begins to massage my right leg just above the knee.

First there is a long sweeping motion with both hands that ends on the upper inner thigh. Then she trails back down rotating both open hands in different directions in an effort to increase the blood supply.

"Hey, you can do that again. That's cool."

She nods and repeats the move only a little harder this time.

"Thanks. I like that one."

"Don't mention it, babe."

She uses her thumbs to work her way up gouging and kneading the muscles. Kind of uncomfortable but still enjoyable.

Next it's both hands with thumbs nearly touching as she digs in the thumbs at the highest part and the fingers on the outside and inside of the leg. In a milking motion she repeats this over and over.

She says softly, "This is supposed to force blood up the leg toward the heart."

I grin, "Oh, really. I guess that's why my heart is heating up. And I thought it was because you turn me on so much."

She changes to my other side by anchoring one knee and swinging her other leg over me and follows with the anchor knee.

Wasting no time she repeats what she did on the left leg. I'm loving every second of it. After repeating the milking maneuver she spreads my legs and gets on her knees between them.

She smiles with her lips slightly parted. Sexy. "Now, I have to tell you this: you may choose to end this party at any time. Just tell me you've had enough. If you don't tell me I must assume you're enjoying yourself."

I don't reply as she again retrieves the oil bowl. She leans forward and drips some from the bowl on my chest, breasts, stomach and upper leg while smoothing it out with her other hand. Likewise she oils her own upper body and legs. She replaces the bowl and studies me pensively.

"I forgot what's next," she frowns.

"Come on, Link. Will you just do me?"

She giggles and cups her hand under my left knee and bends it just enough to where my foot is flat on the beach. She lightly slides her hand over the oiled leg before bending over and kissing the inside of the knee. Moving up a few inches she kisses again. Then again and again as she moves up the leg. She stops short of the upper thigh.

She bends the other knee, sliding her hand over the oiled leg, then she kisses—many of them and I am beginning a slow boil. Reaching the upper inner thigh she smiles and slowly lays a hand on my hot spot. With the heel of her hand she applies a slight pressure as she watches my reaction.

"More please," I beg.

She follows with more pressure and a twist of the hand as I squirm a bit in reaction.

"More, Link. I want more. Do it hard."

She obliges bringing a combination of pure pleasure and almost unbearable pain. The electricity spewing between us is palpable and I feel as if I'm being drowned in sparkly white energy that will explode at any time. And I want more. Now.

Suddenly she stops the pressure.

"No, don't stop," I cry.

She ignores me as she takes the bowl and dribbles more oil on my chest, breasts and stomach before doing the same with my upper legs.

Setting down the bowl she spreads the oil over my upper body with her palms, followed by the upper legs. She retrieves the bowl and standing on her knees between my legs spreads additional oil on her own shoulders. Then over her chest area. Now her belly and upper legs. We both are definitely well oiled.

I watch and wonder as she spreads yet more oil on my chest and stomach. Suddenly she's lying on top of me squirming around to get just the right fit—the right feeling. Feels pretty damn good to me.

"What do you think?" she grins "Does this feel good or what?" She squirms a bit more. "Wow."

I laugh as I attempt to squirm underneath her. "This is so fucking erotic," I gush. "Can you wiggle a little more please?"

"How about a little body dance?" she laughs.

I grasp her behind and pull her closer as we both glide back and forth against each other in our own little exotic tango, my slippery tits against her slippery tits. Damn I love this.

"Shit, Link. This is unbelievable."

She chuckles as she starts to get off of me. I pull her back.

"Not yet. We can't let this moment pass without enjoying it to the hilt."

"You're right. Let's dance." We continue our little back and forth slide and suddenly we are kissing, tonguing, biting and moaning. And giggling.

Eventually we have to come up for air and we laugh as she slides off of me.

"That we'll have to do again sometime."

"When?"

She nods positively, "Soon. Real soon. You know, that reminded me of when we were going to school at TCU—one of those things you missed—a group of ten or twelve of us occasionally had what we called a Wesson Oil party. It was girls only. We all got naked and it was an anything goes deal that started out with everyone getting soaked with Wesson Oil. It got really wild sometimes."

"Yeah, you seemed to have enjoyed a lot of stuff that I didn't. I guess I ran with the wrong crowd."

She smiles, "Yes, with my future husband. Okay, babe, my turn," she announces as she lies or her back with her legs in a welcome spread. "Do me."

I smile as I oil up her legs above the knee. I sit straddled on her left lower leg and lay both hands side by side just above her knee. I slowly run them up her slippery leg toward the top of the leg and retreat to the knee and repeat, harder this time. When I reach the top of the leg I accidently lose the grip with my right hand and it somehow slides into her warm wet spot. She flinches and grins.

I feign seriousness: "Oh my, sorry Link. How clumsy of me. Shit happens. I'll be more careful."

171

She looks at me warily and shakes her head. "But you're not promising are you."

"Why of course I promise. You know me, I wouldn't hurt anyone unless they wanted me to."

She smiles, "I want you to."

"Oh . . . oh. Okay, hurt it is." I move over and sit on the bottom of her right leg.

"Wait, you aren't finished with my left leg are you? I thought I was going to get some more hurt?"

"Just be patient. The big hurt may or may not be coming."

I repeat the same moves and lightly touch her sensitive area before retreating to start over. This time I tweak it a little more and the next time even more. She squirms a bit but says nothing.

Forget this shit. I move between her spread legs, bend her knees, pushing her legs into the full missionary position. I insert two fingers and find the clitoris. I pinch and twist it gradually increasing the intensity.

She moans from deep in her throat and grasps my shoulder. "Yes, Gina. Harder. Hurt me, please."

I remove my hand and move closer to her while still on my knees. Pushing her legs back as far as possible I balance on my left knee and bend the right and place it on her vagina. Soft and easy I press the knee forward bringing a groan. I press the knee harder and she flinches, but she grasps the knee and pulls it even harder.

"Oh yes, Gina. Push harder!" she yells. "Please! Harder! I want it harder! Now!"

I do as she says but I wonder how long I can keep this up. She just might outlast me. I pound the knee against her and she pulls even harder. How much of this can she take?

"More, push harder. Fuck me harder! I'm coming! I'm coming! Aggh! Yes! Yes!"

This is killing me. I can't possibly go any more. I withdraw my knee and practically dive into her, my lips and tongue surrounding her clit. I suck, bite, pull and squeeze her clit while she rhythmically pounds her hips against me. I'm wondering who is going to holler uncle first. I can't breathe.

"Harder, Gina, fuck me harder! Oh! Hurry, Gina! I'm coming! More! Yes, yes, aaaugh! Oh stop, please stop."

I gladly roll away from her as her legs sink limply to the beach. I chuckle to myself. That was like, hurt me, hurt me. Stop.

I lie on my side watching her slowly come back to the life. Her eyes closed, she smiles. "Thanks, Gina. You get the prize."

"Oh, really; and what would the prize be?"

She opens her eyes and renews her smile. "Me."

Before I realize what she is doing she gets up on her knees, turns me over and spreads my legs. She thrusts two fingers into my welcome spot sending energy pin–balling throughout my body.

I'm so powered up and strung out that I know this is going to be short. I grasp two hands full of her curly red hair and pull her head down between my legs.

"No excuses, lady. This is my time. Hurry."

She removes her fingers and pushes up and back both of my legs. Her lips and tongue find my clit and I wonder how long I am going to last before I completely explode.

Link is working as if it's her last meal and I am enjoying every nanosecond. I pound my hips against her mouth and she groans but carries on.

"Link, I can't last! I want to come now! Harder!"

She steps up the pace and I feel pure sexual energy spewing out of all my pores. And I am hot—flaming hot. I feel my body caving in on itself and bordering on complete disintegration.

"Now, Link, now! Oh, I'm coming! Just a little bit more! Oh, right there! Yes! Yes! Uggh!"

Damn, what the hell was that?

"Wow," is the only thing I can say.

Link laughs. "You can say that again."

"Wow."

Gina De Georgio

TEN

I love Saturday night at the club. Since Pep left it has become my weekly kickback time. And, damn, next week I'll probably miss it because I won't want to wrangle the kids by myself since Link and Jonathan will be in Houston at the opening of her show.

I'm sitting alone in the bar as Link has left for a few minutes to talk to Preacher and Jonathan is sitting at the bar talking to some guy I don't recognize. Jeez, I wish I could go with Link to Houston on Monday to help deliver her art work. It would be great to wake up next to her.

I wake well before daylight and the room is dark except for a small streak of street light leaking through the curtain. Oh my. Even though we romped deep into the night, the energy is still sparking between us. I move next to her with her back against me. The heat of our bodies quickly multiplies as it joins together in one massive human stoked furnace. And her smell is intoxicating as usual. I put an arm around her and lightly grasp a breast to find her nipple as hard as a pebble. Huh? Is she also turned on?

"What took you so long?" she whispers as she lays a hand over mine and squeezes it tighter against her breast. "I've been waiting for you for over an hour."

I giggle and press my body closer to hers. "It seems like you're always a step ahead of me. I promise to make up for lost time."

I run my finger down across her belly and mingle a few seconds in her silky pubic hair before gently nudging her legs apart. I deftly bury two fingers in that hot and moist canyon.

"Oh," she moans as she turns over on her back to get the most of my attention.

I don't disappoint. I find her clitoris and squeeze lightly with my fingers, bringing that groan that I like hearing from deep in her throat. I can't wait any longer. I remove my hand and push her legs farther apart and bend her knees. I quickly move between her legs and bury my tongue in—

Once again I'm rudely jerked out of my trance by Jonathan clearing his throat. He is sitting across from me casually sipping his wine. Oh shit.

He grins with eyes twinkling in amusement. "Must be fun. You seem to zone out a lot."

I shake my head dejectedly and present a smirk of a grin. Oh what the hell; go with the flow. My grin changes to a wide smile for his benefit.

"It's called survival. You could at least have given me a few more minutes before interrupting so I could get to the meat of the fantasy." I giggle and put a hand over my mouth. "Oh, did I say meat? Must have been a pretty meaty dream."

He cocks a curious brow and tilts his head but doesn't respond.

"What, John boy? What were you going to say? Out with it."

"Okay, so why don't you tell me about your fantasy. What were you dreaming?"

I'm hung up on his lips and possibly drooling. He gestures with hands spread waiting for my reply.

I present my sexiest smile. "Be happy to, John. But I have a condition: I'll only tell you in a bedroom of your choice. It'll be a show and tell if you get my drift. *What are you doing, Gina? Just give it up.*

I ignore my muse and wait on Jonathan's response. He bows and slowly shakes his head but doesn't respond. Damn he's sexy. I'd give anything to spend an hour in bed with him. Or since I'm wishing let's make that four hours. Or more.

"I thought as much, Johnny. You aren't going there and I respect that." I shrug absently. "I least I try to respect that. But I must tell you that someday when you least expect it I will conquer you before you even realize you've been had." *You wish.*

Jonathan's lips curl into that funky grin but he doesn't comment as Link joins us.

She peers quizzically at her husband as she sits down. "Are you going to be had, John? Sounds like Gina is out to get you."

Jonathan chuckles and waves for the bar lady. "I guess you could say that." He winks at me but doesn't volunteer additional information to Link.

When the waitress leaves with our drink order Link cocks one perfect brow for her husband's benefit. "So who do you get to dance with first, old man?"

"No bueno de nada. I'm not going there this evening. If you guys want to dance go for it."

"Sounds good to me," Link nods and winks at me. "But I don't think the good people of Lake McQueeney Country Club and Ski Resort are ready to see Gina and me grinding it out sexually on the dance floor. They would probably again flood the stairway to see this spectacle."

Jonathan chuckles but doesn't respond as he scratches behind his ear. "So, Gina, did you meet your Thursday deadline with the next column?"

"Done, boss. I've received some great questions and I can't wait to see the responses I get. And Monday's second column will have the questions and answers I've made up including your threesome jewel. I'm certainly looking forward to the feedback in the next few weeks."

Link nods positively. "Me too. Perhaps the comments you receive will encourage our man to participate in our own little private and highly erotic ménage `a trois."

Jonathan forces a lame smile and shakes his head. "It would more than likely be a ménage `a trough as in cattle trough. So don't count on it ladies. I think I'll just

enjoy my sexy wife if you don't mind. That is less traumatic I'm sure."

"How can you be sure?" asks Link. "How do you
know it's traumatic if you've never tried it? It might be the
greatest sexual experience you'll ever have." Link grins
playfully at her husband. "It might be the best thing since
the Internet."

I watch Jonathan as he smiles lovingly at his wife.
"Ma'am, I think I'll never know because I'm going to stick
with the wife I share a bed with if you don't mind."

Jonathan then eyes me, grins and points a threat-
ing finger. "And you, Ms. Rabbit, I suggest you quit trying
to run my sex life and ruin my marriage. *Comprendes?*"

"Si, senor. Te comprendo perfectamente," I reply
with a smug smile for John and a wink at Link.

"Well, Link. I guess we had better leave him be.
We certainly don't want to interfere with his glorious sex
life . . . or his marriage."

She smirks and dismally shakes her head. "I
guess." She pats Jonathan on the shoulder and smiles, "I
still love you anyway."

"Well, I certainly am glad we finally understand
each other."

Damn he's dripping with sexuality. I have to have
him. And the sooner the better. I'd screw him right on this
table in front of his wife and the rest of the world if I could.
But it's not just him. Hell, I'm to the point I'll take any
male that I can get as long as he can walk straight and has
a relatively clean body.

Nut case, my caretaker deadpans.

Link tilts her head at me and smiles. "Are we really giving up on providing this lost man the experience of
a lifetime, Gina?"

We all laugh and Link resigns, "Well folks, I hate
to end this beautiful enlightening conversation, but we
have a van to load first thing in the morning. I suggest we
gather the kids and head home."

Eight o'clock Sunday morning. "Damn, Link,
don't you think this van is too big for the job at hand?"

178

Like me in my black bikini she is definitely not dressed for packing a van. In her extra skimpy yellow bikini she is more suited for a little swimming or an advertisement for a sexual partner.

Nice looking ass when she bends over. I try not to drool on me or her because John is close by silently watching. However, I'm sure he knows what's been going on between Link and me. He's got to. So what's to stop me from scarfing her box right in the back of this van?

That would be a sight for sure—Link and me getting it on while Jonathan is standing by taking notes. Or maybe video with his cell phone.

Get real, Gina. Bug off will you.

"You would think," Link answers, "however for the Austin show I got a smaller van. After adding all the heavy padding to protect the paintings it was barely big enough. And this time there are more paintings and some are much larger."

I can tell this is going to be a major undertaking as she carefully places each boxed or crated painting and surrounds it with enough padding to insure their safe and undamaged arrival. She refuses any help other than for John and me to deliver the next painting she points out.

We mostly watch her pack. Well, I mostly ogle her and Jonathan in that rag of a swimsuit he wears. I'll take a romp with either but if I have my druthers it would definitely be Jonathan because of the yin yang factor. I am really hurting for male companionship—and the sooner the better. I'm going freaking crazy.

Have you tried prayer, Gina? You need big time help. Just go away will you.

I come out of my daydream to find Jonathan grinning at me. "Fantasyland, Gina?"

"Just bug off, Johnny," I bark, surely heard down the lake. "I certainly don't need your sarcasm." But you can screw me if you want.

Jonathan holds up his hands defensively however his grin is still in place. "Whoa. Touchy, touchy."

Link has stopped her work and is looking out of the sliding door of the van to check out the animated chatter between her helpers. She presents a comical stern frown.

"Hey, girls and boys, let's try to get along in work and play. If I have to come out there and separate you two, you will have hell to pay. Now, kiss and make up." She shakes a threatening finger at us and returns to her job at hand.

We exchange a what—the—hell shrug and smile but no kiss. Dammit. Maybe I should take my keepers advice and try a little prayer? God, send me someone to love. No, not necessarily love; send me someone to shack up with. I'll be waiting.

"Alright guys, give me the biggest one you have. *Carnival* will be—yeah, that one. Bring it to the back door."

Jonathan and I pick up the painting grated in a heavy pasteboard box. He walks backward toward the van door. When we reach the door I push lightly and he crashes into the van much to Link's consternation.

"Come on people! If you drop my painting there will be a blood—letting I assure you."

John glares daggers at me but says nothing in his defense as we slide the painting into the van. I chuckle at him, "Kind of clumsy, John boy. If you like I'll move the van up a couple of feet so you don't run into it next time."

"Just shut up and do your job, woman."

I present him with a smart salute. "Yessir, my captain, sir."

Jonathan frowns dismay at his wife: "Do I have to work with this bitch?"

Link looks absently at me and then Jonathan. "Will you two kids get along? I'll tell you what; just don't talk to each other . . . or even look at each other for that matter."

Jonathan and I merely grin at her.

"Link, what is the price you're asking for this painting?" I ask.

"*Carnival*, let's see. The gallery people will give their opinion but it will probably be around five thousand. Interested?

I nod. "I've looked at that painting for three weeks now and it is really growing on me." Oops, how can I look at the painting for three weeks if no one is allowed in the studio? Oh well, it's like I said: John has to know what's going on between Link and me. If he caught my litttle slipup he certainly didn't show any reaction—nor did Link.

"Yeah, I'm interested in *Carnival*, but I won't have that kind of dough until my ship comes in, particularly since I'm going to have to sell my kids to buy Pep's half of the house."

Link looks toward Jonathan and winks. "I'll tell you what Gina; if *Carnival* doesn't sell during the show it's yours for a price I will reveal later."

"Interesting. About how much do you think that might be?" I query knowing full–well it'll be much more than I can pay.

Link winks at Jonathan. "I just might have to take my price out in hide if you get my drift."

I sneak a look at Jonathan as he cocks a curious brow for his wife's benefit.

Don't go there Gina, my zookeeper pipes in.

"Oh, that sounds interesting." I reply softly as I turn to go back to the waiting paintings. John follows.

After a moment John says, "Wow, hide takes in a lot of territory—skin, fur, pigskin, leather, buckskin."

This is getting out of hand but what the hell. I might as well say it since I'm sure he is thinking it. I shrug at Jonathan and look him directly in the eye. "How about sex, John? Isn't hide a term for sex?"

Jonathan nods his affirmation. "Yeah, you could say that."

Links voice bellows out the van door. "What are you guys talking about? You seem pretty damn serious."

John calls back, "We're just wondering what you meant by hide."

Without replying Link disappears into the van and we hear her giggle. Momentarily she calls out for the next painting and we oblige. Nothing else is said about hide. Probably best.

It's eleven–thirty and we can see the end in sight. And Link was right; every inch if the van was needed. Even the front passenger seat. I guess it's a good thing that neither I nor Jonathan is going because there would be no place to sit.

Perfect timing as our gang of four kids arrive announcing they want to go to the Sunday buffet at the country club. That's seems like a swell idea as no one wants to scrape lunch together for seven hungry people. I know I don't.

And Link and I are already dressed for the Sunday noon parade of semi-covered bikini babes. Only John has to change into what he calls his dress bathing suit.

The kids are instructed to meet us at the Bales' boat at twelve. In the meantime we will finish the last details and Link will be ready for her seven o'clock liftoff in the morning. She hopes to arrive at the gallery at Houston's Galleria by eleven o'clock.

Jonathan and I watch Link stuff her small suitcase onto the front floor of the van and I suddenly feel a deep sadness to see her go—even to the point that tears well up in the corners of my eyes. What the hell is the matter with me?

Be aware of your feelings, my guardian declares. Huh?

I watch them share a peck of a kiss and brief hug. Then it's my turn; I hug Link ladylike but no kiss. I release her and strangely feel I should get away from the two of them. Now.

"Be careful, Link. Text me when you get there."

I have to leave before I lose it. "John, see you at the office," I inform as I turn and run to my house as tears begin to flow freely down my cheeks. I'm sure they are wondering what's with this crazy woman. Hell, I'm also wondering the same thing.

After getting the kids off to school I have just enough time to shower before leaving for San Antonio by nine o'clock. It is also gives me time to collect my thoughts and hopefully make some rhyme or reason of my emotional episode at seeing Link off.

I receive no answers so I put it out of my mind, kind of looking forward to the second edition of my column this morning.

When I arrive a couple of minutes late the others except for Jonathan are sitting around the table drinking coffee and, wow, thumbing through the various publications that carry my column.

Jonathan exits the restroom and joins me as I pour myself coffee from the pot in the conference room's kitchen nook.

He views me curiously as he refills his cup. "Are you okay? You were acting kind of strange when Link left."

"Yeah," I answer gloomily shaking my head. "I don't know what came over me. I nearly lost it. That's why I ran away. I didn't want Link to leave with a picture of me coming apart because she is leaving. It didn't and doesn't make since to me. I had no reason for that . . . whatever it was."

"Are you going to be alright? You don't have to be here you know."

I force a smile. "Yeah but I can't miss seeing this new column and hearing the feedback from the others."

As Jonathan and I take our seat the responses come forth rapidly.

"Great questions, Gina."

"It's going to be interesting to see what kind of response you get from *Auto Whirl*. The kind of folk that read that rag can't possibly be interested in those questions, but you never know."

"But they now have the opportunity to send in their own question. 'Anybody know how to get rid of that musty smell in my car? It's so bad I have to drive with the windows down.'"

By the same token the *Women in Charge* readers would probably be turned off by the car guy's question.

"Or *Gay Time*."

"Or *Gym Rat*."

"They might need something to cover up the body odor aroma in their car." Laughs all around.

"All in all it's a good start, Gina. I personally hope the response is what you expect." That was number two exec, Josh Butler looking over his wire rimed half glasses propped on the end of his nose. He is actually smiling at me. That's great.

"Thanks for the input, guys. And also the stuff you are writing in the blog. Some of it is quite amusing. Some of it is crazy. I like it. Maybe it will stimulate people to get involved. That was a great idea, Josh."

"Okay people," Jonathan nods. "On to other things. I received a couple of phone calls from the owners of *Hunter's Almanac* late Friday. Although they have a long and successful track record, the last several years they have made some bad decisions and turned off some of their readers and advertisers.

"Bottom line, they are on the verge of bankruptcy and are hoping they can unload the company to some sucker—us. I told them we would listen to what they have to offer but we want complete access to the books and employees."

"Chapter Seven or Eleven?" Chris Hunter interjects?

"I gather they are not interested in reorganization. Apparently they feel they are too far gone. If they file, it is their intention to just walk away."

Josh chuckles, "Then we wait and buy what's left over after the judge guts the place."

Jonathan nods his agreement. "That certainly is one option but not the only one for sure. That's why we need information from them as quickly as possible."

"Time frame?"

"This is where quickly comes in. They want an answer in two weeks at the most. Their lawyers are holding off the creditors for now but don't know how long they can."

"Got a plan?"

"First off, Darren, you are going to go over their books for the last three years and see if you can get a handle on what's going on and perhaps if it is feasible for us to get the rag back on its feet." Jonathan grins at his accounting guru. "Piece of cake, Mr. Boyd. You should be able to whip that out in two or three days."

Darren dejectedly shakes his head and grins, "Yeah right, John. Try two months. I suppose I have free rein."

"You have it. Put all your people on it and raid other departments if you need extra help."

"Alright, Chris, do your research on their advertising. Contact those that have placed ads in the past. Ask if they would consider rerunning ads with a new owner."

"Jesse, you've got the easy job. See if this rag is worth the time and effort. Can we make a go of it if we take over the company?"

"Josh, since you have the most experience you'll be on call to help each of them in any way you can."

"Next, Gina it is your job to coordinate the whole show—to keep everyone on track so there is no overlapping of research. We don't want two or three people or departments working on the same thing. Everyone is to contact her daily and let her know what the progress is or what problems arise.

"Lastly, if we don't get their complete cooperation in receiving the information we want, contact Gina or me and we may walk away. If we find they are holding back information that we need or they are covering up information, same deal."

"Do you think this is worth the effort?"

Jonathan chuckles and shrugs, "Probably not but it also might be a bird nest on the ground. We'll do our due diligence. Any questions?

"None? Good because I don't have any answers. Remember two weeks, so get you a schedule and we'll meet Friday week to get your findings and hash it out."

"Why don't we just buy a Margarita Machine for the office?" I wonder as John and I hover in the bar at El Cabrito. "We spend a bundle here on Ritas and Marys."

John salutes with his glass in the bar mirror located behind the liquor display. "That would be never ending. Next we would have to have a Bloody Mary machine

185

if there is such a thing, and then there's the barrel of scotch."

My phone beeps a text message notification. I check as Jonathan sips on his straw watching me in the mirror.

"She made it to Houston without any particular problems. Apparently she copied both of us as she says she will call you tonight."

"I left my phone in the car. I'd like to eat my enchiladas without being interrupted."

"Well shit!" I exclaim softly.

"What now?" he grins quizzically.

"That means I can't harass you while you're eating enchiladas?"

"You never give up do you?"

"Can we at least share wine together on the dock." And anything else you want to share. I'm easy.

"It depends on who brings the wine."

I giggle. "Oh I will. About twelve gallons. That should be enough."

"Nice try but I don't get wine drunk."

I shake my head in dejection. "Bastard. You're no fun at all."

He doesn't reply and I watch him in the mirror wishing I could assault him right here on the bar and in front of the bartender.

I reach over and place a hand on his thigh and grin mischievously as he watches me suspiciously in the mirror. The electricity is there, zapping me all the way down to my sensitive place. "Do you think I can have my enchiladas now?"

He laughs and shakes his head. "I was going to say yes to whatever you asked."

I slowly shake my head in disgust. "Yeah, right. Of course, John."

I find Jonathan on his dock with his and my kids. I bring a bottle of wine and one glass as I see he has a glass in hand.

He exaggerates a look of disappointment. "Just one bottle. What kind of deal is that?"

"Hey dude. I'm not going to waste good wine on anyone unless I can see a legitimate chance of a payoff. I want to get bang for the buck . . . or is it, I want to get banged."

Jonathan doubles over laughing and spills most of his wine.

The kids, close by watching the antics of two crazy adults, are giggling. As if on cue they all jump into the water and head for Monica's.

I refill Jonathan's glass and we sit quietly contemplating the lake. Inside my hormones are raging and I am hurting for some attention. Just touch me please. It's to the point I've got to get laid and soon. I don't think that Link could even help me if she were here. I need a male. Now.

Jonathan breaks our uneasy silence: "I think we should have a threesome."

"Asshole. That's not funny, John. You don't throw a drowning woman a rock. No jokes please."

"Oh, sorry," he retorts with a shrug. "That was cruel wasn't it?"

I tilt my head and present the sexiest smile of my drama repertoire. "You could probably make amends if you wanted to"

"Probably not."

"Can we talk about something else?"

"Good idea. What do you want to talk about?"

"When the execs get all the information about *Hunter's Almanac* who makes the decision on what to do?"

"We go through a lot of steps when a major decision has to be made. First off, each one will present what he has found and will answer questions from me and the others.

"Then I get each of the five's recommendation, and the others can question how the recommendation was reached. After everything is cussed and discussed the buck stops here. I make the final decision. If it is a wrong decision the onus is on me. After all it's my company."

"So what is your gut feeling right now?"

"I don't want any part of it but that's why we are doing the research. So it won't be a crapshoot."

"Sounds to me like a crapshoot anyway."

"It's just money."

"I'll bet the present owners don't agree."

"Absolutely right, Gina, it's not just money when you need some and there is no way to get it."

"Umm, oh well, John. It has been fun talking to you this evening. I can't think of anything else I would rather be doing with you."

He shakes his head at my sarcasm.

"Kind sir, I need rest so I think I'll hit the sack early. If you will give Link my best when she calls. And tell her I'm not really crazy."

"Will do."

"Will you point my kids in the right direction when they show up? It's getting close to their bedtime also."

"Done, Gina. Happy fantasies. Goodnight."

I haven't had a chance to review the column in the various rags and that is my plan before going to bed. By myself of course. John, you're missing the best fuck of your life. Any dude out there want some deluxe no holds barred feminine entertainment? Damn I'm in a shitty mood. I don't think I can even conjure up a good fantasy.

Opening *Fashion Week* to page thirty the column jumps out at me.

HUTCH TALK WITH THE ITALIAN RABBIT
by Gina De Georgio Wabbit

Hey, out there, Gina here. I'm so glad you're reading my new column. This my second issue is being published in eleven different magazines, four of them in languages other than English, all under the banner of Bales Publishing. Depending on the magazine the column will be published weekly or monthly.

So what's happening? What am I—or should I say we up to? I say we because we all have an important question that we want answered and we all seem to have an answer to someone else's important question.

Well I hope to give you that opportunity with this column. Before we get to the first questions you've submitted let me briefly give you some simple rules. It's going to be somewhat like a blog.

One week I will publish the question you send to me in the WHAT'S YOUR QUESTION? section and you'll get your answer from the masses out there in the WE HAVE AN ANSWER section of a later edition.

Of course you can refute the advice or even clap back in a later column.

What's the subject? Are your questions limited to certain areas? This is the great part. Anything you want to ask about go for it. Ask what you will—be it lovelorn advice, movies, sports, politics, food recipes or personal hygiene for that matter. The subject of your question is wide open.

Political correctness is not an issue so tell it like you feel it is. Of course you can expect rebuttal or castigation and a bit of clap back if justified.

One last thing: as there will not be room in my column to answer all your questions, I will include most of them in my blog. That way you can ask and answer questions by digital technology.

Please send any questions, answers or comments to any of my social media sites listed below.

Here are this week's questions (Note: As this is my first column with questions, I will attempt to answer each in this week's column. I will not answer questions in future columns as that will be your job. Feel free to add to or protest my answers and your words will show up in the answer section of future columns).

On Facebook I have this old friend that posts boring unflattering selfies and pictures of her animals, her food and other craziness several times a day. I've hinted for her to stop to no avail. If I unfriend her or block her posts I will probably lose her as a friend. What can I do?
Lester in Detroit (Gay Time)

189

Gina De Georgio

Gina's answer: Simple, unfriend her or block her posts. She will never know as she will not be notified.

What do I do when my wife teams up with my neighbor to coax me to join them in a ménage `a trois? I don't think I want to go there. Even if I participated I would have no idea what to do.

Ganged up on, Boston (Men's Life)

Gina's answer: Is your neighbor male or female? Two males and one female is not a good combination. Two females and one male is cool. You do have a choice of whether you participate in a threesome. They should respect that choice.

I read where most of the grated cheese you buy at the supermarket is not one hundred percent cheese as the package says. Most have wood pulp, cellulite and other fillers. What's a person to do if you can't trust the food peddlers?

Lost in the woods, Denver (The Foody)

Gina's answer: Hey, Lost, it makes you wonder if you can trust anyone these days. I guess don't eat isn't a good answer. Folks, I need your help on this one. Send me your answer or comments on the media below.

The Rabbit

MY SOCIAL MEDIA
Website and Blog: italianrabbit.com
Email: gina@italianrabbit.com
Facebook: Gina De Georgio

ELEVEN

T he kids are out the door and headed for the school bus when my mobile phone rings. Checking out caller ID it's Pep. Of course my heart skips in anticipation. However I would as soon skip this call.

"Hey Pep. What's up?"

"Morning Gina. Say, if it's alright I'd like to drop by and pick up my muzzleloader. I've joined this club and my first meeting at the shooting range is tomorrow night."

"Sure. What time?"

"About ten o'clock if it's convenient for you."

"That's cool because I'm going to be tied up late in the afternoon."

"Hey, great. See you at ten."

I hang up without response. Well, I'd just as soon not deal with him but I'd better get used to it. We still have life to go.

I take stock of my appearance and decide that I need to be a little more presentable just in case.

My mentor comes charging forward. *Hold it, hold it. Just in case of what? You are okay just the way you are unless you're looking for trouble. And you don't need trouble with that man.*

I shake my head cheerlessly at my muse. Just go away. I can handle this. My keeper shakes her head in disgust.

Searching through my wardrobe I look for something Pep hasn't seen—something new. Yes, that's it. Perfect. It's a frilly, blue cotton, sleeveless blouse with matching white loose fitting shorts. And I'll go barefooted.

Excited at my choice—why?—I undress and slip them on. I look at myself in the mirror and decide the outfit needs a slight adjustment. Reaching up I unbutton the top two buttons of the blouse. That should work.

My mentor is not happy. *Idiot. No, make that stupid idiot.* Jeez, just leave me be. This is about me. All about me.

At two minutes after ten the doorbell rings and I feel my pulse rate kick up a notch.

Opening the door I find myself face–to–face with Pep. As usual he rekindles that sexual desire not only for him but for any male.

I am speechless as my pulse quickens and a powerful energy rages and heats up my being. I'm overwhelmed with a craving for the man standing in front of me dressed in his usual dress pants and dress shirt without a tie or jacket.

I can't help myself. I want him and I want him badly. My keeper doesn't give up: *Just don't make a complete fool of yourself.*

"Gina, are you there? Hello," Pep says with a grin as he waves his hand in front of my face.

"Oh, sorry. Come on in," I mumble in embarrassment. "I guess I tripped out."

As he enters the house he tilts his head as he studies me. "Do you do that often?"

I force a thin smile and shrug innocently. "Probably more than I'd like. It's kind of a fantasy deal. It owns me I think."

"A fantasy deal?" he quizzes.

I don't answer as I focus on his sugary lips. I momentarily get back to the present. "I have fresh coffee if you like." *I also have anything else you might desire.*
Just stop it, Gina.

"Hey that would be great." He follows me into the kitchen and sits at the table.

"Jameson?" I ask absently as I set the coffee in front of him.

"Please," he says with an easy smile and his eyes locked on mine sending little prickles throughout my body. How many times has that happened in the past and where is it headed today?

I retrieve the bottle from the cabinet. As I pour the liquor in his coffee I present my best sexy smile as my heart hitches up a beat and that familiar energy traipses down my spine and spreads throughout my body. Where do I go from here? What do I say? What do I do? How can I get this man into bed with me?

My keeper is glaring at me while tapping a foot and pointing a threatening finger. *"No, don't go there, Gina. It will only complicate matters. You know you will regret it."*

Of course I ignore her. The only thing important at this moment is getting laid. I must however be careful not to embarrass myself if he isn't game. Didn't my muse just say something to that effect?

During a momentary silence as he sips his coffee he fixes those dreamy eyes on mine and I melt. I have this urge to kiss him but hold back. I feel like I am suffocating and I force myself to breathe deeply and release a long sigh.

He cocks a sexy brow. "You okay?"

"Uh, yeah," I answer hardly above a whisper.

He sets his cup down and resumes studying me with pursed lips and eyes that appear to be caressing me. "You said your fantasies own you. What's that all about?"

I'm sure he's aware of the tears welling in the corners of my eyes as I search for an answer to his question. Well shit, here goes and there may be no turning back:

"I have this . . . this monkey on my back I guess you could call it."

I gaze into his eyes as he tilts his head. "I don't quite follow you," he asks. "Monkey? What kind of monkey would that be?"

Don't go there, Gina. It's not worth it. You don't need sex that badly.

Again I pay no attention to my guide. All I care about is now. I need relief at whatever cost. I need to fuck and be fucked. And there is only one man available and it just happens to be Pep—ironically the only person that has experience in satisfying me.

My heart is pounding out of control and my whole body has become a quivering mess. Well this is a hell of a gamble but I've got to go for it. I move over in front of him as he looks up at me suspiciously. My eyes on cue tear up again.

"The monkey on my back is a lack of sex, Pep." I say flatly as I bend over and deliver a soft lip-nibbling kiss.

Yes, yes, I silently scream inside. He doesn't resist. I kiss harder forcing my tongue into his parting lips and he joins in as he places a hand on my cheek next to my ear. He runs his hand up to my ear and mingles his fingers in my hair.

The kiss, his smell and his taste are sublime but I end it momentarily and step back on unsteady legs while looking directly in his eyes. I declare firmly: "And only you can remove the monkey. Pep, you and I are about to renew an old acquaintance. We are going to fuck right now, hard and long—like we've never fucked before."

His eyes widen, filled with surprise and it's his turn to release a nerve calming breath. Cocking his head he gazes at me intently.

"Sounds like fun, but not necessarily good in the long run. You've got to understand, it won't change our situation. I have chosen to go another way without you and that will not change."

Jeez, thanks for saying that. "And I don't want to go back to where we were either. It won't work. I have accepted that. Right now I just want fun and games; I want to be fucked. No strings attached."

He smiles wryly and I frown at his reaction.

"Do we need a written contract you think?"

I take him by the hand and tug; he stands. "No, Pep, we don't need a contract." I pull him toward the bedroom and I tilt my head back toward him with a smile. "All I want from you is for you to screw me and I fully intend to return the favor royally. Think you can handle that?"

His eyes flare and I sense his breathing hitching up a notch. "Probably."

"Good, I'll happily release my monkey to you."

By the time we reach the bedroom my whole system has gone into overdrive or haywire mode—whatever.

When was the last time I was on the verge of getting laid by a man? It had to be over two months ago and ironically with the same man that I'm going to bed down right now. That last time turned out to somewhat of a dud however. I don't even remember. This time it will be no dud.

My whole body is rising to a boil and seething with desire. My breathing has stepped up but I feel as if I can't get enough air in my lungs. And I want to get–off on Pep immediately. To hell with the preliminaries. I want him now, hard and fast.

We turn toward each other in the same instant and our bodies clash together as we pull each other closer, clawing and grabbing at each other.

"Oh God," I gasp as my hands trail down his back to his ass. I pull him against me harder and he follows. I love the feeling of his hands locking me against his full erection. I feel like I'm going to explode and we are still dressed. I plead, "Please hurry, Pep. I can't wait. I need you to fill me up now."

In the midst of a tongue twisting lip biting kiss it's as if we are in a violently choreographed dance. I desper-ately claw at his shirt buttons and he rips my blouse off without bothering with the buttons.

Somehow he unhooks and removes my bra in one motion as I throw his shirt aside. I fumble with his belt buckle and zipper and pull down his pants.

"Are we in a hurry, Gina?" Pep chuckles breath-lessly as I push him back on the bed and slip off his shoes and socks. I pull off his pants to reveal the welcome bulge in his black bikini underwear. "We have plenty of time."

I remove my shorts as a massive exhilarating shiver engulfs my body. "Of course we do, but that comes later," I respond hoarsely.

I feel like I'm going to come completely undone any second now. I nudge him to lie back on the bed as I place a finger under the band on each side of his bikinis and slip them down his legs and off.

I am quickly at his side on my knees. I grasp the girth of his erection with both hands. Shit, this is fantas-tic—the familiar combination of velvet softness surround-ing a hard yet semi flexible shaft. I drop my hands to the base and take a full measure of this magnificent instrument in my mouth and suck feverishly—the feel, smell and taste sending me even closer to complete oblivion.

"Shit, Gina," he moans. "You're killing me. Slow down." He runs a hand along my upper leg and deftly runs it through the leg opening of my panties to find my raging scorching fantasy spot. Inserting two fingers he finds my clit and squeezes between his fingers.

I have lost all interest with my job at hand as I feel as if I'm falling, losing all contact with myself. My whole being is blazing in pure desire in a desperate race for relief—that long awaited explosion and calming of yin yang energy.

I can't wait. In an instant I pull his hand away and remove my panties as I mount him, thrusting my hips against his as I fully take him into me. He joins me as we pound against each other—in, out, push and draw back, recklessly seizing each other with pure abandonment. It is wonderfully exquisite as I feel I'm in a race with myself to reach the highest ever feeling of pure joy—massive orgasm and ultimate sexual relief.

This is suddenly all about me—about how I feel. About my desires. About what I want. About my enjoyment. My relief. I fly higher and higher as my soul openly sores with me bringing us closer to—

"Oh God!" I cry as I throw my body against Pep as if I'm trying to punish him. I feel my blood rushing through every inch of my body, flying higher and higher, the heat blazing unbearably hotter. I'm at the edge of exploding—disintegrating. As I thrust myself against Pep again and again, I know I'm about to lose it.

Pep senses the same: "Go for it, Gina. Take it all," he encourages.

That's all I need to send me over the edge: "Oh, shit? Aggh? Oh my God! Aww, yes!" I lose complete control of my body and muscles as I crash one last time onto Pep and melt.

Momentarily I return to reality. Lying flat against him I feel that familiar chest hair tickling my cheek. "Damn, what the hell was that?" I whimper.

Pep chuckles, "That was quite a spectacle. I'm glad I was a part of it. It was a little too fast for me though."

I slowly come down from my high as my breathing calms. "Thanks, Pep. Sorry I was in such a hurry. I kind of left you behind."

I can still feel his fantastic erection filling me up and I know that he didn't get–off on me. Well I can certainly remedy that.

"Now you're turn," I whisper as I lift my body a bit and drop back down on him, bringing a moan from deep within him. "And what special something can I do for you, Mr. Wabbit? Anything you've been lacking lately?"

Uh–oh. Maybe you shouldn't get too personal. He might not want to share what his new woman lacks, particularly with you. Wow, I'm surprised that my keeper is involved in this little party.

Apparently no offense taken he adjusts his body beneath mine as he grasps my hips. "I think you know what I like. Go for it."

Damn he feels good. My heart again kicks up a beat and my blood is heating up as I eagerly gear up for more. Am I enjoying myself? Of course. I've been on the wagon too long and I certainly have a few more rounds left for today. And tomorrow if possible. And the day after.

Jeez, I like the control of being on top performing whatever dance I like. My hands find his ears and move up to clench his hair on both sides. I pull his hair as I slowly kiss him on the check and run my tongue down to his upper neck and under the chin. All the while I am slowly and rhythmically pumping my hips as he slides in and out of me. Oh my, this is fantastic and I want it to last this time. I want to savior every thrust.

I run my tongue up over his chin mingling momentarily in his beard. It is soft but oddly prickly and such a turn–on, as if I need to be turned on more than I already am. I move up to his lips and plant biting kisses increasing in intensity.

Now I part his lips with my tongue and find his tongue waiting for that dance that is always a sexual delight. Sucking, biting and pounding hips is the order of the moment and we are wallowing in it to the hilt.

A long low moan comes from deep in his throat that in all our years together I have never heard. I am intrigued as I step up my action to see if I can increase his new way of expressing his pleasure.

He utters another deep moan and steps up his hip action. "Oh, shit, you feel fantastic. Harder, Gina."

I oblige as I raise up off my knees and plant my feet flat on the bed. As I squat over him, it is now all about him—not me as I am not striving for my own immediate relief as before. I raise up slightly withdrawing his erection from me and easily drop back down taking him in to the hilt.

"Again," he whispers.

I repeat, harder this time. When I drop back down he meets me with a thrust of his own hips. Oh my, the clash is incredible as it sends shock ways reverberating all over my body.

Pep squeezes my hips between thrusts and moans, "You feel good. Don't stop."

Well I can certainly do that. I raise up and fall back against him, harder this time. "How's that?" I whisper. "Do you want more?" I raise up and crash back against him—even harder. Then again. Again and again.

"Stop, Gina," he urges. "I don't want to come yet. You feel too good for it to end."

Well that's a switch. Where were you six months ago, bub? My keeper is cheering. *Hooray, a little touch of bittersweet victory, Gina.*

I feel his heavy breathing as I lay quietly with my swollen nipples soaking up the feeling of his sensuous chest hair. His smell is intoxicating and the energy sparking back and forth between us is amazing. Again, where were you six months ago?

He lifts me up and off of him and turns me over on my stomach. He spreads my legs and stands on his knees between them. Placing his hands behind my knees he urges me to bend them up under me, raising my hips for an easy target.

I know what's coming and I look back at him and bite at my lip. He moves up toward me and slowly enters me, his erection sending shock waves through me as I receive it in its entirety. It is more than fantastic.

"Take that," he grins.

"Oh . . . yes. Anytime," I groan. "Harder, please." I am helpless to participate in this position but it is incredible. It is like being his willing captive or prisoner—and I love it. "Give it to me. Go hard."

And he does. He withdraws and hesitates, then buries his erection to the hilt as a shockwave courses through me. I look back at him and grin. "Is that all? Is that the best you can do?"

He chuckles as he withdraws and barrels back into me. I try to thrust my hips back against him at the point of impact but it is useless. I am truly at his mercy—his captive—but I'm loving every second of it. "More," I moan.

Again he crashes into me. And then again. Harder this time. I'm dying a slow death and it is astounding. I wonder if I'll be able to walk tomorrow. I giggle in my ecstasy, "Can I have a little more please?"

Pep laughs as he withdraws from me and falls over on his back. "You win on that one. I can't go anymore or you'll lose me. I'm about to explode."

"Go for it, dude."

"No. Not yet. I want this to last".

Wow, I am suddenly in charge. I smile at my temporary lover, my ex–husband to be. "I think I can revive you for another round."

He doesn't answer as he gets off the bed and stands. He offers me a hand to follow him.

He turns me around and stands behind me. "Bend over."

I do as I'm told and he pulls me back toward him with his hands clutching me on my pelvis in front just below the waist.

"Oh my," I cry out as he thrusts his erection into me to the hilt, sending an explosion engulfing me. My entire being experiences a massive short circuit as my knees weaken and I feel my body crumbling—falling.

He holds me up and laughs. "Still with me, woman? Had enough of this?"

Gina De Georgio

I catch my breath as I regain my balance. "You are fantastic," I groan. "You can do that all day." I brace myself with a hand on each knee and press back against him. "More, fuck me hard . . . and don't stop."

"Shit!" he exclaims as he rhythmically resumes his pace. "You're made of steel."

"Harder, Pep. Just shut–up and screw me."

"Yes ma'am. I'll be coming at you."

He picks up his speed as he pounds into me harder and harder. My legs weaken and I grasp the edge of the bed for support.

"Harder, Pep! Don't stop! My God this is fantastic. Harder!"

Without comment he continues to thrust against me and I hear his breathing increase and he emits a small grunt from deep in his throat each time he thrusts.

I feel him losing it and urge him on knowing I'm also about to get–off on him. "Harder, Pep! Harder! I'm coming! Come with me!"

I feel myself going over the edge and I can't wait for him. I brace myself against the bed as he pounds harder against me time and time again. My whole body seems like it will explode any second and I don't know if I can remain standing as I soar higher and higher.

Just as I am about to crash and burn I sense he is going to join me as he groans louder with each breath and his rhythm is slowly shutting down.

"Oh, damn, here we go, babe! I'm coming!" he shouts as he again picks up the tempo, breathing harder with each thrust.

In unison we spray unintelligible expletives of pleasure just before he delivers one final body slamming blow that propels both of us forward onto bed, he on top of me. However spent we both break up laughing at our zany tumble together.

We rest quietly as our breathing slowly returns to normal. He moves off of me on his side and nudges me over with my back to him, wrapping an arm around me to cradle one breast. I feel secure but I know it will not be for long. I enjoy it nonetheless.

Momentarily he chuckles. "Damn, that was new for us—some crash landing."

I choose not to reply other than pushing myself back against him. Yes it was new and probably the last new thing we do together—in bed that is.

We lay in peace with each other as I silently relive some events and things out of our past that somehow spring up involuntarily. Here we are, so close in this instant but so very far apart in the future.

It is sad—so very sad—but I can't help but hope that it is going to be okay for me in the future. At the very least I will strive to make it that way.

After a few more minutes of silence I wonder if this little party is over. I assume it is but I'm not in any hurry if there's a possibility of more. What is he thinking? I know, don't ask a man what he's thinking—particularly in this situation. I might not want to hear it.

A few more minutes pass and I suddenly feel a stirring against my hips. I know from experience what this is and I welcome it. I press back against him and he responds in kind.

Thank you. I do want more. I want all you can give. I feel my senses revving up and a hint of electrical charge bubbling around my heart. I am anxious for this little bout to move forward but I will hold back to see what develops.

His erection is in full bloom as he presses it against me and kneads my nipple with his finger until it swells into a grape sized nodule.

"Oh shit. Is there more?" I whisper.

"Think you are up to it?" comes his return as he nibbles at my ear lobe.

I chuckle and bring my hand back and grasp his hip to pull him closer like I have done a thousand times in the past. "I probably won't be able to walk tomorrow but damn right I'm up to it. Wear me out. Hurt me. Throw me in the lake when you're through. I'm ready and willing."

My mechanics are clicking in and I can feel the pulse picking up in response to my quickening heartbeat. Energy pockets are effusing all over me, particularly in my belly and in that low, very low hotspot.

Pressure from Pep's knee urges my legs to part and he slides his upper leg between my legs. He coaxes me to turn my body upward and backs his body away with his head toward my feet, his upper knee bent on my belly. This leaves a direct however awkward angle for his penis to enter my hotspot.

I grasp the knee of his upper leg and use it as a lever to assist him in slowly entering fully into me. It is delightful yet somewhat uncomfortable due to the angle of his erection pressing against the front wall of my vagina.

But Pep is the master of patience and tenderness in bringing me to the height of sensitivity without pain. Slowly he moves in and out under my guidance and control by pushing and pulling on his knee. He is watching me for any hint of discomfort and backs off when necessary.

And the whole show is right before us. We not only enjoy the physical part, we can view it right in front of us. The pleasure appears to double or triple as we watch it unfold.

And it does: He backs off under my knee command and slowly reenters at my calling. With each move the sensual pressure rebuilds and it feels as if I will ignite at any time from the unreal pleasure mixed with real pain. However I can turn the burners up and down with his knee and the senses flow and ebb with a mixture of pleasure and pain.

"Oh, my . . . yes, Pep. Jeez, I've forgotten how this feels. Can we do this the rest of the day?" With every move I'm involuntarily elicit a groan of pleasure and I can tell that it is feeding his pleasure.

"I don't think so," he answers as he draws in a full breath and releases it. "We're surely going to go up in flames at any minute and probably burn the house down in the process."

"Sounds good to me. That would solve a world of problems don't you think?" I take a deep breath then pull his knee toward me. "Please don't stop . . . Oh, God, that's great. Yes, Pep, good, oh yes. Harder."

We pump away to our moans and groans of sheer pleasure. I feel the heat in my body shoot up and cool off at my command. This is better than fantastic. Too bad it's going to end soon. Probably with us forever.

"Hey, I'm about to lose it again," Pep says urgently.

"Hold off just a minute and I'll be ready to join you."

Suddenly he withdraws and hops out of bed. Going to the closet he retrieves a special pillow and returns.

"You seem to know your way around here," I muse.

"Yeah, kind of." He assists me in lifting my hips and places the pillow underneath to force my hips up in an angle.

"You think this pillow still knows what to do?" he grins. "It's probably out of shape."

"The pillow will be fine. It's me that probably can't pull this off. Do me and we'll see," I demand, bending my knees and reaching for his hips. I guide him over me. He spreads his knees and wraps his arms around my bent knees so he will be able to adjust my hips to the proper position to give his erection the right slant.

I pull his hips toward me and his erection easily slides into me and rests against my front vagina wall. Pep pauses and watches my reaction before slowly moving his penis softly in and out.

I nod my approval as the heat in my body is again on the rise. I pull his hips indicating I want more pressure and he obliges.

"Oh, that's great. Yes, right there. Easy. Great." The senses are building ever higher but bordering on pain. I want more and nudge his hips harder.

"You okay?" he asks as he increases his stroke and pressure on the front wall. His eyes study mine as he can easily turn this experience into unwelcome pain or profound enjoyment.

"Oh shit, Pep. Oh, harder." I moan as I adjust my hips for better sensitivity. "Oh, right there. Yes, a little bit more . . . yes, fuck me hard. Please, harder. Aww, yes."

Suddenly, he shuts down. All I'm receiving from him is heavy breathing. I'm caught between potential frustration and the bottom falling out.

"No, I need more. Don't stop. Please."

Sensing my predicament he smiles and offers me a hand. He assists me off the bed and leads me over to the dressing table.

"How about a little table dance? This, woman, is the finale."

"You're on, dude," I reply as he backs me into the table, grasps me under my hips and lifts me into a sitting position on the table.

He grasps my legs behind my knees and lifts while bending my knees and pushing my legs back against me. I respond by placing my hands on his hips and pull him toward me. He pushes forward and we kiss—first softly then with renewed passion, sucking, biting and tonguing until we have to stop to take a breath.

"Shit, I've got to get-off on you one more time," I whisper hoarsely. "Right now."

Suddenly he drops to his knees and while pushing my legs back he parts my hot spot with his thumbs. He mouth coverers my clit and sucks lightly, gradually increasing in pressure. A wave of energy engulfs my body and I push against him. Now between sucks he circles my clit with his tongue—then back to sucking. It is taking me higher and higher and I can't imagine lasting much longer.

"Harder, Pep. I want to come now," I gasp. "Harder. Oh, yes . . . jeez, hurry, Pep. Now."

He backs off and smiles while breathing heavily. "Hold on. I want to come with you."

"Better hurry," I moan. "I can't last much longer. Hurry, babe."

He grins as he opens a drawer of the dressing table and takes out a bottle of lubricant. Cracking open the plastic top, he says, "This is going to be one big sloppy orgasm."

"Oh yeah. Show me, but hurry. I want it all, right now. Fuck me hard."

He fills his hand with a generous portion of the oil, sits the bottle down and rubs his hands together. He rubs his hands over my breasts and my heart leaps into a higher gear pushing my pulse even faster, spewing hot blood throughout my system.

"Oh . . . more, yes. That feels fantastic." It strangely reminds me of my and Link's message session.

"No problem, madam." He grins evilly and picks up the bottle. He dribbles it from the bottle on my breasts while pushing it around with his other hand. He dribbles and pushes it on my belly, pubic hair and then a generous portion on my fantasy place. Then on my thighs. And it is so sensuous.

I take the bottle and follow the same route working my way down to his erection. After emptying the bottle I work the oil over his erection with both hands taking extra care to squeeze and pull at the right times to bring him to full readiness for our final romp.

"Oh yes, baby. I like that. Squeeze harder. Yes. Yes. Let's fuck. I'm ready."

I place his erection in that hot spot and grab his hips and pull him toward me as he thrusts forward. The greased pole slams into me and we groan, our slippery bodies pressing and sliding against each other.

He draws back and I assist him into banging against me again—harder this time.

"Oh, yes. Come on," I beg as he plows into me. Oddly I feel like I want him to hurt me. I need him to hurt me.

He partially withdraws and rams forward with my increased assistance.

We are a cacophony of groans and moans as we cling to each other's slippery upper body while pounding each other with our oily lower bodies.

"Oh, yes. Come with me, Pep! Hurry! God, I'm ready! I can't take anymore!"

We step up the pace and our bodies clash recklessly —grunting, laughing and crying out in pleasure together.

Pep yells out, "Just a little bit, babe! Come to me! Fuck me! Yes! Now!"

We go harder and harder. Higher and higher until the bottom falls out and we soar in pure bliss—an unbelievable place I have never been before.

We cling together not talking. Heavy breathing is all we have left and I'm sure that will subside sometime today—maybe.

A moment later he whispers softly, "Damn."

"No, Pep. Exquisite," I answer with a smile. I slowly push him away to find his erection has completely disappeared.

I widen my smile as I step down from my perch. "Magnificent performance, Sir. Do you hire out?"

He doesn't answer as he gathers his clothes and shoes scattered around the bedroom.

Strange. Our little tryst is over. It's odd we've been married for over fourteen years and until recently the sex was fabulous. Then, after we split we somehow end up in the sack and the sex is off the charts. Figure that. Goodbye yesterday, hello today—but there is no tomorrow for us. So long and good luck. And thanks for the good–bye fuck.

I fetch him a towel and he attempts to wipe the oil off of his body.

"You can shower if you like."

"No thanks. I'm going to the gym. I'll shower there."

We are in the midst of an uneasy silence as we dress. This party is definitely over. Back to abnormal. That means the divorce feud will continue soon. Oh well.

I pick up my torn blouse and pitch it toward him with a grin. "Well so much for a new blouse, but the experience of having it ripped off of me was well worth the damage."

Again, no reply on his part as the uneasiness in the room closes in. How do you say thanks and goodbye to someone you've just fucked that you shouldn't have, but it was sensational and in all likelihood it will never happen again?

As he finishes dressing I say casually, "So, you've joined a gun club. Sounds like fun."

"Yeah, I need to get a little male bonding."

"Umm. Maybe you can forget to take the gun and come back tomorrow to get it." *Nice try, Gina.*

A smile and wink are his only reply.

I shrug indifferently, "Bye Pep."

"Bye Gina. See you Friday."

"Friday it is. The kids will be ready." I smile at the suddenly distant man preparing to take his leave. "Thanks for the roll in the hay. You are a lifesaver." I won't remind you that you were the cause of my predicament to start with.

He smiles and shrugs as he turns to leave.

"The muzzleloader," I call out to him.

Finally cocktail time. The kids are fed and doing their thing. Now me. How long has it been since I could kick back and enjoy the best part of my day without having continual sexual frustration grating on me? I don my white string B and head for the shore.

"Hey mister," I greet heartily as I join Jonathan and his kids on his dock. He is dressed as usual—shirtless and shoeless in his tattered red trunks. He still looks good enough to eat. I wish.

Before he can reply the kids ask where Bunny and Don are.

"Probably watching TV. Why don't you guys join them?"

Suddenly they are off and running across the lawn.

I sit and set my Chivas on the table next to Jonathan's wine bottle. I grin and tilt my head toward him. "What say you, sir? Did the day treat you well?"

He gazes at me curiously but doesn't comment. Damn, this guy can just look at me and he drips with sexiness. What is this? Didn't I just sex out earlier?

He finally nods absently. "I don't have any complaints. You seem to be in a chipper mood. Apparently you didn't have one of your usual, shall I say, overly frustrating days."

You can say that again. I smile easily and he glances at me curiously. "I did not. Have you talked to Link?"

"Yeah. They are on schedule with getting the gallery set up. They hope to have it ready by tomorrow afternoon."

I grasp my hands together and shake them. "Oh, that's great. Is she returning afterward?"

"Only if she can get home before dark and she isn't too tired to drive. She says it will probably be late Thursday morning as planned."

"How is the gallery turning out? Everything to her liking so far?"

"She's happy. She didn't elaborate further." He grins, "She did ask if you showed up to scratch on my bedroom door."

I giggle and bite at my lower lip. "And your answer was?"

"Of course it was no."

I force a frown of disappointment. "Oh, I haven't told you. Last night, or was it early this morning, I knocked on your bedroom door but you slept right through it." I smile my open mouthed, I think, sexy smile as he gloomily shakes his head. "John boy, you are missing so much."

"Yeah, I'm sure. So, since I haven't talked to you today, how is the *Hunter's Almanac* project going? Good, bad or otherwise?"

"Everyone seems to be rocking along on schedule. Darren is bitching about his audit. *Hunter's* has gone through three financial officers in three years and the present one has only been on board for three months.

"Darren says this woman doesn't know—what was his term?—jack shit about what's going on financially in the company. She told Darren that she would've been long gone weeks ago if she had a place to land."

Jonathan merely shakes his head with a hint of a grin. "Doesn't sound too good. What do you think?"

I cackle and act surprised, placing both hands comically on my cheeks. "Hell, how should I know? I just work here."

Jonathan belly laughs and studies me curiously. "Damn, Gina, it's your job to know. That's what you were hired for—to solve problems, to intervene in major disputes. To . . . hell, I don't even know what your job description is. Or if you even have specified duties with this company. Do you get a paycheck?"

I twist my lips and squint in thought. "Umm . . . I guess that's why I'm one of the higher paid employees. Isn't that the way it is with big companies? The higher you are on the pay scale the less anyone knows what your job is. Or even who you are for that matter."

Jonathan is silent as he looks out over the water. "Damn I love this lake."

I keep quiet because I'm curious about what direction he is going to take our conversation.

"How many hours a week to you work anyway?"

I try to keep a straight face. "A lot, sir."

He grins, "A lot, meaning, say forty, fifty. What do you think?"

I present my most serious face and count on my fingers for his benefit. "Probably, maybe, could be about twenty, give or take."

Jonathan again studies me with a perfectly arched brow. "Shit, I wish I had your job. You must have a good union. How did you manage to land a job like this?"

"Blackmail sir. I had something on the owner of the company, and I intend to make him pay the rest of his life."

"Uh–huh. And benefits? What kind of freebies do you get?"

I delay my answer while I feign deep contemplation. "Just about everything one would want. There's one benefit I don't get that would make me a whole lot happier camper."

"I can't imagine what that would be."

I tilt my head and eye him with pressed lips. "I would like a whole lot of sexual harassment."

"Sexual harassment? Let me be sure I understand you. You want to be sexually harassed?"

I smile, "That would be correct. More sexual harassment."

With a weird smile Jonathan gazes at me incredulously. "Wait a minute. If you want to be sexually harassed it would no longer be harassment. It would be sexual exploitation. You want sexual exploitation as a job benefit."

I smile as I stroke my chin. "That would work, John. How about setting aside an hour a week, or more, of sexual exploitation for any employee who wants to participate? I'm sure morale would skyrocket."

Jonathan chuckles as he refills his wine glass. "I can't believe we're even having this conversation."

I shrug my shoulders indifferently.

"So why are you in such a rare mood today? Usually tension is spewing out of every pore, but today you are laid back and enjoying badgering me. What's the deal?"

I grin and answer smugly, "Sex, John."

"Sex?"

I hug myself and giggle, "Yeah, Gina got laid today. I'm a new woman—at least for a while, a whole day or ten hours maybe. Or eight."

Jonathan lowers his chin and peers up at me smiling. "You did the big S today? On company time? I'm jealous."

I flash my sexiest smile. "Well, Johnny, you had your chance and blew it. I had to go after my second choice."

"Well, fantastic. Congrats on finally getting a little after all those empty days. Are you going to tell me who shot me out of the saddle?"

I slowly roll my eyes and pat him on his bare knee—my third knee of the day. "John, dear, you can't get shot out of the saddle if you aren't riding the horse. Remember that for future reference."

"Oh, I guess you're right. Now, who was the lucky lad that laid the desperate maiden?"

"I'll give you three guesses and the first two don't count," I grin spreading my hands.

John sadly shakes his head. "Oh shit. Not really? Please tell me you didn't. That should muddy the water. His idea or yours?"

I nod positively with a smile, "Mine. I cornered him and he didn't have a chance. Or a choice for that matter. It was my call and he went along, I assume for his own survival."

I pause but John doesn't reply as he gazes at me with a straight face and a hint of a smile.

"I enjoyed the best sex I've ever had. I'm surprised I can even walk. I was spewing orgasms like one of those automatic rifles. It was amazing. We did stuff we'd never done before. I was hungry and I ate. In fact I gorged myself."

"Uh-huh, all that. *Star Trek* sex—you went places you've never gone before." Jonathan pauses in contemplation. "So, are you guys going to get back together or what?"

"Oh no, John. We agreed in advance—he wants to continue living with and fucking his wonderful new babe, and I told him there's no way I could live with him. Our time together today was just fun for old time's sake. Nothing more."

"Good decision, Gina. Do you desire or have an agreement to do this again?"

"I don't think that will happen. But I'm glad we did it. It was fantastic."

"The divorce is not on hold?"

"No. The divorce time table and accompanying feud will continue as before."

Jonathan squints his eyes and twists those yummy lips in thought. "Let me see if I can summarize this: the whole deal is kind of crazy. First your longtime husband shacks up with another woman for months on end.

"He eventually succumbs to her demands to have him move in and be at her disposal constantly other than when he can sneak away from you.

"Then about six weeks go by and you coax him right back to your bed at which time you enjoy the best sex imaginable. It appears that you've gotten a bit of revenge."

I shrug stoically. "It may be revenge but it's kind of empty if she doesn't know it."

"Well?"

"Well what, John?"

"Are you going to tell her?"

I stare at Jonathan without expression. "You've got to be kidding. There's no way I'm going to open that can of worms. If she throws him out for shacking up with the woman he left to live with her, he might be looking to move back to me. That's a no. I don't even want to deal with that."

Jonathan draws his brow together in a frown as he considers my remark. "Yeah, okay. You shouldn't go there. Maybe he will tell her?"

"Just like with me he'll probably tell her in about a year don't you think?"

John softly grabs my leg above the knee and squeezes lightly and of course it sends chills cascading through me. Shit, a little higher please.

"Well anyway, I'm glad you've finally gotten some relief from—how can I say?—your sexual demon. I know it was eating on you."

"It was that, John. I do feel relief and I now know I can carry on without selling myself out to some insouciant male including my ex."

Jonathan tilts his head and smiles. "Insouciant? If I recall that means unconcerned or uncaring. Do you think males are uncaring?"

"In general—don't get me wrong, John. This isn't about you—males don't give a rat's ass about the women they are hitting on. It's all about them and what they want and need. If they get turned down or turned away, they just move on and find some other willing woman to accept their bullshit and their glorious semen."

I watch as John stares at me blankly. After a moment his eyes widen and he grins while egging me on. "Wow, Gina. I'm curious. Tell me more."

I would love to do that. I pause as I formulate what I want to say. "John, about six weeks ago I got fed up with what was going on with me sexually. I had this virile mate that was more interested in shacking up with a stranger than he was with me.

"What's with that? My only option was to sit and wait on this male—my special male—to decide I also have sexual needs and wants. I had to wait and hope that I would again become a part of his life including his sex life.

"Well, it didn't happen and I was left frustrated in this abyss waiting for relief from an incredible lack of sex." I pause and purse my lips in thought as I tap a finger lightly against my check. "Then it came to me. In fact it came to me on the morning that Pep and I split up. I realized that I was rotting away; I had to get on the offensive and make something happen for me sexually.

"Since Pep and I got together years ago I had basically become passive, allowing him to call the shots because he was always ready to get a little. In my college days I was hyper aggressive and it worked to perfection because there were plenty of males that didn't know shit about sex. They were my prey and I was their teacher. I controlled everything—I called the shots."

I grin thinly at Jonathan and shrug my shoulders. "So, on that morning before Pep left I made up my mind to get laid." I smile at the man sitting next to me. "And since you've been my first or second choice since college days you became my target, hence my hitting on you."

Jonathan chuckles and answers sarcastically, "Thanks a lot, Gina, for including me in your little escapade. I must admit I was somewhat surprised at your actions."

"That was my coming out party. I decided I had to be proactive if I was going to ever get laid. It wasn't going to happen if I didn't take charge. Just like in college."

Jonathan nods perceptively, "But I'm not one of your college guys that didn't know shit about sex. So it didn't exactly happen the way you wanted did it?"

"Jeez, you're telling me. I definitely didn't get the cooperation from you I expected. I thought I could march right into your office, point at the sofa and we would get it on. There's no way you wouldn't take care of me."

"Umm . . . ."

"Is that your only comment?"

"Pretty much."

"Okay, I decided that I was going to get into the hyper aggressive male mode." I present a huge smile for Jonathan's benefit. "Since then I have probably driven you crazy with my continual sexual suggestions, innuendo and downright demanding that you and I shack up."

"Tell me about it. It's been comical sometimes, but I'm honored that you find me desirable."

"Link has even noticed my craziness and we've discussed it." I look out over the lake in thought as he waits for more. "Sometimes I even think she is encouraging me to hit on you. And that is certainly cemented by her never ending threesome suggestions."

He nods his understanding as I wait to see if he'll comment. "Umm, yes this whole situation is kind of crazy. I sometimes think I'm the only one of us three that is not participating."

"So, Johnny, why aren't you participating?" I ask with wide eyes and an evil grin.

"I just don't feel right about it, but I wonder about the whole deal."

I tilt my head quizzically. "Wonder what?"

"It hasn't slipped by me that you and Link have been kind of tight since that first evening when sparks were flying between you guys during and after your hug on the dock."

He studies me for a moment as my hormones click in because of his dreamy eyes and yummy lips. Damn, don't my hormones ever rest? You would think after today they would take a day off. Or at least a few hours. Maybe.

He continues: "I gather that you guys are getting it on."

I gaze at him and wonder just how much he knows and what I dare divulge about Link's and my passion for each other. I finally release a long winded sigh and look Jonathan in the eye. I resign, "Yes, John, we are," I answer flatly.

He nods at my answer but shows no emotion. I've always thought he was aware and this reaction pretty much backs that up.

We quietly survey the shoreline across the lake while lost in our own thoughts. This is totally idiotic passes through my mind.

My keeper cannot let this go by: *Yeah, Gina, you are shacking up with your best girlfriend, all the while trying to coax her husband into bed. And, along with you, she and her husband don't appear to have a problem with the whole scenario. This is so weird. Am I the only one that's sane?*

After an uncomfortable silence Jonathan frowns. "Shit, I wonder what the hell is going on with all of us. It seems like something is just not right and the hammer is about to come down. Why do I feel that way?"

I study Jonathan uneasily. I have felt the same thing for some time but I thought it was just me wallowing in my own marriage and sex problems. But he is right: it's kind of a mutual energy thing. It feels like we are caught up together in some strange web that is destined to drastically change us. Why is that? I have absolutely no reason to feel this way—but there's no doubt I do.

"Well, John boy," I resign. "I sense what you are saying has some basis, but there's not much we can do about it, particularly when we don't know what the hell it is. But tomorrow is a new day and after my good fortune today I intend to live it to the fullest."

"You have a schedule for tomorrow?"

"Yeah," I answer as a matter of fact, "I'll follow you into the office in the morning. I have a quick meeting with the *Hunter's* research group then I need to get my column ready for Thursday. After that, if my illustrious boss isn't game for any extracurricular fun, I hope to buy him lunch at this Mexican restaurant I've heard about. They tell me they have this waitress that is to die for sexy— or cheese enchiladas if you prefer. Or both."

"Sounds like you're giving up on this evening. The wine, uh, scotch is waiting. We can make a night of it."

"No John, I think I'll go lick my wounds from today's joyous activities. If I walk away bowlegged you'll know why. Of course if you desire to add to my injuries I'll certainly entertain . . . no, I don't think that's a good idea."

Jonathan laughs, "Gina, There is a limit. Perhaps you should come and breathe a bit before plunging right back in."

"Hey, John. I've always been told that you have to make hay while the sun shines."

"It's dark, Gina."

"Hey, dark is good. You can do a lot of exciting things in the dark. Want me to show you?"

"Gina, just go home. You need some rest. You may not realize it but dark is also for sleeping. Go get some."

"Goodnight, asshole."

"Send my kids home, Gina."

"Umm."

"There certainly wasn't very much enthusiasm over the *Hunter's* issue. I think everyone is more or less against the whole deal right now. It'll be interesting next week to see what they come up with."

I'm sitting across the desk from Jonathan and we're sneaking a Bloody Mary before we head out to Margarita country. Isn't this a great job and boss I have?

John nods but doesn't comment. I get the impression he is also against the deal but you never know about him. He has reversed himself in the past in situations like this, going against all logic and the people that advise him. Time and time again he makes a profitable decision for the company. I for one won't be surprised whatever route he chooses to go. It'll probably fly.

He strokes his bearded chin in quiet contemplation and I am fixed on his hand wondering how it would feel stroking my face.

For God's sake, Gina. You just got laid big time yesterday and you're already obsessing over sex.

Bug off. I like sex. I want more.

Jonathan takes a sip as he peers at me blankly. I can match that. I also sip then lick my lips before presenting a sexy smile for the man of the hour.

"I'm tempted to ask what you're thinking," he says flatly, "but usually it's the same old song and dance so I don't think I'll go there."

He flips a hand indicating a change of direction. "Did you get your column on its way?"

"Yes sir, it's put to bed." Now can I put you to bed? "It's becoming a lot easier as long as I keep up daily with all the correspondence coming my way."

"You're getting some good material from the masses?"

"I am totally happy with the response."

"Interesting stuff?"

"Yeah. Some is downright crazy. This is going to be a lot of fun. I wish you had gotten me into this years ago."

"Umm," he answers as he again strokes his beard in thought.

I wait for him to continue. Sir, would you please do that to me? I muse to myself.

"Things come spewing forth whenever you're ready. I don't think you would have done this whole deal if you weren't shall I say forced into it—it was your time to shine and here you are."

He smiles thinly with a firm nod. "Link and I are certainly proud of you and extremely happy that it's working for you."

Damn, here come the tears. "Well, thank you both. I certainly couldn't do this without you guys. I would have a hell of a time going through this divorce without you holding me up. You are literally propping me up in so many different ways."

I wipe my tears with a hastily retrieved tissue. He salutes with his Mary and takes a long sip as he peers over the rim with those dreamy eyes. I salute back and gulp my Mary.

Gina, you don't gulp Bloody Marys. Get with the system.

In defiance of my mentor I take another big gulp. So there. Take that.

Jonathan has built that steeple with elbows on his desk and his hands in the prayer position, the tips of his fingers resting against his bearded chin. He chuckles. "Better slow down, babe. You have Margaritas yet and a drive home."

"You mean I can't sleep here on your sofa?"

"Shit, you never quit. Of course you can sleep on my sofa—by yourself."

"Damn, Johnny. You're no fun at all. Can we go eat now?"

"No fantasies?"

"No fantasies. I promise. Maybe."

* * * *

217

"We're getting pretty good at this," Jonathan nods as he raises his wine glass in toast to the lake. "Marys in the morning, Margaritas at noon and wine or scotch in the evening. We're becoming a couple of sots."

I raise my merlot glass to the lake and exaggerate clearing my throat. "To grand old Lake McQueeney. May it never run dry—and may we never run dry."

"Well said, Gina. We make a great drinking couple." He toasts me.

I toast him. Damn, we are about to burn the toast. "We could be great at a whole lot of things if you would only participate."

He shakes his head cheerlessly at me before his cell phone beckons. He answers: "Hey, lady. We've been waiting on your call. How did it go today? . . . Yeah, we thought as much when you didn't call earlier. . . . Uh-huh, so you are up and running? . . . Oh, she did. That's really great. . . . We can expect you when? . . . About noon it is then. . . . Absolutely, we're going to break out one of our better boxes of wine. . . . Of course, she is sitting right beside me holding my hand. . . . Well she certainly is trying, but, but and more buts. You know how that is. . . . Okay then, I can't wait for you to be home. . . . Yes ma'am. Of course. . . . Alright. Drive carefully. Bye."

As Jonathan lays his phone down on the table, I feel very sad and tears fill my eyes. What is this? What is the matter with me?

Jonathan looks at me curiously and I merely shake my head. "Don't ask. I don't have any idea what's up with me, John."

TWELVE

The kids are hardly out the door and I head back to bed. What the hell is the matter with me? I should be happy since Link is returning today and we can get back to our crazy form of normality.

I am depressed big time. And for no reason that I can figure. Well I haven't got time for this. Just thirty minutes of moping then I have to get moving and contact each of my *Hunter's* group to make sure everyone is on the proper page. After that I should have time to get my daily column work done by the time Link arrives. By kicking it up a notch perhaps Link and I can celebrate a bit this afternoon.

> *Gina Wabbit   10:33AM*
>
> *Hey, babe. I trust you are on the road. I'll be waiting for you. Let me know when you get close. Be careful please.*
> *Gina*

I no more than send the text when this irritating depression again raises its ugly head. I can't put a name on it, but it is not actually depression; it's more like a foreboding of I don't know what. Damn, I've got to quit this fretting over nothing. It is a waste of time. But what the hell is distressing me? I can't let it be.

My keeper pops up to give her two cents worth: *With any thought or feeling that you are presented, you should stand back and heed with the tools, the senses you have available to you.*

Now what the hell is that supposed to mean? So I'm sensing something isn't right. Now I should stand back and heed. Heed what? This is bullshit.

Gina Wabbit   11:58AM

Link, where are you? You should be close. Call or message me. Will fix lunch for when you arrive.
Gina

Come on, girl. Holler at me. You've been on the road long enough. I don't need the suspense.

Gina Wabbit   12:40PM

John, heard anything from Link? Way overdue.
Gina

Jonathan Bales   Date: 12:55PM

I just called Link. No answer. Perhaps she made a pit stop to eat or pee—or both. I also sent a message. I will keep trying.
John

Answer your phone, Link. Pick up please. . . . No, I don't want to leave a message. I want to talk to you right now: "Link, it's one–forty. Where are you? John and I are concerned. Return this call as soon as you can."

Gina Wabbit   1:46PM

Link, we are concerned. Please get in touch.
Gina

Well here I am. It's two–thirty and still no Link. The last thing I need is for the doorbell to ring. No, I don't want to subscribe to anything, thank you. Now go away.

I open the front door to find Sheriff Charife, hat in hand. "Well this is a surprise" I motion for him to enter. "Jerry, it's good to see you. What brings you out to the lake people?"

"Hi, Gina. I guess you could say I'm here on business," he answers professionally with a straight face and serious eyes.

My heart drops. Suddenly I don't want to hear what Jerry has to say. "Don't tell me that you're here about Link," I say softly as I dismally shake my head.

"Yes, Gina. She's been in an accident. Close to Gonzales. The Department of Public Safety called the Bales' home phone and got no answer. They contacted our dispatcher and asked if we'd send a deputy by to notify John where she is.

"I intercepted the message and when I saw it was Link I decided to come by myself to give John the news so he could respond."

"Shit. Shit, shit, shit," I mutter with tears beginning to pool in the corners of my eyes. "Is she okay? Where is she?"

"She was airlifted to Guadalupe Medical Center in Seguin. I don't know the extent of her injuries but I asked DPS to fax an accident report. As of five minutes ago we haven't received it.

"I called the hospital but she was still under examination or treatment and the doctors haven't issued any type of report on the extent of her injuries. I'm headed over to the hospital after I leave here."

Tears increase big time as I realize that all the dreams Link was having and all the cautious premonitions we all were experiencing could very well have been warnings of a real life event.

I can tell Jerry is uncomfortable as he stands there silently.

"I'll contact John and I'm sure he can be at the hospital within an hour. Our four kids are due home from school soon. I'll get them squared away and head over to the hospital, too."

I slowly shake my head as the tears are now flooding down my cheeks. I don't bother to wipe them away.

"Jerry, we've been having dreams and premonitions of something happening to Link for several weeks now, but we were at a loss as to what was going on or what we could do about it. Now I feel completely helpless—like it's my fault I didn't prevent this."

Jerry nods and I perceive tears collecting in his eyes as well. Since our first year in college we have always been on each other's radar and now, suddenly, we are entering another chapter—possibly not a pleasant one.

I finally wipe the tears with the back of my hand. "Jerry when you get the accident report would you come by the hospital and give John the details?"

"Yeah, I'll be there. I have a big stake in this too. You guys have always been at the top of my favorites list."

He exhales a long tension filled breath. "Are you okay? Do you want me to hang here with you for a while?"

I force a smile and grasp his elbow. "No, I'm okay. The best way you can help now is find out about the accident for John's benefit."

He nods and I sense that he is about to lose it emotionally.

"Go, Jerry. I'll be okay."

Suddenly he is gone.

Now, Jonathan. I sigh and search for my phone.

"Hi, JB. This is Gina. . . . Really, not too good. Link has been in an accident and I need to talk to Mr. Bales if you will put me through. . . . Yes, I will. Right now we don't know how bad. . . .Okay, thanks, JB."

"John, Gina. I have bad news. . . . Yes, she has been in an accident near Gonzales. . . . Jerry came by to notify you. He didn't have any information on her condition or any details of the accident. . . . She was airlifted to Guadalupe Medical center. . . .Yes, hopefully the doctors will have it figured out by the time you get there. . . . Jerry will be there to meet you. He hopes to have a fax of the accident report soon. . . . Yes, I'll be there before you. I'm going to call Griffin and have her come by and supervise the kids in case we're hung up at the hospital. . . . Alright, hurry but be careful. . . . Bye."

Damn, why didn't I take heed of all the messages we have been receiving? But what could I have done differently to prevent this accident? Well, I can't help but believe I could have done something. Link, please don't be injured badly. I'm so sorry.

*   *   *   *

As I search for a parking space I wonder, jeez, how many times have I passed this hospital on the way to the super market? I've never once considered the drama that must be going on here on a daily basis. Well I'm going to be part of the drama now whether I like it or not. I only hope it is a small drama. We're coming Link. Hang in there.

I approach the information desk and the volunteer looks up and smiles. "May I help you?"

"Yes, ma'am. Uh, you've had a car accident injury airlifted here an hour or so ago. The name is Link Bales."

She checks her records. "Yes, if you'll go all the way down this hall it runs into the nurse's station of the Surgery Center. They'll give you any information you need."

"Thank you." The tears appear as I walk down the almost empty corridor, my heels clopping away on the tiled floor. Like any hospital the smell suggests a combination of sickness, medicine and disinfectant. It gives me a tinge of nausea but I ignore it.

I approach the nurse's station and wait as no one appears to be aware of my arriving. I can wait. I assume I'm going to do a whole lot of waiting in the next several hours.

A nurse approaches. The somewhat heavy woman in her late twenties or early thirties eventually acknowledges me. "May I help you?" she asks stoically.

Be nice, lady. I need nice right now. "Yes, I'd like to inquire about Link Bales, admitted a couple of hours ago."

"Are you a relative of the patient?" the impatient nurse asks indifferently.

"No ma'am. I'm a close friend. Her husband will be arriving in a few minutes. Do you have a report on her condition?"

She answers gruffly, "I'll notify the doctor and he will speak with you as soon as the husband arrives. You may have a seat in the waiting room until he comes." She gestures toward the waiting room as if I am a bother to her. I wish I had three slaps a day I could use without consequence; I would probably use all three on her.

Thanks bitch. Without sneering too much or making a scene, I clomp toward the waiting room. It is void of people with a television blaring some courtroom show. I look for a way to turn it off but I'm unsuccessful; I am able to cut off the volume. I sit and close my eyes as I try to visualize a positive outcome for this whole drama.

Momentarily Jonathan taps me on the knee. "The doctor is coming in a few minutes. You okay?"

I shake my head no as Jerry appears in the doorway. "Folks," he nods seriously as he shakes Jonathan's hand. "John, I'm glad you made it so quickly. Have you talked to the doctor?"

Jonathan shakes his head with tight lips and concerned eyes. "He's on the way. We don't know anything."

"I received the accident report." He shakes his head sadly. "It was bad, John. I have a copy for you to take with you, but I'll summarize it for you."

He hands Jonathan two sheets of legal sized paper that Jonathan folds and slips into his back pocket.

Jerry continues: "About fifteen miles on the other side of Gonzales, apparently Link had a blowout of the right front tire. They judge she was going the speed limit of seventy miles per hour at the time.

"The van veered to the right onto the gravel shoulder and they believe she over compensated in turning the wheel to the left trying to right the van. She lost control of the van and it turned over several times before crashing into a large oak tree just off the highway. The van was pretty much totaled.

"When the EMS arrived she was unconscious and was still unconscious when the chopper arrived. Since it is only about fifty miles to the hospital they got her here very quickly I assume."

I watch as the color drains from Jonathan's face as he realizes the severity of the trauma that Link experienced. I have to sit down to quell my own sudden nausea. This is not the worst it could be but we don't know the whole story.

The sheriff steps to the side as he spies and acknowledges the doctor entering the waiting room. John, although ashen, looks toward the doctor and offers his hand. I force myself to my feet and join the small circle.

"You're Mr. Bales?" the doctor asks while shaking Jonathan's hand.

Jonathan nods as the doctor follows: "I'm Doctor David Morgan. I am the brain trauma specialist here at Guadalupe Medical Center. I was assisted in my examination of your wife by two other highly trained head trauma specialists."

Jonathan's only response is a nod. He doesn't look as if he can go further and I'm tempted to ask him to sit down. I silently wait.

Morgan continues: "We have made a number of scans of her head and found several areas of concern. First, this is a closed head injury meaning there are no open wounds. However when the brain is violently jolted back and forth in the skull upon impact it falls under the diagnosis, concussion, of which there were several in her case.

With every word spoken by the doctor Jonathan becomes more crestfallen. I want to put my arm around him to comfort him but stand back. Who's to comfort me? I don't know if I want to hear anymore.

"In addition to bruising or tearing brain tissue, bleeding or swelling are some of the greatest risks associated with closed head injuries of this sort. According to our tests it is acute with your wife.

"If not relieved by surgery, brain swelling can cause severe or fatal brain damage."

Jonathan doesn't ask so I do: "Will you be able to relieve the swelling with surgery?" Jonathan perceivably nods at me.

"We've already performed some preliminary surgery to relieve some of the swelling but much more is needed. We'll start this with your permission."

Jonathan sneaks a peek at me and nods at the doctor. "Of course. We want you to do all you can."

"Is she conscious?" I ask looking to Jonathan to see if he reacts negatively to my intrusion.

"No, she is not. As far as I know she has been unconscious since the initial impact. Although her condition is extremely serious and we really have no idea if she can survive even after our surgery, her being unconscious is not a particular problem in itself.

"Although we have not discussed this, we may want to induce a coma medically if she does regain consciousness. The body heals better and quicker if the patient is not conscious."

Jonathan studies the doctor: "Do you have a bottom line. Will she recover?"

Dr. Morgan's brow furrows as he slowly shakes his head. "I have to say again, this is extremely critical. We could easily lose her—you need to know that. We have no miracles. All we can do is relieve the swelling the best we can and she has to do the rest."

With sad eyes Jonathan stares at the doctor. "No percentages?"

"No sir. We can't even guess. All of these injuries are different so we have nothing for comparison. Pardon my bluntness but this is a crapshoot at best. You have to understand that."

Jonathan exhales a long winded sigh. "Other injuries?"

"The trauma people are looking at that right now. So far there's several problems—both arms broken, one in several places. Shoulder fractured. Countless ribs. I'm sure there will be more. But right now our focus is to get the brain injuries repaired."

"Go for it," Jonathan resigns quietly.

Morgan nods. "We'll give it our best shot and keep you posted all along the way. This is going to take us several hours so bear with us."

Dr. Morgan leaves us and John's eyes tear up. I remember Link saying that in one of her dreams Jonathan was crying at her funeral. She said, "And John never cries."

Jerry puts one arm around John and the other around me. "Hang with it, guys. Keep me filled in on any changes and call if you need anything. Anything at all."

As is his way the sheriff is abruptly gone, leaving John and I alone together wondering what happens next. We take a seat next to each other and hold hands silent in our own thoughts.

After about five minutes I release his hand and pat him on his knee. "There's nothing we can do here and it may be hours before we hear any kind of report from the doctors. We really need to tell the kids, particularly yours, what's going on."

Jonathan shakes his head with a drawn brow and sadness filling his eyes. "Yeah, but what do I tell them?"

I shrug, "Sooner or later they have to know the basic truth of what's going on. You don't have to tell them that she might die unless they ask. They do need know the truth without the gory detail."

"I suppose you're right. You think we need to tell them together?"

"It would probably be best if you handle yours and I handle mine. It's really two different deals." I pause and frown my concern. "However you want to handle it, I'm game. Just tell me what you want of me. This is all about Link, you and your kids. I'll do whatever."

We agreed that we should wait until the kids are bedded down before we return for our vigil at the hospital. Griffin offered to handle that chore while Jonathan and I spend a few minutes on the dock. It is going to be a long waiting spell and it is as well we first unwind the best we can.

Griffin will be spending the night and getting the kids on the bus in the morning before she heads to her own classes at TLU. We told her of the chance we'd need her to move in with one of us permanently until this all settled down and she readily agreed.

"How did it go with the kids?"

Jonathan doesn't answer as he sets his wine glass on the table and refills it—already his third glass. This whole thing is massive for me so I know he is dying on the inside. I wait quietly.

"Better than I expected," he finally answers hardly above a whisper. "I don't think they see the significance of what is happening or what could happen to them in the near future as a result of this accident. Maybe that is just as well.

"I wish I could join them in their mindset but I know the reality of what's happening. Our world could change in an instant."

I don't respond and we enter into an eerie silence, each weighing the magnitude of our own personal stake in what is happening in a hospital only a few short miles from where we sit.

I finally grasp Jonathan's hand and our eyes meet. "You okay?" I ask lightly squeezing his hand.

He returns the squeeze. "Right now, I'm getting a handle on everything. If she doesn't make it, I don't know. I've never lost anyone this close to me."

It crosses my mind that at this very moment the three of us would be sitting right here enjoying our wine and each other had there not been a blown tire on a van fifty miles away. But we are only two and there is a great chance we will remain two. I personally dread the thought. I want Link here and I want her here now. And I know Jonathan wants her here. I sense that if Link doesn't make it through this, Jonathan is going to be totally devastated.

His cell phone rings and he retrieves it from his shirt pocket. "Hello. . . . Yes, ma'am. . . . I will. It'll take about fifteen minutes. . . . Okay, I'm on the way."

He hangs up. "Shit, this is not good. Dr. Morgan wants to talk to me." Jonathan releases a long sigh of tension. "We'd better go."

I follow him up to the house regretting having to take each step. It hasn't been long enough for extensive surgery. This is not good. I hope I'm wrong. Please let me be wrong.

After informing Griffin we are on our way. With Jonathan driving, I can see he is very concerned. The mood is doom and we ride silently hoping we never get there.

Entering the long corridor we walk swiftly toward the Surgical Center reception desk.

The nurse acknowledges us with a cordial smile and asks us to follow her. She opens an office door a few steps down the corridor and motions for us to enter.

We are face to face with Dr. Morgan who rises from his chair behind the desk and waves his hand toward two chairs for us to sit. His facial expression shouts bad news is coming. We sit as he glances at some papers in front of him. I think to myself, there is nothing on those pages you need to look over. Just say it.

He does with a sad shake of the head: "I'm sorry, Mr. Bales, we lost her. She just couldn't hang on. There was too much damage for her to overcome."

Jonathan merely stares at the doctor. I see tears pooling in his eyes. My eyes aren't exactly dry either. I slowly shake my head as I reach over and take Jonathan's hand.

What do you say when they tell you your wife has died. Not much. What do you say when they tell you your best friend and lover has died. The same. Well, here we are, lost in our own silence. We can't go back. She's gone. Damn. There is indeed nothing to say. Let's get the hell out of here.

Isn't the doctor supposed to say some choice words at this point? Is there no protocol for this situation? Who knows? Neither I nor Jonathan have ever been here before. Say something Dr. Morgan. Anything.

John has had enough. He rises to his feet and I follow. He offers his hand across the desk to the doctor. He says hesitantly, "Thanks, Dr. Morgan. We know you did all you could."

Morgan nods but does not speak. I follow Jonathan out of the office and we make the long walk down the corridor toward the exit hand in hand, both silently crying unwiped tears. The misery starts.

Jonathan and I spent the better part of the night getting filthy drunk on his boat dock. There was very little talk. We just needed someone to be with rather than being in bed alone and crying while looking at the ceiling.

Jonathan was a total mess. He sat silently slumped in his chair hardly breathing as he gulped down my shared scotch. Occasionally he would sniff a bit and eventually blow his nose. I guess I was pretty much following his lead.

We finally gave up about sunup. Then he began stressing over the dreaded task of telling the kids of their mother's death as I fixed him the basic breakfast of coffee and Jameson. More liquor; that's what we needed, right? We had consumed enough in the previous eight to ten hours to get the whole neighborhood looped. Why stop at breakfast?

Well, eventually he got the kids up to get it done and I left to do the same at my house. He had a much harder task than I did. Mine came off as good as could be expected.

Jonathan said it wasn't very pretty, particularly when the kids refused to believe it. Eventually the crying started and John had to trek back and forth between their bedrooms to do whatever you do to pacify a kid that just lost a mother.

After about an hour they calmed down enough to ask about the details of her death. He told them the best he could including the gory details as he knew them. They seemed to take it without too much grief, probably because they see the same thing on television daily.

We kept the four kids out of school. At noon I asked Griffin to take them down to the local fast food center to eat. I gave her instructions to bring Jonathan and me a Big McSomething from her choice of the burger joints. I couldn't imagine us eating anything but you can only use alcohol as your fuel source for so long. Of course we didn't eat the burgers.

After threatening him with his life I finally convinced Jonathan about twelve–thirty that there were certain things he needed to do in spite of his grief to prepare for the days to come.

In the early afternoon Cory came by to take Griffin and the four kids skiing. We've decided that we have to keep them busy and that will be Griffin's mission. She cut her classes today at TLU and has agreed that she should take over the guest bedroom at the Bales' for at least a few days. At memorial time she'll move out because we're sure to have both homes full of guests for one night at least. Then we'll decide what her schedule will be.

I called Pep and asked that he postpone picking up the kids until next week so they could be here for Johnny and Jody. He was shocked when I told him of Link's passing as was everyone that we've talked to today. Pep said he would attend the memorial. That's interesting: in her dreams of her funeral Pep wasn't in attendance. As if that makes a difference now.

Jonathan made arrangements with a local funeral home to handle the cremation. He also called the hospital because we left without giving them any information on insurance and whatever else they need.

We made a short trip to the Ski Club by car for a talk with Preacher. He not only agreed to preside over the memorial service, but also offered the club facilities for the ceremony. Jonathan insisted on feeding the attendees so Preacher is going to have his crew come in and prepare several buffets for what we expect to be about four hundred people.

Jonathan chose Tuesday for the memorial service at eleven–thirty in the morning. Immediately I called Bales Publishing with the news of both Link's death and the memorial time. Jonathan has decided that the local Bales' operation will shut down on Tuesday for those that want to attend the memorial. With spouses and children, that will total about one hundred fifty from Bales.

Jonathan made the call to the gallery in Houston and broke the news about Link so they could plan to go it alone during the opening reception. He mentioned that if there are any paintings left after the show closes, he'll decide at that time what is to be done with them.

The manager of the gallery suggested since Link's paintings are so popular, they might consider raising the prices since there will never be any more Link Bales' work available. John left it up to them to decide.

I called the Seguin, Houston, Dallas, Austin and San Antonio newspapers to arrange for the obituary to run on Saturday, Sunday and Monday. Following that we set out to contact all the relatives on both sides of the family. Link's parents were extremely upset and shocked. They will probably fly in from Georgia on Monday and leave on Wednesday. Jonathan's parents and a brother will drive in from Dallas on Monday afternoon.

We got it done. We pretty much accomplished the must do items and made decisions about others to get them in motion. Jonathan is not doing well emotionally but I have us both on a mission to keep us occupied and our minds off of Link's death the best we can—that's both sad and impossible. Will someone please smooth my feathers?

By five o'clock, with my list fulfilled, Jonathan with weary sunken eyes asked me if I'd go sit with him on the dock. Drinking time I assume. There's going to be a bit of that in coming days, at least on my part. I told him we'll have our dock time, to just sit tight. We have people to feed and it won't be fast food. Griffin volunteered to take care of the meal.

This is going to be an interesting group for dinner—Cory and Griffin, Jonathan and me, and four kids. So we are eight, not particularly related for the most part but all on the same page except for Jonathan.

He's out sitting on the back steps drinking—what?—a beer. He never drinks beer. And he looks so sad. Jeez, he's wiping tears. Oh, Link, where are you when we need you? Please go hold his hand. Help him through this. Help all of us.

As Griffin and Cory drive to the supermarket to buy a smoked ham and readymade potato salad, I join Jonathan on the steps. I sit and lay a hand on his knee and glance sideways at him. Without expression I ask, "You okay?"

After a long moment he releases a long–winded sigh. He is looking more haggard by the minute. "This is rough. I feel worse now than I did last night. I wonder how long this is going to go on."

I don't respond as I wonder the same thing. I do know it is going to be a while before either of us are going to heal and move forward. Particularly him.

He shakes his head in dismay. "I think if it weren't for the kids I'd wander off and shrivel up against a tree somewhere and never be found."

I pat Jonathan on the knee and offer a bit of encouragement. "The kids are going to have a very hard time adjusting to their mom being gone. I know it's going to be rough on you but I urge you to be aware of their needs right now. Jack, Bunny and I will help the best we can but most of it is going to fall on your shoulders."

Jonathan is quiet for a moment and I can see his facial expression change into a giant curious question mark.

"What John. What's on your mind?"

He twists his lips under pained squinty eyes. "This beer tastes shitty. How can anyone drink this stuff?"

I laugh and he follows with a chuckle. The first levity we've had today. I stand and go back to the kitchen and return with a mug of merlot. I hand it to him, take the beer and pour the remaining half on the lawn then sit back down beside him.

He gathers his brow in a frown and toasts me with the wine. "Gina, thanks for you guys hanging with me. I can't see myself doing half the shit you're doing for me. It would be more of a disaster than it already is."

I nod as I notice Griffin and Cory's return. I again pat Jonathan on the knee and stand. As I head back to the kitchen I reply, "John, you and your kids are really special. You always will be."

I think oddly as I enter the kitchen, now will somebody please give me a hug; I hurt too.

Cory must have read my mind. He hands me a Chivas and water and points to the breakfast bar. "Grif and I will get dinner on the table. You rest and get drunk. You've had a long day. You deserve it."

I grasp the drink, sit and nod my thanks as tears pool in my eyes. Griffin's eyes have also clouded over. I wonder if she was aware of Link's and my relationship.

A few minutes later the table is set and Cory calls the kids from their television show in the living room. I retrieve Jonathan and we settle around the table and quietly pass around the ham, beans, potato salad and dinner rolls straight from the package.

It is eerily quiet and I finally break the silence. "Thanks Cory, thanks Griffin. There are six people here that certainly appreciate your help . . . and love."

"Amen to that," Jonathan says softly.

They don't reply but smile at each other. Griffin's eyes tear over. These kids are mature beyond their years.

After Griffin and Cory have cleaned and stored the dinner dishes, Cory announces to the kids that it's movie time at the King Ranger Cinema in Seguin. As fortune would have it *Captain America: Civil War* is showing and the kids have been clamoring to see it. Momentarily they are off.

Jonathan and I gladly settle for the dock and a couple of drinks or more. It's been a long emotionally taxing day for the both of us and we are content to sit quietly and listen to the Friday night cacophony on the lake—if only for a moment.

I take a long deep breath and exhale it evenly in hopes that it will calm my nerves. No help. "One day down, Johnny."

Jonathan doesn't reply as he absently scans the lake. What is he thinking? He drearily shakes his head and tears bank in his eyes.

He speaks softly, hoarsely, barely above a whisper with extreme sadness in his eyes. "Do you have this feeling that we could have prevented Link's accident? Ever since we got home from the hospital last night I have been beating on myself that—shit, I should have done something."

"Yeah, John, me too. You and I talked on several occasions recently about this feeling that something was not quite right with Link." I pause in thought. "There's more that I haven't told you, John. Link was having dreams about her pending death for a couple of months."

John stares at me incredulous. "Why didn't she say something to me?"

"She didn't want you to be concerned since there appeared to be nothing that could be done about the dreams. She and I researched death dreams and it seems everything we read, those so called dream experts generally agreed that death dreams just indicate a change coming in one's life, perhaps an emotional one."

"The dreams were the reason you expressed concern to me?"

"Yes, they were."

Jonathan nods in thought. "Well that kind of supports my feelings that we should have done something."

"Since last night I've been thinking the same, but what could we have done? Nothing, John. Not a damn thing."

Jonathan is silent for a moment as he looks up staring at the top of the cypress trees in thought. "You realize one of us could have been with her. She declined my suggestion that one of us go along."

I nod slowly with my brow drawn in thought. "Maybe she sensed that something was going to happen to her; we'll never know."

"I've thought the same thing. This whole deal is getting into the unreal, weird, subconcious—what is it?—spiritual mumbo jumbo."

After a moment I reply, "John, certain people might tell you, just because you can't see or really fully grasp what you're feeling doesn't mean it doesn't exist."

"Umm . . . so what's the purpose of her losing her life? What's with that? How is that supposed to affect me, you and the kids?"

I pat Jonathan's knee for the third time and remove my hand. "Probably in this situation all you're going to get is some old worn out adage."

"And that would be?"

I force a chuckle. "How about, everything that happens to you in life—the good, the bad, the ugly—is meant to happen."

Jonathan tilts his head and forces a thin smile as he glances at me curiously. "Thanks for that, Gina. That's really going to help us through this. You may as well say shit happens and we're all swimming in it for a purpose. Whoopee."

I force a chuckle of sorts: "Yeah, and I suppose you can add, all the shit that has happened is leading us to this very moment—no, make that this very glorious celestial moment, John."

"There you go."

We are silent for several minutes. "I don't know about you, dude, but I'm so tired I feel like I'm going to drop right here."

Jonathan forces a smile. "No sleep will do that to you. I hope both of us sleep tonight."

"What is your plan for tomorrow?"

"Nothing. How about you?"

"I have a few hours work tomorrow and Sunday on the column. I've got to keep ahead of the game, particularly with the massive early part of the week ahead of us. You and I are going to have a heavy schedule on Monday, Tuesday and Wednesday with guests coming in from all directions. That'll surely carry through Wednesday.

"Tomorrow and Sunday I think we need to keep the kids busy. Maybe more skiing if we can get Cory to do a repeat of today. It might be a good idea to take the kids to the Saturday night feed at the club. Perhaps we can get Griffin and Cory to do that also. If they can't I don't mind taking them, but you may not feel up to facing all those curious people."

Jonathan bows his head in thought. "Probably not. At this point I just don't want to do anything but deal with my misery. I'm considering not going to the office next week.

"I don't want to be bothered with anything. I'll make the decision Sunday or Monday. I'm surely not going in on Monday. I must warn you, I might ask you to do your usual second in command duty and fill in for me for however long I decide to be out of the office—one day or one year."

"You're the boss. I'm just your lame brained employee. I'll do whatever you require."

Out of the office for one year? I hope not. Oh, well. I'm sure it's going to be a roller coaster ride for a while and I will handle whatever he desires.

What about me? Yeah, I know, every experience I have is meant to happen. Meant to happen. Meant to happen.

Jeez. *You go girl*, my keeper, coming out of hibernation, pipes in. Where the hell have you been?

I stand and smile at the miserable man sitting in front of me. "John, I can't take anymore. I've got to crash."

He reaches up in tears and takes my hand. "Good thinking. I think I'll hang out here for a while. Good night."

I hesitate as he doesn't release my hand. "Will you be okay? I'd hate for you to fall in the lake and drown because I left you alone."

He grimaces. "Maybe it's meant to happen, Gina."

"Good night, sir."

"Good night again, Gina. I certainly hope you sleep well."

"You, also."

As I trudge up the walk toward my lonely house a thought comes to mind—I haven't had one sexual desire in over twenty–four hours. I guess I'm free. Not.

The weekend presented no particular drama as we all attempt to cope with the death of Link. Saturday morning I assisted Griffin in making breakfast in the Bales' kitchen and later worked until noon on the column.

To give Cory and Griffin a break I took the four kids to Burger King in Seguin for lunch. Jonathan chose not to go and spent a large part of the afternoon in his home office doing who knows what—other than grieving. He looked pretty ragged out after not sleeping for the second night.

In the afternoon Cory and Griffin took the kids skiing. I went along for the ride for a while then spent time on the column. Cory and Griffin took the kids to the club for dinner and they stayed until about ten o'clock. These two kids are a lifesaver for Jonathan and me.

Saturday late, Jonathan and I sat on the dock getting soused. When the children came back from the club he told everyone goodnight and headed off to his bedroom. He was not doing well but what do I know. I don't have any idea how someone copes with the death of a mate. Perhaps he's just going through a normal or usual process. To me he appears to be having a very difficult time.

All I can do is be there for him and his kids in their transition to being without their wife and mother. I sat on my dock and sipped on my Chivas feeling very sorry for myself. I don't think I have ever in my life felt so alone and useless.

I certainly could have used someone to lean on about one o'clock in the morning. I even had the fleeting notion of sneaking into Jonathan's bedroom and laying quietly beside him—or even in his arms. But my keeper protested as that would be pushing Jonathan where he is definitely not ready to go. Maybe he never will be; he won't have the desire to have anything to do with the likes of me.

Of course for once I listened to my subconscious. I will give Jonathan all the space he needs. Sometime later I went to bed. I don't have any idea what time it was. All I know is it was foggy and I was polluted to the hilt.

Apparently I made it to bed without help. And when I woke up this morning still dressed as last night, I seemed to be in one piece—but definitely not at peace with myself. I really hurt for and terribly miss Link.

Then today was kind of a replay of Saturday. I worked on the column in the morning and at noon Griffin, the kids and I headed for one of Seguin's pizza dumps. We are certainly pigging out on fast food.

Griffin and I sat at a separate table and she shared with me that she was aware that something pretty special had been going on with Link and me. She urged me to come to her if I needed someone to lean on or even a private sounding board.

We certainly clicked because we both teared over. It was an unexpected magic moment for me. I felt so much better after talking with her. At least I am not completely alone.

Cory came over later and they took the kids out skiing again. For dinner Cory put hamburgers on the grill and we had chocolate ice cream for dessert.

I have spoken very little to Jonathan as he has been holed up in his office the majority of the day. So, after the dishes are put away I approach Jonathan drinking wine on the back steps and offer him my hand. He smiles faintly and stands. We walk down to his dock with arms loaded with booze and rebooze.

We no more than got settled in our deck chairs when a clap of thunder rumbles above us and a sudden gush of rain threatens to drench us. At least it is a good reason for a quick laugh as we retreat to Jonathan's boat in the covered boathouse.

It is unreal sitting here in a comfortable boat going nowhere while beginning to get crazy drunk and the rain pounding on the tin roof of the boathouse.

Jonathan leans back and rests his head on the back of the seat and closes his eyes. He is looking so old and worn out that I wonder how long it's going to take for him to recover from the pain he has experienced the last three days—or if he ever will.

I study him as I sip on my scotch. His grief and sadness permeate the air around us. And I am helpless to do anything but suffer with him. Please, Link. Help me make him better. Me too, Link. Make me better. Help us both to get through this.

The ever present tears gather in my eyes as I watch his shallow breathing. I want so much to comfort him. And I want him to comfort me, but I can do nothing except stand by and watch. Apparently the same is true for him.

What if he, Link and I had actually had a threesome before she died? Would it have made a difference to Jonathan and me right now? I think it would have made a world of difference. We would be on a completely different plane—a familiarity with each other, a memory of desire and shared passion creating a bond that we don't have now. An open door for each other that is now closed. Well we tried, Link. You really tried.

"Jonathan, you okay?" I ask softly when the pounding of the rain on the roof lets up.

Without opening his eyes or lifting his head, he takes a sip of wine and toasts me with the glass. I can almost see a thin grin. "Slow boat to China."

My tears make their appearance again. "I understand for sure. Shall I cast off, sir?"

He actually smiles and opens his eyes. "I don't think this river goes to China do you?"

I nod as I wipe my tears with the back of my hand. "It does if you want it to."

He sits up and studies me with penetrating, compassionate, teary eyes. "We've been on that slow boat many times over the years, you and me."

"Yes sir, but I think this is going to be the mother of slow boats don't you think?"

"Yes, I'm three days into this and I can tell it's not going to be fun. I'm glad you are riding with me, but I don't think at this point we're going to be much consolation for each other."

'At this point' rings in my ears. He said, 'at this point.' Maybe there is hope for us getting together. I set my drink down on the floor of the boat and gently take his wine and set it next to my drink.

I take both of his hands into mine and look him directly in his eyes. I try to speak but the words are locked in my throat way down deep. I swallow as my tears increase along with his.

"Jonathan, I have to tell you this, and you have to listen and remember in the coming days and weeks." I pause telling myself to not to lose it completely. Just tell him what he needs to hear at this time. "I hurt for you extremely. And I know you are hurting inside like you have never hurt before. No one should have to go through the grief you are experiencing now and in the future."

I pause and try to collect myself as his tears run freely down his cheeks. "John, please know that I love you. I didn't know it at the time but I have loved you since our time at TCU.

"Now, here we are: both of us are in a place that's unfamiliar to us and we are both hurting terribly inside. I promise I'll ride this slow boat to China with you no matter how long it takes, and I'll continue to love and help you the best I can. That's because I do love you very much. And I want nothing in return other than for you to accept my help because of who we were together and who we are now together."

Jonathan lightly squeezes my hands, releases them and wipes his tears. He leans over and places a soft kiss on my cheek. His teary eyes gaze into mine and he says softly:

"Thanks, Gina. I needed to hear that and I'm glad you shared that with me. I do need you. More than you think. I guess, right now, you're the only person that really knows me. That knows my feelings. That knows what makes me tick."

He pauses and with a glimmer of a smile wipes his tears with one hand and mine with the other hand. "And I do need and want your help getting me through this. I will do my best in my misery to return your help, because I love you and I know you feel all alone right now."

I grin at Jonathan. "Wow, are we a mutual admiration society or what?"

He kind of chuckles sadly. "I'm glad we had this little chat. I think we both needed to hear what was said. Perhaps we really can help each other."

"So, perhaps we should end this little confessional and try to get some decent sleep for a change."

He shrugs, "I wish. I think I'll just sit here for a while in my super expensive boat and get highly wasted."

"Can I go with you?"

"As long as you like."

A quick nod. "So, I'm assuming you're not going to the office tomorrow as planned."

"There's more, Gina. I have decided that I'm going to take some time off to deal with my stuff and I want you to take over at Bales in my place."

Crap. I certainly didn't want to hear that. I don't ever want to be in that position at Bales. There are too many people that have the experience that I don't have from all different angles.

"How long do you think, John?" I mumble.

"However long it takes I guess."

"Well okay. I said before I'm at your disposal until you get over what is sure to bug you for a long time. I'll do what it takes."

"Good. I'd hoped you wouldn't bolt on me."

I scratch my head as I take another gulp of my scotch. "I have to say this, John, and again I am only looking at this from my own prospective. Wouldn't you be better served by going to the office every day and losing yourself in your work rather than moping around the house being miserable?"

"Yes, I've thought about it and maybe in the long run you're absolutely correct. But on the short side I don't want to make any decisions about anything other than those that have to do with regaining some semblance of the life I had just a few days ago."

I definitely don't agree but it is my position to support him the best I can both on a personally and business level.

"Alright, John. It's done. However I need to ask a few questions about what my job is. First, do you want me take over and do just what I think you would do? Or do you want me to be in full command?"

"You will be in full command. It's your deal. Handle it without me."

"Are you sure?"

"I'm sure. I have full confidence in you."

I slowly shake my head, gather my brow in a full frown and purse my lips. "If I remember correctly, about Thursday a decision has to be made concerning the purchase of one *Hunter's Almanac*. You would normally be making that decision, but now it becomes my decision. I can blow two or three million bucks right there."

"Uh–huh."

"Is uh–huh all you have to say?"

He grins. "Yes, ma'am."

"Okay, I've been elected queen of Bales' world. When do I start?"

"Tomorrow."

"Tomorrow. Are you going to inform the board of your decision?"

"No, you are. I don't want to be bothered."

I stare at the strange man in front of me. "You are dropping out aren't you?"

"Pretty much."

"And you don't want to know what's going on in your company?"

"Pretty much."

"John, I know you are miserable and hurting inside, but I have to tell you, you're fucking crazy. You don't want me to ask you anything or tell you anything about what's going on?"

"Pretty much."

"So, tomorrow morning I'm going to march into our usual board meeting at ten o'clock and announce to a bunch of shocked men that I am their new boss and if they don't like it they should just suck it up. Is that correct?"

"Pretty much."

"Sir, I hope you won't regret this decision.

"I won't."

"One last thing: do you think your kids are up to going to school tomorrow?"

"Yeah, they need to get back into the thick of things."

"Kind of like their father, huh? Good night, John. Sleep well for a change.

"Good night, Gina. Good luck. Are you okay?"

"Pretty much."

Gina De Georgio

THIRTEEN

Pulling over on the shoulder of Interstate Ten I open my cell phone to Favorites and touch Office Jonathan. John's secretary answers.

"Good morning, Pat, This is Gina Wabbit. . . . Say, Mr. Bales will not be coming in this morning but will you call all the board members and tell them that the board meeting is still on at ten o'clock. . . . Yes. I will be in charge of the meeting. . . . I'm on the way now and will be there by nine–thirty. . . . Okay, and if you haven't already, would you make coffee in Mr. Bales' office. . . . Hey, Pat, that's great. . . . Okay, bye."

"Well, let the show begin," I mumble to myself as I pull back on the highway to San Antonio. There's going to be a ton of people wondering what the hell is going on. Me included.

As I get within blocks of Bales I pull into a parking spot in front of Donut Express. Getting out of the car the smell of freshly cooked donuts assures me that this is good idea.

I carefully place the large box of assorted sugary donuts and jelly rolls on the back seat of my Mercedes. I wonder if this is going to be interpreted as a woman's touch, peace offering or downright bribery. Whatever. If I'm going to run this company I'm going to do it my way, even if it turns out to be a disaster.

Luckily Clement the security guard is out patrolling the parking lot in his cart. I flag him down and coax him to carry the donuts up to Jonathan's office in exchange for his getting his pick of one of them. JB also chooses one as my apology for not having the time this morning for our usual visit.

As the officer and I step out of the elevator Pat eyes me curiously and expresses her usual meek greeting. You best be nice to me, woman. I'm your new boss. Do I feel all powerful or not? Probably not. I am scared out of my skin at having to go before the group of four this morning. I truly hope I don't wet my pants.

After an agonizing moment of looking over the donuts the officer finally chooses one and prepares to leave.

"Clement, on your way out would you ask Pat to join me please?"

He nods. "Yes ma'am. Uh, thanks for the donut." He leaves quickly. I wonder what he is going to think when word reaches him later that I am his new boss.

"Yes ma'am, you wanted to see me?" Pat asks flatly as she stands in the doorway. She is dressed in her usual impeccable outfit, a knee length pleated brown skirt and a sleeveless beige cotton blouse with an attention grabbing plunge of the neckline. She is wearing high dollar dark brown leather stillettos.

I have a fleeting question regarding how she pays for all those expensive clothes on her meager salary. Contrary to my past beliefs about her not being capable of having a decent relationship with any male, maybe she is being kept by one. A rich one.

I speak, reminding myself to be nice. "Yes, Pat. Please come in. Would you like coffee and a donut?"

She lays a hand on her stomach and grimaces. "I'd love a donut but I've been putting on some weight and that's got to stop." She crosses over to the coffee pot and pours a cup while watching me out of the corner of her eyes.

"Thanks for making the coffee. Do you do that daily?"

"Yes, I do. I've forgotten a couple of times and Mr. Bales gives me a hard time about it."

She gazes at me with large brown eyes while gathering her lightly penciled brow. "I was so sorry to hear of Link's death. Is Mr. Bales doing all right?"

"I don't think he is handling her death too well but I don't have any experience in that area to compare. The

246

reason I want to talk to you is, he no longer works here. At least for a while."

Pat's jaw drops as her eyes express confusion. "I don't understand."

"He's decided he needs some time away."

She is definitely shocked. "What about . . . will I still—? My job?"

"Yes, you still have your job with the same duties you have now. You'll just be working under someone else."

She stares at me dumbfounded with her sensuous mouth agape. "Who?"

"You'll be working for me. In fact I want you to be my assistant," I reply seriously with a firm nod.

Her eyes widen and her mouth remains partially open before she attempts to compose herself. She doesn't comment and I wonder exactly what she's thinking. It's obvious she never has cared for me and she has virtually ignored me as long as she's been Jonathan's secretary. Now she works for me. How does she slice that? I'm loving it. Take that, bitch.

Back off Gina. Be nice, my advisor is barking.

You can nearly see the little wheels turning in Pat's brain as she shakes her head. Suddenly a little light turns on in her eyes and in marches the new Patricia.

She actually presents a real full–dimpled smile— the first time I've seen it. "I'll be glad to work for you, Mrs. Wabbit. Will you be working out of this office?"

Amazing. "Partly. I will still be using my fifth floor office as well. I'll use this office for meetings like the Monday morning board meeting. You will still be on this floor and I'll always let you know where I am in case I'm needed."

"Will you be giving me additional duties?"

"Actually yes. I don't have a lot of experience in this job. You have much more than I do, so I hope you will consent to guide me along—show me the way if you will. You will be kind of like my assistant. Can you do that for me?"

Who is this new suddenly confident woman that is smiling genuinely at me? "Yes, but I don't . . . I don't understand. It's obvious we have never . . . you know—"

"Liked each other, Patricia."

She grins hesitantly. "Yeah, maybe worse."

"I assume your name is Patricia, right?"

"Yes."

"But everyone calls you Pat."

"They do."

"Do you like the name Patricia?"

"Yes ma'am."

I reach out to shake her hand. "Patricia, from now on to me you are Patricia. Is that alright with you?"

She grasps my hand firmly. "You will be the only one that calls me Patricia but I would like that."

I feel a familiar yet strange energy spark between us before I release her hand. "And I prefer that you call me Gina. Okay, I'll get with you before lunch to discuss the how and what of our job relationship. For right now I would appreciate your not telling anyone I'm the new boss because you are the only one that knows.

"After the board meeting your first duty will be to message the company employees worldwide." I slip open my notebook, take out a page and hand it to her. "There will be two different messages—one for those that work locally about the memorial service, Mr. Bales stepping down and my taking over his job, and about a paid holiday tomorrow. The other message for the global employees will be different, telling of Link's death, the management change and our local closing tomorrow. Okay?"

"Yes. I'll send them when the meeting is over."

"Good. I appreciate your support." I look at my watch. "Jeez, it's just about meeting time. Please don't bring this week's publications to the meeting. We have enough ground to cover without them."

"Yes ma'am. Is that all you need right now?"

"I would appreciate it if you would sit in at the meeting."

Again her mouth drops in surprise. "But I'm not on the board. Won't they—?"

I grin as I cut her off. "Bring a pad. Act like you're taking notes."

Wow, another face crossing smile. "Yes ma'am," she beams.

She is barely out the door when Josh Butler and Jesse Ferro arrive. After the usual greetings they head for the coffee. Upon seeing the donuts they mumble something to each other and turn and look at me. I shrug and smile. They dig in.

Darren Boyd is next, followed immediately by Chris Hunter. Upon greeting us they both see the partially eaten donuts of their colleagues.

"What's this?" Chris asks while sticking a finger in the jelly of Jesse's roll. He licks the jelly off his finger. "Wow, who's responsible for this good stuff?"

Nobody answers so Chris and Darren head for the coffee station. They return momentarily with coffee and two donuts each. Everyone becomes quiet as they gorge themselves.

Their food sinfulness is interrupted by the entrance of the newly confident Patricia. A brow or two is raised when she takes a seat on one of the three vacant chairs and sets her coffee and legal pad in front of her. I wink at her and she projects that wide dimpled smile. Damn, she is a looker when she smiles. And sexy. The guys certainly notice. Particularly Chris who is studying her with penetrating blue eyes.

I walk over to the coffee urn and fill my cup and a carafe. Returning I refill Josh's cup and place the carafe in the center of the table. Another raised eyebrow or two. What the hell is Gina up to?

Well, here goes. Should I stand or sit? I'd better sit just in case my legs nervously collapse underneath me. I take a long sip of coffee and every eye in the room is focused on me. I feel a wave of confusion emanating from the men sitting in front of me.

It's Patricia's turn to wink and smile at me. Of course she knows what's going on.

I clear my throat and present a forced smile. "Gentlemen, as you know, Mr. Bales wife Link was lost in a van accident on Thursday morning. Jonathan, uh, Mr. Bales is taking it extremely hard. In fact I fear personally that he is going to have a very difficult time in the next few weeks or even months.

249

"I have spent a large amount of time with him and his kids since late Thursday afternoon when we heard of the accident. As most of you know I and my kids live next door. He and I have been good friends since our college days together. We, my kids and I, will keep close watch on the Bales and help them through this the best that we can."

I pause and sip my coffee to collect my thoughts. "Since we have released very little information about her accident I want to give you a brief account of what happened. You are welcome to pass this information along. As you may well know, Link was an artist—a painter. Her work is appreciated all over the southwest, particularly Houston, Dallas, Austin and San Antonio.

"She had delivered paintings with a rented van to a gallery in Houston for a solo show that opened on Saturday. Returning to Lake McQueeney she had a blowout on the right front tire, lost control of the van which rolled over several times and hit a tree. Unconscious, she was airlifted to a hospital in Seguin where she died several hours later during surgery.

"I have no way of knowing what it is like to lose a loved one but thus far the grief is overwhelming for Mr. Bales."

I take another sip of my brew. Darren refills his cup from the carafe and I pass mine down for him to top off.

"We have arranged with our local country club on Lake McQueeney to have a memorial service for Link tomorrow at eleven–thirty. After the service a buffet luncheon will be served for all attendees that desire to stay and eat with us. By the way, we expect somewhere near four hundred to attend.

Mr. Bales has arranged with the club to remain open until four o'clock and he suggests that you and your family—kids are certainly invited—to spend the rest of the day having fun in honor of Link. The club has a game room for the kids, a beach for swimming in the lake and it also has a large swimming pool, golf and tennis if you choose. There will be rooms set up for you to change into swimwear.

"By the way, Mr. Bales has no problem with you and your family dressing casually for the memorial—in fact he encourages it.

"We have ordered several kegs of beer that will be provided free to Link's guests as long as it lasts. There will also be an open bar to use at your expense." I smile, "Sorry, Link said not to provide you booze other than beer."

There are several chuckles. "Good thinking," Josh nods.

You will receive a notice today before noon with directions to the country club. Now, as Mr. Bales feels that most of the local employees, their spouses and kids will wish to come to the memorial, I am going to shut down local operations completely tomorrow."

It certainly didn't go unnoticed that I said that I am going to shut down operations as the four first stare quizzically at me and then at each other. They have to feel that something important is coming down.

"The closing procedure will be in the message you receive before noon. It will include what you tell those in your department about the message they will leave on their company cell phones. The message on the company land lines will be handled by JB through the main switchboard.

"All and all, this building will be locked tight tomorrow. Absolutely no one will be on duty, and no one's pay will be docked for this work holiday."

I pause and look over the group as they watch me knowing there is more. "In support of Mr. Bales, I encourage each employee and his or her family to come to the memorial. He wants to honor Link but also expressed that she would want everyone to have a good time in sending her off. Come early if you like. We'll have coffee, soft drinks and pastries starting about nine–thirty."

I quickly look each in the eye. "Questions so far?"

None. Well, here goes: "Next, Link's death has necessitated a change in the administration of Bales Publishing. As of this morning, Jonathan Bales will still remain the owner of BP but is no longer going to be on the campus in his CEO position."

I pause and see concern on each person's face except for Patricia. "Overruling my objection, Mr. Bales has appointed me to take over his position. I didn't then and I don't now want this job. He insisted and said my loyalty to him should win out."

There are four definitely shocked faces staring at me—as they should be. However, no matter what they feel, it is what it is and I definitely will not apologize for honoring Jonathan's wishes. I wait for comment.

After a long tense silent moment, it's the one with the most experience and logical choice for the job—Josh Butler: "Uh, not to take anything away from you, Gina. I think we question Mr. Bales' choice as the experience and tenure of everyone in this group certainly outweighs yours."

"Your concern is well taken, Josh. And I agree. I personally put that question to Mr. Bales and he pointedly said that he is choosing the person that he feels is best for the job regardless of those that might feel slighted. He also said that if I didn't take the job he might bring in an outsider."

I pause and study the faces staring at me. "Other thoughts?"

Chris clears his throat and slightly lifts a hand off the table but decides against speaking. "Out with it, Chris. This has to be settled before this meeting is adjourned."

"Gina, I fully support his choice as it's certainly his to make, but I'm concerned about the future of this company and even our jobs if he's leaving permanently. Do you think he's going to sell the company? If that's the case everyone sitting at this table including you may be without a job."

"Absolutely, Chris. Let me briefly tell you what I think is going on with Mr. Bales. Bottom line: he is a mess. He thinks the misery he's going through is going to last forever and he's kind of given up.

"He's not suicidal by any means but extremely down on life. He feels like he's lost everything and he doesn't care to deal with the blessings that he has. I urged him to come to work to get his mind on something else but he completely refused.

"I asked him how long he intended to be away. He said perhaps a year or more."

I pause and bite at my lower lip in thought. "Personally I don't believe it. This is just my guess but I think he will get himself together in a short time and decide he wants to get back to work.

"No, I don't see him selling this company. He may not realize it but his kids and this company are all that he has. He will come around; I have no idea when. Right now I'm more concerned about his kids than I am about this business."

I pause for more questions. None forthcoming I add: "To show you his state of mind, after he told me to take this position I asked if I could come to him for advice when we needed it. His answer was no, just handle it. Just take charge. No matter what the problem is he feels like we will do the right thing. If we don't do the right thing or make a wrong decision he said that was not a problem.

"I questioned him about the Hunter's *Almanac* decision coming up. He said that you all would have a handle on it. Get the information and make a decision. It won't be wrong. He didn't want to discuss it additionally."

I spread my arms. "Any other?"

They don't look happy but they have no more questions. "All right. What are my expectations of you? I really want you guys to carry on like you've done with Mr. Bales here. You do your job as usual and handle all the problems the best you can.

"If you need an executive decision I will make it. Otherwise I will leave you alone to do your job; I have no intention of getting in your way or micromanaging. For the most part I will be working out of my office on the fifth floor. We will use this one for meetings and what have you.

"No one knows Mr. Bales and his procedures better than Patricia, so she will be assisting and guiding me. She will also be joining us at these board meetings at my request.

"If you need me quickly you can call me on my cell or she will know my whereabouts. Like Mr. Bales my door will always be open and I suggest you tell it like it is when you deal with me—good or bad. I've been cussed at before and I'm sure it'll happen again. I'm not into coming down on anyone that is keeping me afloat.

"Questions, anyone?" I pause and cock a curious brow. "Okay, we'll meet Thursday at ten at this table. I assume you will have the info and recommendations for the *Hunter's* decision. We'll hash it out and see what happens. By the way, Mr. Bales said he doesn't want to know what the decision is. I find that extremely interesting.

"Gentlemen, thanks for coming and I hope I can count on your support. I assume you and your families are coming to the memorial tomorrow. Be careful out there, please. This company certainly doesn't need another accident like Link's. This meeting is adjourned."

Three of the guys leave without comment. Chris joins Patricia and me. He extends his hand and while we shake he trains his penetrating blue eyes on me. "Hang in there. They will come around. Call me if you need any help."

"Thanks, Chris. You don't know what that means to me. I don't want to be in this position, but I am and I intend to do my best with your and their help."

We walk out to Patricia's area and Chris mentions to Patricia that he would pick her up if she wants to ride with him to the memorial service. She declines and after a short goodbye Chris is off to the elevator.

"All right, lady, let's get those messages out. I have to pick up Link's parents at the airport and I certainly don't want to be late."

The last time I saw Link's parents, Jethro and Grace King, was when they visited three summers ago. They are getting along in age; I judge them to be in their early eighties. Jethro retired from farming their four hundred acres and now leases it to a farming conglomerate that pays him more than he used to make without the hard work. He says very little but is the type you definitely listen to when he does. In Jonathan's opinion it's because Grace doesn't give him a chance to talk.

Grace still maintains her duties of tending a small vegetable garden, chickens, fruit trees and keeping house for the two of them. She is active in her church and has held a position on the board for over forty years. She has missed very few meetings and is very outspoken when she feels her church is drifting off course. In fact she is outspoken about everything whether she is right or not. She is certainly Link's mom but the red hair has long ago turned gray.

I arrive at the San Antonio International Airport in plenty of time but have difficulty finding a parking spot in short term parking close to the terminal. There's no way I want them to get lost in the terminal so I take off my heels and actually sprint. Reading the incoming schedule I find that their flight has arrived fifteen minutes ago.

I slip my heels back on and walk quickly to Corridor B security check where incoming passengers are funneled through a narrow hallway on their way to baggage. I can't possibly miss them there.

Perfect timing: following a large group of incoming passengers are two old folk trudging absently along holding hands and pulling their carryon carts. It is apparent they are not bothered by the hubbub of a giant airport.

When they get near I step out in front of them and present a welcome smile. "Hi, Jethro, Grace. I'm glad you made it in okay."

They both stare blankly at me before Grace smiles her recognition. "Jethro, it's Gina."

I extend my hand first to Jethro, then Grace. I'm taken aback by their fragile hands when I grasp them and it reminds me of JB's hand. I guess that's part of getting old—skinny vein–streaked hands as well as wrinkled and liver blotched skin.

She is dressed in your typical calico loose–fitting granny dress with a beige cotton blouse. Her shoes are black lace up oxfords polished to perfection. He is wearing apparently home–sewn blue denim trousers, a light blue chambray shirt and what is probably his Sunday go to meeting black shoes.

They both wear wire rimmed glasses and Jethro wears the old style hearing aids that protrude from his ears. These people are definitely old but appear to be hanging in there.

It is readily apparent to me that it is good that they have each other. It also saddens me that they have to experience the tragic death of their only child during their lifetime.

Jethro merely smiles as Grace does the talking. "Hello, Gina. We're so glad you could pick us up. We would never be able to get to the lake by ourselves."

"It was no trouble at all. I was in town already. Jonathan would have come to get you but I made him stay and work on the memorial plans since I was close by anyway."

"Let's find an exit where you can wait while I get the car and pick you up. It's parked a long way from here and I don't want you to have to walk."

"Oh, Gina," Grace scolds. "We may be old but we can still walk. It may take us a while but we'd get there for sure."

Jethro nods his agreement.

I smile compassionately. "No, we've got a long day ahead and I don't want to wear you out. I'll get the car."

I nest them on the first bench that is convenient to picking them up and head to the car. No sprinting this time.

Opening my phone I punch Jonathan's number. There's no answer so I leave a message: "John, the package has arrived in one piece at the airport and I'm walking to get the car so I can pick them up curbside. I don't know if they've had lunch or not so we might be a couple of hours getting home. Gina."

It's my lucky day. The car is exactly where I left it. I never park in an airport parking lot without my car moving to another space where I can't find it.

I negotiate the pay booth and head back around to the passenger pickup area. The traffic is relatively light and I find a place to pull curbside directly in front of the Kings. I get out of the car to help them load their carryon luggage. I quickly open the trunk and join them. They look at me like I'm a complete stranger.

Jethro finally smiles. "Gina's back, Grace."

She looks at him curiously and then at me and smiles. "Gina, you're back."

I'm beginning to think this old couple shouldn't be traveling beyond the local supermarket without a chaperone. Well, they made it here and I'll keep an eye on them as well as arrange for an airline escort to make sure they are boarded when it's time to return home. Jeez, I hope I never get old.

I grab their luggage before they are able to get up, put it in the trunk and open the front and back door of the car for them. It is their job to decide who sits where. After a moment of bickering she decides that she will sit in the front with me. She has difficulty getting in and he shrugs as he slowly takes his seat in the back. Maybe I should say, his usual back seat to her.

Everyone settled in I pull away from the curb and head for Loop 410. The traffic is light. I glance sideways at Grace. "Did you all have a good flight?"

Grace grins. "Great. That lady asked if we wanted coffee or some other beverage. I told her we both wanted one of those bloody drinks."

I chuckle to myself. "Do you mean Bloody Mary?"

"Yes, Gina. That's it. Have you ever had one? They are really good."

I think to myself, have I ever had a Bloody Mary? How many Bloody Marys a week do I have? "Yes, I've had one. I liked it. Did you just have one on the plane?"

"No, we had two each. They taste like tomato juice with lemon and something hot in it."

Jethro jumps right into the conversation. "Three. We had three, Grace. Don't you remember? That lady asked if we ever had three before and you said, every day."

Oh, shit. No wonder they are spaced out. Maybe they are not so old after all. They are simply drunk. Three Bloody Marys, even though small, would space out a seasoned drinker. What would they do to a nondrinker?

"So, Grace, do you have an occasional alcoholic beverage?"

"Oh, no ma'am. Reverend George says alcohol is the drink of the devil. He says a little Communion Wine is okay though. Why do you ask?"

"Oh, uh, just curious. You think maybe you'll have another of those Bloody Mary drinks when you fly back home?"

Grace turns and looks at her husband. "What do you think, Jethro?"

He projects a wide smile. "Of course. And we ought to see if we can buy some at the grocery store. We could have one every morning with breakfast."

Oh, my. Thanks, Southwest Airlines.

"Have you folks had lunch? Did they feed you on the airplane?"

"Just some of those pretzel things and some peanuts. They were grown in our hometown. Can you imagine? They fed us our own peanuts."

"Umm, would you all like to stop and get some lunch? It's going to be a while before dinner."

Grace turns and I see Jethro in the rearview mirror shake his head. "Not me."

"Me neither. No, we're okay, Gina. So I guess you can go on home."

"Okay folks, home it is."

After riding silently for several minutes on Loop 410 on our way to Interstate 10, Grace touches me on my knee. "Gina?"

"Uh-huh."

Do you or Jonathan have some of those Bloody Mary drinks at home?"

Southwest Airlines, what have you done to our fragile elders? Reverend George, I think you have a couple of sinners and they don't even know they're sinning.

"I'm sure, Grace. I'll tell you what: I'll have Jonathan put out the ingredients on the table with a recipe so you can make your own."

Oh, me. Talk about the great awakening. I've got to see this. Probably a YouTube moment.

The rest of the trip was uneventful and mostly silent. Link's death wasn't mentioned and that was fine with me. I certainly wouldn't know what to say to an old couple that has tragically lost their only child.

When we pull into Jonathan's driveway I glance at the dash clock. Two o'clock. Now if the rest of the day goes as well as it has so far I'll be content in spite of the circumstances.

I honk for Jonathan and he comes out the front door and waves as he approaches. He looks more old and worn than he did this morning. Grief isn't treating him well. He opens both the front and back door for his in–laws.

He takes Grace's hand and assists her out of the car. "Hello, lady. Give me a hug." As they hold onto each other Jethro climbs out of the back seat and waits.

I stand by and watch this unwanted reunion and silently dread the next two or three days.

After a long moment Jonathan and Grace release their hold on each. They both have tears pooling in their eyes. Now me.

Jonathan forces a smile and takes Jethro's hand. "Good to see you, old man."

Jethro shakes Jonathan's hand with a hint of a smile. "Johnny, sorry about your loss," he says flatly.

John nods and releases Jethro's hand. "Our loss. Let me get your bags and we'll go in."

I open the trunk and assist by removing one of the bags and commence to drag it up the walk toward the front door. Jonathan follows with the other and the old folks slowly bring up the rear. I wonder if the Vodka is wearing off.

I pause and Jonathan passes me to open the door. I follow him inside and down the hall to the guest bedroom. The Kings silently follow.

"I think you'll find everything you need. If there is something I haven't thought of just say so and we'll get it."

They nod and I can't help but say, "A couple of nice cold Bloody Marys would be great, John."

The Kings smile and Jonathan looks at me in confusion. "What? Uh, never mind," he says to me.

"Later, dude," I smile at Jonathan and wink at the old couple.

Soon the four of us are out sitting outside on the patio drinking iced tea that Jonathan had previously made for this sure to be awkward moment. We sit quietly looking down at the calm lake. A light breeze is blowing and the midday temperature is perfect. If only the subject was a little more pleasant. I wait for Jonathan to take the lead.

I watch him puff out a breath of building tension and make eye contact with the Kings who are sitting in the cushioned, white wicker swing holding hands.

Jonathan clears his throat and gazes at the old folks with tears in his eyes. "I am so glad to see you, but I wish it could be under better circumstances. If you feel like I do, you must be dying inside.

"I have never felt this hurt and alone. I wish I could take away your pain but I cannot. I'm having a very difficult time accepting that this is actually happening to us—both of you, Jody and Johnny, me and even Gina and her kids."

He pauses and I'm sure he's hoping for some comment from the Kings to move the conversation along. There is not a dry eye on the patio.

It is Grace. "Reverend George reminded us yesterday that Link is in a much better place and we should be happy for her. She is home. That doesn't mean that we shouldn't grieve for her . . . that we shouldn't miss her, but it is in God's plan. We should accept her passing the best we can and carry on. That's what she would want . . . or does want."

She pauses and I wonder if those words hit home for Jonathan. Probably not. I know it doesn't soothe my hurt. Maybe it will later.

Suddenly Jethro says softly, tears running steadily down his cheeks, "The pastor said it's all God's will—everything."

Grace's beams up at her husband through her own tears.

Jonathan doesn't comment as he sneaks a sideways glance at me. Recalling our earlier conversation I can only wink at him. I wonder if their getting soused by Bloody Marys was God's will—everything.

My caretaker is shaking her head: *Get a grip, Gina. This is serious.*

After a long silence Grace asks while dabbing at her tears with a hankie retrieved from her pocket, "You have the memorial all set up, do you?"

Jonathan nods, "Pretty much. As a favor to us the proprietor of our local country club is handling all the details. He is as a retired clergyman happy to officiate. Gina and I have given him all the details he needed about Link that he didn't already know." He pauses and adds "He will do a great job, I'm sure."

I nod in agreement as I head to the kitchen to get the tea pitcher. As a second thought I quickly plate cheese, bits of ham, fancy crackers, pickles and olives for the Kings to snack on. When they come down from Bloody Mary high they will surely be hungry.

As I set the plate on the glass topped white wicker coffee table in front of them and refill their tea glasses, Jethro smiles and quickly finger picks the cheese and crackers. Grace is not far behind and I regret not stopping and force feeding them after picking them up. Well hopefully this will hold them over until Griffin and Cory provide us dinner.

After some brief talk about the details of the accident the Kings announce that it is nap time and take their leave with Jonathan showing them the way. A moment later he returns.

He sits and looks wearily at me while biting his lower lip. He looks so sad and unhappy. I wish there is something I can do to make him better but there is nothing. Same for me. Here we are: Link's husband and lover sitting across from each other missing her together. Weird.

"What are you thinking, John?"

He slowly shakes his head, forces a false smile at me and asks, "Do I have to think right now?"

He pauses and looks at me sadly. "Gina, thanks for what you are doing. Without you, Griffin and Cory I would have come undone completely. I wish so much that Wednesday was over so it would be done and everybody can get on with . . . with whatever."

I choose not to comment because I'm sure he wasn't fishing for a reply. He merely wanted me to listen. I can try to do that.

"So, John. Do you want to hear what went on at BP today?

He shakes his head gloomily. "Since you are here in one piece I assume you survived. That's all I want to know."

I slip away from Jonathan to go home and change out of my work clothes into something casual before the kids get home from school. They arrive promptly at three–thirty. "Hey guys, how did it go today?"

Bunny answers with her usual shrug. "Okay, Mom."

"Jack?"

"Pretty good. But this morning everybody was asking about the accident. Jody and Johnny were getting kind of ragged out about it, so me and Bunny told everybody to shut up about their mom's accident."

"Jody and Johnny got through the day pretty well then?"

"Yeah, they got through their classes okay. At lunch we had to tell the kids again to leave them alone."

"You think it was all right that Jonathan sent them to school today so soon after their mom died?"

Bunny nods, "They did better today at school than they did yesterday at home."

I smile at both. "Thank you for helping them. I would appreciate you both hanging close to them in the coming days. It's going to be hard on them adjusting to not having their mother around."

"We know, Mom," Jack replies. "You've already told us twice. We'll take care of them."

I run my finger across my mouth to zip it up. "I'm sorry. I know you're trying to take care of them. They need you right now."

I pause as they wait for anything else I have to say. "Okay here's the plan. We'll go over to the Bales for dinner tonight. I don't know how many people are going to be there but I picked up the kid's grandparents at the airport so they will be there for sure.

"Jonathan's mother and father and I think his brother and maybe his wife are due about now from Dallas. They are driving in. That's about twelve right there and maybe some others that I don't know about."

"Wow, that's a lot of people, Bunny exclaims. "Where are they going to sit at dinner?"

To start with Griffin, Cory and some of their friends will be cooking here at our house and they will bring the food over when it's ready. We won't be sitting at the table. It'll be kind of like a buffet. You fill your plate and go sit . . . wherever—on the boat dock if you want."

"Are Granddad and Granny coming tonight?"

"No, they are not that far away so they'll drive in tomorrow in time for the service.

Jack is figuring on his fingers. "That's a lot of people. Are some staying here?

"So far, no one is staying here. Jonathan's mom and dad and brother are staying in the lodge at the country club. We have several more rooms there if we need them so I don't think anyone will be staying here unless Griffin wants to stay here to get a quick start on breakfast."

At four o'clock Griffin and Cory arrive with a couple of friends to cook dinner for sixteen people. They're loaded with a cooler of beer and seven plastic sacks of groceries and three flat boxes.

The kids have already said that this is about the Bales family. They intend to cook and serve twelve people dinner. After that is taken care of, they will clean up, then eat at my house.

They have decided on lasagna as their main course with vegetable salad on the side and freshly baked Italian rolls. Dessert will be warmed apple pie with either melted cheddar cheese or vanilla ice cream.

After giving the kids a brief tour of the kitchen I get out of their way and let them have at it. Griffin directs traffic as the kids set out to have their meal ready to serve by seven o'clock.

Making sure they have everything under control and no longer need my assistance, Jack, Bunny and I head over to the Bales.

Jody and Johnny are sitting in the living room with their grandparents that they haven't seen for quite some time. They are in animated conversation about school and there is a great deal of laughing about the kids exploits.

I interrupt to reintroduce Bunny and Jack to Grace and Jethro whom they haven't seen for three years.

"My, my!" Grace exclaims. "You two have grown so much. What are you feeding them, Gina?"

I make sure my two are dutifully visiting and leave to find Jonathan. I stop in the kitchen and get a wine glass and head out the back door. He is on the back patio sitting near the wicker table sipping on merlot while he gazes out over his lake.

"Mr. Bales. How's it going?" I greet as I sit beside him and fill my glass from the half empty bottle.

He smiles and rests his hand on my knee, sending that familiar bolt of energy zipping down my spine to that crazy distant place. "Just hanging in there and wishing this whole show would end."

I release a light breath of tension as I lay my hand on his knee and squeeze lightly. "Yeah, myself. We'll still have two more days after today, then you can figure out what your new normal is going to be."

He sadly shakes his head and removes his hand from my knee as I silently beg him to leave it there. All I want is just a little attention. Nothing more. I think.

"Umm, I don't know where to start on that little chore. I guess I have no choice however."

I squeeze his knee and remove my hand. "Just go with the flow, John. Go with the flow."

That's easy for you to say, comes my guardian's tweet. Just leave me be, please.

After a moment of uneasy silence I smile and John spreads his hands. "What up, Gina?"

"I have to tell you what happened this afternoon with Link's mom and dad. You could probably use a good laugh about now."

"Go for it. I indeed could use a little levity."

"When I picked them up at the airport they really seemed out of it. They didn't recognize me to start with and I felt it was because they we just getting old."

I pause while John waits. "Well, they told me that when the stewardess asked them on the plane if they wanted refreshment, Grace ordered Bloody Marys not knowing exactly what they are.

John flashes a grin and cocks that familiar brow. "My in–laws, the teetotalers ordered an alcoholic drink? I wonder if lightning struck nearby."

"That's not all. They liked them so much they each had two more."

John chuckles. "Shit, it's a wonder you didn't have to carry them to the car."

"You're telling me. Anyway on our drive home Grace asked me if we could make them a Bloody Mary. I told her you could probably do that but I suggested that they ask you to show them how to make one for themselves—you know, set the ingredients out for them. Let them discover the Vodka and let the fun begin."

Jonathan slowly shakes his head and grins. "I certainly don't want to tell them that they've been drinking the evil hooch, but if they find out for themselves—they don't have to admit it to us if they don't want to. I love it. Let's do it."

"Maybe if you write out the basic steps and leave the ingredients for them to sort through on the table, we can step back and watch. This is going to be a major shock and we should take care to not laugh."

I follow him into the kitchen and he sits down at the table and carefully writes out the directions. He places the sheet of directions on the table and behind it he sets a bowl of ice and a bottle of Uncle Tom's Bloody Mary Mix. Behind the mix he places a stalk of celery and a pepper shaker. Last, the punch line to our little charade, he sets his one liter blue bottle of Skyy Vodka.

Jonathan's eyes actually brighten in anticipation. He rubs his hands together. "All right. Here we go."

I follow him into the living him and he stands behind the kids. Jody is telling her granny and grandpa an animated story. Story ends and Jonathan gains Grace's attention.

"Yes, John?" she queries.

"Umm, Gina told me that you want to learn how to make Bloody Marys for you guys. Are you sure you want to do that? That's a pretty strong drink."

Grace's eyes sparkle and Jethro grins. "Of course we do. They charged thirty bucks for six drinks on the plane. Surely we can make them cheaper than that."

She glances sideways at her husband. "What do you think, Jethro? You want another Bloody Mary?"

"Sure 'nuff. Let's do it."

"Good," Jonathan says while clapping his hands together. "I have the recipe and the ingredients set out on the kitchen table. All you have to do is follow my directions. It's quite simple."

Jethro is already getting up and extends his hand to help Grace. They hobble off toward the kitchen.

Jonathan calls out to them. "You all read the directions and check out the ingredients and I'll be there shortly in case you need help. Gina and I need to talk to the kids a moment."

The kids are watching us curiously as we grin at each other. "You guys stay right where you are right now. Gina and I are playing a joke on the old people."

Jonathan and I approach the kitchen door and peak in, careful not to be seen by Grace and Jethro. They finish reading the instructions and, one at a time, check out the ingredients while making comments about each one. Then Jethro picks up the Vodka and his jaw drops to a full gape. He points at the label and Graces eyes widen in shock.

Jonathan and I pull away from the door and rejoin the kids while suppressing a laugh. The kids look at us puzzled but don't say anything. What kind of joke is this?

Momentarily the Kings come out of the kitchen and Jonathan asks the kids a meaningless question as a diversion. The kids exchange eye rolls.

"What do you think?" Jonathan asks Grace.

She fidgets a bit and her eyes are troubled.

"Is something the matter, Grace?" Jonathan asks seriously making a point to lift a brow.

Grace looks at Jethro and he nudges her with a finger to her ribs. "Tell him, Grace."

Jonathan plays it to the hilt. "What is it, Grace?"

"I'm afraid . . . well nobody told us. We didn't have any idea . . . we didn't know Bloody Marys had, you know, alcohol. We don't . . . Jethro and I don't use, don't drink liquor."

Jonathan places a hand over his mouth in mock surprise. "Oh, I'm sorry, Grace. I thought maybe you had changed—that George, uh, Reverend George had changed and allows you to have a cocktail on occasion. But you're right. Those folks on the airplane should have told you that you were getting an alcoholic drink."

An uncomfortable situation is saved by the bell— the doorbell. Jody runs to the front door. Opening the door she is greeted by her other grandparents.

"Hey, Grandma, Grandad. Wow! And Uncle Bob and Aunt Shirley. Come in."

She steps aside to let the guests in as Jonathan approaches and takes his mom into his arms. Then he hugs Shirley and shakes the hands of his dad and brother.

"Come in, folks. The party is just beginning."

There is a round of greeting with my bringing up the rear after Jethro and Grace.

"Come on out to the patio and we'll break out the bottle of your choice." John announces as he winks at Jethro and Grace, "If that's okay with you, Grace?"

Grace blushes and nods. Jethro smiles. How could she object—an old sot that she is? Just don't tell Pastor George.

We congregate on the patio and I take orders for their drink of the day. I send Bunny next door to bum a beer for Bob and return to the kitchen. I load a tray and it's back to the patio with glasses and bottles of merlot and chardonnay, I set them on the table and step back for them to serve themselves.

I ask the Kings if they want iced tea or whatever and they decline. No, Grace, we don't spike the tea. And Reverend George will never know your little sin unless you tell him. They would probably be better off the next couple of days if they would mellow out with a little wine or a Bloody Mary.

Oh, well. This show is indeed on the road. We should reach the top the hill about noon tomorrow. I look over the group and find Jonathan staring at the lake sadly. Lots of sadness in this group. Me too.

I sneak away and head to my house. The mood is entirely different here. The kids are in a party mode as they drink Mexican beer and cook Italian food. The couple helping out are the best buds of Cory and Griffin. They are members of the junior class at TLU and are living in the same apartment complex.

Leslie and Denny are both on athletic scholarships—men and woman's basketball. And they look the part. He is six foot seven and she is six foot two, an Amazon of a woman but beyond beautiful in every sense of the word. He's not bad either. At least he would be on my radar if I was twenty years younger. But, then again, I think every male over the age of twenty is on my radar. Helpless. *You've got that right, Gina.*

Anyway, it looks to me like they are on schedule with dinner. It certainly smells like it. Leslie and Griffin return to the Bales with me to scope out how they are going to present the food. They decide to use the dining room table for the buffet.

After I introduce them to the group they ask if anyone wants a beverage with their dinner other than what they are drinking now. The kids and Kings agreed that iced tea would be great for them. The others elect their wine and Bob sticks with Cory's Mexican beer. Griffin and Leslie return next door.

Jonathan is slowly walking Link's parents down to the dock and it strikes me that with Link gone Jonathan is all they have left. Sad.

I join the group and seek out Jonathan's father and mother. Both in their late seventies, they are trim and apparently fit. Barney is taller than Jonathan but they share many of the same features. His beard and hair are salt and pepper, and his hair, unlike Jonathan's, is medium in length and well–coiffed. And he is sexy as all get out. But what do I know?

Tex is striking. Any women in her seventies would love to look like this lady. White hair in a short pixie cut frames deep blue eyes. She looks like she has stepped right off the cover of a fashion magazine. Jonathan mentioned that several years ago he tried to get her to pose for some pictures for a feature on older women in one of our fashion rags. She would have none of it.

Now Bob. The first of the two offspring of Barney and Tex Bales is older than Jonathan by two years. They definitely don't look like brothers. Bob has many of his mom's facial features highlighted by the same blue eyes and trim build. It is apparent that he spends time in the gym. He is sexy but Jonathan more so. Of course I'm a bit prejudiced.

Bob, like his brother was assisted big time by his parents when he was getting started in his business. He owns one of the larger long haul trucking businesses in the southwest. He has made a statement several times: "As long as we can buy diesel, I'm good no matter what the cost."

I wonder about Bob's wife Shirley. Jonathan often calls her Bob's trophy wife. She doesn't relate too well with me but in her defense we haven't been around each other very often. Long and lithe with shoulder length straight brunette hair and a perfectly tanned body she is a beauty that's for sure.

No doubt the Bales are an interesting bunch. Of all the Bales I like Jonathan the best however. That's probably because we have interacted over a lot of years. Perhaps we can still interact some in the future after we send Link off. *That's terrible, Gina.*

I top off Barney's wine and he nods his thanks. "Barney, did you stop by the lodge and get checked in?"

"Did that. Nice little room. Looks to be very comfortable."

Tex interjects, "And that Preacher guy is something else. Nice as can be."

I chuckle, "Yeah, we're lucky to have him. He's a fantastic man. He will definitely give you the shirt off his back if you need it. There are countless stories of his helping people that just happen to cross his path and are in need.

"He and Link have . . . well, had teamed together to provide a Mexican Thanksgiving Dinner to the homeless or those that don't have the means to celebrate with food like we do. They feed a thousand people every year, and it's completely financed by donations and the workers are all volunteers. Preacher told Jonathan and me Saturday that Link is irreplaceable. He doesn't know what he's going to do without her ramrodding the dinner."

Bob follows, "Preacher mentioned that he is officiating at the memorial. It seems to me John made a good choice."

"Yes, he's definitely got experience. Years ago he founded and financed his own church. We don't know much about it and he won't say, but apparently it had a very large congregation. For whatever reason the board voted to ask him to leave and returned his original investment in the church."

"Interesting," Barney says while stroking his beard just as his youngest son does.

I shrug absently. "Well, that was ten years or so ago. At this point Preacher is so well–respected and trusted in this community, I don't think anyone cares about his past."

Jonathan and the Kings return from the lake as Griffin's group and the four kids begin bringing our dinner across the lawn from my house. Jonathan opens more wine and sets the bottles at the end of the building buffet spread.

Griffin shakes her head at Jonathan and moves the bottles to a table in the corner of the kitchen. "Sorry, John. We need more room at the table for what's coming."

Jonathan shrugs and flashes a real grin as he backs off. "Whoa . . . sorry, lady. I'll get out of your way. Carry on."

Griffin smiles and plants a kiss on Jonathan's neck bringing chuckles from us bystanders.

Momentarily the buffet is loaded and Griffin announces dinner. The four kids are encouraged to lead off followed by the Kings. At Cory's urging the kids tote their plates and drinks down to the dock to eat.

The meal was fantastic and the dessert of freshly baked apple pie from Mom and Pop's Pastries in Seguin was beyond good, particularly warmed up with two scoops of vanilla ice cream placed carefully on top.

After assuring Griffin that we have eaten all we can possibly eat and that the dinner was a complete success, her helpers began the task of cleaning up. The rest of us head to Jonathan's dock for after dinner drinks.

At nine o'clock we agree that we should get to bed early as tomorrow is going to be long and taxing. Jonathan, the kids and I see the Bales off and make sure the Kings are bedded down. We encourage the kids to watch a movie at my house, and thank Griffin's group as they prepare to leave.

Now it is back to the dock for Jonathan and me with two armloads of goodies—two bottles of cheap merlot, a thermos of ice, a bottle of water and a flask of Chivas Royal Salute. We know it is going to be a long night for us.

Gina De Georgio

FOURTEEN

My boat will easily hold eight so we all load up around nine–thirty to head to the club. We are definitely a gloomy bunch for good reason. This is going to be a goodbye and none of us wants to be there. I don't know if it'll be closure or not but it has to be done. I think Jonathan wanted the casual, have some fun if you can, easy way out. I agree. Let's say so long, have a beer and get it over. I'm sure Link is also okay with that.

Before I back the boat out of the lowered lift I turn and look at the kids on the back seat. "Okay guys. Do you have everything—swim suit, towel, phone, whatever?"

I get silent nods. "Okay, when we get there leave your stuff in the boat so you don't lose it. You can pick it up later if you decide to swim."

Jack pipes up, "What about our phones? Can we take them?

"Only if you have a pocket to put it in. And while swimming keep it with your towel. I'll have my phone if you need anything. Oh, be sure to turn your phone off during the service."

I back out for the short trip to the club. When we near the club boat docks, it is apparent the guests are already arriving as adults and kids are sitting down at lake side enjoying the sweet breakfast served by Preacher's staff.

Everyone is dressed casual, some in jeans and others in shorts. I guess I'm a step above in white cotton Capris and a pink tee with a light blue rabbit on the front. My sandals are rose Beaumont Lasers.

Jonathan chuckles, "Lots of people. Bring them on. The more the better."

Grace, largely quiet during the ride points at the dock. "Look, there's Barney and Tex."

She and the kids wave as I ease the boat into a slip and shut down the engine. Jonathan quietly ties the boat as his mom and dad approach to help the Kings disembark—no easy task.

Jonathan, in white jeans, blue plaid shirt and brown deck shoes offers me a hand to help me out of the boat. It certainly is easier getting out of the boat in pants instead of a skirt.

"Let the show begin," he whispers in my ear as I stand beside him. He spies several Bales employees and leaves me to join them, extending his hand of welcome.

Even though Griffin made us a hearty breakfast two hours ago, the kids and I decide to check out the sweets. I certainly could use a cup of hot coffee right now.

As I follow the kids I am greeted by several Bales people with way more respect than I have ever received before. It's amazing how becoming CEO can change everyone's concept of you. Hey, guys, I'm still the same Gina you ignored last week. Oh, well.

Oddly enough I come up behind Patricia at the sweet table. I pause to see what she does. She takes a napkin and places a sticky pecan roll on it.

I whisper in her ear, "Uh–oh. Sin, sin."

She is startled and drops the roll on the table. She turns and grins in surprise, "Gina, you just saved me from myself. I want it but I don't need it. I'm so weak."

I laugh. "Hey, don't miss out on a sweet like that on my account. Go for it."

She shows her sensuous dimpled smile. "No. You saved me. You've provided just what I needed. Thank you."

I return the smile but mine isn't as sexy I'm sure. "Wow, it sounds like we're talking about something besides a pecan roll."

She pauses and her partially penciled brow furrows. "Uh, it does, doesn't it."

"Come on. Let's get coffee."

I grab her by the hand and pull her along with me to the coffee station while checking out her designer casual wear. She is wearing loosely fitting, cropped pants with a draw string waist, a red stretchy button blouse cut low enough to lightly accentuate her ample breasts. Her sandals are Balenciaga Studded T–Strap Sandals. She is one sexy lady.

"Did you come alone?" I ask as we fill plastic Styrofoam cups at two different urns.

"Yeah, I don't have any close friends at work, mostly because I am stationed in Siberia by myself. And no one would dare come up to the seventh floor to visit with me for fear of running into Mr. Bales."

"Chris was certainly interested in your coming with him. He seems like a nice enough guy."

She shrugs and shakes her head in disgust. "For me nice enough may not be enough. For the last year since his divorce he has asked me out several times. I wish he would just give it up. He won't take no for an answer."

"Oh, okay. Follow me." I lead her to the boat and hand her my coffee as I board. She hands both coffees back to me and I set them down to extend my hand to steady her as she boards. Our touch sends a light electrical charge passing between us as she steps into the boat.

"Wow, this is cool. Is it yours?" she asks as she picks up her coffee and sits on a white vinyl seat.

I twist my lips in thought. "I haven't thought about that. My divorce is final later this month and I assume I will get the boat since I'm getting the lake."

She frowns quizzically in surprise. "I didn't know you're getting divorced."

"The only one at the company that knows is Mr. Bales. He lives next door to me here on the lake."

She reaches out and touches me lightly on the arm, genuine concern marks her face. "Are you all right? Are you okay with getting the divorce?"

"I'm adjusting to a long list of things. But it's coming along. Link and I were best friends. Now I've lost her too. Everything is just piling on me right now. And then Mr. Bales pushed me into a job that I don't want. But I'm good. Thanks for asking."

"Well if you need anything, ask. I'll try to help."

I study her briefly. "Thanks, Patricia. You know, in the last twenty four hours you and I have certainly made a big change in our attitudes toward each other."

She shakes her head as she clicks her tongue. "I think we were a couple of bitches."

I laugh. "Speak for yourself woman."

"No, Gina, we were a couple of bitches. Both of us."

I curl my lips in thought, then nod. "You're right, Patricia. Two bitches."

"Hey, you folks are certainly talking serious down there while hiding out from the party. Permission to come aboard, Captain?"

"Hey, Johnny. Come on down."

Jonathan steps into the boat and extends his hand to Patricia. "So apparently you're getting along with your new boss. She's already coaxed you onto her boat. That's not a good sign. Has she told you all the things she has done on this boat?"

She smiles with those sugary lips and winks at me. "No, Mr. Bales, but I think I can take care of myself."

"Oh, okay. And now you can call me John, being that I can't fire you."

"I can do that." She touches him lightly on the shoulder. "John, I am so sorry for your loss. I hurt for you as many others do. If there is anything I can do, please ask. I can certainly never repay you for all you've done for me."

Jonathan tears over and he retrieves his handkerchief to wipe his eyes as we watch. He checks his watch. "Damn, still forty-five minutes to go."

He sits and studies both of us. Damn, Jonathan, not now. He's sexy even when he's sad.

"Good time for a Bloody Mary, huh, Johnny?"

"I think I have to be sober for the next couple of hours, then all hell is going to break loose. It's going to be a bloody circus—Bloody Mary circus that is. I'm certainly not drinking that stinky beer you talked me into ordering."

I chuckle as Patricia looks on curiously. "I'll bet tonight on the dock you're going to get pretty much wasted."

Jonathan slowly shakes his head. "If I make it that long. This might be your turn to pour me into bed, Gina."

"Umm, we'll see." I turn to Patricia. "For the last five nights we have been drowning our miseries together on one of our boat docks. It has been pretty disgusting." I turn back to Jonathan. "Maybe tonight will be the last time we get sotted. What do you think?"

"Don't count on it. Hell, we've been getting polluted long before either of us experienced all this shit. I don't see us stopping anytime soon do you?"

"Well, my divorce is going to be final in about three weeks."

"I don't think that's going to get rid of your biggest demon."

I place a hand on each of my cheeks and feign surprise. "Oh, I thought you were going to rid me of that demon, John."

Jonathan merely stares at me. "You never quit do you?"

"No sir." I turn back to Patricia who I'm sure has been wondering what the hell is going on between Jonathan and me. "Don't mind us, Patricia. We're both crazy. If we hadn't been such good friends since forever, we would've probably killed off each other years ago."

"Certainly sounds like it," she grins. "I hope you guys make it through the next few months. I can certainly see that you need each other's help."

Things grow silent. I find Patricia staring at me and I wink at her. She winks back.

John watches us and sadly shakes his head. "Damn, what's with you two? If it's not one thing it's another. Okay, children, I think it's time to head to the big going away party."

Reaching the restaurant of the club I am taken aback by the crowd of people. I search the front of the room for the reserved section where Preacher has set up a lectern with a picture of Link attached to the front. I spy Mom and Dad and make my way toward them. I am unaware of Patricia and Jonathan drifting away. My parents smile as I approach.

"Hi, people. Have you been here long?" I bend over and hug them both at the same time.

"We just got here, Mom answers. "I'm glad you had chairs reserved for us. Looks like it's standing room only."

"We prepared for four hundred. It looks to me like they all showed up." I sit in my reserved chair next to Dad and turn to look for my kids who are going to sit next to me. I spy all four kids congregated around Pep in the far back.

After a moment I excuse myself and head back to get the kids moving.

"Pep," I greet shaking his hand while trying to not think about our tryst last week. "Glad to see you made it."

He smiles but doesn't respond.

"Okay, people, it's getting close to starting time. You best come on down and take your seat."

I wave a faint goodbye to Pep and the kid's follow me down to the front row. They take their assigned seats, my kids next to me and the Bales sit next to where Jonathan is going to sit. On the other side of Jonathan's vacant chair the Kings are already seated as are the four remaining Bales on the far side of the Kings.

As the time nears Jonathan walks in with Preacher and takes his seat. Preacher steps up to the lectern and his audience is suddenly quiet.

He is wearing blue jeans with a light blue tight fitting work shirt and blue athletic shoes. Like the kids have said, his tanned body appears to glow as he presents a wide toothy smile for those assembled to honor Link.

He walks around to the front of the lectern and studies Link's photo momentarily. He turns toward his audience while pointing back at the picture.

"Link Bales. My good friend. My helpmate. My antagonist." He drops his hand and returns to the lectern. "We are here this morning to not only say goodbye; we are here to remember and honor her."

"I will start by telling a little story about how I met this lady over ten years ago. As many of you know, Lake McQueeney County Club used to be called McQueeney Ski Club and Restaurant. For those that experienced eating at this establishment back then, restaurant was too kind of a word. Dump would better describe it."

Preacher pauses and smiles at the chuckles echoing around the crowded room.

"Umm, more old timers here than I thought. Well, anyway, I had the opportunity to buy the restaurant and one hundred surrounding acres. It was my hope to build a golf course and turn the dumpy cafe into part of a country club for Seguin, McQueeney and Lake McQueeney.

"Well, first things first. I immediately set out to gut the old restaurant and turn it into an upscale restaurant, bar and boat ramp.

"So I don my work clothes and boots and I am amongst the hired workers sweating away trying to help undo the old. In comes what I thought to be a teenager. Dressed in short shorts and tank top, this person is smaller than petite with this unbelievable curly red hair. She demands that one of my workers show her the way to the owner of this establishment. The worker points me out on the other side of the room and this person stomps her way over to me.

"The closer she gets the more I realize this little person is no teenager. By her carriage and—excuse me— adult woman's body, I quickly realize, however small, this is a fully grown woman."

He pauses and smiles. "'What are you doing here?' she asks. Taken aback, I don't answer, but I do glare at her. 'Well, what's going on here?' she repeats.

"Hey, I try to get along with everyone, but don't come onto my turf and demand anything of me. 'What does it look like I'm doing, ma'am? We're playing a basketball game. Can't you see?'"

Preacher pauses to let the chuckles subside.

"'That's not funny,' she retorts. I'm like, I don't know who you are but just go away please.

"She doesn't give up easily: 'I really like this place and I don't see why you're tearing it down.'

"'Ma'am, we're, as you say, tearing it down so we can rebuild it bigger and better, okay?'

"'Oh, are you sure?'

"'I'm sure. Now, I need to get back to work if you don't mind.'"

"'Okay, I believe you, but I'm going to keep an eye on you.'"

"'Go for it, lady.'"

He pauses and grins as he slowly shakes his head. "I should have never said that. This woman, Link Bales, showed up every morning to make sure I was doing what I said I was going to do."

Preacher pauses for the scattered chuckles to subside. "I finally had enough of this daily intrusion, so one morning when she showed up about nine o'clock, I push a wheelbarrow with a shovel in it up to her.

"'Look lady, if you're going to hang out here every morning, you may as well make yourself useful.'" I hand her the shovel. "'That pile of junk in the corner over there needs to be taken out to the dumpster. After that I'll find something else for you to do.'

"Ladies and gentlemen. I want you to know: without comment she dropped the shovel in the wheelbarrow and pushed it toward the debris. By noon she had completely hauled away the waste and even swept the area with a broom. She left without comment."

He grins in thought. "There's more. The next morning she arrives dressed in work pants, ragged out shirt, baseball cap and heavy duty work boots. She showed up every morning for over a month and worked for nothing. She just wanted her restaurant rebuilt as soon as possible.

"People, that was the Link that most of you don't know. Since then she had turned into the mellow just–trying–to–get–along Link that we lost last week."

I take a sideways glance at Jonathan to see him nodding his agreement. There are tears welling up in his and his kids eyes. He has his arm around Jody with his hand resting on Johnny's shoulder. I also see Bunny's eyes tearing over. I put my arm around her and rest my hand on Jack's shoulder.

"Since that time, Link and I have been in close contact and have worked together on many personal and civic projects. Several years ago she took over our mission to provide a Mexican Thanksgiving dinner to over one thousand homeless and needy people each year.

"With this job one can't just show up on Thanksgiving morning and open the doors. Link worked year round to solicit donations of money and food to pull this off. Many of you know this because she pestered you for your help, both in dollars and in volunteering on the big day. That was Link.

"I know of several instances when, at her insistence, she and her husband Jonathan anonymously helped someone in need of physical or financial assistance. Several times I called on Link to help me out in some of my crazy endeavors and, without complaint, just like with the shovel and wheelbarrow, she showed up with her work boots on. That was Link."

Preacher looks down at his notes on the lectern and curls his lips. "Let me take you on a brief tour of Link's life. In 1980 she was born in the same bedroom which her mother had been on a four hundred acre farm in south central Georgia.

"Her mother and father, Grace and Jethro King, are here with us today to honor their daughter." He gestures toward the Kings. "Link graduated from high school in Tifton in 1997 and immediately took the big step of enrolling at Texas Christian University, a long way from home. Her eventual degree was Master of Fine Art.

"She married fellow student Jonathan Bales in the summer after their junior year in 2000. They graduated from TCU in 2001 and began Bales Publishing in San Antonio later the same year. They moved to Lake McQueeney in 2005 with their one–year–old son Johnny. She gave birth to a daughter, Jody, in 2008. Link passed on Thursday, April 28, 2016 approaching the age of thirty–seven.

"Link's life was both public and private. She got carried away with the private—but for a good reason. A friend relayed a story to me about her need for complete solitude and privacy. Five or so years ago, Jonathan was forced to build her an artist studio next to their home to give him, as he said, 'a little sanity and organization in my home.' It appeared that every room of their home was cluttered with art materials such as easels, canvases, finished work and works in progress. That was Link.

"Upon completion of the studio she invited all her friends and neighbors for a tour of her new workplace. That was the last time anyone including her husband has been inside. Every work day since then she disappeared inside to work five hours without interruption from the outside world. That was Link."

Except for me. I must have been pretty special. *You got that right, Gina.* Now I'm mingling my tears with everyone else's. Damn, Link why did you leave us? Why did you leave me?

"Link's art work is enjoyed and purchased throughout the southwest. She had two or three gallery shows every year and usually all her work was purchased before the end of the show.

"She had a show open in Houston on Saturday, three days ago. After word got out about her accident on Thursday, the thirty or so paintings in the show sold out by Sunday afternoon. That was Link.

"Link the wife and mother. Those of you that are members of this club know firsthand the influence she has had on her children and her husband as well as our children. Her family was a top priority and she gave it all she possibly could. That was Link.

"Watch out water skiers. No teenager on this lake, male or female, could hold a candle to Link in a head to head contest of skiing skills. They long ago have stopped trying. Who wants to be embarrassed by this tiny dynamo on skis?"

Suddenly there is a smattering of clapping by the teens in the audience that quickly grows until all the youngsters have joined in the celebration. Now the adults are joining in. Finally the clapping ends only to be replaced by chanting from the youngsters:

"Go Link go. Go Link go. Go Link go. Go Link go. Go Link go."

I glance at Jonathan. He and our four kids are looking back at the audience smiling. Good, they need something to smile at about now. It comes to mind what Jonathan had said about the teenage boys on the lake:

'Link's testosterone army.' I can say, they are sending her off well.

Preacher smiles as he holds up both hands for everyone to settle down. Order restored he says, "Ladies and gentlemen. That was all about Link. Go Link go."

He becomes more solemn. "Jonathan asked that I keep this celebration short because Link would have wanted it that way. So be it. I would like for all of us to join together in a moment of silence. This time is for those of you that would like to be with Link to send a silent prayer, to send her your love, to say goodbye. Please join me in the silence."

And the moment is silent except for a muffled cough here and there. Preacher clears his throat and I see tears gathering in the corners of his eyes.

"I want to say one last thing about Link. Last Thanksgiving Eve, she and I were frantically finishing up the last minute details for the next day's meal when she made a comment that has stuck with me. She said, 'You know, Preacher, sometimes my life seems like an evening at the carnival. There is so much to see and do, but I don't have near enough time before it's over and they shoo us away.'"

Preacher pauses to collect himself as the tears continue. "Link, the gates have again closed big–time on your carnival. However, on another plain I'm sure you will have all the time you need to experience your carnival."

Preacher smiles as he wipes the tears streaking down his cheeks with the back of his hand. "So here we are. If I know you, Link, you're impatient to be on your way. On behalf of your family and friends I want you to leave with this: I love you. We love you. And have a great trip. You deserve it."

Preacher stands before the group silently for a moment. "Jonathan requests that all of you stay and have a buffet lunch with him and his family. My staff are setting up four buffet tables on the outside patio as I speak. The buffet will be served when this service ends.

"Lastly, this is not only a memorial; today would have been Link's thirty–seventh birthday. In celebration Jonathan has arranged that the club be available to each of you until four o'clock following the meal. All amenities of the club will be available including the golf and tennis facilities.

"Beer will be available for the adults and soft drinks and tea will be available to all others. The bar will be open for you who want a cocktail." He pauses and grins: "However, Link has sent word that you have to buy your own booze other than beer. At two o'clock, German chocolate cake and ice cream will be served on the patio to celebrate Link's last birthday.

"Folks, on behalf of the Bales family and the King family, thank you for being here to honor Link today."

As is his way, Preacher is gone in a flash and suddenly the huge room is filled with conversation. I glance at Jonathan and he is holding on to his crying kids. He glances at me with a hint of a shrug. He is also crying. Next to him the Kings are silently holding hands as they stare at their daughter's picture on the lectern. The remaining Bales have disappeared into the crowd. Me, at this point I don't have any tears left. I do hurt. I hurt badly. Dammit, Link.

Well, the biggest part is over but it doesn't get any easier for the rest of today. I predict that tonight and tomorrow won't be any easier. Soon the four kids drift away, I assume to eat. They will have to be on their own. I am physically and emotionally bushed. I sit back down in my chair thankful that my parents have also left for the buffet. I need a moment alone.

With elbows on my knees I bow my head with fingers on my temples and a thumb on each cheek. I close my eyes. Shit, what a day. And we still have hours to go.

"Are you okay?" comes a soft voice to my right.

I open my eyes to find Griffin and Cory sitting on each side of me. I blink, look each way at them and offer a painful grimace.

"Hey, guys. Yeah, I just need a little relief from all the tears and misery. Thanks for stopping by and asking."

Griffin smiles and lays a hand on my knee. "What can we do?"

I scratch the top of my hand and force a smile. "You guys are already doing more than we could possibly ask. John said last night that there is no way he could get through this without your help. Someday I hope we can repay you in some way."

Cory stands, wanders a few steps away and turns back to say tersely. "We are here to help and we don't expect any payback. What's next?"

"After tomorrow maybe we can start getting back to normal after everyone leaves. The rest of today, tonight and tomorrow I guess it's more of the same."

"That's good for us," Griffin nods. "Gina, just tell us where to be and what to do. We're at your command."

"Okay, after the buffet is broken down, Preacher's crew is going to fix us a care package of the leftovers so you guys won't have to be cooking except for breakfast in the morning. If you'll pick up the food and bring it to John's that would be great. You can go in the boat if you like."

"Done."

"Thanks. After four o'clock, if there is any beer left over, John said you guys could take it and have a party at TLU if you like. Preacher is aware of this and he suggests picking it up with a truck if possible. However, there may not be any left so don't get your hopes up too high."

Cory smiles. "Wow, that's great, but what about tonight? You'll need us won't you?"

"We'll manage. And you guys need a break. The kids are going to be ready for bed at dark and as far as feeding the same people as last night, I'll spread it out for a second buffet."

Griffin frowns her concern. "Are you sure?"

"I'm sure and I hope there's plenty of beer to spread around. If you can fix us breakfast at John's in the morning it would be great."

Griffin and I stand and she hugs me. "I'll bet you'll be glad when this is over."

"You're right. My problem is, when is it ever going to be over? What do you say we go get some of this free food?"

When we reach the buffet the lines have dwindled and the kids wander away on their own after saying goodbye. After a few minutes with a full plate of mostly vegeta-bles I spy Mom and Dad eating at a small table in the cor-ner of the patio. I join them.

"Interesting program, huh?"

Dad chuckles. "That Preacher guy is something else."

"He's always the life of the party. You don't know what he's going to come up with next."

Mom frowns. "Link must have been really special to the kids on this lake. That response from them couldn't have been rehearsed."

"When we sat on the dock in the evening, there was always a different boat of kids stopping by to see her. They usually ignored John and me."

"We talked to Pep a while ago," Dad says.

"That's interesting. What did he say?"

"He just wanted to say hello and he hoped we are doing well. Are you two going to make it final this month?"

I shrug my indifference. "It's a happening thing. I'll holler at you when it's done."

Mom smiles and grasps my arm. "Are you okay, dear?"

"Mom, I really don't know what I am. I was good until Link—her accident—now everything is screwed up. And on top of that, I haven't told you but I have even more craziness to deal with."

I pause and they wait. Finally Dad shrugs his shoulders and spreads his hands. "What?"

"John has stepped down from running BP and ap-pointed me CEO."

Both of their jaws drop in surprise. "Well, I'll be damned," Dad mumbles. "Wonders never cease. Are you up to it?"

I grin with a quick shake of the head. "No."

He laughs. "Sure you are. I have never seen you back down from anything. This is no different."

Mom nods her agreement.

"Well, I guess we'll see pretty quickly. Friday I have to make a decision that could make or lose about three million."

"Three million dollars?" Mom exclaims covering her mouth with both hands.

Dad howls, "I love it. My daughter taking over the business world. I've got to see this."

After a few more minutes of banter, Mom and Dad decide they've had enough excitement for the day. They spy Jonathan and want to wish him well. After a quick goodbye hug they leave to catch up with Jonathan before heading back to the Hill Country.

I eat alone. Maybe Link is close by.

Patricia strolls by, beer in hand but doesn't see me. I call out to her. "Hey, lady!"

She turns and frowns. "What's with you? Don't you have any friends? Can I sit?"

I chuckle. "I'm finally getting a free moment. But yes, please sit and stroke my fevered brow."

"What did you think of the service?"

"Fine, I guess. I'm glad that square is checked and we can move on to the next drama."

She lays her hand on mine and smiles with those honey soaked lips. I feel a faint glimpse of energy course down my spine. I try to ignore it.

"Are you going to make it through this?" she asks as she squeezes my hand and releases it, her beautiful brown eyes locked on mine.

"Umm, I don't think I have much choice." I eye her drink. "Beer looks good. Do I want one or go the hard route?"

"Beer's free," she grins. "But of course it's chocked full of carbs. It seems like all the food and drinks I like want to add some pounds on my belly. I'm hopeless."

"So far I don't have that problem. I can drink like a fish—which I do—and never gain a pound. Maybe some-day it will catch up with me though. If it happens I'll prob-ably get fat because I'm not giving up the hooch. That's the way I lose myself."

Patricia grins, "You could switch to grass."

"Grass always makes me want to eat more."

"So you've enjoyed a bit of weed on occasion."

"Since college we have mellowed out on grass now and then, but a good scotch is my first choice, which I'll probably start on pretty soon. It's too bad John is too cheap to provide his guests with something besides beer."

"Why didn't he provide the hard stuff?"

"He thinks I'm a lush and will run up the tab."

Patricia chuckles. "Not really?"

"No, not really. He doesn't mind spending some bucks to feed the guests at his wife's going away party, but providing cocktails would get pretty expensive if two hundred people drank two or three each."

"Good point. So what's it going to be? It's on me."

"Dang, I'm liking you more by the minute. Since you're buying I think I'll have a Chivas Royal Salute with a splash of water."

She grins, "Maybe I should take my offer back. That sounds kind of pricey."

I nod and lift an orchestrated brow. "Since I'm your new boss you should think of it as an investment in your job security."

"It sounds like you can be bought."

I chuckle, "You can get anything you want from me with the right booze."

Suddenly she gets up. "Anything? Damn, I can't pass this up. I'll return. Don't you dare leave." She is off to the bar.

She returns with two drinks and grins as she sets one on a napkin in front of me. "That anything takes in a lot of territory. Just remember, one drink equals one anything. I intend to collect."

I laugh and touch her on the hand when she sits. "Maybe I should be careful what I promise. Well, thanks anyway. I'm surprised that you're joining me. Most people don't care too much for scotch."

"I don't. I'm just trying to get on your good side."

"Kind of an expensive gesture but well received. I think it's working."

She lifts her glass. "To my new, uh, friend."

Our eyes lock as we sip.

"Wow, that's smooth," she exclaims and takes another sip. "I think you've won me over."

I raise a curious brow and wink. "If that's all it takes, you're in trouble."

She nods with a cute grin. "Maybe. Maybe not."

We quietly nurse our drinks while looking over the crowd. Everyone appears to be having a great time in spite of this being a sad occasion.

Patricia says softly, "Happy birthday, Link."

"Umm."

After a few minutes I feel the need to mingle. "Let's walk, Patricia. I really need to check on Link's parents. I hate for them to be left alone. Not now."

We stand and walk slowly through the crowd pausing to sip on occasion. We note that people are really enjoying themselves. That is good. That is how Link would want it. We find Jonathan sitting at the bar nursing a Bloody Mary.

"Mr. Bales," I smile. "You appear to be hitting the booze rather early today."

He raises his glass to us. "As you are also. I suggest you speak for yourself, woman." He points his drink toward Patricia. "Who is this woman tagging along with you? She's a knockout. Is she available?"

She smiles and I answer, "I don't think so. Neither are you."

He nods and replies dryly. "Good point. How about you, as if I didn't already know. Are you available?"

I feign anger and lash out with an evil grin, "Just leave me be, Jonathan Bales. Don't even go there."

Jonathan merely shrugs and Patricia stares at us as if to ask, what's with these two?

"Time to move on, Patricia." I lay a hand on Jonathan's shoulder. "Are you okay, Johnny? We can hang around and keep you company if you want."

"I'm hanging in there. No, you all don't need to stay with me. I can check out the crowd if I need companionship. Will you check on the Kings? We might need to shuttle them home for their nap time."

"That's my plan. I'll ask them what they want. If they've had enough, I'll have Cory take care of getting them back to your place."

"Good idea," he said as we collect our drinks off the bar and head toward the partiers.

289

We find the Kings lakeside sitting on a bench silently looking out over the water.

"They look so sad," Patricia whispers as we approach the old couple.

"Grace, Jethro, are you two doing okay? Do you need anything?" I ask.

Jethro doesn't react but Grace forces a limp smile. "Hi, Gina. I think we're okay, right now. Who is your friend?"

"Grace, Jethro, this is Patricia Goodwin, John's assistant at BP. Patricia, Grace and Jethro King from Georgia—Link's parents."

Patricia smiles and nods as she shakes each elderly hand. "Pleased."

I ask Grace. "Can we get you some refreshment—tea, coffee, soft drink, Bloody Mary?"

Both of them smile while Grace shakes her head despondently. She wags her finger. "Now, Gina, you know we're not going to do that, so don't you be tempting us like those ladies on the plane."

I smile. "I'm just funning you a little bit. I know you don't drink that stuff. Any other drink I can tempt you with?"

"I don't think so. Maybe later. We're just resting here a little bit."

"Whenever you want I can have Cory run you back to the house so you won't miss your nap."

Grace smiles openly. "We would like that. We just don't want to put you out. You've got other people to help."

"No, Grace. You and Jethro are our number one guests. Whatever you want, we'll try our best to provide it."

"You are so sweet. Link told me one time that she wished she could be like you."

She did? Wow, that's news to me. Was that before or after our time in bed? *Stop it, Gina.*

"That's nice to hear. Again, when you are ready to go, let us know. We're going to have to stay around here for two or three hours."

Jethro touches Grace on the arm with a finger. "Well, tell her, Grace."

"Tell me what, Grace?"

Jethro shakes his head. "Crazy old woman. She wants to go back now. She just doesn't want to be a bother."

"Grace are you ready to go now?" I ask semi–sternly.

"Yes, Gina," she smiles. "We're ready if Cory isn't too busy."

"It's done. Come on, Patricia, let's find the boat driver." I take Patricia by the hand and drag her away.

"Glad to meet you," Patricia calls back and the Kings wave.

After searching for Griffin and Cory for a few minutes, we finally find them in the game room with the four kids.

After introducing them to Patricia, I ask, "Hey, can I ask a big favor?"

"Anything. What do you need?" Griffin answers.

"The Kings are kind of worn out and it's their nap time. Can you run them back to the house in the boat?"

Cory exclaims, "I'll never get tired of driving your boat. Let's go."

Patricia and I lead them back to the Kings who are already slowly making their way to the boat. It takes us a few minutes getting them loaded with Cory receiving them in the boat and Griffin carefully guiding them off the dock. She follows them in and makes sure they are seated and ready as Cory unties the boat. He starts the engine and after Patricia and I exchange waves with the Kings, he slowly backs out. I'm kind of glad to see them go as that is one less responsibility I have for the next three hours.

Patricia and I sit on the nearest vacant bench and I wonder where I left my drink and was it empty?

"Are you doing all right?" Patricia asks as she touches my knee with a perfectly manicured finger, sending those familiar charges rippling down my spine and other places. Come on, get a grip I tell myself.

"Yeah, just trying to get my second wind." I glance sideways at her without speaking.

She tilts her head with a grin. "What?"

"You shouldn't feel like you have to hang out with me. There's a lot I can be doing here. Go for it. I'm okay."

She presents that sensuous smile. "Maybe I like hanging out with you."

I chuckle. "Funny, last week I was ready to slap you upside your head. Now, here we are making nice with each other."

"I guess no one ever introduced us properly."

I grin and bite at my lower lip. "I guess not. I think it's my turn to buy the drinks. Want another?"

"Damn, Gina. I have to drive home. I don't want to end up like Link." She thinks for a moment while I watch and wait. "You know, you and I may not have this chance to hang out with each other and get polluted ever again. Buy me a drink, please. I'll sleep in my car tonight if necessary."

"Same stuff?"

"Yeah, that expensive scotch."

"Come on, lady. Maybe we can sit at the bar and pick up a couple of guys."

"Whoa, I don't see you doing that," she replies as I drag her toward the bar.

I shrug as she catches up with me. "Okay, a couple of gals then."

As we find and perch on stools at the end of the bar she replies, "Interesting. I think you and I need to have a little talk about what our preferences are."

I shrug indifferently. "Easy for me. I play the field."

She slightly parts those fantastic lips. "I'll bet you do." She motions for the lone bartender. "We'll have two more, please."

William, the usual night time bar keep, nods at me. "Hello Gina. You doing okay?"

"I'm doing good so far, Bill. Thanks for asking."

He turns his attention to Patricia and fixes her with a stare and a hint of amusement in his eye. "You said that you want two more. That would be what?"

Patricia partially opens her mouth in mock surprise. "What kind of bartender are you anyway. I just ordered two drinks an hour ago and you've already forgotten me and the drinks I ordered."

He grins and shakes his head. "No ma'am. I'll never forget you. I'll probably die with your image emblazoned on my brain. But I don't remember the drinks you ordered. I've only served about fifty drinks in the last hour."

I watch for her comeback. She tilts her head curiously and says pointedly, "Bartender, are you coming on to me? Are you trying to pick me up? My image emblazoned on your brain. What kind of line is that?"

He chuckles. "I just tell it like I see it. You don't have to buy it if you don't want to."

"Oh, it's a lost cause anyway."

"Why is that?" he asks.

"I like women."

He woefully shakes his head. "Well crap. My lucky day. Now, what were the drinks you wanted?"

"Write this down for future reference. I want two Chivas Royal Salute with a splash of water."

"Yes ma'am. I should have known." He leaves and we silently watch him prepare the scotches. He returns and places each on a napkin in front of us. "That will be twelve dollars not including the tip which better be pretty high for your tormenting me."

I chuckle. "Put it on my tab, William, and add a fair tip. It's not my problem if you can't tell the difference . . . well, you know."

We sip our scotch as we gaze at each other in the mirror.

Momentarily she taps a finger on her temple in thought. "You already knew didn't you?"

I nod slowly and hold my glass up to salute her.

"How did you know?"

I smile with a tilt of my head toward the mirror. "Patricia, let's just say I wasn't born yesterday."

"Oh." She pauses and I wait. "Are you . . . ?"

"Am I what, Patricia?"

"Do you prefer men or women?"

"You can't tell?"

"Well, I guess not. I've seen the way you and John interact. I can see that you both have—I don't know exactly what—something going on with each other. But, then I see another side of you. Like I feel attracted to you, and I think you're attracted to me."

"Maybe that's because I like it all. I can play it both ways."

"Oh. I can't do that."

"Because?"

"I think all men are jerks," she answers emphatically.

I cock a perfect brow for her benefit. "That's probably because they are."

She shakes her head. "But you don't believe that?"

"Right, I like men . . . and women. But I prefer a man over a woman because of that yin yang thing. I'm not against having a little fun with a woman by any means, but I will never agree to be in a live together partnership with a woman because it may interfere with my search for a male I'm compatible with. My problem is, for the last few months men and I are strangers."

"Since you split up with your husband?"

"Yes."

"So what now?"

"I don't understand the question."

"I guess I mean, how are you handling your situation?"

"My situation is so chaotic right now, I just try to make it to the next day and see what happens. But you can only live on dreams and fantasies for so long. Sooner or later something real has to happen. I want some fun and tender loving care. I want to hold on to someone for a while—man or woman."

I tilt my head in a sideways glance to study this stranger sitting next to me. "Why are we even having this conversation? It's a dead end street."

She stares into her drink in deep thought. "I don't know. It hit me yesterday when you told me that you and

I would be working together. I suddenly felt a strange kinship with you, like we could be friends or whatever. So here we are."

"Or whatever takes in a lot of territory."

Patricia smiles. "Yes, it does."

Again we are gazing at each other in the mirror. "So tell me, Patricia, how long have you two been living together?"

She appears stunned as her jaw drops in surprise. She suddenly laughs uneasily. "How did you know?"

"I didn't until now. You just told me. So how long."

"I don't know; three years maybe."

"She's an older woman. Highly paid professional type I presume."

"Come on. How do you do that? Nobody knows this. Are you psychic?"

I laugh easily. "Psychotic would be more like it. I'm just guessing. You drive a Mercedes SUV and your clothes are top of the line. Someone's got to be helping you purchase that stuff unless you're running drugs or something."

"Oh."

"So, why are you hiding her?" I quiz.

"She doesn't want anyone to know because of her professional status."

"Which is?"

"She's an instructor at the medical school and lead neurosurgeon on the staff at Southwest Regional Hospital."

I widen my eyes in surprise. "Wow, I'm impressed. Her age?"

"Fifty six."

"Umm, does she like younger women or do you like older women?"

"Probably a little bit of both."

I take a sip of my drink in thought. "Someone might say you are a kept woman. What do you say to that?"

She nods and twists her lips in thought. "In the beginning, no. Now, probably yes."

"Because?"

"Well, at first it was kind of exciting because of who she is. The sex wasn't all that great but it kept me basically satisfied because there was a lot of it. And she kept buying me all this neat stuff. And we were a couple if only in private.

"As time passed we've had less and less sex and it isn't all that exciting anymore. I need more, much more, but it seems she only wants a basic sexual fix every couple of weeks or more. It's driving me crazy."

Patricia shrugs absently as she watches me in the mirror. "So, yes, I do feel now that I'm being kept. I don't understand why she even wants to be in this relationship if sex isn't involved. I don't know what's with her."

"Why don't you leave?"

"I tried to not too long ago. She talked me out of it by allowing me to see others as long as I didn't do it too much."

"Have you seen others since her offer?"

"No, since living with her I've decided that my next, uh, sexual partner is going to have to be pretty damn special. That person hasn't come along."

"Then leave."

"I guess I can't take the plunge. My situation does have its perks—a fancy car, extra money to spend and a closet full of nice clothes. Umm . . . I guess I am kept."

"But basically there's no sex."

She grins. "Basically there is no basic sex."

I chuckle at her in the mirror. "Wow, I thought I had problems. Your life is as shitty as mine."

She merely nods in agreement.

I hold up two fingers to William and he nods. He soon brings us two drinks and sets them in front of us. "Do you guys want me to call the fire department later to resuscitate you?"

We ignore him as we stand to leave. "Put it on my tab, Bill."

"Yes, ma'am."

As we stroll away, I comment, "I guess I'd better go greet my employees like a good leader would do."

"Yeah, I guess you had better, Gina. Or we can find us a place to sit and get filthy drunk."

We mingle and greet the likes of Josh Butler who gives me a cold shoulder, Jesse Ferro that at least smiles, and JB, who congratulates me on the new job. Then we ran into Bob Couser dressed in his usual unacceptable office garb. He's always appears excited to see me.

Chris Hunter is very cordial, offering an enthusiastic handshake. I note that Patricia reacts by offering a limp hand. What's with her?

Chris, about six foot two, has a chiseled and tanned body. He keeps his brown hair short and his face is accented by deep blue eyes that appear to be devouring you when you grab his attention. I have never been around him when he wasn't the most charming. In conversation he studies you as if he's making mental note of everything you say, and he is sexy. Dripping sexy.

I noticed after our board meeting yesterday that he appears to be gaga over Patricia. I see the same today, but she appears to ignore him no matter how he tries to coax her into basic conversation. That's curious but I assume it's because he isn't special enough—he's not a woman. Oh, well.

I shrug compassionately at Chris as we prepare to move on. "Glad you came, Chris." Patricia turns and walks away without a simple goodbye. Interesting for me. Confusing for Chris I'm sure.

I had hoped to run into the Bales but they are nowhere in sight.

"Come on, Patricia. Let's go out to the parking lot."

She follows without comment. She stops to take a sip of her drink and catches up smiling.

Once in the parking lot I search the porches of the lodge rooms and find what I'm looking for. Patricia follows me through the rows of parked cars. We stroll up the walkway toward Bob and Shirley sitting on lawn chairs under their porch roof.

"Gina, did you get your cake and ice cream?" Bob asks as we join them.

"Damn, we were sitting at the bar and completely forgot." I gesture toward Patricia. Bob, Shirley this is Patricia. She is John's assistant at BP. Patricia, this is Bob and Shirley Bales, John's brother and his wife from north Dallas."

After handshakes we are invited to sit with them.

"How are you doing, Gina?" Bob asks.

"Let's put it his way. I'm ready to go home. I've had my fill."

He chuckles. "Myself. At least we can hide in our little rented castle. Dad and Mom should be out soon. They are taking what he calls a power nap."

After a moment of silence I ask, "Say, Bob, when you all come over for dinner this evening, I wonder if you will do Patricia and me a favor."

"Sure, what do you need?"

"Well Patricia and I have been imbibing a little more than we should and I think both of us are not going to be fit to do anything shortly. So when you come over later could you drive Patricia's car over. She is going to stay in my spare bedroom tonight because I don't think she'll be fit later to drive back to San Antonio."

I sneak a glance at Patricia and she lifts a brow and smiles.

"Sure, be glad to. Patricia, walk me out to your car and show me how to drive it. Then you can get as stewed as you want. I promise I'll get it over to Gina's without wrecking it more than once."

Bob follows Patricia down the walk to the parking lot. I remain behind. Soon John's mother and father join us.

"Gina, how's the party going?"

"Hi, guys. I'm playing it low key but I think everything is going well. We have been spending a little too much time in the bar however. I know John is. He started drinking Bloody Marys as soon as he had lunch."

"Yeah, we noticed," Tex comments, "but I guess that's as good a way as any to help him through this. He appears to be extra miserable."

"What's Bob up to? It looks like he's found him a stray woman in the parking lot," Barney asks as he gestures toward Bob and Patricia. Shirley laughs.

"He's going to drive a car over to my place when you come over for dinner this evening. Patricia, John's assistant at BP, is going to stay over with me tonight because we've already had too much to drink for her to drive to San Antonio."

They join us and Bob drops the car keys on the coffee table.

"Barney, Tex, this is Patricia Goodwin. Patricia, John's parents." They shake hands.

"Get it figured out?" I ask Bob.

He chuckles, "Kind of complicated but it's doable. I think I want a job in John's operation if his employees knock down enough to buy that kind of transportation. That thing costs more than one of my rigs."

Patricia merely smiles and winks at me.

I stand. "Well, Patricia, let's go see if we can rescue John from the bar. Either that or we join him."

"We'll be over directly," Barney calls out as we walk down the walk. I wave over my shoulder."

Patricia calls out to them: "Glad I got to meet you all. Thanks, Bob."

She lightly jabs a finger in my ribs. "That was certainly a surprise."

"And what would that be?"

She presents that dimpled saucy lipped smile. "That I'm staying with you tonight."

"I couldn't let you spend the night sleeping alone in the parking lot. I would have felt that I had to join you for protection, and I'm not sleeping in your car. I don't care how fancy it is.

"Hold it just a minute, Patricia." We stop at the edge of the parking lot and I take my phone from my back pocket and speed dial.

"Hi, mom. What do you want?"

"Hi, Bunny. Just checking to see how you guys are doing"

"We're at the pool."

"Did you get ice cream?"

She laughs, "We all had two bowls. No cake."

"Are Jody and Johnny doing okay?"

"There are okay, Mom."

"Are you going to stay at the pool until time to go home?"

"No, we are going back to the game room. Is it alright if we don't change back into our regular clothes?"

"That's alright. I'll call you when we're ready to leave."

"Bye, Mom."

I resume walking with Patricia. "So, anyway, where were we?"

"I guess I get to experience the madness on the dock tonight, huh."

"Yeah, that probably will happen."

"Umm, and will you pour me into bed like John says if I drink too much?"

I laugh as we enter the patio area. "You'll probably get the same attention that I got one night from John and Link after I couldn't walk straight."

"What was that?"

"They had to practically carry me home. They undressed me and put me to bed with me ranting at them the whole way. I even fussed at John about him getting me naked and then was too chicken to take care of business. Link laughed.

"I slept for about ten hours. The next morning I woke up with Link sitting on top of my naked body in her bikini."

Patricia giggles. "Wow, sounds like fun. I think I need another drink."

I laugh loudly as we approach the bar and partiers turn to see what the joke is. Jonathan looks up from his Bloody Mary as I announce, "Let's get this party over with and go home, John."

I lay a hand on top of his head and he smiles at me by way of the mirror.

"How's the Mary, Johnny?"

"Oh, is that what I'm drinking?" he quips as he salutes us with his glass.

"What do you think, Patricia? Should we hang with the scotch or switch to John's drink?"

She grabs John's Mary and takes a long draw on the straw, then licks her sexy lips and smiles. "I'll have one of these, please." She sets his drink on the bar in front of him and sits on the stool next to him.

I take the stool on his other side. "Hey, William, can we have some service down here, please?"

Patricia adds, "Bar guy, we need two drinks."

He glances at Patricia without expression when he arrives. "I'll bet you do. I remember this time: two Chivas."

"Wrong," she retorts. "Two Bloody Marys, and put them on my account."

"Look, lady, you don't have an account."

"No problem. Put them on Gina's account." She nods at the bartender as he glares at her.

"Gina, you had better keep this woman away from me. Someone is liable to get hurt." He smiles as he heads down the way to make the drinks. People at the bar are snickering at the display.

Jonathan glances at Patricia and arches a single sexy brow. "What's with you, lady? You and the tender know each other?"

"Our paths have crossed a couple of times."

Again Jonathan glances sideways at her and frowns. "How many scotches have you had today?"

She winks at me and I wonder where this is heading. She counts on her fingers. "I think three?" she says, but looks at me for confirmation. "Maybe four?"

Jonathan gazes at me in the mirror as William sets our Marys in front of us. "Who gets to drive this woman home?"

I see her grin in the mirror as I answer flatly, "No one, Johnny boy. She's staying with me."

He glumly shakes his head. "That figures. The drama starts. Whose idea was this?"

"Chivez Royal Salute," Patricia interjects with a dimple–riddled smile.

"Oh boy," he says absently. "It's going to be a great time on the old boat dock."

I add: "Just think, John, we have the makings for a threesome."

Patricia laughs while glancing at me.

"Just leave me alone, Gina. I don't want to hear your damn threesome bullshit." He looks at the clock above the mirror. "Just thirty–two minutes to go. I want to go home."

The four other Bales join us and order drinks. Jonathan salutes them in the mirror with his Mary.

Barney places a hand on Jonathan's shoulder and squeezes. "Are you going to make it?"

"Probably. I just need a couple more drinks, then I'm good."

"Hang in there." Barney joins the other Bales at a table as their drinks arrive.

I find Patricia studying me in the mirror. I tilt my head and raise a curious brow. She smiles and winks. Something crazy is sure to happen tonight. I hope it's good and I hope I show up. Maybe I should back off the hooch a bit.

In comes Griffin and Cory. He grins as he approaches Jonathan. "Looks like a keg and half left. We brought my lawn trailer to haul it. We're going to have a pool party at the apartment complex tonight."

"Great Cory. I'll ask Preacher to announce a last call for beer. Then you can go ahead and take it if you want."

Griffin announces to me, "The dinner for this evening is waiting for you at Jonathan's."

"Good. The next phase of the day is set to start."

The announcement is made and Cory and two friends hover around the kegs waiting for the signal to go.

Getting close to four o'clock the partiers slowly begin to leave, several stopping by to give Jonathan parting condolences.

I beg three large Styrofoam cups from Bill so our Marys can travel as we begin to wrap up this part of the day. Preacher approaches on cue and we give our profound thanks for all he did for Jonathan today. I call the kids for our boat ride home.

A moment later we board—Jonathan, me, Patricia and four kids. Jonathan unties while I start the engine. After Jonathan is seated I slowly back the boat out of the stall. Several stragglers including the Bales wave goodbye from the shore.

John is sitting next to Patricia. I make eye contact with her in the rearview mirror. "When was the last time you were on a boat?"

She grins, "This morning."

"Never mind, smart ass." I slip the gear into forward and the boat slowly moves toward home. I keep care to go at a very low speed because of my high state of intoxication. I hope I can dock without crashing into it.

I look back at Jonathan to find him with his head buried in his hands while Patricia is rubbing his back. I wonder if there is time for a nap for all of us before dinner. I wish. I take a big slug of my Mary.

Gina De Georgio

FIFTEEN

Perfect. Jonathan announces that he is soused enough that he just might be able to take a nap. Since the other Bales aren't going to show up for about two hours he'll have ample time.

I walk down to the dock and tell the Kings that it is going to be naps all around for a while and they agree that they will guard the fort while we do so.

I inform the four kids that if they don't choose to nap they should swim or watch television at either of the houses. Quietness is the order of the day if they are in the house. They choose the lake since they already have their bathing suits on.

Jonathan disappears into his bedroom and I take Patricia by the hand and we walk toward my house.

I take a sideways glance at her and smile. "Hey lady, would you like to join me in my bed for a nap?" I ask as I wrap an arm around her waist.

She stops and gazes at me with the usual sexy smile. "Umm, that's a hard question. I guess I would have to answer yes and no."

"Yes and no. I don't understand?"

She teasingly smiles. "Yes, I would like to join you in bed, but no, I don't want to take a nap."

"You want to go to bed with me but there won't be any sleeping."

"I hope not."

I smile as I take her hand and pull her toward the house and open the back door for her.

"Nice home," She says as we enter.

"This is not the time to be talking about nice homes. All you have to be concerned about is does the bed meet your needs of the moment?"

Her eyes widen and she purses her lips. "Yes ma'am. Whatever you say."

I open my bedroom door and sweep my arm for her to enter. She walks over and presses a hand against the mattress, turns and smiles at me. "Okay."

I reach out and pull her toward me and she throws her body against mine. The energy flowing between us is already about to explode. "Damn, I've been wanting to taste your lips all day."

She grasps my cheeks in her hands while presenting a sensuous open–mouthed smile. "Well go for it. I want you to taste everything. And hurry, please."

Our lips clash and our mouths open to frantic tongue sucking, twirling, and biting. The moan from deep in her throat invites me to push further, to take everything and give up even more. My hands caress her body feverishly and I try to touch all of her at once, searching and then moving on for more.

She releases my cheeks and runs her hands down to my breasts, squeezing and pinching, rubbing and pulling through my shirt. Now she runs her hands behind me and grasps my hips pulling me even closer.

I push her away from me and smile. I grasp the top button of her blouse and slowly unbutton it. "I need to take this off before I tear it off."

She grips the lower hem of my tee to pull it up and over my head. As I work my way down unbuttoning her blouse she slips my bra straps off my shoulders and down my arms and slides the bra around to unhook it. She tosses the bra aside and caresses my breasts.

"Oh, my. That feels good. More, more."

Taking hold of both sides of the neck opening I slip her blouse off and pitch it on the bed. Her frilly designer bra is fastened in front and with a twist of my thumb and finger her breasts are free if only for a moment. I recapture them and gently knead her nipples that begin to swell under my touch.

"Your tits are fantastic."

We move on; now the pants. Together we fumble at the other's waistline. I release her draw string with a slight pull and in one quick motion she unsnaps my pants and runs the zipper down.

"Damn, we're fast," she giggles.

In unison we drop each other's pants to the ankles, step out of our sandals and remove the pants.

I push her back on the bed and, with one knee on the bed, I raise myself up next to her. I pull her close to me. I kiss between her breasts and move up to her neck and behind her ear, then across to her mouth.

She hungrily returns my kisses and runs her hands behind my head. With a fist full of my hair she pulls my head back as she moves her kisses down to my neck. "Oh, you smell so good. You taste good. I want you now."

"Not in a hurry are you." I force her to release the hold on my hair and guide her head down to my breasts.

"Yes, I need you now. It's been too long. Please hurry. Please fuck me, Gina."

"Yes ma'am." I run a hand down over her belly and slide a finger under the waist of her thong. Raising myself up on both knees I place the other hand on the opposite side and run the panties down. I bend her knees and slip them off.

I grab each leg above the knee and slowly work my hands up the leg to find that warm moist spot below her silky hair. I press and massage lightly with two fingers until I find that welcome opening. I easily push the fingers deeper as she groans in delight. I withdraw the fingers slightly then push deeper. Again I withdraw and push harder.

"Oh, yes, that feels so good. Don't stop."

I don't comment as I step up the pressure—in and out, in and out. She begins to push her hips with each thrust as she grasps my hand to guide the tempo. In and out, in and out.

I withdraw my fingers, spread her legs and bend her knees to position myself between her legs. When my tongue enters into that welcome nest she gasps in delight. I find her clitoris with my lips and lightly suck, then run my tongue around it, then suck even more.

"Oh, Gina, hurry. I want to come now," she pleads. "It's been so long."

I oblige. I put both hands beneath her hips and tilt them up for a better angle. I run my tongue around her clit followed by sucking. I increase the pressure and the tempo as she thrusts her hips against my mouth.

Her breathing intensifies and I push on, trying to bring her to the edge.

"Oh, yes, please, harder. Fuck me harder, Gina. Just a little . . . more, harder, I'm coming. Ahh! Ahh! Ahh! Oh, Shit! Enough, stop! Gina, stop!"

I can do that. I need to take a breath. I straighten her legs and roll over one to lie beside her.

With her eyes closed her breathing begins to settle as she grabs my arm and squeezes. "More, more," she says as she opens her eyes and smiles. "That was marvelous."

She pushes me over on my back and straddles me sitting on my belly. She leans forward and kisses me with little nibble kisses working all around my mouth. Then she kisses harder and lightly bites my lips. Her lips feel delightful against mine as I knew they would from just looking at them. It's if they were made just for kissing.

She opens her mouth and runs her tongue between my lips to tangle with my tongue. Slowly she steps up the titillating tongue movement as she reaches back behind her and buries a lone finger into my fantasy place.

"Oh, that's great, Patricia. You can do that all day, every day."

She renews the pressure on me, twirling her finger around my clit. She smiles at me with those dreamy lips. "Enjoying yourself are you?"

"Damn right and don't stop."

She lifts herself off of me onto one knee and spreads my legs with both hands.

"Bend," she says, pushing my legs back with my knees completely bent. She grabs a pillow and commands me to lift my hips. She places the pillow under my hips and pushes my legs farther apart. She places her hands on the fold at the top of my legs and spreads my vagina with her thumbs creating an easy target for those lips.

Her lips are suddenly caressing my clit sending little bursts of light throughout my body. She steps up the pressure and sucks until I feel like I can't take it anymore. But I don't dare ask her to stop; this hurts so good.

"Oh, Patricia. That hurts but please don't stop. Harder, make me hurt. I want you to hurt me. Please, harder."

She does as told and I wonder how much more of this I can take. "Oh, stop. Please." I laugh. "No, no. Don't stop. Harder, harder."

She elicits a muffled giggle but doesn't miss a beat. She pushes on.

"It's not funny, woman. I want more. I want you to hurt me. Harder. Oh, I'm coming. Just a little bit . . . yes, don't stop. Please fuck me harder. Aggh. Oh, yes! Aggh! Uh, uh, oh! Now, now! Yes!"

Suddenly I feel my whole being falling, tumbling and bursting into complete nothingness. It's done. Relief and calmness at last.

She backs off, removes the pillow and straightens my legs. Sitting next to me she waits as I come back to reality.

I open my eyes to see her smiling at me. "What have you done to me? You're a killer. I want more."

She giggles. "Does that mean that we've passed the beginners test and we can move up to bigger and better things?"

"Gets my vote for sure."

She leans over and kisses me lightly with her sweet lips. I grab the back of her head and force her to kiss me harder. Then I release her.

She shakes her head and flashes a wide smile. "I can't believe this. Yesterday we hardly knew each other. And what we did know was shitty. Now we've had the most fantastic sex. How come we didn't do this sooner?"

I chuckle. "Our stars weren't aligned yet."

Patricia pauses in thought before her reply. "I don't think my stars have been aligned for a couple of years now. Everything I've touched turned to crap." She snuggles next to me and places a kiss under my ear. "I can't believe I'm still with my, uh, magnificent partner after experiencing today what's out there waiting."

I grin. "They aren't out there waiting, ma'am. It's just me. You hit the jackpot today." I pause in thought. "Well maybe our luck is changing—concerning our sex lives anyway."

"What now? Do we have time for more?" She smiles with those sexy lips. "Surely we do."

"I wish but we'll have all night long to chase each other around the bed. That is if we're not too drunk to enjoy it."

"How much do you think I should cut back on the booze tonight? Maybe two percent?"

I laugh. "Drink what you will. It makes no difference to me, but you'd better be able to take good care of me . . . or else. You don't get a chance like this every day."

"Oh, Okay. So what's next on the schedule?"

"We have to lay out the dinner spread and I have to make a quick trip to Chilo's Taco and Margarita Heaven. It's only a couple of blocks. It won't take long if you want to ride along."

"No, I don't think so. I really need to call Beverly."

"Beverly is the lady of your past, right?"

"Yeah," She answers pensively.

"You have a problem with telling her you are not going to be home tonight?"

"No, I have a problem telling her that I'm moving out as soon as possible."

I laugh and kiss her on the cheek. "Wow, that must have been great sex for you to immediately up and leave your longtime lover."

Patricia doesn't answer as I get up and begin dressing. She follows.

I walk directly to my car with her a few steps behind. I get into the car, close the door and run the window down. "Well, go for it. You knew this was coming so follow through. No compromise and take no prisoners."

She nods without a reply, turns and returns to the house. I back out and pull away. This could be an eventful few days coming up.

When I return she is sitting on the front step. I expect an action report but get none. Perhaps she isn't ready to tell me.

I sit down beside her, take out my phone and consult contacts. Finding the person I want I punch call. She answers. "Griffin, has the big party started yet? . . . Oh, these have to be late night. I wish we could come. I haven't been to a college beer party in who knows how long. . . . I just wanted to let you know, you don't need to come over to fix us breakfast in the morning. I've already ordered tacos for the whole group. Nothing to fix. They just dig in. If they have a problem with that, too bad. . . . Now you can sleep in if you like. . . . Okay, bye."

I slip my phone in my back pocket and turn my attention toward Patricia and wait, trying to keep my face neutral.

"It's done."

"Damn, that was quick."

"Yeah, I actually got through to her while she was on break."

"She didn't fight back?"

"Beverly said she was prepared because she knew it was just a matter of time. She took full responsibility for the split. She said she didn't live up to her end of the bargain and apologized for that."

"I can't believe that was so easy."

"She definitely helped. I had to say very little." She pauses and slowly shakes her head "I think my planets are definitely aligned. She asked if I wanted to take the car."

"Really."

"Yeah, she had already talked to the bank. The payoff on the loan is about twenty thousand. The bank said that they would refinance that amount for me with nothing down. That payment would be two hundred more or less a month."

"Jeez, she's giving you—what?—that car has to be worth close to seventy thousand new. She's giving you at least forty thousand."

Patricia grins, her eyes dancing with enthusiasm. "She said that I earned it. There may have also been a little bit of guilt on her part."

"You earned it? You must have been providing more than basic sex."

"Maybe to her it was the greatest sex ever. Now, all I have to do is stop by the bank in a few days and sign some papers. Then notify the insurance company—"

I interrupt, "Let me guess. The insurance policy is paid up for a year."

"Yeah."

"I suppose she didn't write you out of her will either?" I ask sarcastically.

"Well, dang. I should have asked," she laughs.

We are quiet for a long moment. "Patricia, how much does John know about your living arrangement with Beverly?"

"I made him aware at the very beginning that I was living with a woman. He never asked about the particulars and I didn't volunteer anything."

"Do you want him to know that you're moving out?"

"I don't feel the need to tell him but I don't care if he finds out. It was what it was. And I'm certainly not ashamed of it. It was kind of cool if you look at it from the outside."

"Not so much from the inside."

"Whatever, I not going to look back."

I smile and squeeze her hand. "You're just going to ride your Mercedes into the sunset."

Patricia laughs and kisses me lightly on the lips. "Yeah, that. You want to come along with me?"

"At this time, my dear, I'm not going there. You know where I'm coming from with my male and female relationships and that won't change."

She nods and smiles. "I certainly understand that and I have no expectations from you other than a bit of erotic banging once in a while if you desire. I certainly would like a lot of that. Who knows? Maybe a time will come when I want to approach a male relationship. I suppose I have the same options that you do."

I spread my hands. "Really?"

"Well, something major would have to happen to my attitude about men for that to happen."

I slowly shake my head as I wonder how we came so far together in such a short time. "This is all so crazy.

We've been in bed with each other one time and we're making rules like it's going to last forever."

"Right, isn't it cool?" she grins. "I think we should go for it. We can always go in a different direction tomorrow if either of us gets a better, or should I say more suitable deal."

Do I want this? Yes. "Sounds good to me. A fantastic romp once in a while would be nice—that's all I desire. Do you agree?"

"I accept," she laughs and sticks out her hand for me to shake.

Weird. I take it and kiss the back of it softly. "We need to get dinner ready to serve but I have a few more questions."

"I'm liking this," she smiles as she kisses her hand in the same spot. "Especially since the stars are gathered in my house. Go."

"I don't think you have a house for your stars to gather in. Do you have a plan where you are going to live?"

"Probably get an apartment close to work."

"Alright, I have a suggestion: why don't you move into my spare bedroom for a while until you decide what you want to do. Of course I don't think it would be a good idea to make it forever, but it would be a place to hang out until . . . you know."

Patricia responds with dimples. "I really think you are my stars. It's as if you showed up to rescue me from my last few fucked–up years. My mind was made up as soon as you asked. Yes, and thank you. I want to do that, to stay here until I can figure out what I really want to do." She lays a hand on my knee. "If ever you get your fill of me I'll leave at your request with no hard feelings—just love and gratitude."

"Good, it's settled, but you should know I don't provide fancy cars or clothes."

Patricia shakes her head dejectedly. "Damn, you've just messed up a perfect day."

"Yeah, right. We'll get a plan going to move you as soon as possible. Do you want to stay here before you move you stuff?"

"Oh, yes. I don't even want to face Beverly. I'll stay here."

"Okay, let's shoot for Thursday after work. Do you think with our two cars we can move all your stuff with one trip?"

"All I have is a lot of clothes, shoes and bathroom type stuff like makeup, hair dryer and the like."

"Let's see. In the morning when you go by to change into office garb, bring what you'll need until Thursday. Also bring the bathroom stuff. After that pack everything your car will hold. Surely we can accomplish the move with three carloads. Take your time in the morning. I'll probably be there close to nine and I'll have JB intercept our calls until you show up.

"Now, as to John. Since he and I are so close, our relationship is going to affect him. He will be curious about what's going on so I think it would be a good idea to lay it out for him—past, present and even hopes for the future."

She nods with a bit of concern. "Is this going to cause a problem with you and John? I know you have something special between you. I don't want to get in the way of something between you two that might develop in the future."

"First off, John is free and easy, even with his mate. He knows me well and is fully aware that I need companionship, male or female, and respects that. There is a great chance he and I could get together in the future so I don't want to flaunt whatever relationship you and I may have, but then again I won't hide it."

I wait for comment but I get only a nod. "Alright, we're going to have to get moving to get dinner on the table. There's more I want you to know about John and my relationship, his expectations of his mate including—I'm sure you've wondered—threesomes. Which brings up Link's part in all of this and what was going on behind the scenes both before and after her accident. It certainly was crazy at times.

"Maybe we can have lunch together tomorrow. I'll give you more insight on John and we'll cement plans for your moving here. I think it would be a good idea to tell

John tonight about my new roommate. He definitely will not be surprised."

She follows me over to John's kitchen to find him sitting at the table drinking a Margarita. I stop and study him without greeting.

"Equal opportunity drinker are you, John?" I smile and pick up his glass. Tasting it, I shake my head. "More salt." I set the glass back on the table. "So, why are you drinking a Margarita and not a Mary or merlot? And how did your nap go, anyway?"

Patricia has moved across the kitchen to the stove to boil water for a pitcher of tea. As she lays out the tea-bags she keeps a curious eye on us.

"Shitty, I didn't sleep a wink. Then I give up and decided I need a drink. Lo and behold, the maid didn't buy enough makings for Bloody Marys."

"So, fire her, John. There's no reason you should put up with total incompetence."

I sneak a sidelong glance at Patricia to find her smiling. John doesn't answer as he takes a measured sip of his brew. I guess there is something to drinking a foul tasting concoction to slow down your consumption.

"I think I have enough Bloody Mary mix to get you through the night, John. After you take the Kings to the airport in the morning you might want to drop by the store and stock up on booze and mixes. I notice your Vodka is running low and you might get a couple of bottles of high priced scotch to keep your neighbor happy."

He forces a smile for our benefit. "You'd better make me a list because I refuse to get into the thinking mode for a while."

I grin at Patricia. "Oops, you should never say that to a woman that likes her libations. I'll make you a list, sir, and it will be a long list."

Jonathan salutes with his glass. "Bring it on."

Patricia, what do you want to drink? We have all the usual."

She winks at me and it isn't wasted on Jonathan. "I think I'll hold off for a while."

"Good idea."

Jonathan exhales a long sad breath. "Come on now, folks. You can't let me drink alone. Not today."

I slowly walk over behind Jonathan and put my hands on both shoulders. I bend and kiss him softly below his ear. "John, the night hasn't even started. We will not let you drink alone."

He crosses his chest with one arm and covers my hand. He doesn't comment but we are aware of tears welling up in his eyes. This man is hurting—badly.

I remove my hands and join Patricia. "John, you'd best move as we need to arrange the food on the table."

Sighing he rises and heads for the door. We watch as he sits down on the steps. He wipes the tears with one hand as he holds his nasty drink with the other.

I've got to get that man a decent drink. I exit the backdoor and touch Jonathan's shoulder as I walk by on my way to get Bloody Mary mix at my house. I return and he shows a hint of a smile and a big nod of his head when he sees what I am carrying.

It takes only a moment to make a Mary if you have the right ingredients. It's done. I take it out to Jonathan and exchange it for the Rita. He nods and takes a big gulp. Mission is a success.

Back to the job at hand we finish arranging the food and set out plates, napkins and silverware. We step back and observe. Both of us shrug and grin at each other. That part was easy, but we will have to warm up some of it in the microwave later.

I prepare a couple of glasses of iced tea and hand one to Patricia. She eyes it skeptically and gloomily shakes her head.

"The price we pay?"

I smile and kiss her on the cheek. "I guess it's a matter of priorities. Do you want to get drunk or do you want to get laid?"

She lays a fingertip on her temple and grins. "Can I get laid right now, then drink scotch?"

Without answering, I take her by the hand and we join Jonathan on the patio.

As we sit next to him on the steps he notices the tea and raises a curious brow. "You guys on the wagon?"

"Just coasting right now, John. It's going to be a long night."

He eyes us both and purses his lips with a lone cocked brow. "Uh–huh, I bet it is. Am I invited?"

I part my mouth as if in surprise. "Of course you are invited, John. There're so many things three people can do together."

Patricia eyes us as Jonathan glumly shakes his head. "Just leave it be, Gina. Just leave it be."

I chuckle and jab him in ribs with a finger. "You're just no fun at all, John."

He salutes me with his glass. "And don't you forget it, Gina." He takes a big gulp of his Mary. "Excellent drink. Thanks."

The Kings who had been watching television with the kids join us. They had helped themselves to the tea.

After greeting them Jonathan comments: "It's going to be a long day for you folks tomorrow. Are you up for it?"

Jethro eyes Grace for her answer. "We're packed and ready to go. When do you think we should leave?"

"Your flight is at eleven, so I guess we should head out about eight. That way we'll have time to arrange with Southwest's curbside people for assistance getting you to your flight."

"We don't need help. We can do alright."

"No, Grace, I won't have it. It's going to be a long way to the flight gate. They will carry you right where you need to be in one of those golf cart type vehicles."

Grace objects, "We don't want to cause trouble for anyone."

"It's not trouble, Grace. It's their job to assist those that need help."

"Everyone acts like we're old and can't help ourselves."

John cheerlessly shakes his head and clicks his tongue. "Guess what, Grace. You are old and you do need help."

Jethro smiles and nods his head.

She presents a toothy grin. "Okay, Johnny. We'll do what you want because we don't want to be any trouble for you."

Jonathan rolls his eyes for Patricia's and my benefit. I wink at him and smile.

We sit and sip our drinks. Soon the Bales join us through the patio door with the kids trailing behind. They had already stopped at the drink table and chosen wine.

After greetings all around they drag up chairs and we sit quietly viewing the lake. It's relatively calm on the lake considering the teens took a holiday to attend the memorial.

Bob quietly returns to the kitchen and returns with two bottles of wine. He refills everyone's glass even though they had drunk very little.

He gestures toward Jonathan's glass. "Bro, you need that Mary freshened up?"

Jonathan studies his glass for a long moment. "Probably not. I still have a couple of swallows left. Gina said that I only get three refills and if I refill too soon I lose three hits in the long run."

I shake my head at Jonathan. At least after this long day and week he still has a little levity in him.

I waggle a finger at my friend. "John, don't link your uncontrollable, excessive, nasty, filthy, dirty drinking problem to me. As everyone here knows, nobody controls you. No one should even attempt to tell you what to do, and everyone here knows that you are your own man. I'm not your keeper. So there. Leave me out of any conversation about your drinking problem."

Everyone is laughing, including the Kings and kids sitting quietly to the side.

Jonathan studies me as the laughter dies down. "Oh, okay, Gina. Would you do me a favor?"

"That depends. What do you want?"

"Would you refill my drink? I can't get up."

As everyone watches for my reaction, I stoically shake my head and flip him the bird. As I should have expected the laughter returns, even the Kings and kids.

Jonathan's eyes widen as his jaw drops. He spreads his hands. "Does that mean no?"

318

I stand. "People, dinner, the same as you had for lunch will be served in five minutes."

Patricia follows me into the kitchen and we microwave the meal as quickly as possible.

Bob is not far behind and he drops Patricia's car keys into her hand. "I was tempted to abscond to Mexico," he grins. "But there wasn't enough gas in the tank."

"Thanks, Bob." She stuffs the keys into her back pocket and resumes her heat–it–up work.

Just when everything is ready to serve the others join us. The kids and Kings silently fill their plates and we follow. They head back to the patio and Patricia and I bring up the rear.

"This is much better than at noon," Tex comments with a sharp nod.

"How's that?"

"We didn't have to wait in line for fifteen minutes."

We eat quietly for a few minutes and I comment softly: "It would be nice if you folks eat everything on the table so we don't have to store it."

No comment so I continue: "Tomorrow morning we are going to have a taco breakfast at six–thirty if you guys want to stop by on your way out."

"I don't think so," replies Barney. "We probably won't get moving before nine and we'll stop along the way for breakfast. Thanks anyway."

Another round of refills disposed of, the Bales plead extreme fatigue and announce it's time to leave. We follow them out to their car and there is a round of hugs, a hang in there guy and several more I love you. We watch as they slowly drive away.

Back in the house the Kings express their desire to turn in and I suggest the kids do the same since they've had such a long day. There was no complaint as the Bales headed for their bedrooms and mine traipse across the way to theirs.

John sits at the table in the kitchen and stares sadly at the floor. I shrug at Patricia. "I don't see there is a whole lot to save as far as food. I suggest we get the biggest garbage sack and chunk it all, particularly since all the serving bowls are disposable.

She nods her agreement and opens up the dishwasher. She counts the plates as she rinses them and sticks them in the dishwasher. "Thirteen," she grins. "That should mean there are only thirteen glasses plus a whole bunch of silverware."

I finish bagging up the food waste just as she snaps the dishwasher door closed.

Suddenly Jonathan springs into action. "It's time for the grand finale of the day."

"What's your drink of choice, sir?"

"I think it'll be merlot." He grabs two bottles and an empty glass out of the cabinet and heads down to the dock alone.

We watch him from the patio as it hasn't quite gotten dark yet. Now our attention turns to each other. I study Patricia until she looks at me directly and spreads her hands. "What?"

"Have you been laid yet today?" I ask.

She slowly and dejectedly shakes her head. "No ma'am. I haven't gotten any for the last three months. It's gotten to the point I just don't care anymore. I may as well give up on sex. It's not all it's cracked up to be anyway."

"Would you like to get laid if I ask really nice?"

"What would I have to do?"

"I really don't know. I guess you can just lie there if you want."

"Then the answer is no."

"No?"

"The answer is no."

"Why?"

"If I can't get passionately violent, just forget it. I'm not going there."

"Oh, what do want to drink?"

"That expensive scotch. I forget the name."

Come on. She follows me to my, to our house. I grab the bar ice storage canister and a closed pitcher of water, and hand them to her. I grasp a full bottle of Royal Salute and two glasses for me to carry.

Then we are off, slowly trudging down the walk-way just as dark is setting in and the moon is making its presence.

Jonathan has set up three chairs around the table and is sitting in the middle chair. We set our supplies on the table next to his wine and I crack open the scotch. As I don't use jiggers, I lay in about an inch and half of scotch and follow it with a bit more than a splash of water. I add five cubes of ice to each and slide in a stirring straw.

Handing one to Patricia, she stirs it and offers a toast to both Jonathan and me.

"Folks, we are now closing a very sad day. It is my hope that you, John, can soon put it behind you. I know that Gina and I will help the best we can. Salute."

We take a quick swig and set our glasses in front of us on the table.

"John, I don't know why but Patricia has been looking forward to this, her first night on the dock. It appears she has heard some rumors about what goes on down here. She wants to see for herself."

John chuckles. "I don't know. I guess we can bore her to death. As far as drama is concerned, probably not, unless you guys have a story to tell to liven things up."

He knows. Yes, we have a story to tell to liven things up, but he already knows or at the very least suspects.

Patricia watches me and waits for me to lead. She's not ready to go there at this point but knows it is going to get there.

I sip my scotch and remind myself to take it easy. There will be no pouring anyone into bed tonight unless it's Jonathan. Wouldn't it be interesting to put him to bed unconscious and pile in behind him? Early tomorrow morning would be a classic for sure. But that isn't going to happen.

After a moment of silence I speak. "Johnny, in all your wisdom, do you have any idea what is happening with Patricia that could affect both you and me?"

He ponders. "I think I can rule out slow boat to China. I do suspect that what has happened around here the last six days could cause some monumental changes for you and me . . . and our kids. And there is every reason to think that outsiders could be drawn into our little net. We definitely have a vacuum here now that Link is gone. The big question becomes: how is that vacuum going to be filled?"

He pauses for comment and neither of us volunteer. He continues: "However if something presents itself even before the dust settles today, we can't ignore it.

"Things don't always happen at your convenience. Sometimes things happen when it's time, and you can't disregard it." He chuckles, "We talked about this very thing a few days ago. We kind of laughed at the time, but again, you can't turn your back."

He picks up his wine and sips once, twice, again. He sets the wine on the table and folds his hands as he looks out over the dark water. I guess the ball is in our court but I wait. I can feel Patricia looking at me in the dark.

He continues. "There is something going on here and I think it's good." He grins and pats me on the knee. "It can't be you, Gina. You are never going to get your mess cleaned up."

I chuckle along with Patricia. "Thanks for the vote of confidence, John."

"You're doing all right and things are going to change for you very soon. I have felt it for some time. As things are going to change for me whether I like it or not."

He pauses and tilts his head to gaze at Patricia. "So, I guess the subject of this evening is you, Pat. Did the rich lady throw you out or what?"

The silence on our little part of the lake is broken as we all three laugh. Patricia retrieves her drink and methodically sips. We wait.

She wraps her hand around her long flowing hair in the back behind her neck and nervously twists it. She then swivels toward John and flashes that juicy smile.

"Kinda. Actually I left her."

Jonathan waits for additional information but none is forthcoming. "Let me take a stab as to why. She wasn't providing the favors she advertised when you came on board?"

"I was given a lot of favors that I didn't ask for, but the one favor that was a part of our agreement disappeared after a year or so."

"No sex?"

"Or very little. No excitement."

"How old is she?"

"Middle fifties."

"Man, that's really, really old. Past her prime. Sexually antiquated," he jokes. "So, the breakup must have been difficult for you."

"I thought it was going to be. But she knew it was coming so she was prepared for it."

Jonathan drinks more wine then refills his glass. "I guess you'll have to go buy a car and rent a place to live."

"She gave me the car I was driving."

Jonathan looks at Patricia with a brow raised in curious surprise. "You're kidding! She gave you the Mercedes?"

"I have to refinance what is left on the note."

"And that would be?"

"Twenty thousand."

Jonathan pauses as he does the math on this fingers. "She giving you fifty thousand of equity in a car as you leave?"

"As I see it, after three years I earned it."

"Good investment. Now, living quarters. Got any idea what you are going to do?"

"It's already been arranged."

Jonathan chuckles and slowly shakes his head. "I should have known. The plot suddenly thickens. When are you moving in?"

Patricia sneaks a look at me and I shrug. "We're going to decide that tomorrow. It will be before the weekend because I would like to do it when she's working."

Jonathan pats her on the knee. "Well, there goes the neighborhood. I think both of you have made an excellent decision. You both have my full support as if I have any say–so about what you do."

It's my turn: "John, since you and I have kind of decided that our two families will hang close for a while this will not be a problem. I still think we should combine

323

evening meals and such to lessen the load on the adults and give support until we get back on solid ground. Patricia is okay with that and will do her share."

"Sounds good to me." Jonathan looks out over the water in thought. "Damn, is it still Tuesday?"

I chuckle. "Yeah, it feels like we've lived three days today. I'm glad it's close to being over."

We're silent with our own thoughts until Jonathan clears his throat. "Hey, you guys are something else. As long as I have been observing you two, you've never had a kind word or even smile for each other. Several times I thought you were going to get into a real cat fight. Now, suddenly in a little over a day, you're falling all over each other as if you're lifelong friends. What happened?"

Patricia jumps right in: "Sometimes things happen when it's time."

We laugh, not necessarily because of her statement but because we have cleared another little hurdle to the satisfaction of all involved.

I'm caught up between my desire to hang out on the dock and getting Patricia into bed as soon as possible. I take a big slug of scotch. Sex will have to wait. Now is Jonathan's time.

I pat him on the knee and allow my hand to linger there. He covers my hand with his and it feels good—at least to me.

Patricia stands and strolls to the far corner of the dock and rests her sandaled foot upon a planter as she looks out over the lake. The moonlight catches her silhouette as she takes a sip from her drink.

John whispers, "That is one fantastic looking woman. I hope you can help her get a life to go along with the package."

I nod in the dark but don't comment.

Momentarily Patricia returns and pats Jonathan on the shoulder as she sits. It crosses my mind that Jonathan has lost a woman that has been in his life for over fifteen years. She won't come back. She can't be replaced. Yet on the day he has ceremoniously said goodbye to her, he is surrounded by two other woman that want to help ease his pain and to help him adjust and go forward.

Can we help him? Perhaps not. We will try in spite of our own baggage. In our own way we all have each other. And that has to be worth something—if only to provide an occasionally nudge and even a shove once in a while.

But there are boundaries on both sides. I know there will be times that there will be no appreciation shown and even a few leave–me–alones will surely pop up.

Bottom line: how much can I or we support him and how much does he want to be supported? I already know he will not be hurried. I have to remember that because it is very important. He shouldn't be hurried, as much I would like to help him to get through this as quickly as possible.

There is no easy journey through this maze. If it were easy it wouldn't be necessary. You would just run like hell to the next chapter of life and screw the last part.

So what do I do? Do I press forward with compassion and help, and expect little, or do I do nothing and expect a lot? It's probably somewhere in between the two. Maybe. Speaking for myself, I will tag along on Jonathan's slow boat to China the best I can and expect nothing in return. However I can't kid myself, I would like the maximum payoff.

Jonathan lightly squeezes my hand that is resting on his knee. "Kind of quiet, lady. Are you okay?"

"Yes, John. I was just thinking about a quick healing for you and an end to your misery so you can move on. I know that's not the way it works, but that's what I wish. I hurt for you John. I also suppose that is no consolation to you, but I do hurt for you."

Dammit, that wasn't supposed to bring his tears. But I guess that's okay. Maybe there's a quota of tears that have to be shed. *Get a grip, Gina*, my zookeeper tweets.

After a quiet moment of Jonathan wiping his tears with the back of his hand, Patricia breaks the silence:

"This has certainly been a crazy, crazy day," she says stoically.

Jonathan and I look at each other and start laughing which brings a puzzled look to Patricia's face. "I really wasn't trying to be funny . . . I don't think."

I glance over at her and grin. "We laughed because crazy doesn't even come close to what today was. What should we have expected? As far as I'm concerned, it was bizarre for me, and you certainly had a lot to do with that."

Patricia smiles at me as Jonathan looks on and says. "We can always go back to where we were yesterday and start over."

"I think not, mainly for you, Patricia. You finally did something I think you wanted to do months ago. I think that is a huge turning point for you and it's going to work out in a way that you least expect."

Patricia chuckles softly. "I don't guess I get any previews of what's next, huh."

"No crystal ball here."

Jonathan chuckles. "Timing, timing, timing."

Jonathan and I are already connected with my hand on his knee. He places his hand on Patricia's knee and clears his throat. "Say children, why don't you go do your thing and I'll just hang here for a little while before I go start the rest of my life."

"Are you sure, John? This is your day until you can't go anymore."

"Thanks. You two, along with Griffin and Cory, have saved me the last six days. Now go."

We don't leave and I release a long tension laden sigh. "I think I need a dip in the hot tub. How about you, Patricia?"

"Sounds good to me."

We all stand and Patricia and I take our time in hugging Jonathan. "You okay, John?"

"Yeah, just enjoying holding on to you guys."

"Goodnight, John boy."

"Goodnight, John."

"Goodnight girls. Have fun."

As we turn to leave Patricia stops short. "John, we would be happy for you to join us in the hot tub if you want."

I explode in laughter and Patricia is dumb-founded.

"What did I say? Did I say something I shouldn't have?" She looks first to me then John who is dismally shaking his head.

John protests: "Gina, give me a break. Where did you find this 3–D copy of Link? She's taking up right where Link left off."

"In more ways than one, John. In more ways than one. It's uncanny."

I grasp Patricia's hand and pull her along while she protests, demanding an explanation about what just happened.

"Night, John boy."

It doesn't take long for us to strip down and wade into the hot tub, drink in hand. We sit in front of a cluster of jets that spray against our backs. Patricia raises her legs and lays them over mine.

"And what is this all about?" I ask as I take our drinks and set them on the edge of the tub. I lay my hand on her belly and slide it down to mingle my fingers in her silky pubic hair.

"Presentation is everything. I'm sure you're going to figure out what to do."

I turn her head toward me and slowly place light biting kisses on her fantastic lips and gradually press harder. I force her mouth open with my tongue. My tongue finds hers and we begin that sucking dance of twirling tongues.

I drop my hand below her pubic hair and nudge her legs apart. Quickly I enter a finger in that soft nest bringing groans from deep in her throat. I find her clit and encircle it with my finger while gradually increasing the pressure.

I quicken the pace as I am spurred on by her heavy breathing and increasing groans. I want her to come and I want her to come now.

I withdraw my finger and gently nudge her legs off of mine. I grasp the nearest elbow and turn her toward me to take the other. I urge her to stand and then sit on the top edge of the tub. With a hand on each inner thigh I spread her legs and bend her knees, providing an easy target for what comes next.

"Hurry, Gina, fuck me. I want you now."

With her hands on my shoulders, she pushes me down and my tongue finds that juicy opening. I run my tongue around her clit before sucking, gradually building in pressure.

"Oh, yes, Gina. That's what I want. I'm ready to come. Now, Gina. Harder, please fuck me harder."

I hear her gasp and she pulls me closer. "Just a little. Yes. Oh! Aggh! Oh, Agh! Oh, my God! Yes!"

Suddenly she goes limp and releases my shoulders. I lower her legs to assist her back into the tub. She buries her head under my chin as her breathing gradually quietens. "Shit," she mutters.

When she comes back down to earth, she whispers softly, "Thanks, Beverly. That was great."

She giggles when I don't bite.

SIXTEEN

Well it's done. I feel a ton of relief that the memorial is over as I travel Interstate Ten toward San Antonio. I am a bit played out for sure as Patricia and I frolicked in the hot tub until two, then played for a while in bed before we both finally cratered.

We all pretty much left Lake McQueeney at the same time after eating our breakfast tacos and seeing that the kids made it to the bus. Jonathan seemed to be more at ease as he hustled the Kings into his car for the trip to the airport.

Patricia was a mess—but a happy mess. She is on a mission to get to Beverly's, bathe, dress for work and load what belongings she can in her car.

Arriving at Bales I hustle inside to find JB beaming. She extends her vein streaked fragile hand. "Congratulations again on your promotion."

"Thanks, JB, but I don't see it as a promotion; I see it as being pushed into a job that is nothing more than a giant pain in the ass."

She lays a comforting hand on my shoulder. "You'll do okay. In time you'll grow to enjoy it."

"We'll see. Pat is running a little late so you'll need to monitor her phone. She should be here by ten."

JB nods her understanding. "Where can I reach you?"

"I'm going call the fifth floor office my base unless there's a board meeting or other big meeting, then I'll be on the seventh. Pat will stay on the seventh for the time being."

JB stares at me puzzled. "Why don't you just move to the seventh? It such a nice office."

"I want to leave it just as it is in case Mr. Bales comes back."

"Oh, I thought he's gone for good."

"I really don't know, JB. I think he'll be back but I don't have any idea when."

I turn for the elevator when she doesn't reply. "See you, JB."

I get settled in and read over last week's column published in *Fashion Week* magazine. With each column I am becoming more relaxed and feeling less tension and pressure over deadlines and actual column content.

With more and more questions and answers arriving over my social media, I find that as long as I keep up with it daily it is quite easy. This past week has been entirely different and I have fallen behind. Now, hopefully I can get back on track.

Before Patricia comes in I want to finish up this week's column for tomorrow's deadline. When she gets here maybe she can give me some insight about what I'm supposed to be doing in this high powered job I inherited.

"Hey, *Conejo*, where's *Juan*?" Juanita greets after Manuel shows Patricia and me to our table.

"Hi, Juanita. I'm afraid that John doesn't work with me anymore. He's decided he needs some time off. I gesture toward Patricia. "Juanita, this is Patricia. She works in my office."

Juanita takes Patricia's hand and shakes it. "I am most happy to meet you."

She turns and eyes me suspiciously. "No. *Juan* wouldn't quit. He liked his work. Is he ill? Perhaps I should send him a special order of cheese enchiladas."

Oh, shit. She doesn't know. I reach up and grasp Juanita's hand and she searches my eyes warily. "Link died in a car accident late last week."

Instantly Juanita's eyes tear over. She stares at me as she slowly shakes her head. "Oh, my God. That poor man. He must be overwhelmed in grief. I too am devastated."

I release her hand and she wipes at the tears that suddenly flow freely down her cheeks. "I must talk to him to express my sorrow. I'm sorry, I have to go. I'll come back in a little while and serve you. I need to be alone with myself right now." She quickly disappears.

Patricia gazes at me in confusion. "Wow, John and Juanita must have been very good friends."

"For years. I don't know the whole story and John refuses to talk about it, but I do know she has only one child, a son that's about fifteen–years–old. When he was four–years–old he had some form of cancer that was considered terminal.

"I understand that at Link's insistence John footed the bill for her to take him to M.D. Anderson Hospital in Houston. I think that Link drove them because Juanita was terrified that she would get lost in Houston and that she wouldn't know what to say to the doctor.

"Long story short, the kid pulled through and without John and Link's assistance there's no way that would have happened."

I rattle around in my purse and take out John's business card. I turn it over and write John's home address and cell number.

Momentarily Juanita returns under forced composure. She nods with a tight smile. "I'm sorry. I am shocked. I need to help if I can. He is part of my family. I'm sorry I didn't get word so I could have gone to the rosary service. It was when?"

"Yesterday. I'm sorry Juanita. I should have called. It was in the newspaper over the weekend. I just thought that everyone would see it."

"No matter now. I will call him," she nods determined.

I hand her the business card. "His phone and address are on the back. I would suggest that you send him a note first. Then after a few days or a week call him. Right now he's just too miserable to handle any calls, but you should do what you think is best."

She studies the card as tears reappear in the corners of her eyes. "Thank you, Gina. Would you tell him today that I'm thinking about him and I am grieving along with him. I love that man."

"I will do that, Juanita. As soon as I see him today I will deliver your message."

Juanita releases a long ragged breath and forces a smile. "Now perhaps I should take your order so that you can get back to work on time."

"I'll have the cheese enchiladas please with flour tortillas."

"That good for me also," Patricia nods.

"And drinks. Will you be having a Mary?"

"Not today, Juanita. I'm supposed to act like the boss so maybe I shouldn't do that. How about bringing us iced tea."

She nods and is off.

"Damn, I can't believe I let that happen. I called everyone John wanted. I guess he forgot Juanita. I feel really bad about her not getting the message about the memorial."

Juanita stops by with a tray of drinks, leaves two teas and exits without comment.

We sip on our tea and I wish I could have a Mary. Well, it's not going to happen until later this evening.

I study Patricia, wishing I could get her in the sack. "Ma'am, that was one hell of a day . . . and night wasn't it?"

"It was that for sure. I just can't believe that happened to us out of the clear blue. I would have laughed yesterday morning if I sensed even a suggestion of what was getting ready to play out between us. My whole body has been singing all morning."

I'm fixed on her sugary smile and have the urge to lean over the table and have a bite of it. But I hold back lest the whole restaurant catch me at it. "I think it would be very difficult for us to go back and write down every little spark that flashed between us. All the emotions we shared like we had been doing that forever. I can't wait until tonight for a replay."

"That is a happening thing, I guarantee."

Juanita brings two plates of enchiladas and a warmer of tortillas. She nods and is on her way.

"How did it go this morning? Did you get a full load?"

"Yes, I did. It's pretty easy when there are no boxes to pack. Just pick up an arm load out of the closet, throw them in the car and repeat. It took about six trips to fill the car."

I toy with my enchiladas as she watches in amusement. "Don't play with your food, daughter. You will make Mommy angry."

I lay down my fork and stick my tongue out at her. "Are we going to be able to finish off the move with two car loads tomorrow?"

"Yes, ma'am. Easy. I need to pick up a couple of boxes for my shoes. I brought all the bathroom stuff like cosmetics today so I'll have the means to make myself presentable in the morning."

"Great. Now what?"

"I want to know right now; what is all the drama over a threesome?"

I smile as I study her. Damn, she's beautiful. What could have possibly happened that turns her off to men? I can see why it is so frustrating to them to get completely rejected by her.

"I waited to explain because there is a little history involved that will take a few minutes. I didn't want to give you bits and pieces because of Link's part. It's kind of sad, but also amusing because of John's complete rejection of the idea.

"About a month ago Link started having dreams that she was going to die. They got worse as time went by and in spite of our research that indicated they didn't mean pending death, she just could not escape them. She actually thought she was going to die." I drearily shake my head. "And she did.

"So she decided that she needed to make sure that John was taken care of after her death by finding him a mate. As you might guess, the potential mate she chose was me."

Patricia's jaw drops and her eyes widen. "Damn, that's weird. What did you think?"

"Yes, that was weird, however at that time I was high and dry sexually so it sounded pretty cool to have even a thought of a potential male sex partner.

"To achieve this she felt like she needed to get John and me in bed together immediately, so when the transition came we would already be on familiar ground. She decided the best way to do this was a ménage `a trois."

She tilts her head and studies me quizzically. "Jeez, Gina, this is totally bizarre. What did you think about having a threesome?"

I pick up my fork and absently stab at my enchiladas. "Originally I was completely against it—totally turned off. But as time passed I began to come around because I was starving for some male sexual companionship, even if it was John.

"From the very beginning John was against a threesome. He didn't even like us joking about it as you've seen. But Link and I wouldn't let up. We continually manipulated our conversations to the punch line—threesome."

"I assume it never happened."

I chuckle. "Not even close. I wish it had. Link felt that John and I would be on a totally different playing field after she died because of our sexual familiarity with each other. I'll never know if that's true."

"As long as you and John have been such great friends you guys have never had a sexual relationship?"

"We've hit on each other but were always on a different page." I shrug with a drawn brow. "I've wished a thousand times that we had but we didn't, so that's the way it goes.

"It's going to be an interesting time for John and me for sure. I would jump in the sack with him in an instant but I don't have any idea what's with him—what he's thinking.

"The only thing for sure is, it's going to take him time to sort things out before he's ready to go forward with me or anyone else." I grin and touch Patricia on the arm with a finger. "Hey, maybe you'll be the chosen one."

She gloomily shakes her head. "Hey, woman, you leave me out of this equation. I'm not having anything to do with men, now or ever."

I gather my brow and fix her with a curious frown. "Not even someone as special as John?"

334

"Not even."

"You must have been involved with some real ass-holes."

She affirms, "Frigging jerks. All of them."

"Sometime you'll have to tell me about them."

"Maybe not."

I squeeze her arm and those familiar sparks crackle throughout my body. Shit, do I ever stop this madness? "Okay, I'll leave that subject alone. From now on it'll be just you and me."

She shows her wide dimpled smile. "And John."

"Not a threesome though. I really don't think I want to go there anymore."

"If John is a male and I think he is, me neither."

"John neither . . . also."

I catch Juanita's attention and she stops by with the check. "Thanks, Juanita. Again I am so sorry you weren't notified of the memorial."

She nods and forces a thin smile. "*Conejo*, I know you will keep an eye on *Juan* for me. If there is anything he needs let me know and it will be provided." She is gone as quickly as she came.

"Alright, babe. It's time to get back to the office."

As we stand she reminds me to call Griffin.

"Oh, yeah. Thanks. I'll do that as soon as we get back. I want her to cook tonight if she can. John is in no condition to cook and you and I have to unload your clothes and drink scotch. We won't have time for cooking. What do you think?"

Jonathan joins us as we unload Patricia's car. He sips on his Bloody Mary as he watches but doesn't volunteer to help. After we return for the second load he grins as he slowly shakes his head.

"What is it, John? Do you have a suggestion?" Patricia asks pointedly, her lips pressed in mock defiance.

"Just an observation."

Patricia sets her scotch on top of the car and faces Jonathan with both hands planted on her hips. "And that would be?"

"You guys could carry more if you would set your drinks down and work with both hands don't you think?"

Patricia drops her mouth open feigning surprise. "Well, damn, why didn't I think of that? For your information, Mr. Bales, we happen to be working while we drink—not drinking while we work.

"Think about it. There's a big difference there. We just want to do something with the free hand while we drink. Do you want to know the drunkard's motto?" She reaches in the car for more clothes.

Jonathan shrugs, "I suppose this is something I need to know. What, pray—tell is the drunkard's motto?"

With clothes draped over one arm, she grasps her scotch off the top of the car with her other hand and turns toward the house. "The drunkard's motto is . . . oh, I forget. It has something to do with drinking, though."

Jonathan drearily shakes his head and trudges back toward his house. I trail behind Patricia laughing.

We two one–armed laborers are pretty fast and we finish the job posthaste. We eye Jonathan on his patio and join him.

I gesture toward the kitchen. "What are Griffin and Cory cooking, John?"

"I have no idea, but it smells pretty good. And I am not about to complain even if they are serving stewed rat. I'm just glad they're cooking."

"Umm, I guess we shouldn't be too nosy but I'm hungry. Those cheese enchiladas didn't last very long. Patricia, how about moseying in and sneaking a look."

She grins and grabs my and Jonathan's glass. "I think it's time to refresh our drinks. I shall return."

"So you went to *El Cabrito* for lunch."

"Yes sir, we did, and I have something sad to tell you: Juanita wasn't aware that Link had died. She was devastated. She was crying huge tears."

Jonathan drops his head and lightly knocks his temple with a fist. "Damn. I can't believe I didn't have you call her. She is so special."

"Yes, she regretted not coming to—get this—the rosary. I told her it was my fault because I thought she would see it in the obituaries. She's okay with it. She's just sad for you and wants to share your pain.

"She wants to call you to say how sorry and grieved she is, but I told her to hold off for a few days until things settle a bit."

Jonathan nods sadly. "I should call her but I just don't want to be bothered by anything right now. Remind me in a few days."

Patricia returns with the drinks. "I don't think it's stewed rats. Looks and smells more like fried chicken. The kids came snooping around complaining about how hungry they are right now. Griffin told them for every minute they hang around the kitchen, dinner will be five minutes later. They left right away."

Jonathan counts on his fingers. "Let's see, how many members of this family tonight?"

I name them off: "Four kids, Cory and Griffin, us three—awfully large family you have here, John."

"Yep, and I'm missing one more."

Patricia and I see the tears welling up in his eyes. What can we do? Nothing.

Seconds later Cory calls out, "Dinner, guys."

When we get inside the kids have already crowded around the table filling their plates.

Griffin announces above the chatter of the kids, "It's just as well with this number of people to feed that we continue to serve it buffet style."

"You're in charge, Griffin," I answer. "You set it up any way you want. You won't hear us complain." I grin and shrug, "Well, maybe the kids, but Patricia tells us you perfectly handled them raiding your kitchen."

She laughs and points at Johnny. "Johnny, what happens if you cause too much trouble?"

Johnny grins, "I don't eat."

Eventually everyone has a full plate and we're sitting around the patio quietly eating.

"Fantastic, guys. Thank you for a great meal." That was Jonathan. "I hope you guys are going to be available for a few weeks."

Cory and Griffin nod with a smile. "We'll be here when you need," Griffin follows.

"How did the party go last night?" I ask between bites of mashed potatoes and gravy.

They chuckle and Griffin looks to Cory to answer. "It got out of hand pretty quickly. Word spreads extra fast over the campus, particularly when free beer is involved.

"As far as we could tell about two hundred people showed up and the two kegs emptied within an hour or so. We had to pass the bucket around to get beer money for a run to the store. I think we had to go back to the store about three more times."

Griffin exaggerates a nod. "It was a fun party though. Those last minute parties are always best. All over campus today people were talking about it. They were calling it Link's party."

Dinner over, Griffin, Cory, Patricia and I gather the dishes and fill the dishwasher before they scamper off to another campus party. Griffin explained that with the end of the school year approaching, everyone wanted to get in one last party. She also reiterated they would return each and every night until we either got tired of them or their cooking.

Summoned by a call from Monica, the four kids head down to her house for cake and ice cream to celebrate her birthday.

Of course the three of us, arms loaded with drink, head for the boat dock. The only confusion is whose dock is going to enjoy our company tonight.

We settle in and quietly enjoy the light breeze as it passes through gently swaying the cypress trees. The scotch is smooth and the merlot must be pretty good because Jonathan hasn't complained. And we miss Link—at least Jonathan and me.

"I notice you laid in a ton of alcohol, John. It must have cost you a bundle."

He raises his wine glass to me. "Worth every penny, my dear. Every frigging penny."

"Any problems in taking the Kings to the airport?"

"No, the Southwest people quickly loaded them on the back of one of those carts and we barely had time to say goodbye. They called after the flight and said a neighbor had picked them up, so they are home safely.

And Grace wanted to make it clear, they didn't have a Bloody Mary—or two."

I chuckle, "They probably needed a Mary as much as any of us do."

Patricia takes a sideways glance at me. "I take it they don't drink."

Jonathan and I chuckle and he replies, "During their flight in on Monday, they had three Marys each, not knowing they were alcoholic. Needless to say when Gina picked them up they were three sheets to the wind. And they wanted more until we filled them in on the sinning they had been doing."

Patricia laughs, "You're kidding. I love it. I wish I could have seen that."

I add, "They were just a wee bit embarrassed to say the least."

Jonathan shrugs, "I wish Link could have seen that. She would be rolling on the deck in laughter. She used to say her parents drove her crazy sermonizing about drinking the evil juice."

We drift into quiet again, lost in our own thoughts.

Jonathan chuckles, "Hell, Link did see her parents plastered. She had a better seat than we did."

Patricia and I laugh. "Of course, John. Of course."

The kids come roaring back from Monica's and we march them straight to bed. We're looking forward to the end of the month when school is out and the kids can stay up later and sleep later.

At Jonathan's urging Patricia and I also decide to call it a day—at least until we can crawl under the sheets together. I don't think there is going to be extensive play time as we are still pretty exhausted by yesterday's activities. But there will be play time for sure.

Heeding my instructions by phone, Clement the security guard meets me when I park to help with the pastries. He immediately sizes them up to see what his choice is going to be. Then JB chooses the same one and they argue over who has first dibs. He rides with me up the elevator to the seventh floor.

The elevator opens to find my smiling assistant decked out in her usual to–die–for outfit of cream slacks, nude patent Trotters Paulina Pumps and an orange ruffled sleeveless blouse. As usual, the top two buttons have been intentionally left unfastened drawing attention to two of her better parts. This woman is a knockout. It's a shame she doesn't care for men.

"Good morning, Ms. Wabbit. Good morning, Clement."

"Good morning, Ms. Goodwin. I trust you had a restful night at your new home."

"Yes ma'am. Very restful and entertaining. Thank you. The coffee is ready. Shall I get you a cup?"

"That would be great with a jelly roll. Perhaps Clement would like a cup also."

As Patricia passes me she whispers, "Anything else I can do for you just let me know. I aim to please."

I whisper my reply: "I would like to eat you but I'll have to settle on a jelly roll right now."

Clement takes his coffee and donut, says his thanks and heads for the elevator.

Patricia is eying the pastry she brought with the coffee. "Will you share your jelly roll?"

"No ma'am. Get your own."

"Damn, you're no fun at all. You must have had a bad night."

I grin. "*Au contraire*. I scored. And scored again."

"Wow, who was the lucky participant?"

"I don't know. Just someone who wandered in off the street. I didn't get her name."

"Umm, do you think she will return for more?"

"Probably. She left her underwear so I assume she will return for it. At that time we'll see about more."

"She left her underwear. What did you do with it?"

"I put it under my pillow. I like the way it smells."

"That's kind of kinky isn't it?"

"What difference does it make? Nobody knows."

"Oh, by the way, I have a problem"

"And that would be?"

"I'm missing some underwear."

We laugh and hug—a long sensual hip grinding butt grabbing hug.

The elevator door pings and we quickly release our hold on each other. Darren and Josh exit the elevator, mumble their hellos and head for the coffee. The next ping brings the two remaining members, Jesse and Chris. Jesse heads for the coffee and Chris joins us in his quest—as Patricia says—"to pester me."

He extends his hand in an enthusiastic greeting. I note that Patricia reacts by offering the same limp hand as she did at the memorial. What's with her?

"Good morning, ladies. I trust things are going well," Chris bubbles, zeroing in on Patricia—and the cleavage. "Nice outfit. I'm impressed."

I watch as Patricia stoically mumbles good morning. This is ridiculous. He's just being nice and she acts like he has some sort of contagious disease. I feel so sorry for him. If I were a man and she completely ignored me it would only happen once and I would disappear. At the very least he hangs in there. I wish I could help—both of them.

He touches me lightly on the shoulder. "Cool blouse."

I grin. "Walmart."

"Walmart has everything you need. What do you say we get this show on the road?"

I follow him to the coffee pot to refill my cup. I fill the carafe, head for my place at the head of the table and set the carafe in front of Josh. Patricia takes the same seat as the last meeting and buries her head in her I-Pad.

I sit and sip my coffee as I look over notes prepared yesterday afternoon. I clear my throat and make eye contact with the four gentlemen sitting around the table.

"Our purpose today is to make a decision on the possible purchase of Hunter's Almanac. The way I see it we have three options.

"First, we take over their debt and pay the present owners the two million they are asking.

"Second, we wait until they file bankruptcy and contact the trustee to see if we can work out a deal with the judge that's beneficial for us.

"Third, we walk away.

"After your presentation I understand the final decision is mine to make. Bottom line, that may be true but I'll weigh my decision heavily on your input. If you cannot come to an agreement and you are split down the middle, it will definitely be my decision.

"If you are split 3–1 or 4–0 that will also weigh heavily on my decision. Regardless, I will take full responsibility for the final decision and you will not be held accountable for any negative consequences that come out of this meeting. That will be on me."

I pause and smile while looking at each as they stare at me stoically. "If what we decide here today in the future turns out to be a profitable decision for the company you will get your full measure of praise for your input along with any possible bonuses or rewards."

I look over the group. Still stoic. "Any questions so far?

"No. Okay, before we begin let's have a little poll. How many of you have already made a decision before hearing what the others have to say?"

I wait until all have shook their heads positively. "I guess that's good. Alright, let's start with you Darren. I assume your time in the accounting department was somewhat frustrating."

Darren is in his early fifties, with a sad face accentuated with dark sunken eyes. His dark hair is thinning prematurely and his bald spot is growing. Unlike most of BP's employees he wears long sleeved dress shirts with colorful ties even in the heat of summer. He is known as a no nonsense guy that will tell it like he sees it—typical accountant.

Darren chuckles and woefully shakes his head. "It's a frigging circus over there. They've changed chief accountants three times in three years with the last being on the job only three months. She's completely lost. As far as I can tell the books are not up to date, payroll is a mess and employees rush to the bank on payday lest the money run out.

"They are losing about one hundred fifty thousand a month which in a year's time would be well over a million. They are in debt about four million right now. Neither of those figures would be a big deal for us if we can get the company on the road to recovery.

"One of the big drains moneywise is the owners that make a ball of money and neither does a hell of a lot to earn it. They of course are going to be long gone one way or another."

Darren pauses momentarily in thought, then clears his throat as he runs a hand over his bald spot. "My bottom line: we can probably bail the company out of debt for about four and a half million. I don't see paying the two owners anything. I also don't think they actually believe they can walk away with anything. BP is known as a big spender but we're not stupid.

"I can give my vote on the accounting end of the deal right now. It's a go if we can take over the company and its debts. There are really no big monetary outlays except for handling the debt.

"By the way, the employees over there see us as a Godsend. They are all concerned that the business is going to fold and they will be out on the street."

Darren folds his notes in front of him and takes a swig of coffee.

"Questions anyone?" I ask.

Chris nods curiously. "If we wait for bankruptcy do you think we can get a better deal since much of the debt will be wiped out?" I notice that Patricia listens and watches attentively when Chris speaks while she appeared bored when Darren spoke. Interesting.

Darren slowly shakes his head. "Not necessarily. The judge and trustee are going to try to get as much of the creditor's money back as possible. So, in the beginning the price will be close to what it is now—four million. Later on they will have to drop the price to get rid of the company, at which time the creditors will suffer.

"I need to say at this point that if we decide to wait for bankruptcy, there might be a bidding war with others that want the property. So that would be the case for taking over the company and debt of four million now."

I wait. "Others?"

"Okay, Chris, you're up."

Unlike Darren and me, he elects to stand. Patricia watches closely and he sneaks a glance at her with those penetrating blue eyes.

"It's pretty simple. They've lost about one–third of their advertisers in the last year. Some of the others are wavering but about fifty percent will hang in there for sure.

"In talking to those that have quit running ads in the last year many would consider coming back. I've talked with all of them and I think we can hold on to those that are wavering.

"By the way, many of these are companies we have worked with in the past. They like working with us. That goes a long way.

"Within a year I predict we could increase advertising revenue at least twenty–five percent. That makes the company profitable right there."

Chris sits and again glances at Patricia. She looks away. What's going on with her?

"Questions?"

"Alright, Jesse, will it work?"

Jesse Ferro. Short, bull dog appearance, pug nose. Would pass for an old boxer. He's head of publications. He also elects to stand.

"Thanks, Gina. Yes we can make it work. First we revamp the whole rag. Give the hunter's something they can get their teeth into. Once we make the changes, we send the new magazine to all those that have dropped their subscription with a juicy deal to get them back on the list. We can do this. We've done it twice in the past. It'll take about a year.

"Also this: we have access to a raft of company magazines where we get cut rate deals to advertise." He smiles. "I'm sure many that read *Gay Time* would just love to subscribe to *Hunter's World.*" He sits and folds his arms.

"Good, Jesse. Any questions?"

"No. Okay, Josh, you've been keeping your ear to the ground on this subject for over a week. Do you have anything to add?"

Josh Baker, the old guard, pushing sixty, over weight and obviously not healthy. He is usually disagreeable and cantankerous, especially now that I am sitting in the chair he feels belongs to him. He chooses to remain seated, peering over wire rimmed glasses perched at the end of his nose.

"Nothing other than everyone seems to have a handle on the issue. I must admit I wasn't too enthused coming into this, but now I at least know how I want to go. Good job, gentlemen."

"Questions for Josh?"

"None. Okay, let's see where you stand. All we need is a simple yes or no.

"Number one. We take over the company and debt and offer the present owners two million to squander. What say you?"

I scan the guys. "No one's interested. I'm not interested either."

"Number two. We wait until bankruptcy and try to work something out with the judge and trustee.

I point two fingers of each hand at the gentlemen sitting in front of me. "Two and Two. We have a stalemate. I will delay my preference at this time."

"Three. We walk away. What's your pleasure?

"All of you vote no.

"Well, it looks like we have a stalemate on the wait for bankruptcy issue. Unless there's another option that we didn't list." I look over the group and see Josh grinning. "Okay, Josh, let me guess: we need to change number one, right?"

"Yes, Gina. We make an offer to the present owners to take over the business and its debt of four million and pay them zip, nada—clean out your desk. Put your stuff in a cardboard box and get out."

"Great, Josh. If they would go along with this it would save a lot of jobs because an outright bankruptcy would probably close down the business completely.

I add, holding up a cautious finger. "However, we have to keep in mind this is not going to happen overnight. The owners might want to take our offer, but they still want that two million. So they'll more than likely wait until closer to bankruptcy in hopes that we will blink first—which we won't."

I pause. "Questions?"

It's Jesse: "If this doesn't work, we still have the possibility of picking up the pieces in bankruptcy, right?"

"That's right. Okay, what's your pleasure on going with number one without paying the present owner's anything?

"Yes, yes, yes and yes.

"You have done your part and I agree. This is my as well as your decision. I'll approach the two owners early next week to give them our offer with no timetable as the bankruptcy will determine that. I'll arrange for five million in financing with the bank in case we have to act fast.

"If that doesn't pan out the next option is to see how we fair in the liquidation of the business. Since your vote was two–two, I'll be the deciding vote. I will be in favor of entering the fray to give us a chance, however small, of pulling this off.

"If all of the above fails, we will be forced to walk away. However, we will know we have done our due diligence. Any questions before we adjourn?"

I nod and smile. "Very productive meeting, gentlemen. I will keep you posted on any progress or surprises. Thank you."

The four guys wave at me and leave together. As we follow them out to Patricia's desk I notice her watching Chris. He turns, smiles and points a finger at her as he enters the elevator. She looks away. She certainly is acting strange. Could this be the beginning of the lesbian world losing a mainstay? I think not. She's going where she's going and I don't see anyone changing that. However, I'm going to sure as hell try.

I drop my column on her desk for the Thursday deadline. "Will you get this to the designated people before we leave this afternoon?"

"Consider it done. What else?"

"Do you have the contact information on the guy John deals with at Federal Bank? I need to see if they'll accept me as a representative of BP."

"Yes, I have it. By the way, congratulations on a perfect meeting. I am impressed as all get out."

I grin and kiss her on the cheek. "Well, thanks. I was pretty good wasn't I?"

She searches for a moment on the computer and writes down a name and phone number. "This should be the guy. Do you want me to make an appointment for you to meet with him?"

"I'll call him first. I just don't think I can drop in off the street and work out a loan deal for us. They want to deal with the top and in reality that is not me."

"You have to get the job done but you don't have the clout to do it."

"You know what. I don't think I have any clout at all. I wish I could ask the owner."

"Why don't you?"

"He told me not to ask or tell him anything about what goes on at BP. He doesn't want to be bothered."

"Umm, so what are you going to do if the bank wants to talk only to him?"

I throw up my hands and shrug with a smile. "Beats the hell out of me. Maybe you and I can do a noon-time bank robbery—you know, stocking masks, big ugly guns—think AR-15. Maybe a bazooka and even a couple of those women's pink pistols. Do you think they keep five million in the teller drawers?"

"Probably not. We'd have to kidnap the president of the bank and make him let us in the vault."

"Should we get small bills or large ones? And how would we carry it."

"I guess we could stop at Walmart and buy one of those toy wagons with sides on it."

"What time to you think we should leave here to get you moved?"

"You're the boss. We leave anytime you want to go."

"I may be the boss but, remember, I don't have any clout. I can't just up and leave anytime I want."

"In that case let's just sneak out."

"Good idea. Let's see, I have several phone calls to make. I'll get that done and we'll leave about three. That way we'll have the cars packed and be home by five or five–thirty, in time to watch Griffin and Cory cook."

"Sounds like a good plan. What about lunch?"

"Damn, it's just about noon. Time flies when you're having fun. Do we have great jobs or what?"

She grins and pinches my cheek. "We have great jobs. One of my workmates is a tiger in bed. When do we get to screw on that leather sofa in the conference room?"

I chuckle. "The boss is not supposed to fish off the company dock."

Patricia studies me quizzically. "What does that mean?"

"The boss does not fuck the employees."

"Does that mean I'm not going to get laid on the sofa?"

"I know this Mexican place down the road a piece."

Patricia pouts her big lips. "That's not the answer I wanted to hear."

After notifying JB that we were sneaking out and to intercept our calls, we get to Beverly's Condo about three–fifteen.

I step out of my car and squint up at this huge fancy building, shielding the sun with my hand. "Damn, which one is Beverly's?"

Patricia laughs. "It's all Beverly's. That's her home. All of it."

"Well, you sure have taken a step backward moving in with me. That's no condo. It's one big– ass house."

"In some ways, yes. In other ways a big no." She grabs two boxes out of her back seat and we walk through a large wrought iron gate, then she keys in the code to open double extra–large doors that lead into a foyer. In the middle there is a staircase with a hallway on each side. Off to the right of the foyer is what appears to be a living room or library and on the left it is a dining area with doors to what is probably the kitchen.

Patricia is watching for my reaction and I merely shake my head. "Your lonely mansion on the hill."

"You've got that right. Do you want the usual tour?"

"No, I'd just as soon get your stuff and get the hell out of here if you don't mind."

She giggles as she hands me a box, takes me by the hand and drags me behind her upstairs.

Walking into what was her bedroom two days ago I'm a bit floored. I thought I had a large master bedroom, but hers was twice as large and it's not even the big one. I don't comment as I follow her into the closet that is bigger than most bedrooms. It has a connecting bath and huge tiled walk in shower that I'm sure ten people could fit into.

"I guess everything goes, huh?"

"Everything."

I spy what looks like a cut out newspaper theatre advertisement stuck on the mirror with tape. I pull it off as she watches.

"Umm, are you a fan of Adele?"

"Yeah for several years. I was hoping to go to her concert at the AT&T Center next week but I waited too late to get tickets. An hour after they went on sale I went online and they had already sold out of everything in my price range. I'm not about to pay one thousand dollars for a concert ticket, and that's one of the cheaper tickets located a half mile from the stage. Floor tickets go for as much as five thousand."

"So, you're not going?"

"I guess not. She's in Austin in October. Maybe I can get tickets for that one. I'll be waiting online as soon as they go on sale." She takes the ad from me, looks at it and shrugs before pitching it in the wastebasket.

"Are you ready to do this?" she grins.

"Ready. Just say what?"

"Okay, woman. Just take everything not tied down and we'll have it all loaded in a few minutes."

She starts by changing from her heels into athletic shoes, then she loads shoes into one of the boxes we brought up. I wrap as many clothes over my arm that I can handle and head for the stairs wishing I had thought to bring other shoes. On my way back up I meet her coming down with the box of shoes.

As soon as I get to the closet I go to the bathroom and take the Adele ad out of the trash and stick in my pocket. Then it's another load of clothes. She returns and starts to fill the other box with shoes and I head downstairs with my load.

In about twenty minutes we have it all loaded— the last two loads of clothes had to be stuffed all the way to the roof in both cars. She slams the doors shut and turns to take one last look at the condo.

"Say bye."

"Bye."

I grin and pat her on the back. "When one door closes . . . ."

She smiles as we both get into our cars. Starting up I follow her back toward Interstate Ten for what will be a short trip home.

I feel relieved that the move is almost done. I feel relieved that the board meeting was a success. I feel relieved that I have somebody to physically love on again until my dream is fulfilled—if that ever happens. Shit, I even feel relieved that I have survived fifty–three days since Pep left. There's only eighteen days until the divorce is final. That will be a huge relief.

I certainly could use a cool smooth Chivas Royal Salute and water about now. And a quiet time on the dock. Maybe even a threesome. Not.

Yahoo, go girl, comes that familiar echo from my keeper. Where have you been lately?

We pull into the driveway and park side by side. We start unloading and I'm wondering if the meager closet in the guest room is going to hold all of her clothes. When we come out after delivering the first load, Jonathan spies us and without comment pitches in to lighten our job.

We finish the job quickly but had to put a large amount of the clothes in the hall closet. I assume she will get it organized later. I have no idea how she can wear all the clothes she has in a year's time. But that's neither here nor there for me. I'm just glad she's moved in and close to me.

We follow Jonathan over to his kitchen where he already has our scotch ready to splash. I'm tempted to ask if he was lonely today, but I decide to not go there since I already know the answer. We traipse down to his dock with drink in hand.

We silently sip our drinks and I wonder where the kids are. I assume Jonathan has the kid thing under control. He has nothing else to do.

Griffin and Cory shout from the patio and wave. After we wave back they go inside to start dinner. Damn, it's nice to be able to sit down here where it's so peaceful and have someone else do the evening cooking.

"It's been a long day," I comment. "I'm glad it's over."

Patricia agrees, "Me too."

Jonathan doesn't comment and I wonder if he is curious about what happened at the board meeting this morning. Well, he's about to get an idea of what happened, like it or not.

"Hey, John boy, I know you don't want to hear about what's going on at BP, however I'm having a minor problem. I'm going to need your help."

I glance at Patricia and find her grinning. I stick my tongue out at her.

Jonathan is silent as he casually looks out over the lake. Don't make this hard for me, Jonathan. You have to do this if I'm going to be able to do the job.

He takes a sip of his merlot, sets the glass on the table in front of him and clears his throat. Patricia is slowly shaking her head and smiling.

"Having a problem doing your job? What's the deal?"

"I need five million dollars," I reply stoically.

Silence for a minute, then two, three. "Umm, I see. Doesn't Darren have this kind of money in the company accounts?"

"You know he doesn't, John. He says he has trouble making payroll. He said for me to do what you would do—go to the bank and take out a loan."

His lips move slightly; is that a grin? "Go for it. You don't need me for that."

351

"Tell that to Homer Johnston at Federal Bank. He said that they don't have any idea who I am and what my position is within the company. He said for you to come on down and they will work with you as usual."

"Umm . . . what do you need five mil for?"

I shrug and wink at Patricia. "Just company stuff. You know, daily working capital."

"Oh, okay. I'll give him a call in the morning so you can work with them. I'll probably have to sign some type of agreement or contract for that amount, but it won't be a problem. BP is one of their best customers. I'll let you know in the morning after I talk to him what you need to do."

"Good, then Patricia and I will be headed for Brazil. Five million should last us a couple of years don't you think, Patricia?"

Patricia responds emphatically, "Yep."

We watch as Jonathan dismally shakes his head. "Nope, you can't do that unless you take me with you."

Gotcha, John: "It'll never happen, John. You have told me time and time again that you don't do three-somes."

SEVENTEEN

Well I have procrastinated long enough. Here it is Friday, my fifth day as the first woman CEO of powerful Bales Publishing, and I still haven't made one courtesy phone call to the BP partners worldwide to let them know I'm here if needed. Today I also have to get the bank loan squared away, however that hinges on Jonathan's phone call and may have to wait until Monday.

First things first. I have read over the Adele concert ad that I fished out of Beverly's bathroom trash. I don't know if I can pull this off but I'm certainly going to try.

Okay, internet search, don't fail me. Let me try, *Adele San Antonio concert*:

It suggests *www.adelesanantonio.com*: All they have available is floor seats varying between three and five thousand dollars a pop. I'm not going there for sure.

Alright, *www.ticketnetwork.com*: Same high dollar seats.

AT&T Center Box Office: Jeez, you have to be a high roller at these prices.

www.ticketinventory.com: Nothing.

www.StubHub: High dollar only. Damn, this is a lost cause.

www.seatgeek: Forget it. This concert is definitely not for your common middleclass bloke.

www.ticketliquidator.com: Hold on. They've just refunded two tickets, first row balcony. Well shit, nine hundred dollars each. Umm, do I want to pay that just to hopefully get a romance started? Go for it. I click the square to buy. Good, I'm in. Hooray for Gina.

Hooray for stupid would be more like it, my keeper laughs. Just go away. I don't want your input, thank you.

Credit Card information: Done.
Deliver to: Gina Wabbat, Bales Publishing, 340 Austin Highway, San Antonio, Texas 78209.
Shipping method: I check *Special overnight mail.*
Expect delivery: Monday morning by 10:30 AM, May 9, 2016.
Your order is being processed. Thank you.

This sure as hell better work. I can't believe this; did I just blow eighteen hundred dollars? Oh, well. It's done. Don't look back.

Alright, I've put it off long enough. Time to call some folks. I'll do this until Patricia and I head out to lunch, and perhaps by then I will have heard from Jonathan.

It's three–fifteen and I've just hit Interstate Ten for my appointment in Seguin at four. So far, the day has gone well. And it looks to end well.

After purchasing the Adele tickets, for two hours before noon I made calls to the partners worldwide and was received cordially. I was also able to finish my list of calls after lunch. I'm happy.

I got the call from Jonathan right before noon. He talked to Homer Johnston and they've devised a plan where the bank will send the paperwork for the loan to Jonathan and he will immediately sign and return it to the bank.

I did have to give Jonathan the figures we came up with to buy out Hunter's Almanac. The amount of the loan we are asking is slightly above that to allow for wiggle room.

Oh, something else: the bank will accept a letter from Jonathan giving me full authority to make transactions with the bank in the future without Jonathan having to sign off on it. Jeez, maybe now I do have some clout.

However, the bottom line is the same as before—deliver me. I don't want to be CEO of this company.

I reminded Jonathan to be on the lookout for Pep as he is picking up Bunny and Jack about three–thirty. He promised he would check them out to see if they have included everything that Pep requested for their weekend campout with their backwoods dad. I hope it doesn't rain.

Right after Patricia and I returned from lunch I received a call from Bill Jenkins. He asked me to stop by his Seguin office about four to discuss the ongoing negotiations he's having with Pep's lawyer. He indicated that things are going smoothly and they hoped to have a settlement agreement ironed out well before our court date in two weeks.

He said he was happy with the progress but it wasn't about him, so I needed to understand and agree to everything. Same for Pep. I can't believe this divorce might go to court without a huge knockdown, drag out fight.

I pull into the driveway right behind Patricia. She flashes that sexy smile as she opens my door for me.

"Hey, babe. How did it go with the lawyer guy?"

I exit and squeeze her shoulder. "Excellent if everything holds up. The good news is I am not going to have to go in debt to purchase his half of the house. It looks like I'll even run off with a great deal of securities."

She grins and pokes me lightly in the belly with a finger. "Great, you've had a pretty good day except for having to go to lunch with that bitch that works for you."

"Oh, do that some more but a little lower please. Actually I've had a great day so far. I fully expect you to make sure it continues into the night."

"Count on it. We can start right now if you want."

I chuckle. "With two kids, two cooks and a lonely old fool on the premises that might pop in at any time, I'd just as well wait until the moon is shining if that's okay."

We stroll into our kitchen arm in arm and set our purses and my satchel on the kitchen table.

"I want some scotch pretty soon, but I have to change out of this office garb first."

She follows me into my bedroom and assists me in removing my blouse. I watch her warily but eagerly anticipate just where she is going. Hell, I know where she is going and I like it. Now she slips off my bra, takes a breast in each hand and slightly squeezes my nipples.

"Hey, don't stop," I moan as I unbutton her blouse, strip it off and pitch it on a chair. I leave her to close the door. When I return we remove our shoes. I push her back on the bed and fall on top of her.

I remove her bra and run my hands down to her skirt waist. Rising to my knees I run down the zipper, nudge up her hips to slip the skirt down and over her ankles.

Getting off the bed I remove my skirt and panties, lay back on the bed on my side facing toward her feet. I spread her thighs as I run my fingers under her thong and insert two fingers into her warm and inviting nest. She groans as I encircle her clit before removing my hand to slip off her thong.

Now she spreads my legs and kisses my inner thighs. She inserts a finger in my fantasy spot and does a replay of what I just did. It is exquisite and a bolt of energy surges through my body, heating my blood and splashing in my sweet spot.

As if on cue, we are all mouths and vaginas eagerly clashing, sucking and tonguing feverously. I know by her moans and gasping for breath that she is already nearing the brink and I am right with her.

Harder and faster we go, trying to bring each other over the edge at the same time. "Oh, hurry" I moan between sucks. "Come with me, woman."

She murmurs a muffled, "Yes, yes, now, please."

Suddenly I lose it in the same instant that she grasps my hips and pulls me closer in her now familiar full body explosive spasm followed by glorious release.

We cling to each other and our breathing begins to calm.

"That certainly was a quickie welcome home, Patricia."

"Yeah, I couldn't wait until tonight."

I chuckle. "Maybe we should rest—take a little sexless vacation?"

"Is there a problem if I want you all the time?" she pouts.

"Absolutely not. We've both been through a long dry spell and I'm not about to back off. I want to fuck and be fucked. And the more the better."

"Good. That's what I want to hear . . . and do."

"Now can I have my scotch?"

Patricia giggles as she gets out of bed. "Maybe we should get dressed first." She opens the door a crack to make sure the coast is clear and runs over to her bedroom with her clothes and shoes in her arms.

Later we meet in the kitchen and prepare our drinks for a quick trip to the dock before Griffin and Cory announce dinner. Damn she looks scrumptious in her black string bikini. If I was a guy I would be making a fool of myself trying to get in that bikini with her. Shit, I'm going gaga over her and I am a woman—the last time I checked anyway.

I remove a sheet of paper from my satchel, stuff it in the back of my yellow bikini bottom, grab my drink and trek across the lawn. Poking my head into Jonathan's kitchen I ask the cooks if they need help. Of course, they don't. I join Patricia on the dock. Jonathan and his kids are nowhere in sight.

We don't speak as we suck on our scotches and she draws little circles on my inner thigh with her finger.

"A little higher, please," I grin.

"Earlier it was a little lower, please. You are never satisfied."

"I take all I can get because you never know when the well might run dry . . . or better yet, we'd better make hay while the sun shines. Whatever."

Patricia chuckles as she removes her finger from my thigh and salutes me with her glass. "I'll drink to that."

"Drink to what?" Jonathan says as he quietly joins us. "Damn, you guys look sexy as hell. There was a day not too long ago that I would be sniffing around trying to choose between the two of you."

Patricia giggles. "You don't have to choose, John. Take both of us—"

"At the same time," I interject.

Jonathan shakes his head cheerlessly as he takes a chair next to me and sets his wine bottle on the table. "Just leave me be, guys. As usual I don't need you haranguing me about a threesome."

I pat him on the knee. "Get my kid's off to the wilderness okay?"

He chuckles. "I wish I could see this safari without participating. Pep was dressed in camouflage like he was preparing to go into battle."

I slowly shake my head. "I hope the kids survive."

Jonathan cocks that sexy brow. "Just the kids?"

I shrug as Patricia looks on. "Hey, I'm moving on dude. He's no longer a priority. Two weeks from now he will be history and I will be boogying down the road."

"I guess it's easier when you have a bed partner, huh," he replies as he reaches across me and slaps Patricia lightly on the knee.

She raises her glass to Jonathan and winks at me but doesn't comment.

"Speaking of history in two weeks, I received some great news from Bill Jenkins today. He called and asked me to drop by on my way home."

Jonathan widens his eyes and spreads his hands. "If Bill has great news in the old divorce arena I've got to hear this. Lay it on me."

I reach my hand into the back of my bikini bottoms and draw out the paper, smell it for Patricia's benefit and unfold it. "Okay, the two lawyers have hit the high places on the divorce settlement and Pep and I agree on what they've come up with so far. They hope to have a complete agreement long before going to court so it will be just a formality—sign the papers in the judge's chamber and go home."

I read off the paper: "Here are the assets to be shared. The house, furnishings and dock is worth one million two hundred thousand. The boat's value is seventy thousand. The cars are worth about sixty thousand each, and the securities as of this week are valued right at one million one hundred thousand.

"Now, this is the shocker in my favor. When you and I were discussing our property value before, we completely left off Pep's business assets."

Jonathan holds up a finger. "I guess that's one reason you have a lawyer."

"Right. Anyway, when Pep and I married, the real estate holdings and the business itself were worth two hundred thousand. Today, they are worth over one million five hundred thousand. So the real estate business and holdings have gained one million three hundred thousand of which half is mine."

"Damn," Jonathan's mouth drops. "We were concerned that you wouldn't have enough value in your half of the settlement to buy his portion of the house. Along with getting the house, boat and one of the cars, how much are you going to walk away with?"

"About five hundred fifty thousand in securities. Pep, along with his business, will get about the same in securities. In essence, I will get the house, the boat and my car plus half the securities. Pep will get the real estate business, his car and the other half of the securities. Pretty clean deal."

Jonathan nods positively. "That's super. You don't have to go into debt to keep the house."

I grin. "And you won't need to lend me the money for the house. I still appreciate the offer."

"I really wanted to do it so you would be indebted to me for the rest of your life. I would own you." Jonathan pauses and studies me curiously, lewdly. "I still want to own you, but since you are so rich, will you marry me? I'm also okay with being a kept man."

"With all I have going for me now—expensive home, luxury car, big expensive boat and CEO of a major company—I don't think so. I'm going to have a line of gents out there wanting a piece of me. I might have them pay me to get in the lottery for my favors."

I wink at Patricia and she flashes her dimple laden smile.

"Okay," John asks, rubbing his hands together. "What about the kids?"

"Pretty cut and dried. For each kid he pays one thousand a month support until the month of their eighteenth birthday. Starting January of each year the monthly support will be raised by five percent over the previous year despite what the amount of inflation or deflation the economy records.

"He will also provide medical insurance and pay all medical bills above what the insurance allows. I will take care of all other expenses for the kids including a place to live, food and clothing, ski camps, country club membership—everything. As far as college or higher education is concerned the kids will have to negotiate with the two of us at the time."

I refold the paper and slip it back in my bottoms and smile at Jonathan. "That's about it, John. I think it's great."

He smiles. "Sounds like it. I'll bet that's a load off your shoulders, huh."

Suddenly we hear this banging coming from Jonathan's patio. We turn to see Griffin beating on a pan with a wooden spoon. She waves for us to come.

Jonathan collects his phone from his ragged bathing suit pocket and speed dials.

"Dinner."

Instantly we see Jody and Johnny running across lawns from Monica's. They beat us to the house. Our nine are down to seven for the next two days and it makes it a little more comfortable around the dining room table.

Griffin and partner have outdone themselves. They have put together a complete Mexican dinner of enchiladas, crisp tacos, beans, tamales, Spanish rice and flour tortillas. Oh, yes, guacamole and chips. There is very little talking once everyone is served.

Everyone stuffed, Griffin and Cory commence the cleanup, the kids head for the TV. Jonathan, Patricia and I head back to the dock with an arm load of liquor.

I renew our drinks as they wait. I have trouble with the bottle opener and Jonathan impatiently takes it from me.

"It takes a wine drinker to open the merlot or cabernet . . . whatever." He has the cork out in a jiff and pitches the opener on the table as I fill his glass.

I take stock of Jonathan. He looks a little better today but still has deep circles around his eyes and a face that looks tired and shriveled, probably from lack of a good night's rest for over a week.

I stare at him and he spreads his hands for me to speak. "Okay, John, you seem to be in a somewhat pleasant mood. What did you do to keep busy today?"

"Well, initially I really didn't want to go here yet, but the quicker I handle some of the stuff on my plate the quicker I can move on."

He pauses and we wait patiently without comment.

"I'm probably going to need both of you to help me out tomorrow or Sunday or maybe a little bit of both. I want to get Link moved out of the house and I want to go ahead and clear out the studio while we're at it."

I nod. "That's going to be rough on you, but you're probably right. Do you have a plan?"

"Early next month all the local art groups are getting together to have their annual sale at the exhibit hall on the fair grounds. Each group sets up their own area to sell all of their member's surplus or excess art supplies, art work, fabric and whatever they want to dispose of. The money they make goes to that particular group after expenses are paid.

"I've convinced the local art groups to take all of Link's supplies and paraphernalia, and set up a separate area to sell it all. The proceeds are to be divided by all the groups participating."

"Sounds good, John. Link would be proud I'm sure."

"There's going to be very little we have to do other than cleaning up the studio after they've hauled all the stuff off. They are coming Monday morning to move it all. All that will be left is the bed, a small desk, a little table, a couple of portable shelves, a television and a chest containing the bed linens and towels."

"Do you have plans for the studio?"

Gina De Georgio

"I'll probably get some basic furniture like a sofa and some chairs to turn it into guest quarters. What do you think?"

"That would be great." In fact I would like to try out that bed with a different person than before.

"You guys might take a walk through tomorrow or Sunday and see if there's anything you want."

"Maybe a leftover painting or something."

"For Link's clothes and other possessions I have already taken the jewelry and some other items I want to keep. I don't think the clothes or shoes will fit either of you but you might go through them. Maybe there will be some accessories you would like. You never know."

I ask, "What's the plan for the remaining clothes, shoes and accessories?"

"You two are taking the kids to the club tomorrow night for dinner I assume. Ask Preacher. He'll have the perfect solution, but whatever, we do not deliver. It has to be picked up. All of it. It's all or nothing. And I want it out by Thursday night. That will give them four days."

We turn quiet and drink. And drink we do. About ten o'clock we're surprised that Jonathan elects to turn in. He needs to. If only he could sleep. He hugs first Patricia, then me. Despite his misery he feels very good to me and I want to wrap my legs around him. I linger in his arms but he breaks it off. Well, whatever. Patricia takes it all in. She's well aware of what's going on with me. I'm glad we had a clear understanding before she moved in.

After Jonathan leaves we spend a few quiet minutes sipping our scotch. Eventually we decide that drinking would be more fun in the hot tub. We scramble over to our hot tub, refill our drinks and wade in. Off come the bikinis. We drink a little while she sits in my lap.

After a spell I've had enough. I take her glass and set it on the tub edge along with mine. Then we do other stuff. Have you ever considered all the neat things you can do in a hot tub? We've started keeping a list.

The first task of the day—breakfast. Let's see, three adults and two kids. In Jonathan's kitchen I cook scrambled eggs with sausage, gravy and biscuits. I dice to-matoes, onion, cilantro and jalapeno to make *pico de gallo* for the eggs. They waste no time in scarfing it up. I don't get too much feedback but it must have been good as there is absolutely none left. A good start for the weekend.

The kids have fled to Monica's and we can hear chatter and splashing as they swim off Bedford's dock. We are having our Jameson coffee on the patio as Patricia and I can't get enough. Too much coffee. Too much liquor. Plenty of sex. What else is new?

I'm beginning to dread pawing through Link's stuff. I hope Jonathan isn't with us. I'd rather eat a bug than go through this, but that's what he wants.

Jonathan looks worn out. He is really suffering—sunken dark bloodshot eyes, gaunt face and an overall haggard look.

"Sleep at all, John?"

He is silent, then replies wearily, "Very little. It's a lost cause. Every day I drag a little more. I need relief."

I watch as Patricia lays a hand on Jonathan's fore-arm and rubs his shoulder with the other. "I have some sleep meds if you want to try them."

He bites at his lower lip and shakes his head. "I hate to go that route but I have to get some sleep soon or I'm going to crater. I'll take some, thanks."

I can't wait any longer: "John, do you want to ac-company us on our survey of Link's clothes and art stuff?"

"I think not. You know, getting rid of her stuff is kind of like there's no going back—it's final. She's gone. And since I'm the one disposing of her prized possessions, I'm responsible for her leaving."

She isn't coming back, Jonathan. I release a sigh of tension. "Don't be so hard on yourself. It may be diffi-cult for you right now, but in the long run it's a passage or portal you have to go through to help you accept what is—to help you heal so you go forward."

He forces a chuckle. "That's what I keep telling myself. It's easy to say but difficult to do. And what the hell does go forward mean? I may be going forward into hell. Or backwards. Or whatever."

I rise and go to the kitchen and return with the coffee pot and the bottle of Jameson. I pour a shot of the liquor in their cups and top it with coffee.

Patricia twists her long hair at the back of her neck with one hand and glances sideways at Jonathan. "I suppose we can sit here all day long and get Jameson drunk."

Jonathan salutes her with his cup. "Excellent idea, but somehow, someway I'm going to have to tackle this problem. The studio is set up with the art group and hopefully you guys can arrange for the shoes and clothes with Preacher this evening."

I lay my hand on Jonathan's and squeeze lightly. "Why don't you come with us tonight, John? It would do you good to get away from here, if only for a couple of hours."

"No," he answers firmly with a grimace. "I can't bear to go there without Link. Someday maybe, but not anytime soon."

I don't respond and I see Patricia shrug.

I remove my hand from Jonathan's and stand. "Alright, Patricia, let's do it. We'll start with the studio."

She stands and follows as we leave Jonathan alone. She catches up with me and I take her hand for the remaining few steps to the studio.

I open the door remembering how I felt just a few weeks ago when I entered Link's private kingdom for the first time in five years. I gesture for Patricia to enter and she stops just inside the door.

"Damn, this is fantastic. You could live here. I remain at the door as she walks around examining everything just as I had done. When she reaches the bed she presses her hand down on it and nods:

"It'll do."

I can't help but laugh heartily. She turns and looks at me curiously. "What?"

"That's the exact same thing I said."

"Did you . . . ?"

"We did. Many times in the last six or seven weeks."

She flashes that big sexy–lipped smile. "That turns me on. I kind of figured you did. Only seven weeks?"

"She rescued me when Pep left. If it wasn't for her I think I would have gone mad."

"Does John know?"

"He suspected in the beginning but didn't say anything. He and Link had this agreement that if either had this urge to shack up with someone else on a short term basis it was okay as long as the marriage wasn't destroyed and sexual business was taken care of at home. Not exactly an open marriage but close."

Patricia's mouth drops slightly and her eyes widen. "Wow, did he ever ask either of you about it?"

"I don't know if he asked her. When Link was in Houston right before the accident, he said he was aware of how close Link and I had become. He asked if we were getting it on and I said yes. There was no particularly reaction from him."

She grins as she studies me. "So how do I measure up?"

"Say what?"

"How do I compare with Link?"

"In bed?"

"Uh-huh."

I chuckle and shake my head. "No fair. I'm not about to go there. Good, better, worse, terrible—any answer I give can blow up in my face sooner or later. So, I don't and won't openly compare.

"I will say this, then the case is closed: You are sensational in bed and I can't wait until the next time. Link was fantastic in bed and I couldn't wait until the next time. That's all you get.

"Now, I have a question for you: who was better in bed, me or Beverly?"

Patricia falls over on the bed laughing uncontrollably and I am immediately on top of her laughing with her. I kiss her—a long open–mouthed tongue twisting kiss with hands grasping at sensitive areas.

When we finally settle back to earth, she says softly, "Beverly of course."

I giggle as I get off of her and stand.

365

"Wait, you can't get up. We have to see if the bed works out okay."

"Not today. John might come in and I think that would be a little uncomfortable for us—and him."

She sobers, "Maybe even like sacrilegious. Can you imagine what he would think if he caught us fucking on Link's bed."

I offer my hand to help her off the bed. "Let's get a look at everything and get the hell out of here."

Well, for a couple of people that knows very little about art we basically don't have any idea what we're looking at. I find a sketch of *Carnival,* the painting that I expressed interest in when we were loading the van. I would still like to have the painting but that's not going to happen. So, I'll take the sketch. That's the only thing I want. I can frame it and tack it on a wall somewhere as my little remembrance of Link.

I wait for Patricia at the door and she soon joins me, shaking her head. "Nothing here for me."

One down, one to go. We head for Jonathan's house. Neither he nor the kids are around. We enter the master bedroom and cross to Link's closet.

I stop short as I get a glance of all the clothes I remember Link wearing. "Oh my, I can't do this. This is Link. I would be ripping her off."

John startles both Patricia and me as he quietly joins us and leans on the closet door frame. "That's kind of how I feel."

We turn and face him without comment.

He has tears gathering in his eyes. "Somehow I feel that to get rid of her treasures, I am getting rid of all our memories in the process. I should be saving all this stuff for . . . for I don't know what. It's really tough."

I don't have any idea what to say to this man that is definitely having difficulty with goodbye. Patricia doesn't either I assume.

I tilt my head and frown at Jonathan, "Let's allow Preacher to handle this—all of it. I know Link would want me to have some of her things, but I just can't do it."

Patricia nods her agreement and follows me past Jonathan into the bedroom. He follows.

"Dammit," he blurts out. "I don't know what I want. But whatever it is I just want it over."

Patricia and I surround him and hug him the best we can. I want it to be over also. I'm sure Patricia feels the same. So, what now?

I reach up with a single finger and wipe tears streaking down his cheek. Even when he's hurting I want to hold and touch him. To lay with him. I release him reluctantly.

"John, I have a temporary solution. It's Bloody Mary time. You go sit on the patio and Patricia and I are going to make the finest Marys ever."

Jonathan forces a thin smile and leaves for the patio. We follow him as far as the kitchen. I ask myself, we can't drink Bloody Marys all day long can we? Why the hell not? I wish Grace and Jethro were here. I'll bet we could get them to join us. Maybe even Reverend George.

Well, to make a long day short, we drank Bloody Marys all day long. We did stop to have lunch when Patricia went to Pizzaria for takeout. Fortunately Barbara Bedford's husband Jeremy volunteered to take Monica, Jody and Johnny skiing in the afternoon.

Finally it's time to load up for Saturday night dinner at the club. I'm somewhat surprised that Patricia and I are still standing upright. I caution myself about driving the boat, but I'll just have to drive extra slow because no one else other than Jonathan knows how. That will have to be high on my list for tomorrow—to teach Patricia to drive the boat.

I approach Jonathan on the patio. "John, come with us. You need to get out of here for a while."

He shakes his head no and does not reply. I sit down next to him and put my head on his shoulder as Patricia watches.

"Come on, John. We want you to go. The kids want you to go."

Another outburst: "Dammit, Gina, will you just give it up. I may never go to the club again, so just leave me be."

I raise my head off his shoulder and take his Mary glass. "Okay, John. I can refill your Mary can't I?" I wink at Patricia and head for the kitchen. I return minutes later with the kids following.

I pat him on the back. "Sorry, John, I'll try to leave you alone. Will you be okay by yourself?"

He nods as he takes the Mary.

"Can I bring you dinner from the club?"

"I don't think so. I'll have leftover pizza if I want something. I'm using alcohol as my chief fuel these days."

You're telling me. We all are. "Well, if you change your mind, give me a call. We'll probably be home by ten."

Jody, Johnny, Patricia and I head down the walk toward the dock. The kids have a soft drink and that reminds me. I head back up the walk and grab my and Patricia's Marys off the table in front of Jonathan.

"Bye, again, John."

He salutes with his Mary as I hurry back down the walk.

Johnny has already lowered the boat into the water and everyone is set to go. I hand the Marys to Patricia, step into the boat, take back my drink and set it in the drink holder.

"Yahoo, folks. Here we go," I announce as I start up the motor and back out. I shift into forward and slowly, extra slowly, pull away, taking care to point the boat in the right direction. I pick up my Mary and smile at Patricia:

"When's the last time you've been on a boat, sweetie?"

"Never have. Will I get seasick?"

The kids giggle. Crazy woman.

It takes a while but we make it without having a collision or anyone drowning that I know of. Patricia, Jody and Johnny do an excellent job of keeping this partially inebriated driver from ramming the boat into either side of the narrow slip and embarrassing myself in front of all the folks watching me dock.

Johnny grins, "Not bad for a woman."

"Watch out kid. You're liable to get walloped beside the head. Right, Jody?"

She laughs. "Mom did that once for saying the same thing to her."

"No she didn't. She couldn't catch me."

"Alright, you guys have your phones in case we get separated. We want to leave here about nine–thirty. We'll probably eat in the bar upstairs if you want to join us. Otherwise eat in the restaurant with your friends. Whatever, please eat something besides pizza or hamburgers."

They are off in a jiffy and I step out and offer Patricia my hand in assistance. "What do you say we get a Chivas and see if we can find Preacher before we eat?"

She flashes that luscious smile but doesn't reply. We head to the downstairs restaurant bar.

As we approach the bar Patricia grins and points out her favorite bartender, William. We find a couple of empty stools and get settled in.

"Oh, crap. My lucky day," Bill mutters as his eyes lock with Patricia's. "Let me guess: two Chivas Royal Salute and a splash."

"Right, Bill," she replies with a syrupy voice. "Say, do you still have my image emblazoned on your brain?"

He grins, "I went in to have brain surgery but they couldn't remove it."

"Too bad, Bill. If you were a woman it wouldn't matter."

"Well, no kidding. That's something I really need to know," he snaps back sarcastically. "I'll get your drinks." He shuffles off.

I chuckle and squeeze her on the thigh. "Be nice. He just wants to get in your pants."

"Yeah, right. Fat chance. He's dealing with some pretty big odds that that is not going to happen."

"I gather. Right now, considering your preferences, I'm just glad I'm a woman."

Patricia flashes that ultra–sensuous smile and I melt. Just as William walks up with the drinks she tilts her head at me and says loud enough for him to hear: "What do you say we go find a closet somewhere?"

He presents a painful frown as he sets the drinks on napkins in front of us. "Come on. Give me a break. That's cruel."

Patricia and I laugh as we toast each other in the mirror.

"Bitches," William mumbles as he trudges off. "Two bitches that could do a lot better than what they've got tonight."

We sit quietly watching each other in the mirror when I catch a glimpse of the man in black. I turn and wave for him to come over.

He grasps my hand and flashes that incredible full–faced smile. Damn, this man is sinfully sexy. I wonder what he's hiding. Is there a secret woman in his life that he has chained in the closet? Even better: I wonder if he would chain me in his closet.

Gina, you still need help. Get a life for god's sake, my keeper comes through loud and clear. Just leave me be. I'm trying.

"Gina, it's good to see you. Did you bring Jonathan with you?"

"He said he's not ready. I brought his kids." I turn toward Patricia. "Preacher, this is John's helper at BP, Patricia Goodwin."

He takes her offered hand in both of his. "Patricia, I'm so proud to meet you. You guys having dinner with us this evening?" He holds onto her hand and she curiously watches him. I can tell he's impressed with Patricia and she with him in spite of his being a dreaded male.

Patricia presents that easy sensuous dimpled smile and it isn't lost on Preacher. "Yes sir, later. John sent us to ask for your help."

"Of course I can help. Whatever John needs."

I interject: "He wants to recycle Link's clothes, shoes and accessories. He will give them to you or a group of your choice if they'll come pick them up. As you know, Link was a fancy dresser but there will be few women that can fit into them."

"Hey, this is great. I know several organizations that would love to have them."

"Good. John thought you would. He only asks that they pick them up by late Thursday."

"Tell John someone will be there about ten in the morning on Tuesday. If there's a change, I'll let you know. Should I call you or John?"

I take out my phone and pull up my number. He adds it to his contacts.

"Okay, guys, I have to keep it moving—you know, people to see and things to do. Tell John thanks and to hang in there." He's gone in an instant.

Again Patricia and I study each other in the mirror. She speaks to the mirror,

"Interesting man. Where did you find him and does he make house calls?"

I chuckle, "Yeah right. As if you would be interested." I grab her thigh and squeeze.

"Umm . . . don't stop. Just curious. You know, I have been so happy the last few days, I would be thrilled to just forget dinner and sit with you, your high powered scotch and the mirror. And I mustn't leave out your high powered body."

I add with a grin. "Or William the unlucky bartender."

"Unlucky is what he gets for being male."

I cock a weary brow. "Damn, you've got it bad. There's some great guys out there that would just love spending a little quality time with you. Preacher and the bartender are two."

She rolls her eyes for my benefit. "Yeah, right. Show me just one so–called great guy."

"I just might do that. Yeah, I just might do that."

She holds up both hands defensively. "Wait a minute now. Don't you be doing me any favors."

I don't reply other than wink at her in the mirror. "I'm hungry. Are you going to eat with me or stay here and pest William?"

"I just might do a little of both." We stand to leave and she motions for William to come over.

She puts a quiet finger up to her lips then cups her hand around her ear indicating she wants to whisper. He tilts an ear toward her and she plants a lingering wet kiss on his cheek.

He is paralyzed in surprise before jumping back and grinning at her. "Someday, somehow, you are going to get yours. Just expect it." He flashes a genuine smile and walks back to the other end of the bar shaking his head.

Is she playing sexual games or is she just tormenting him? Whatever, she's mean. Rub it in why don't you?

As we walk by him with our drinks in hand, she calls out to him: "Just make sure what I get is Chivas Royal Salute, babe."

He grins and waves goodbye to the both of us. This has become a friendly gender war; As far as I'm concerned there will be no winner. Only two losers.

We climb the stairs and the usual table is waiting overlooking the docks below. We order and when our food arrives we silently eat. Patricia has chosen fried quail, wild rice and a vegetable salad. I have the veal cutlet with asparagus and linguini. This is the only real food we've had since breakfast—it seems like three days ago. We follow the meal with a glass of Jonathan's usual merlot. See what you're missing, John.

The rest of the evening is uneventful and we arrive home just before ten. Jonathan of course is across the way alone on his dock. Not for long. The kids sprint up to the house to watch a movie.

"Good evening, Mr. Bales. I trust you have stayed out of trouble since we left."

"That I have," he retorts as he does his usual salute with this wine glass. "No action here except for four boats of game wardens chasing a wayward fifteen foot alligator."

I click my tongue. "John, your life is just so dull. You should let Patricia and I show you how to enjoy life."

He slowly shakes his head and takes a sip of wine. "I'm not going there, Gina, so give it up."

Patricia can't stand being on the sideline. "John, I heard that before I came on the scene you were a real . . . uh—what did they say?—party animal."

He points a threatening finger and grins. "You heard wrong, lady. And whoever told you that doesn't have any idea of who I really am and it's obvious that . . . well, never mind." He sips his wine as he looks out over the darkened lake. Conversation over.

"Preacher has someone to pick up Link's stuff. They'll come by Tuesday with a van about ten o'clock."

"Good. Thanks for doing that."

"Did you eat anything?" Patricia asks.

He holds up has wine glass. Let's see, at least two hundred fifty calories a glass. That make about two thousand calories. I'd say that's enough to sustain me."

I turn to Patricia. "What do you think?"

"Maybe with dessert."

"Aha," John blurts out. "My kind of woman. Are you taken?"

"More or less."

He chuckles. "More being woman and less being man. Is that correct?"

"Pretty much," she grins and winks at me.

"Oh, well. Maybe some other time."

I merely shake my head fiening disgust. "John, you are full of it. But we love you anyway. And by the way, do Patricia and I ever have a proposition for you."

He waggles a finger at both of us and dourly shakes his head. "No, a thousand times no. I'm not going there."

"Just thought I'd ask John. I meant no harm." I rescue his wine glass from the table and take a sip. "Umm, not bad. I don't suppose you—?"

"Of course I do." He stands and walks over to the storeroom and brings back a bottle of scotch, water, ice and two glasses."

"Wow, John, Thanks," Patricia and I say in unison.

"I take care of my support group." He prepares two scotches with his usual drunken flare. He hands one to each of us and toasts with his merlot.

In the moonlight we can see tears well up in his eyes. "Here's to my friends that are loyally standing by me in my time . . . my crazy time in bringing to an end this eleventh day of being lost in my own world. I love you both and I need you both."

We clink and sip.

"Oh yes. And I think I will now consider a three-some with you two ladies."

373

We stare at him stoically. John you are full of shit.

He scratches his head. "Not? he asks."

"Not," Patricia and I reply in unison.

We drink in silence. Patricia grins and sadly shakes her head at me.

"I saw that," Jonathan snaps. "I'm not the crazy one. You two are."

We don't reply.

Sunday morning. Oh, Sunday morning. We all slept late except for Jonathan—he stayed in bed late. No one—meaning Patricia or me—wanted to make breakfast so I headed out to Chilo's to get tacos. As usual they were scarfed up with no complaint.

Afterward the kids headed off to Monica's and we sit on the patio with the usual Bloody Marys. This has got to stop. We've been drinking from morning until late at night forever. After the first drink Jonathan disappears, I assume to his office to sulk. Later Johnny comes back from Monica's, mumbles something about fish bait and heads to the freezer.

Patricia leaves to refresh our drinks just as Johnny passes by and heads down to the dock. Jody joins him and they talk before Johnny retrieves a fishing rod from the storage room. Jody watches as he baits his hook and flips it into the water.

"What's going on down there?" Patricia asks as she sets my drink in front of me.

"Thanks. Looks like Johnny is fishing. Jody is just hanging as far as I can tell. I'm a little concerned about them. I feel that John in his own misery has kind of deserted them. And I have too. They are the ones that really need someone to hang onto and no one is there for them."

"So, why don't you quit concentrating so much on John and try to support them a bit more?"

I think over what she said as I release the usual breath of tension. I take a long drag from my Mary. "Yeah, you're right. I need to do that."

"So what's the problem with right now. Go talk to them and see how they really feel. Maybe you can get some ideas about how to support them."

I force a smile at my friend and lover. "Why haven't you mentioned this before?"

"I didn't move in with you to be your keeper. I don't want to rag on you about anything except sex, and I don't have any need to complain about that except I didn't get any this morning."

I don't comment as I study her. "I'll try to do better. Right now, I think I'll go down and feel them out a bit."

"Want me to come along."

"Probably best not."

She tilts her head and smiles. "Good luck, woman. I'll be watching. If you need a refill hold up your glass."

I'm off wondering just exactly what I'm supposed to say to two orphans.

I join them and we share less than enthusiastic hellos. I sit in the chair next to Jody and everything about her reminds me of her mother. I sit my Mary on the table in front of me.

"Any bites, Johnny?"

"A couple. They must be small. They nibble at my bait until it's gone but they don't take the hook."

Then the silence sets in. I take a sip of my drink and wait. I have no idea what to say or ask.

"I miss mommy," Jody says hardly above a whisper.

Johnny looks back at her and then at me warily.

"How about you, Johnny?"

He looks at me with a pained look. He lays his fishing pole down, walks over and sits in the chair on the other side of me.

"Yes, I miss her a lot. Every day I think she is going to come back but it never happens. She never comes."

I take a sidelong glance at Jody to find her eyes tearing up. I don't know what I'm going to say or do but I do know I'm at the right place. They need comfort from their hurt and Jonathan is not providing that comfort. One way or another I have do that—for them, for me, for Jonathan and for Link.

I spy the swing on the far corner of the boat dock hanging from the cypress tree. I have to be able to touch them if they will let me.

I stand and offer my hand to each. "Come sit by me."

Jody readily takes my hand. Johnny reluctantly. They follow me and sit on each side of me on the swing. I gradually push off with my feet to get the swing moving.

"I miss your mom too, a whole lot," I say softly as I put my arms around them. Jody snuggles into me. Johnny tenses a bit but doesn't move away.

"Like you, Johnny, every day I expect to see her but she's never there. It makes me feel very bad and lonely and I don't have anyone that understands how I hurt. I don't have anyone to tell how much I miss her."

Jody lays her hand in mine without looking up at me. Johnny gazes up and I find tears banking in his eyes. Jeez, I've hit the right note. Just push on.

"Sometimes I just want someone to ask, 'Are you okay?' but no one ever does. Do you guys feel that way?"

Johnny nods and I can see his tears increasing. Jody squeezes my hand just like Link used to. Damn, Link are you here with us?

We are quiet as the swing makes a little squeaking sound with each change of direction. I decide to wait before I say anything else mainly because I have no idea what to say.

Johnny softly breaks the silence. "I want things to be like they were before . . . before. . . ."

I finish for him: "Before your mom died. Me too. Every day I want to see your mom and say her name. But I know it's not going to happen. She has left us and I'm sure she wants us to go on, to live without her. I know that would make her happy.

"I don't want to live without her but I have to. I need to. It's so hard and I've got to keep trying. That's why I need someone to talk to—to tell them I'm hurting."

Again, silence but I can sense little wheels turning in their brains.

Jody nods as she looks up at me with teary eyes. "I will listen to you," she says hesitantly.

"Me too," Johnny follows.

Now my tears. "Will you guys tell me when you're hurting?"

Johnny nods and Jody again squeezes my hand. "Yes, I want to tell you."

"And will you come to me to just talk about stuff—anything?"

They both nod.

"Then I have a big favor to ask. Can I come to you when I just need to talk? Sometimes adults and even Bunny and Jack don't want to listen to me about what I want to talk about."

They both nod and Johnny flashes a hesitant smile. Seeing this, Jody smiles. I hug them closer and both melt into my arms. A small victory for healing.

"Okay, Griffin and Cody can't come today because Griffin's family is having a reunion. Patricia and I will take you guys skiing if you want."

They take me up on my offer and I suggest that we have lunch at the club buffet. They can ski up there and afterward they can ski as much as they like as we head back in this direction.

We skip up to the house and announce our plan to Patricia who readily agrees. I look in on Jonathan to invite him knowing he will decline. He does.

Gina De Georgio

EIGHTEEN

Monday morning, Interstate Ten. Potentially interesting day ahead. Yesterday afternoon went as planned and I definitely feel my talk with Johnny and Jody was beneficial to me and the kids. More so if we make a genuine effort to follow up. Jody even insisted that she sit next to me at lunch. That's great. I certainly can't take Link's place but I can stand in for her the best I can if needed. Jeez, what would I do with four kids?

Since Griffin and Cory weren't able to cook our evening meal I volunteered and asked Jody and Johnny to help me out. They readily agreed and Pep delivered the campers in time for them to pitch in. They had fun cooking but it was one noisy and crowded kitchen. But I think we are onto something. It is time for the kids in both families to start taking some responsibility by sharing household duties.

While we cooked, John had walked down to the dock with his merlot and I suggested Patricia join him to keep him company. She readily agreed. I also suggested she try to get in his pants but she definitely didn't think it was funny. It would've been fun to watch nonetheless. Actually it would be male and female attempting to get away from each other.

I've instructed Patricia to cancel the board meeting this morning because frankly we don't have anything to discuss or decide. I've also asked her to see if she can get me an appointment with the owners of *Hunter's Almanac* so I can present our offer. Probably won't work, at least for a while, but I have to get the ball rolling.

I roll into the parking lot and Clement is waiting in his little cart in Jonathan's parking place next to mine.

I know what he's here for and I chuckle. I roll the window down when I come to a stop.

"What's up, Clement?"

"Monday's donut day," he grins.

He certainly needs a donut. He looks to weigh about two fifty with a large amount of it in his gut. "Sorry, no board meeting today, so no donuts."

"Well, damn . . . uh, sorry ma'am. It's just that you buy the best donuts. I think I've become a junkie."

I laugh. "The first ones are free. The rest are very expensive. I'll get you hooked so you'll have to pay me top dollar for more."

"Yes, ma'am. Well, you have a nice day." He starts up his little cart and whirrs away.

I enter JB's personal domain and she greets as usual offering her fragile hand. "Since you are top dog nowadays I get to see you more. That's good."

"No, JB, that's bad. I don't want to come to work every day. I want my old job back.

"I assume Patricia is here. I forgot to look for her car."

"About ten minutes ago."

"I'll check in with her before I end up on the fifth floor." I turn to leave but stop and turn back. "Oh, yes, I'm expecting a package sometime—"

"Oh, I forgot," she interrupts. "It just came a few minutes ago." She reaches over the counter to retrieve it and hands it to me. "Overnight. Must be pretty important."

"Kind of. Thanks JB. Well, I'm off to see the wizard."

I ride up to the seventh. When I open the elevator door I am greeted by the smiling woman I slept with last night.

"I can't imagine that you have anything to smile about since it's Monday morning and you have nothing ahead of you for the next five days but drudgery."

She tilts her head slightly and presents a wide–eyed smile. "Oh, to the contrary. I have the possibility of having lunch everyday with this sexy lady. I also have a chance of being laid on that massive leather sofa in the meeting room. It should be a fantastic week. How was your weekend, ma'am?"

"Probably about the same as yours."

"Well, in that case I'm very happy for you. What now?"

"You canceled the board meeting I gather?"

"Done."

"*Hunter's*"

"The owners don't get in until after ten. I told the secretary to set you up for eleven. They will call if there's a problem."

"I'll leave here about ten–thirty. It's not far. Say, why don't you go with me and we'll catch lunch afterward."

"Yippy." She claps her hands and squirms in her chair just like a child. "See, it's just like I said. Lunch with a sexy lady."

Damn, maybe the leather sofa is a good idea. "I'll holler at you about ten. Otherwise I'll be holed up on five. See you." I turn to leave.

"If you have time later today, I'd like to show you that leather sofa."

I don't answer as I punch the elevator button to an immediate ping and the door opens. I step inside only to hear:

"I'll bet you would have taken that offer three weeks ago."

The door closes and I impatiently take the short ride down. The door opens and I hurry to my office. Opening the package I find the tickets. I put them aside, leave my office and walk around the corner to knock on Chris' door.

"Yeah, come in."

I open the door to find him surprised to see me. He lifts a brow as he looks up.

"Hey, lady. What brings you to my cubbyhole?"

"Chris, if you don't have something going on right now can you come to my office on this floor for a few minutes?"

His laugh is so sexy. "You forget, you're the boss. Everything stops when you beckon. I'll be right there."

I close the door and head back to my office. I leave the door open and sit at my desk. He stops in the doorway and raises his hands palms up.

"What's going on?"

"Close the door if you will." I gesture for him to sit.

He does. He crosses his legs and fixes those blue eyes on me waiting. Shit, maybe I should ask him to go to the concert with me.

I smile easily at the hunk sitting in front of me. "First off, this is not business. Second, I'm attempting to interfere in your affairs and you are welcome to tell me to bug off at any time and I will."

He cocks his brow but doesn't respond as he stares at me. I feel as if his eyes are penetrating my thoughts.

"Thirdly, I am interfering with my new renter's life and she would have a kitten if she found out. That would be Patricia."

He chuckles and shakes his head. "Sounds like you are up to something devious or naughty."

I smile. "Or both. I really don't know how to start this other than jump right in. I usually wouldn't even consider going here but I think I can help you out and maybe her too."

He grins as he waits.

"Look Chris, I know you have been trying to get a second look from Patricia and in my opinion she has not only been rude to you but she has been downright mean. I feel for you and I feel for her because I would love having someone like you sniffing at my door."

He chuckles. "Close. I'm a bit smitten over her and she won't even speak to me. It's very frustrating. If it was any other woman, I would have given up a long time ago. But there's something pushing me toward her and I'm not going to stop. I can't."

"I have a plan if you're interested. I guarantee it will get her attention. Maybe it won't work but I think if you are patient it will get that second or third look. If you can just get past all these barriers she has put up against men you will win her over."

"She's lesbian?"

"You don't already know that?"

"Of course I know it. I just wanted to hear it from you."

"But that doesn't deter you?"

"Bottom line, she can put all the women in the world against me and I still have the advantage because I have something they don't. Also, I'm a pretty cool guy even if I do say so myself. But it won't happen if she won't open the door."

"Good. I'm glad you shared that with me."

"What's your plan?"

"Adele."

"The singer?"

"Yes sir, the singer." I reach in my top drawer and take out the concert ad.

Handing it to him, he skims over it. "Friday night. That's got to be a hard ticket."

"As she found out. When the tickets went on sale, she waited about an hour to get online. By that time all the cheap seats were gone. All they had left was floor seats at five thousand or better a shot—way out of her range. She had looked forward to this concert for about six months and let it slip away."

"So I assume you have a plan."

I slide the tickets over to him and he picks them up. One look and he looks back at me and grins. "Damn, front row balcony. These aren't cheap. Where did you get them?"

"Some ticket outlet. Someone had asked for a refund and I just happened to be searching that site when they posted them. I jumped on it and scored."

His blue eyes dance for me. "Cool, Gina. This is just so cool. It certainly will get her attention."

I hold up a cautionary finger. "Don't get your hopes too high. I've already learned in the past week she will be a tough nut to crack. Lots of animosity toward men and very vocal about it."

He chuckles, "I guess I'll have to review my salesmanship manual, but I'm game. If it takes a bribe to get her attention I'm all for it."

He pauses and studies me with those piercing eyes. "Why are you doing this?"

"I wish I knew. Crazy I guess."

"Well, win or lose, thanks for helping me . . . and her out. If it works I'll sing at your next wedding. Now, what do I owe you for the tickets?"

"Nothing. This is my gift to her if it works. I do have one stipulation however: if it does not work by tomorrow afternoon I want the tickets back. I can get my money back if I return the tickets thirty–six hours before concert time on Friday."

"Alright, I'll get my special 2016 PowerPoint cranked up and hit her up early this afternoon."

"Again, I have to caution you. This will not be easy. Call on my cell immediately after you talk to her. If she turns you down, I'll work on her from this end. I can say the same things you do and she will hear it differently because I'm a woman—I think."

He cackles, "This is going to be fun . . . and interesting I'm sure." He again looks at the tickets. "I wish I was an Adele fan."

I laugh easily. "Funny, you'll have to listen to Adele's sad, woe is me songs in order to impress your woman. I love it."

Chris stuffs the tickets in his shirt pocket, stands and offers me his hand. "I still don't know why you're doing this but I'm going to give it my best shot. I hope you never see these tickets again."

I release his hand and smile. "There's one last little caveat: if you don't make this work you're fired."

He laughs and those blue eyes sparkle. He turns and leaves. Damn, I wouldn't mind standing in for Patricia. She sure as hell better not blow this.

My cell rings. It's Patricia: "*Hunter's* called. One of the owners is not coming in today so I set you up tomorrow at ten. Is that okay?"

"Well, suddenly I don't have anything pressing for today. If you don't have anything for me I'll get to work on my column."

"Hold it woman. You do have something pressing. You're having lunch with the most sexy and beautiful woman in the whole wide world."

"Oh, that. I forgot. Talk to later, sweetie."

I got mounds of work done on the column and lunch with the most sexy woman in the world was uneventful except for dealing with the still grieving Juanita. I finally told her to call *Juan* and cry on his shoulder. She said she would.

It's one–thirty and Chris just called to say he is about to drop in on Patricia unannounced. I wish him luck and now I wait.

At two my cell rings: "Gina, Chris. She turned me down but I think she was battling with herself. At one time her eyes actually teared over. There's a big conflict going on with her."

"Okay, Chris, stand by. I'll go up right now and see if there's anything I can do."

"Thanks, Gina. I'll be waiting for your call."

Immediately I'm on the elevator riding up to seven. The door pings open and I find Patricia sitting at her desk bawling. Huh?

I walk over and stand in front of her desk. She is so lost in her emotions that she doesn't realize I'm there. I reach over and touch her on the shoulder and it startles her."

I project the biggest surprised look that I can muster. "Patricia, what's the matter. Why are you crying? What's happened?"

"I don't know. I don't know why I'm crying. I just can't stop."

Wow, do we ever have a confused child here. Apparently Chris has opened her up and exposed what she thought were her hard core beliefs about her sexual preferences. It might take a while to get to the bottom of this. I don't have any idea where to start.

"What happened, Patricia? Did someone call you? Did someone say something to you? I don't understand. Can I help?"

She wipes her tears with a tissue being careful not to smear her makeup. Cool. Protect your looks at all cost.

"Chris came by."

"Chris Hunter?"

"Yes,"

"Chris came by and now you're crying. You can chew him up and spit him out without a second thought. What could he possibly say that you can't deal with? I've seen you in action. Nothing bothers you."

"He asked me to go to the Adele concert with him."

"And I assume you told him no. What's the problem with that? It's nothing that you haven't dealt with before, but you're crying. This is not the Patricia I know."

"I don't know why I'm crying, but I can't stop. I don't know what's going on with me."

"Okay, start from the beginning. Chris shows up. Then what?"

She grabs a tissue and blots at the tears as I pull up a chair next to her and sit.

"He handed me tickets to the concert. I noticed that they were very good seats. I was really surprised. Then he asked me if I would go with him."

"You said no. What happened next?"

"He asked, why not? I said that I don't date men."

"And he said?"

"He said that he wasn't asking me to go on a date. He said he just wanted me to go as a friend. He wasn't looking for any type if romantic encounter. He just thought I would like to go to the concert."

"And you said?"

"I said no, I can't. Then he asked if there is some type of lesbian rule that states you can't go to a concert with a friend that just happens to be male?"

"Good question. And your answer?"

"I didn't have an answer. I just told him thanks for asking but I wouldn't be going with him to the concert."

"What did he do then?"

"He smiled and touched me on the shoulder. He said to call if I change my mind and left."

"Were you okay with that?"

"Apparently not. He barely got on the elevator when I started unraveling inside. It's crazy. My feelings are in turmoil. My mind is all confused. I don't know what's going on. I'm just trying to be who I've been the last five years. But I feel like I am rebelling against myself."

I chuckle. "Sounds like your mind is at war with your heart and soul."

"What do you mean?"

"Five or so years ago you decided that you were through with males that didn't treat you like you thought they should. And rightly so. So you made the decision that you were through with them, and that was also good for you. You've been comfortable with that choice for a long time.

"Now comes the dicey part. Your soul all along has not been in favor of your choice but it doesn't interfere. It's your responsibility on the physical level to choose what you want to do and how you do it.

"Oh boy. Then comes the heart's involvement which you have no control over; things get confusing.

"Next, in this mix you add the female temperament in your relationship to the opposite sex and all these hormones on both sides are going ballistic. Crazy things suddenly happen that your mind just cannot control.

"So you listen to your mind while your heart, soul and physical body are rebelling. Your heart and soul disagree with your mind so they, you, cry in frustration."

She wipes at her tears and I offer the tissue box. She takes a handful. "So, what do I do?"

I shrug my shoulders as I shake my head. "You don't do anything."

Through the tears she forces a laugh. "After all this, you say I should do nothing. What kind of deal is that?"

"You asked the wrong question."

"What is the question?"

"So, what would you do—not I do?"

"Okay, what would you do?"

"I don't know."

In frustration her crying intensifies. "Why are you doing this to me? I asked the question you wanted."

"Because I have another very important question to ask before I answer what I would do."

"What is that?"

"You have to give me a quick answer and tell me exactly how you feel."

"I'll try."

"The question is simple: what kind of physical feelings have you been having about Chris lately?"

Her brow draws together and her teary eyes squint in thought. "I feel attracted to him. There's a crazy energy between us that I cannot explain, but it makes me feel good. It makes me want to feel more. It makes me want to be around him."

"You've been suppressing this feeling?"

"Absolutely, I'm trying to."

"Because you don't want to get involved with another male no matter how fantastic this person might possibly be or how the involvement with him could change your whole life?"

"I guess." She pauses as her eyes search mine. "Tell me what you would do."

"Without a doubt, I would go with him but keep my distance. I have to keep in mind that this is not a date. We are just friends going to the concert. However, I'm going to be relaxed and take in his friendship—and that energy that you mentioned.

"I'm going to talk about what comes to mind and listen to what he might have to say. I don't expect or want anything from him. I just want to laugh and have fun with him.

"After it's all over, I will think about it. I will think long and hard about it. I may say, no more; I've had enough. I may say I want to look into this a little more. I might even hazard a casual date with an easy exit. If the physical feelings increase I will acknowledge them but cross that bridge when I come to it. Above all I will be cautiously open to him."

I notice she has quit crying; her tears are dry. She doesn't reply and I don't comment further. The decision is yours, babe. However, the way I see it, if you don't go with him you will regret it. You will regret it mightily. You had better go for it, girl.

Patricia releases a long slow breath and suddenly I know her decision. Her whole continence has changed. That old anti–male barrier has been lifted, if only a bit. It isn't completely lifted by any means but a beginning is good. That alone can set her free. I wait.

"I think I need to call Chris. Do you think he will come back up to talk to me?"

I nod at my lover—perhaps my lover for only a little while longer. "Yes, he will come back. Please tell him what your rules are on the concert trip. You can change them later if you wish."

She dials and waits. "Chris, this is Pat. Could you maybe come back to see me? . . . Okay, bye."

"Alright, I'm leaving it with you, babe. Good luck."

The elevator stops on the fifth floor and the door opens. Standing there waiting is Chris.

He cocks a curious brow and I smile as I step out of the elevator. "You're in dude. Don't screw it up."

He nods and passes a finger over my shoulder as he enters the elevator sending those familiar sparks cascading through me. "Thanks, Gina. I promise I won't."

As usual Griffin and Cory have cooked an excellent dinner. They cleaned up and left immediately after eating because they are in the midst of finals at TLU and want to get in some last minute cramming. Their last day of classes is Friday next week and they are definitely looking for a change of pace even if it is only being nanny and yard man for the Bales and Wabbits.

The four kids have glued themselves to some space movie from Netflix. Jonathan, Patricia and I have headed for his dock for a little boozing.

Jonathan studies Patricia. "Gina tells me that you have convinced Chris to accompany you to the Adele concert. I'm not much of an Adele fan but I think that is going to be a blast."

Patricia smiles easily and sneaks a peak at me. We haven't discussed what transpired during their second meeting today.

"Yes, I think it's going to be fun. I really don't know what will happen, but we have agreed to just go and have fun with no expectations of each other."

She certainly seems relaxed at this point—a far cry from this afternoon. I assume that's good. I guess we'll find out.

"Did you work out any of the details for Friday?"

"Yes and no. First off, he doesn't want me to drive home alone late Friday night and insists on bringing me home. But then he has to drive both ways. I don't want him to do that either. So I guess we'll see."

"Umm . . . I suggest that we stash him in the studio so he can drive back to San Antonio Saturday morning. That way he can spend a while getting smashed with us on the dock before he turns in."

"That's a great suggestion, John. Patricia, you could ride in with me Friday morning and your car wouldn't be hung up at BP over the weekend. This is your deal however. You do what you need to do or what you're comfortable with. You might not want Chris to spend the night here."

She reaches back and runs her fingers through that long hair like I have learned to do, except I kind of grab a handful in the heat of battle.

"That sounds like a good idea. And no, I don't mind his staying on the premises. This situation is so fragile for both of us; I don't think either of us will likely make a wrong move and screw the whole thing up."

Jonathan strokes his beard and we wait while I have a mini fantasy about stroking his beard and everything else.

He replies: "I suggest you throw it out at him and see what he has to say. I kind of think he will go for it because that way both of your concerns will be alleviated."

Patricia silently assents.

Good. Let's keep the ball rolling. I add, "Again, this is not my deal but I would like to make a suggestion: You guys are going to have a few hours to kill after you get off of work before the concert. I understand he latched on to some relatively high dollar tickets, so maybe you can treat him to dinner at some fancy restaurant."

Patricia presents her easy, dimpled smile. "That's a good idea. I was wondering about how to fill that time. I certainly don't want to hang around BP."

"Whatever you decide," Jonathan says, "Gina and I will support you anyway we can."

"I'll talk with him about it tomorrow. If he thinks he might want to spend, I'm sure he'll love the studio. That place is so cool. I'll start the cleanup of the studio tomorrow. Thank you for your offer."

Time for another issue. I sigh and scratch my head. I know Jonathan isn't going to like what I have to say but someone has to do it.

"John, Saturday morning I noticed Johnny and Jody down on the boat dock. I went down to sit with them and see how they are doing. I know that I have been neglecting them and they need all the attention that they can get at this time.

"Well, bottom line, they are both hurting badly over Link's death. In fact Jody started bawling and said that she missed her mom and really hoped she would come back. Same for Johnny.

"Anyway, we talked back and forth and they warmed to me pretty quickly. They said that they have no one to talk to about their feelings and they feel very alone. That's my fault. I should have been more aware of their needs but I was concentrating on us.

"They should be my first concern because . . . well, because they should. At their age they need an anchor— someone they can rely on, to at least hold onto them and comfort them.

"John, I have failed them, and John, I know you have tried, but you have also failed them. They need someone to show them how much they are loved. They need someone to get down on his or her hands and knees in the sandbox with them. We haven't done that."

I have said all I can say. Jonathan is just staring at the deck stoically. Somehow I don't think this is going over well. Patricia, concerned, watches the both of us.

"You're right, Gina. I am screwing up. They need me right now and I've been unavailable. I'll certainly try to do better.

"On the other hand, it's really none of your damned business how I handle this situation with my kids. I don't recall asking you to point out my shortcomings or take over Link's duties. I've asked you before; now I'll ask you again. Just leave me be. I'll handle my kids and I'll handle myself and my grief the way I want. I don't need your help."

He is suddenly silent and the tension is thick. My subconcious pipes in: *Don't say it, Gina. Like he says, just leave him be. For you, this is still about him and his kids. Just back off. He didn't mean any of that. He is merely beating on himself by taking it out on you.*

I sneak a look at Patricia and she agrees with my keeper. She has pressed a quiet finger to her lips and slowly shakes her head. I smile and she nods.

So, what now? Who's on first, comes to mind. I swallow my last bit of scotch, stand up and head for the edge of the dock, handing my empty glass to Patricia on the way. I look back to find her refreshing our drinks.

Patricia joins me and hands me my drink as she puts her arm around me. I look out across take the moon-lit water and take a sip. "Ugh, strong, Patricia."

She smiles. "I figure you need it."

I don't answer as my mind drifts. Two weeks from now I should be a free woman. The divorce will be final. That's got to be a huge turning point for me. I need change. I need good change. Not like the last two months. Well whatever, it is going to be a crazy two weeks and I'm anxious to get it over.

We slowly walk back and sit with Jonathan. I don't want to be here. I have had enough of Jonathan for a while. I need to be elsewhere.

"John, Patricia and I are going to drown ourselves in the hot tub. We'll see you in the morning." He doesn't respond so we both kiss him on the cheek and we are gone with drinks in hand.

There was an Artic chill hovering over the breakfast nook this morning. Something has got to give. At this point I'm not about to apologize for telling the truth. After all, I took my share of the blame even if Jonathan maintains this is none of my business.

Well, it is my business because Link asked me to get involved. I don't think at this point Jonathan wants to hear that Link encouraged me to look after him, and even tried to facilitate a sexual relationship via the threesome.

I think things would be a hell of a lot better between us if he did know, but I can't tell him because I don't want him to think that it is all about me, which is not the truth. Well, maybe a tiny bit.

Jonathan just nodded when I reminded him that Preacher's people were coming at ten. I assume he will handle it. I can't help him anyway because I've just entered the executive suite of *Hunter's Almanac*.

It's a spacious room with expensive furnishings and a lone secretary who smiles her greeting.

"Hello, I'm Gina Wabbit representing Bales Publishing. I have a ten o'clock appointment with Gerald and William Cook."

"Yes ma'am. They are expecting you. Please follow me."

We walk down a long hallway and pause in the doorway of a meeting room.

"Gentlemen, this is Ms. Gina Wabbit from Bales Publishing."

They both stand as I approach and offer my hand. Both appear to be in their late seventies or early eighties. My first impression is they are on their way out and are looking for some semblance of a final payoff. I also have this hunch that they are no longer an asset to the company they own.

"Gerald, William, my pleasure."

The secretary assists me in sitting and offers coffee which I decline. No Jameson.

"Gentlemen, in past talks with you, BP has been represented by its owner, Jonathan Bales. He is on temporary leave because of personal issues. He has selected me to represent BP and I have full authority to negotiate and finalize any and all agreements that may arise with your company."

393

Gerald Cook speaks: "Ms. Wabbit. We hope that Jonathan's issues aren't of a serious nature and we send him our best."

"Thank you, and please call me Gina. I am well aware of your company's financial situation and BP's interest in acquiring it. It was then and is now our intention to offer you an option to sell your company to the Bales group with a buy out of all your debt.

"We are also aware that the clock is ticking and your company is on the brink of a forced bankruptcy. As you know, this in all likelihood will force your company to close its doors and all your employees to lose their jobs.

"It's not BP's purpose to save jobs, however in the process of a business transaction if we can save jobs that is certainly a plus, particularly to your workers."

William Cook: "Thank you for your concern for our employees. Of course we too have no desire for them to lose their jobs as many have worked for *Hunter's Almanac* decades."

I reach in my satchel and slide across three stapled pages to each man.

"This is our offer to purchase your business in its entirety and assume its outstanding debt accrued up until the date of the sale. Gentlemen, this is our only offer, and we are not open to negotiation."

William is looking closely over the offer but Gerald lays it aside. "Your final offer is to take over the debt of about three and a half million, but there is no further cash offered to buy us out."

"That is correct. Our offer is to assume the company's indebtedness and take over the business without compensation to the present owners. We have the means to keep the business running until it can again show a profit. All employees will be retained except for those on the executive level."

William frowns, puzzled. "Would you explain this clause*: From the date that this agreement is offered, no further debt shall be accrued other than that of usual business activities.*"

"That's basically legal jargon. It means, starting today, no other debt will be taken on except for that used for usual business activities as in the recent past. In other words, the company will not take on additional indebtedness by giving employee bonuses or offering buyouts to all types of employees and executives. This includes any retirement packages that aren't presently on their present employment contract."

No, William, you will not be able to quit and have the company take on more debt at BP's expense to give you a golden parachute. It isn't going to happen. If BP takes over this company you and Gerald will get absolutely nothing.

"Gina, I don't see a deadline on this agreement."

"We feel that if you are forced into bankruptcy that will be the deadline because you will not have control after that.

"If you accept our offer, you might consider this time frame so we don't get caught up in a forced bankruptcy. Although we have verbal agreement from our lender, it will take a week or so to finalize the financing after we reach agreement. Also our and your attorneys will need time to meet."

I fold my hands in front of me. "Any additional questions?"

There are none so I zip up my satchel indicating I am ending this meeting.

"Gerald, William, thank you for allowing me to present this offer this morning. All pertinent contact information is included in the material."

I stand and they follow. We shake hands and mumble a few pleasantries and I am gone. Sorry to disappoint you fellows.

I enter my car satisfied that I handled that meeting as well as could be expected. Are they going to take our offer? Probably. Sooner or later they have to realize that they are going to walk away with nothing, but they can save their loyal employees their jobs. For me it's a no–brainer but you never know.

That brings up an interesting question. If I'm still in charge of BP and we do take over *Hunter's Almanac,* I will select a manager to breathe life back into that publication. Interesting. Josh would be the logical choice but he's getting close to retirement. My favorite would be Chris, but I'm prejudiced. Oh, well, we'll see.

I press speed dial. "Hey, babe. I survived the meeting. Everything went well."

"Good. No action here as far as BP is concerned."

"Have you talked to Chris?"

"Yes, I did. He likes the idea of staying over in the studio, and he was very enthusiastic about having dinner before the concert, but we couldn't decide where. Probably something close to the AT&T Center. Whatever, I'll be riding in with you on Friday."

"Do you think I should call John to see how the great clothes caper is going?"

"I wouldn't. Let him stew. He's the one that lost it and he shouldn't be on your case anyway. You have done nothing but help and I don't care how much he's hurting, or how much he misses Link."

I force a chuckle. "Wow, thanks for the advice."

"Well, I'm pissed. He doesn't know what he has in you. Hell, he doesn't know what he has always had in you. He had better latch onto you before you get a better deal."

"He needs time to grieve."

"So grieve. But live at the same time if you have the opportunity. That's what Link wanted. He doesn't have to commit to you or ride off into the sunset with you." She giggles. "He should be riding you for sure. Every chance that he gets."

"Sounds like you're trying to get rid of me."

"If you get what you want. I think you would do the same for me."

If you only knew. "You told me to not do you any favors."

"Yeah, you're right. And that still goes. I don't want you trying to get me hooked up with some jerk, no matter if he is a so-called great guy."

"Whatever. Say, I have a few errands to run so I'm not coming back to the office this morning. Why don't you meet me at El Cabrito for lunch?"

Tuesday night, Wednesday and Wednesday night were more or less uneventful. Johnathan is in a funk and is definitely steering away from me. I have made no effort to make amends and don't intend to. I am cordial and we have our usual dock time but it is different. There is none of the comedic banter. It is just small talk, drink and go to bed at a decent hour.

That is great for Patricia and me because we have been devouring each other every chance we get. We have become even closer as time passes, but I keep in mind that either of us could get the opportunity to bolt if the right male comes along. And with her that could very well be Chris. We'll see.

On Wednesday I did drop in on the other board members to report on my trip to *Hunter's Almanac* headquarters. Most agreed that we would in all likelihood have our offer accepted but we certainly won't be holding our collective breath.

All afternoon I worked on the column to be ready for the deadline. I am feeling more comfortable with the column and each week the volume of communications increases. I can see that soon I might have to hire someone to help me keep up with the increasing workload. It would certainly be to my advantage if Jonathan came back to work and I could return to my old job.

Gina De Georgio

NINETEEN

I sneak a sideways look at the beautiful woman riding shotgun. Patricia glances back and shoots me a furrowed frown with squinty eyes. "What?"

"This is your big Friday. It's going to be a long day. Just checking to see if you're okay."

She turns on her dimpled, big–lipped smile. "I'll survive."

"I hope so. What did you decide about dinner?"

"There's this new fancy steak place not far from the venue. Some of Chris' friends have been there. They said it's great."

"Can you get drunk before the concert or do you have to be sober to understand Adele's songs?"

"I don't know but I'm certainly going to ply myself with a couple of Royal Salutes with a minimal splash."

"I suppose you will be trucking in about eleven. I'm sure Jonathan and I will have drinks ready when you arrive. I wonder what Chris drinks?"

"I have no idea. But when we get close I'll call and let you know. Do you think you and Johnny will be getting along?"

I chuckle. "If I don't make any snide remarks. You know, it's been a long time since we've been alone. That was before you moved in."

"Maybe if I hadn't been around chaperoning you guys, he probably would have been clawing at the buttons on your blouse by now."

"Very funny, Patricia dear. You can also look at it from another angle. If you hadn't been around protecting me, he would've thrown me in the lake."

Patricia chuckles and lays a hand on my thigh. "Probably true since you've been such a bitch."

I cover her hand and nudge it upward—and inward.

She removes her hand and giggles. "I think you'd better concentrate on driving before we end up in a ditch getting it on."

I smile, "Umm . . . you're no fun at all. Are we going to have lunch together or maybe you want to spend that hour meditating so the spirits will be in tune to guide you through this evening?"

"Maybe we should check out the Rainbow Salad bar. I suppose I should eat light for lunch since I'll be munching on steak later."

"So be it. I've got to do something about that trouble brewing in Brazil that I have been putting off. That will probably take all morning to sort out. Then I'll let you know what time we can slip away."

We pull into the parking lot and I assist her with her change of clothes for this evening. "Nice, outfit. I don't think I have seen you wear this."

"Isn't it neat? I've been saving it for a special occasion."

Umm, that's interesting. This is suddenly a special occasion. No comment.

Well, it's four–fifteen. I'm on my way up to seven to see how Patricia is fairing for the so–called special occasion. I find her in Jonathan's office undressing at the sofa with her new outfit laid out waiting.

She smiles her welcome and I lean back against the conference table sensing a lust bubbling up inside me at seeing her stripped down to her fancy thong. No, I'm not going there. The timing is definitely not right. Just forget it.

I see her watching me watching her. I know she is having the same thoughts. She smiles coyly. "What are you thinking?"

"The same thing you are thinking and it's not a happening deal. Just go to the concert with your friend and have fun. Maybe we can get together later—maybe not."

She grins, "Not even a quickie?"

I shake my head. "I've wanted to get laid on that leather sofa too long to settle on a quickie. So, no. No quickie. Wrong time, right place."

She pouts as, for my benefit, she makes a production of pulling on her bright yellow sleeveless blouse designed with a field of red roses surrounded by clumps of green leaves. She buttons it except for the top two. She follows with a coral knee–length skirt and red tangerine Nadira sandals. Who is she trying to impress?

It certainly isn't lost on me. This woman is to–die–for sexy. Of course, she is just going to a concert with a guy friend that she supposedly wants nothing to do with. A guy friend that is also a knockout. What's the final verdict going to be? The way I see it, there's going to be two winners or two losers and it is going to be decided by this sexy lady. The one dressed to kill.

She poses for my benefit. "What do you think?"

"So, you are just going to a concert with a male friend. One you might slay the instant he looks at you. He doesn't have a chance, but I would certainly like to have a bite after all."

"No way, lady," she smiles. "I'm ready to boogie and I am not undressing for you—perhaps later but not now."

"That may be too late, sweetie. John and I are going to be alone and you never know what might happen?"

"Very funny. Probably the same thing that has not happened between you guys for the last twenty years. I don't see that happening tonight, particularly since you two aren't speaking."

I jab a finger at my temple. "Oh, why didn't I think of that?" I hold the same finger up indicating I have more to say. "Do you think you might want to have a threesome later with Chris and me?"

"I'll answer the same way John does: don't even go there. I don't want to hear it. Will you take my clothes with you?"

"Yes, dear. Anything for the queen. Where and when are you guys meeting?"

"Five minutes. The lobby."

"Oh, boy. Can I go too? I want to see what he looks like. Did you arrange with JB for her to take your picture with your arms around each other?"

"I'm sure JB is gone for the day and don't you get any ideas. You can observe but no talking. And no pictures for sure."

"Yeah, it would probably go viral and Beverly would see it. Wouldn't you be in a fix?"

She shakes her head with a tight grin and hands me a box with her clothes. "Follow me. Remember, no talking."

I salute. "Yes, ma'am. I'm at your service, ma'am."

A moment later the elevator door pings open. Chris turns from looking out the window and his jaw doesn't drop—but close. And she too seems to be mesmerized by Chris. Somewhere way in the background I hear the Hallelujah Chorus. Or is it Jingle Bells? Whatever.

"Hello, girls. You look, uh, chipper, Pat."

"Thank you."

Chris smiles at me "Well, Gina, do you want to go with us. I'm sure we can find an extra ticket"

"I probably would if it was George Strait."

"I understand that. Alright, Pat, we'd better go so we don't have to rush dinner. Since you're buying I just might have two steaks."

She smiles and actually takes his arm. My gosh, it is the Hallelujah Chorus.

"Bye guys. Have fun. Call when you're ten minutes out. We'll have drinks on John's dock. What's your pleasure, Chris?"

"Scotch will be fine."

"You are my kind of man."

Big party night at TLU for Griffin and Cory, so we eat leftovers for dinner. The kids retreat for a movie on television, and Jonathan and I do the usual dock caper. We aren't in the most jovial mood but hang out as usual.

In fact, there is very little conversation—just me and my smooth scotch and his usual merlot. I have this urge to perform a lap dance on him but I don't even know what a lap dance is. He probably wouldn't appreciate it anyway. Whatever. So we just drink. A lot.

Jonathan studies me in the moonlight. I like it when he studies me, even if he is in a funk lately. He's still sexy. I wish he would practice it on me.

"So, lady, are you sad?"

"Why should I be sad?"

He shrugs absently. "You may be losing your new-found lover only a week after she moved in."

"Could be, John, but you don't know the whole story about this little concert fling. I instigated it knowing full–well she might want to jump right into the sack with Chris, leaving me high and dry."

"How's that?"

"I want you to know, sir, I purchased the tickets and convinced Chris to ask her to go with him to the concert."

"Really? I'm impressed. You connived to set up your new lover with another potential lover. That's just asking to be shot out of the saddle."

"I'm fully aware of that. But, we have an agreement—at least I do—that if either of us wants a male partner, which is my goal, the other will step aside. If I can help her find a male type match and pry her away from her lesbian ways that's what I will do—even at my own expense."

"Umm . . . it'll be interesting to see how this pans out. I don't know who to root for. It seems to me, you can win and lose at the same time."

I think about that for a short time as I beam in on his beard wishing I could run my fingers through it. Sexy.

He waits and I eventually reply. "True that, John, but I'm confident something fabulous is going to happen to me real soon. I don't know what it is but it's going to be big time. I'm ready and waiting. My stuff with Patricia is just play time so it won't be a super loss if she bolts."

At eleven my phone rings: Chris and Patricia are just around the corner. Jonathan's mood changes as he prepares their drinks.

We soon hear their light chatter as they come down the walk. My eyes lock with Patricia's in the moonlight as they approach. I don't pick up any tale–tale signs of 'yea or nay. She does wink however when they get close.

Jonathan rises to shake hands with Chris. "Welcome to God's country, Chris. I hope you had an enjoyable concert with this lovely lady."

"Hey, we had a great time. I even enjoyed what's her name, uh, Adele."

I hand each a scotch and they sit next to each other between Jonathan and me. I touch Patricia lightly on her hand. "How did it go?"

She bubbles over with her answer: "It was a fantastic concert. The energy level was out of sight. It made the hair on my arms stand up. Crazy."

"So you weren't disappointed."

"Oh, no, not in the least. I'd go back again in a minute."

Chris looks out across the lake with the moon reflecting on the water. "Wow, it's so peaceful here. Gina, do you have a room I can rent also?"

I chuckle, "I don't have any room left in my boarding house, but I'll bet John would rent you the studio. Just wait until you see it. Anybody would want to live there."

I stand and offer Chris my hand for him to get up. "John, let's show Chris his bed for the evening before we all get wasted. Later we might not be able to find it ourselves."

The three of us follow Jonathan up the walk toward the studio. He suggests that Chris get his night bag from his car and we wait. He returns and we continue our walk. Opening the door, Jonathan turns on the light and Chris peers in.

"Now this is home," he beams. "I like it."

As Jonathan shows Chris around, Patricia strolls around the room as if it is her first time here. She sits on the edge of the bed and presses her hand against the mattress and winks at me. I get the message and I want to hop on the bed with her. She fills the room with energy and she is so sexy. Even more now than earlier at BP. She is absolutely glowing.

We finish the tour and stroll back to the dock. Everyone's drink refreshed, we sit and enjoy each other and the lake. It is extraordinarily quiet on the lake for a Friday night, even this late. No boats, even in the distance.

As Jonathan and Chris stand at the edge of the dock in animated conversation, I squeeze Patricia's hand and she smiles.

"Are you sleeping in my bed tonight?" I whisper softly.

"Of course, but that comes later. First you are going to get royally fucked. I can't wait."

I release her hand and place my hand on her thigh. "What do you say we go now? We've visited long enough. If the boys want to continue, that's fine. I don't want to wait any longer. I've been wanting you since this afternoon when you were tormenting me by undressing and flaunting your sexy body."

A little later we announce that we can't stay awake any longer and prepare to leave the boys to their own chatter. I inform Chris that the coffee is on a timer set to go off at daylight if he wants. I also suggest that he sleep until noon if he desires.

Patricia lightly squeezes Chris on the forearm. "Thanks for the fun evening. I'm glad you invited me."

He smiles but doesn't comment.

We're off and undressing before we reach the bedroom.

I wake about ten to find Patricia gone. Well, so much for getting a little in the morning. The sex was out of sight last night. Apparently Chris stirred up some old dormant hormones because this women virtually attacked me, leaving nothing to the imagination. Then she came back for more. And more. Well you get the picture. I am completely spent. But certainly not complaining. Thanks for getting her warmed up, Chris.

I find Bunny and Jack glued to the television. At what age do kids stop watching Saturday morning cartoons? Or do they ever?

I spy Chris and Patricia seated at the table on the patio drinking coffee. I add a gracious amount of Jameson to my coffee and join them.

"Morning, campers. I trust everyone slept well."

Chris greets heartily as he reaches over and pulls out a chair for me. "Morning, ma'am. I slept like a baby. Thank you for your hospitality. It was so much better than having to drive home last night."

Patricia does not speak but squeezes my arm and winks. That's enough for me. At least for right now.

"Are you folks ready for breakfast?"

Both protest that I shouldn't bother, but I stopped at the supermarket on the way home yesterday specifically for breakfast. I am going to warm up the chili I made last night to top off scrambled eggs. I also bought two cans of those super biscuits and packets of homemade gravy. I'm happy.

After two cups of coffee and a lot of small talk, I leave for the kitchen to prepare breakfast. I spy Jonathan, Jody and Johnny joining Chris and Patricia. After a short visit the kids pass by me on their way to join Bunny and Jack. They say a quick hello as Jody pokes me on the behind with a finger and smiles. That's good.

To make it easier I decide to serve breakfast buffet style. After getting it ready I announce to the kids to serve themselves and I join the adults outside.

"Morning, John boy." I pat him lightly on the shoulder from behind and he touches my hand briefly with his fingers. I guess that's better than nothing. Still his touch sends shock waves cascading throughout my body.

"Breakfast is served people. I suggest you make yourself a plate and bring it out here. It is so nice this morning."

Chris and Patricia pad into the kitchen for a plate and I remain with Jonathan.

"Get any sleep last night, John?"

"A little. I find if I drink a lot and stay up as late as I can, I sleep some. Pat's meds also help some."

I grab his coffee cup and head for the kitchen. Returning I set the coffee in front of him and the Jameson bottle nearby so he can add as much as he desires. I follow him, adding a little bit more to my coffee.

"What's on your schedule today?" I ask flatly in an effort to start up some kind of conversation.

He shrugs absently. "Probably the same as yesterday."

"And the day before that," I add without expression.

Chris and Patricia return with full plates.

"Well, thank you for making me a plate, Patricia," I say with a feeble attempt to pull her plate toward me.

She slaps my hand lightly. "You keep your clammy lunch hooks off my plate, woman. Go fix your own."

I chuckle as I get up to head for the kitchen. "Oh, touchy, touchy."

Jonathan shakes his head sadly and follows me to the kitchen.

Soon the four of us sit quietly stuffing ourselves and I wink at Jonathan. "When are you fixing the Marys, dude?"

"An hour ago. They are cooling down in a pitcher in the refrigerator as we speak. I will pour as soon as I finish off this great breakfast. Thank you for doing this."

Chris studies Jonathan with his piercing blue eyes and John shrugs. "What do you have on your mind, Chris?"

He smiles widely. "You people drink a lot. Does it ever stop?"

Jonathan chuckles. "We only drink once a day and no, we never stop. Do you want to try the greatest Bloody Mary you will ever have the chance to drink?"

Chris smiles but shakes his head as he glances at Pat. "No thanks, John. I'm going to hit the highway in a little bit and don't want to . . . you know the story."

"Why don't you hang around here for a while? I assure you we'll provide some basic entertainment."

"Like drinking Bloody Marys," I add.

He steals a glance and winks at Pat. "Hey, thanks guys, but I have a contractual duty that I must perform."

Patricia remains silent. That is good. At least for now.

Chris stacks all of our empty plates to take to the kitchen as Patricia watches him closely. I wonder what the score is but I can't quite read her. I can't wait to hear what she has to say—if she's made any earth-shaking decisions.

Chris returns and walks down to the studio, returning shortly with his belongings. "People, I have thoroughly enjoyed this little visit. Perhaps you'll allow me to return sometime when I can stay longer."

We follow with the customary goodbyes.

"Again, thanks."

Patricia rises from her chair as a signal she will walk him to his car. Their small talk soon fades away.

"What do you think?" Jonathan asks.

I throw up my hands and shake my head. "Who knows? I can only guess."

I'm already on my second Sunday morning Bloody Mary and it is definitely not my last. I again opened my big mouth to John last night and he has not been too amicable to me this morning. But he still makes a perfectly bloody Bloody Mary and keeps me company.

So what happened last night to keep me on Jonathan's bad list? I was a little tipsy when time came to board the boat for our usual Saturday night at the club. Alone with John, I again pressed for him to come with us because of Jody and Johnny's sake as well as for his own healing. In fact I practically yelled at him: "Get amongst the people at the club; you need that!"

He was about ten degrees above unhappy for my intruding in his affairs and yelled back angrily, "Just leave me be, Gina! I've had enough of your trying to push me through this. I'll do it my own way and take as much time as I want."

I suppose he's right but I'm just trying to help. That's what Link wanted so I probably won't shut up. I guess I should worry if he stops making these splendid Bloody Marys.

Patricia is her usual bubbly self but she has not said a word about Chris, good or bad. So I'll wait. I am certainly not going to ask. Right now she is going along for the ride with Griffin and Cory as they take the kids skiing.

The boat comes in at a full clip and Jody releases the ski rope to glide up to the dock. The boat circles around and pulls into the slip to switch skiers. Patricia steps out of the boat and holds up her empty Mary mug and I smile.

John refreshes mine and provides a fresh one for Patricia so I scoot down to the dock as the boat slowly backs out. Apparently she has elected not to go on this round as she is sitting on the dock in a scrumptious black string bikini. I have this urge to touch her, to feel the energy emanating from her.

"Had enough boating for the day?" I ask while handing her the Mary.

She takes a long slow sip. "Damn that man makes a fine drink." Another sip. "It was fun but I need to talk to you about Chris."

About time, lady. I study her for a hint but she shows no signs of what she has decided. After Friday night I can go either way but in the long run I hope she decides in Chris' favor. I wait in neutral.

She releases a long sigh and I see tears gathering in her eyes. Oh, no, she is giving him up.

"I want to see if we can . . . if we can make it work for the two of us. I really want it to work out. I really like him a lot and there's so much more that I'm feeling. It's so new to me. I'm confused about what I feel but I want to feel more. Damn, I want him right now."

Yahoo. She's hooked. She has fallen for this guy big time. Now it's my turn for tears.

"That's a relief, babe," I say as I take her hands in mine. "You are not making a mistake. This is real and you will make this work. Tell me more. When did you know that you wanted to do this—to be with him?"

"At noon Friday when we were at the salad place. Suddenly it hit me. I knew that I wanted to be with him and that I was going to make it work for me. This is about me, because I know if I'm happy being with him then I can make him happy too."

"I kind of felt when you left BP with your arm wrapped around his you had pretty much decided but I wasn't sure. How does it feel when you touch each other?"

"I was determined that I wasn't going to get physical with him Friday so we didn't touch a whole lot. At the concert when our arms touched I thought that I would explode from the sheer energy that passed between us. It took my breath away.

"When we got into the car afterwards I really wanted to touch him and I wanted him to touch me. I now know exactly what they mean when they say she's hot. I was boiling."

I laugh. "I know you were boiling. I was the recipient of the effects of the hormones raging in you. You attacked me. Three times you attacked me. It was astounding."

She presents that big lipped smile and slowly shakes her head. "I have to tell you and I hope you don't get angry. I pretended that you were him. I loved every second of you, uh, him."

I double over laughing and recover enough to hit her lightly in the stomach with my fist. "Damn, Patricia. This is a first for me. And I hope it's the last. Here we are, fucking away and all the while you are fantasizing that I'm someone else, and a male at that."

I lean over and kiss her lightly on the lips. "This certainly puts a new slant on a lesbian affair."

"Are you unhappy with me?"

"I don't know if I'm furious or super happy. I definitely am glad you liked it. Personally I thought it was sensational."

"So what happens to us?" she inquires as she watches me intently.

"Right now that's your call. I like our situation but I will leave you alone if that's what you want. If it was me I would probably tell you that it's over. I want to concentrate on my man."

She nods in thought. "I have enjoyed my time with you so much. I don't want to lose that." Her eyes are pleading. "Can we stay like we are now, at least for a while?"

I shrug, "It's entirely up to you."

She grins in relief. "Then we can still take a nap later?"

"I'd love to . . . as you say, take a nap with you. Have you told Chris of your decision?"

"No."

"I have a suggestion and you can take it or leave it. Take him out to lunch sometime next week. Before you tell him what you have decided, ask him about his past including his divorce. I'm even curious about that. How could any woman leave this man for someone else?"

"Then you tell him about your past. Everything. Don't leave out anything that might cause a problem if he hears about it later. All of it will be out in the open. Take it and live with it or leave it as fast as you can."

She thinks about it for a minute, then there's her big smile. "Good idea. I like it."

"Everyone entering in a new relationship should do that, especially if they are the jealous type which you are not.

"I suggest one more thing. To keep your first date—if you want to call it that—on familiar ground, why don't you invite him to come skiing on Saturday and we can all go to the club that night.

"Later if you decide to stay with him in the studio it will be familiar to both of you. If you want to make waves together you have your choice of two hot tubs."

I pause in thought and she waits. "If you choose to do that and things don't work as planned, you can always come get in bed with me, with or without the fantasy."

With lips pressed in determination she slowly shakes her head. "That isn't going to happen." She pauses and grins. "How about a threesome? Is that in the offing?"

Other than Patricia and Chris sneaking gaga glances at each other, the Monday morning board meeting was boring and uneventful. At Chris' suggestion a short time was spent on my column and where it was headed. They made several useful suggestions and comments. I appreciated their input because the column is not a company deal. Anything to help out the boss. Am I all powerful or what?

We drag through Tuesday and Wednesday at work. I worked on my column Wednesday readying it for Thursday's deadline.

Patricia had lunch with Chris on Wednesday and they hashed out their pasts, and apparently have agreed to live with it. Chris was elated that Patricia is giving them a chance to be a couple. He will arrive at the lake midmorning on Saturday to ski in the afternoon and do the club bit on Saturday night.

Apparently Patricia is dead set on bedding down with Chris in the studio Saturday night as she went shopping for the necessities—candles, two bottles of fancy wine, heavy duty scotch, some fancy lubricant in a tube and exotic massage oil. Oh, yes, and twenty condoms as she isn't on the pill.

She and I are in the studio to make sure everything is in order for the big night. She empties the three plastic grocery sacks of goodies on the bed just as Jonathan walks in. He has to examine each item individually, nodding his approval. The condoms are the last item.

He raises a brow for Patricia's sake as she grins at him: "Damn, Pat, it looks like you are planning on some big time action. Can I watch?"

She flexes that big–lipped sexy smile. "The only way you can watch is if you participate, and we already know your answer on that one."

I give a thumbs up to Patricia. Jonathan merely shakes his head and leaves as we laugh.

Jonathan still hasn't let go of my tirade against him last Saturday evening. He is more distant than ever and seems to be making no progress dealing with his grief and moving forward. It will be three weeks tomorrow since Link died.

Personally I think a good tumble in the sack would do wonders for him. It doesn't have to be a commitment thing—just recreation. And Link specifically wanted that for him. Frankly, I don't get it, and of course I don't get any either.

Thursday was dull except for lunch at El Cabrito with the new lover in waiting. I stopped by Bill Jenkins office on the way home to okay the final draft of the divorce documents. Yahoo, soon I'll be a free woman. A lot is coming down and my life is going to be even more interesting for sure.

It's Friday and Pep did his usual three-thirty kidnapping of Jack and Bunny for a weekend of whatever. He didn't seem to be in a very good mood, but hey, that's not my deal. Just get my kids home safely on Sunday and sign the divorce agreement on Monday. Thanks. Over and out.

Griffin and Cory did the cooking chores tonight. I'm getting used to being waited on hand and foot by these two angels. One of these days I hope to be able to repay them in kind. They cleaned up quickly and headed out to one of their end of year TLU parties.

John, Patricia, Jody, Johnny and I sit down at the water as the sun goes down. Jody is sitting next to Jonathan holding his hand. That is good.

But suddenly there's something better to do. "Jody, Johnny!" comes a shrill call from down the way. It's Monica. "I have a movie!"

Jody and Johnny are gone in an instant.

We silently contemplate tomorrow. Well, there are two of us actually anticipating tomorrow. Jonathan is as grouchy and morose as usual but Patricia is glowing. Me, I guess I'm somewhere in the middle. Although it's early I've already made up my mind to get totally soused tonight and go to bed early with my sweetie—Patricia, not John.

Chris shows up promptly at ten to join Patricia, Jonathan and me on Jonathan's patio. Jonathan retreats to the kitchen and returns with a tall Bloody Mary for the man of the day. He takes a sip, nods appreciatively at John and sets the drink on the table in front of him. He smiles at Patricia and scans her face with those weird captivating blue eyes.

He touches her on the shoulder with one finger and I swear sparks fly between them. I have the urge to put my hand between them to see if I can feel the energy arcing back and forth.

He looks at Patricia longingly "Are you skiing with me today?"

She flashes her big dimple–riddled smile. "I hope to ski with you, among other things. It's been about eight years since I've skied, but they tell me it's the same as riding a bicycle—you never forget. Same with the other things."

Chris smiles smugly. "It's all in the legs."

"Hey, I've got the legs." She grins as she stands and raises up her gauzy red cover–up to reveal a red string bikini and the legs she was talking about. "What do you think?"

We watch as Chris tilts his head and grins. "Looks like they'll do."

"They can do a lot of neat stuff."

We laugh and Patricia makes a production of pulling down the cover up. This woman is sexy and she knows it. Hopefully she can practice it on someone of the opposite sex and the sooner the better.

I wear my favorite yellow bikini. No cover–up for me. Jonathan is shirtless in his usual tattered red bathing suit. He's sexy as all get–out, but what else is new.

Chris is wearing blue jeans, a tight fitting red T–shirt and white canvas deck shoes. He also is one sexy guy. I'm certainly jealous of Patricia.

So it's back to small talk and Bloody Marys. Approaching noon we decide to boat down to the club and have a sandwich before ski time. Chris changes into his bathing suit and we load the skis, Jody and Johnnie in the boat and we're off. Jonathan of course stays home. It's over three weeks, Jonathan. It's time. Whatever.

We linger over lunch and follow up with another Mary. Finally it is agreed that Chris will ski first. He enters the water from the dock and dons the skis. I slowly back the boat out and Johnnie pitches him the tow rope. I stretch it out and he nods his good–to–go and we're off. He pops out of the water and pulls outside of the wake before circling back and popping the skis as he jumps the wake. He is good and I am impressed—with his skiing and his body.

Next up: Patricia. It takes her a while to get set up but eventually she gives her thumbs up. I gun the motor and she pops out of the water, then glides back and forth across the wake, her wet dark hair streaming down her back. Pretty damn good for not being on skis in eight years. I am impressed—with her skiing and her body.

Her athletic legs give out after about fifteen minutes and she releases the tow rope. We circle back around and Chris assists her getting in the boat. She is ever so sexy as her long wet hair cascades down her back and the wet droplets of water on her skin shine like diamonds in the sunlight. Chris eyes me and winks. What have we created for this lucky man?

She smiles at her lover–to–be and touches him lightly on the cheek. The energy appears to be spewing back and forth between them. Are they going to explode? Can they wait until tonight? Probably not. I don't know if I can stand watching them until tonight. Let's get it done.

Jody and Johnny get their skis ready and enter the water to ski together. Soon they are off and we head for home. They drop off at the dock and we circle around and enter the slip.

I decline to ski but encourage Chris to take the boat out to familiarize himself with its handling in case I want to ski later. He and Patricia return about an hour later. There's not much creative activity you can do on a boat in a crowded lake. Oh, well. Later. It's a happening thing for sure.

Gina De Georgio

TWENTY

The sun is beginning to drop out of sight as we prepare to go to the club for dinner. Because I refuse to give up on getting Jonathan out of the house, I leave Patricia, Chris, Jody and Johnny on the patio and walk down to the dock where Jonathan is just starting in on his merlot.

"Hey, John boy. We're getting ready to go to dinner. Do you want to come?"

I wait as he delays his answer. Somehow I feel like I have once again blown it. I'm right.

His eyes flare. "No," he snaps at me. "I told you to leave me alone about it. I'll go when I'm good and ready."

I swallow nervously as my heartrate steps up and my face flushes. I don't reply but I'm not leaving either. I fix him with a stern stare just to see what's next. Nothing, so I wait.

With pressed lips I begin to shake my head slowly, woefully as he watches.

His gaze is unfaltering and his jaw muscles clench, unclench, clench. "Do you have something else you want to say?" He asks tersely.

I wince at his tone and nervously clear my throat followed by inhaling and releasing a deep hopefully calming breath. "Yes, John, I do." My voice is weak and unsteady.

"Link died twenty–three days ago at about this time of day. It was tragic. We have grieved and we will certainly grieve some more. And that is good. The only way we can go on is to do what we have to do to get through it.

"I suppose everyone has to decide on the path that is best for them. You have chosen your path. But your path is going nowhere if you lock out the world around you.

Like I told you earlier, you have to get amongst them—people, your family, your workers, everyone."

Well, he is listening but I have no confidence that what I have to say will phase him.

"You cannot mope around here every day. The only time you have been out is when you took the Kings to the airport, and that is not good. You have to get involved again—and soon."

I trudge on wishing I could just suck it up and leave him to figure everything out for himself.

"I'm not saying you shouldn't grieve. Grieving is necessary hard work. But you have become a drunken hermit. That won't do and you know it. Get back in the system. Get involved with your kids. Run your business. Go out to dinner. Go to McDonalds. Anything."

He stares at me with narrow angry eyes as he dismally shakes his head. "How about fucking my neighbor? Is that part of it?"

No. No tears, my keeper chimes in. *Don't cry over this. Be calm, tell it like it is and walk away.* I raise my voice an octave—not yelling or screaming but close. "That too if you have that desire. That could be part of healing if you want it to be. Particular when that neighbor has been an important part of your life for twenty years."

Suddenly calm, he replies, "Umm . . . maybe I do have that desire, but I also intend to honor and respect the person I lost. There has to be a proper time period for my restraint, and I don't know how long that will be."

Tell him, Gina. Tell him what Link requested from you before she died. He has to hear that.

No, I will not go there because it would sound so self–serving. I do have a desire for him but I will not tell him of Link's request.

I struggle to find words that will get through to him. "I can't argue that, John. Do what you have to do. I'll try to respect that and support you and the kids the best I can."

I can't hold back the tears any longer and there is nothing else I can say. Without further comment I turn and walk up to the house in a full blown bawl.

Patricia leaves Chris and the kids and meets me halfway down the walk.

"What did he say?"

I wipe my tears with the back of my hand. "He said . . . he has to honor and respect Link and he would do so until . . . he didn't know how long."

"Did you tell him about Link's request?"

"You know I can't do that."

Patricia grasps me by both shoulders. "Well, no one says I can't tell him. Go up and get you a stiff one. This might take a while. And don't let the kids come down. They certainly don't need to hear what I have to say."

She releases her grip on my shoulders and marches down to the dock. I walk slowly to the patio where Chris has a scotch waiting.

I wipe the tears and sit with my drink as Jody and Johnny eye me. Soon Jody sits beside me and takes my hand in hers just like Link used to do. Uncanny.

I watch, we watch as Patricia drags a chair over and sits in front of Jonathan. She talks calmly and he listens without, as far as I can tell, any comment.

After a few minutes she stands and pats Jonathan on the shoulder. She makes one last comment before leaving him and calmly strolls back up the walk.

She smiles proudly as she approaches. She stops in front of me and touches Jody on the top of her head with a single finger. She peers down at me and says simply: "Done."

Chris watches curiously but doesn't comment.

Patricia hands Chris her glass. "Can I have a refill? Folks, lets load up the bus. Time to start the night."

Chris hands her the scotch and they hold hands as they stroll down to the Wabbit boat. Johnny, Jody and I also hold hands as we follow along. Johnny carries my drink in his free hand.

We ignore Jonathan on his dock as Johnny lowers the boat. Chris states the engine and we are on our way. Jonathan makes a special effort to look the other way as we slowly ride by. Jody waves but gets no return.

"Crazy bunch of people you're getting mixed up with, huh, Chris?" I ask as we get up to speed. He merely smiles with a shrug. Patricia, sitting shotgun smiles at him and pats him on the knee. He winks. Let the fun begin.

We finish our drinks before we arrive and dock. The kids hit the soda bar and we stop at the restaurant bar for refills. Lo and behold, William is tending and he eyes Patricia standing shoulder to shoulder with Chris as they lean on the bar.

He raises a brow and smiles thinly. "Is this some sort of miracle or just an aberration?" he asks Patricia.

I step aside to get a better view as I know this conversation should get amusing.

Chris is watching curiously as she answers calmly, "You know, Bill, sometimes when you least expect it your life can change in a flash. This is probably not a miracle but it's pretty damn close."

He eyes Chris and replies. "Cool looking dude. You didn't just run into him in a crowd somewhere. So, there must really be a miracle at work here."

She chuckles and gestures with her hand: "Chris, this is Bill. Bill, Chris." She tilts her head toward Chris. "Until you came along, Bill and I were considering running away together. The only reason we didn't is he couldn't stand the company I keep."

They shake hands and Bill replies to me, "Of course we were. I would have been struck down by lightning if that happened."

He turns back toward Chris and grins. "You must have some kind of magic spell over her. I'm impressed." Back to me. "Well, win some, lose some. I guess I'll have to return to the brain surgeon. I can't go on forever with this image."

Patricia and I laugh. Chris scratches his head.

"Okay, let me see if I can get this right: three Chivas Royal Salute with a splash. Is that correct."

We nod and he's off to the mixing station.

"What's the brain surgeon stuff?" Chris asks.

Patricia grins, "His original pickup line was my image is emblazoned on his brain. Later he found out about my sexual preferences. He then told me he went to the surgeon but they couldn't remove it from his brain."

Chris chuckles and shakes his head. "I feel for him. Your image has been inscribed on my brain for months now."

Bill returns with the drinks and sets them on a napkin on the bar in front of us. "On your account, Gina?" She nods.

He turns to Chris. "You want some advice?"

"Go."

"Hold on to her tail. She's a tiger."

We laugh and Chris nods. "I think I know what you're talking about. Thanks."

We scan the restaurant for the kids. They have chosen a table close to our old Saturday night group but far enough away that we don't feel the need to make introductions.

We order and as we wait for the food to arrive we slowly sip our drinks. Somehow the kids have arranged to sit on either side of me and it doesn't go unnoticed by Patricia and Chris. Jody—or is it Link?—covers my hand with hers and smiles—Link's smile.

The food comes and we eat. Speaking for myself, that sandwich for lunch didn't last very long and I am really hungry, even eating a roll that is forbidden by my bikini restrictions. My quail is very tasty. The kids dig into their spaghetti, and Chris and Patricia their grilled chicken breasts.

Barely finished with their spaghetti, the kids are flagged by their cronies and they are off to the game room. We decide to head upstairs for a little more of the smooth stuff.

We settle in at Jonathan's favorite table overlooking the boat slips. The waitress already has an idea what we want but checks in anyway. In a few minutes she brings the scotch.

The DJ plays some dreamy music and before long Chris leads Patricia to the dance floor. It's show time. Their first really close bodily embrace is suddenly in full bloom and I can see Patricia's body melt into his. I can see his hand tighten against her back pulling her even closer. This is real, folks. I can see steam rising from the top of their heads. I might have to get the fire extinguisher.

Gina De Georgio

The song ends and they return hand in hand. I am definitely a third wheel. I wonder if I can coax Preacher into a short dance. Maybe not. I don't know if he even dances.

"Okay, Patricia, I have to know what you said to John earlier."

Her face turns serious. "Yeah, I figured you would. First, I don't know if I accomplished anything. I couldn't read him. At least he listened.

"I'll try to get this word for word. I told him, 'There is something I really think you need to know. And for you to get the full impact of what I have to say, I'm going to start from the beginning: It all starts with Link's dreams about dying. Deep down she really believed she was going to die. Her main concern was how devastating it would be for you after she died and how lonely you would be during your period of grief.

"'She felt that there wasn't much she could do ahead of time. She did, however, think she could persuade someone to stand in for her after her death. And there was only one person that could possibly do this.

"'That was Gina. She was well–aware of the closeness you and Gina have shared over the last twenty years, even to the point of hitting on each other on occasion but never actually having sex. Even though Gina assured Link that she would help out the best she could with you and the kids, that wasn't enough.

"'Link felt that you would not only lose a wife, but you would lose your sexual partner, which was extremely critical. She felt that in your grieving, sex would bring you closer to Gina and buffer your grief.

"'Gina wasn't keen on the idea because the two of you had never had a sexual relationship and it could never happen during that stressful time of grief. Link countered with the idea that she had to get the two of you into bed before she died because this sexual familiarity would draw you two together easily after her death.'"

Patricia pauses and raises a brow aimed at me. "Pretty close, so far?"

I nod as she continues: "'The problem was, John, you didn't cooperate. You could not be coaxed into bed

422

with Gina even though over the years you had strong sexual feelings for each other.

"'So Link came up with a big surprise. She suggested a threesome which left you confused because that just wasn't the Link you know. She didn't want to participate in the threesome, but if she could get you two together by having one, great. At least you two would have a sexual foundation that would draw you together after her death.

"'There was a problem with this. You didn't want any part of it, and you wouldn't change your mind no matter what. You even became irritated when it was mentioned. I can attest to that. So the plan didn't work.

"'The bottom line is, Link wanted you to heal starting from day one after her death. And she felt that Gina could help pull it off. A few days off from work, Link would have accepted but your completely dropping out was not in her plan. She knew you would grieve and hurt, but she also knew you would heal quicker if you stayed in the game with the kids, your work and life—and that included sex.

"'Now, before you bring it to my attention, Gina would love to get in the sack with you, a fact she's made abundantly clear, but this has to be your deal. If you don't want any part of a sexual relationship with her, she is alright with that. She just wants you to get back in the mainstream as quickly as possible—for yourself and the kids.

"'When I mentioned to her that she should tell you about Link's plan, she refused because you might think it is all about her. It is not. She has decided that she is not going to stop urging you to get back on the track as quickly as possible whether sex is involved or not.

"'That is what Link wanted of her and she says, one way or another, she is going to help you get there, for you and the kids. She is not part of the equation.

"'That's all I have to say, John. I felt you needed to hear it even though Gina objected. She is a special lady as you are a special man. I love you both. I don't expect you to reply or answer. We will now be headed to the club.'"

Tears fill my eyes. That was perfect and I am glad she did it. I take her hand and squeeze it. She smiles.

"Thank you for doing that, Patricia. Why don't you guys go gyrate a little on the dance floor? I don't suppose I can get in between you two out there. It's looks pretty inviting."

Patricia smiles, stands and takes Chris by the hand to lead him out to the dance floor. She calls back over her shoulder: "We're not sharing. Not tonight."

I release a long–winded sigh of frustration and take a hefty gulp of my expensive drink as I watch them. They look like they have just stepped out of a fashion magazine. And here I am, Ms. Walmart.

They return from the dance floor and join me without comment. We look over the railing at the people coming and going below. We spy a boat docking with a lone passenger. I turn back to nurse my drink. Patricia grasps my arm without taking her eyes off the boat. I follow her eyes to find John tying up his boat.

I motion for the bar maid. She takes my order and returns with a bottle of merlot and one glass. She opens the bottle and sets it and the glass in front of the chair next to me. As soon as she leaves I urge Patricia and Chris to dance. They know what's about to transpire so they are glad to oblige.

My back is to the stairwell so I look toward Patricia on the dance floor. She nods and I sip my drink as I feel my heartrate kick up a notch.

"May I join you?" Jonathan asks as he pulls out the chair.

I smile and cry for joy inside. "Yes sir, if you know the password. You were expected so I ordered a bit of wine for you."

"Thank you." He pours his glass about half full and sips. "We're going to have to stop meeting like this. People are beginning to talk."

"It only matters if they sign our paychecks."

"Well, since I don't work and don't get a paycheck, I guess I'm okay."

"Me too, since you sign my paycheck."

"Will you dance with me?"

"Only if it's a slow one." I glance out at Patricia and Chris to find them sneaking a peak at us. I nod and smile.

The song ends and another starts up. Jonathan stands and grasps the back of my chair. I stand as he pulls out the chair. I take his offered hand and he leads me to the middle of the dance floor where only one other couple is dancing.

Jonathan greets the couple. "You people look familiar. Do you come here often?"

Patricia and Chris beam but don't comment.

I fold into Jonathan's arms and melt as that familiar bolt of electricity soars throughout my body and splashes into my belly. I'm exactly where I need to be—where I want to be.

I snuggle my cheek against his beard and feel his hand around my waist pulling me closer. Oh, my. Through all the continual yearning, the frustration and the disappointment of the last two months I have wished for this moment.

I tilt my head and look into Jonathan's eyes to find them bordered in tears. His smile is an easy one that I haven't seen lately and I know we have just hurdled a monumental obstacle.

We have lost someone important to us and suffered because of it, and there is more grieving to come, but we really do have each other to help trudge through what remains.

The song ends and we head back to the table. Patricia flashes that unbelievable smile and kisses Jonathan on the cheek. "Hey, stranger. Good to see you out and about."

"Thanks to you. Apparently I needed a swift kick in the ass. I appreciate what you did and said, particularly when you had to know that there was a great possibility I would throw you in the lake."

We sit and quietly sip our drinks. I am suddenly so happy to be here. I touch Jonathan on the forearm and he nods with a thin smile. I think he is too. His whole countenance has changed as if a huge weight has been lifted off his shoulders. He appears to be turning back into the Jonathan I used to know. That is good—for him, for the kids and for me. I think.

I tilt my head toward Jonathan and ask, "You want to eat?"

He grins, "Yeah, I'm really hungry."

I turn toward Patricia. "We're going back to the restaurant. If you guys want to vacate this place and do something more exciting, take the boat and go for it. We'll follow later with the kids."

That smile again. "You've been reading my mind. We do have better things to do. We'll probably have another dance or two, then we're out of here."

Jonathan nods, "Looks like there's fun to be had."

Patricia tilts her hand and lifts a single brow. "And kind sir, what might you be doing tonight?"

"I'm sure I'll think of something. And since it's my first night out it'll probably be exciting."

"Bye, guys. We'll see you tomorrow." Chris says as they head back to the dance floor.

Jonathan follows up. "If you happen to be available we're going to come back for the buffet at noon tomorrow. But sleep or whatever all day if you like."

We walk slowly down the stairs arm in arm. I guide Jonathan to the game room and leave him outside as I go in. There seems to be a thousand noisy kids going tech crazy. I spy Jody in the same instant she looks up at me.

She comes over and frowns. "It's not time to go yet is it?"

"Maybe in a little while. Your dad is here to eat. Maybe you and Johnny can come out and have dessert?"

"Wow, cool. I'll get Johnny."

I leave and take Jonathan's hand to lead him to a table. The kids soon join us and look curiously at their father.

"What? Why are you looking at me like that?"

They both burst out laughing but don't answer as the waitress approaches.

An hour later we make our approach to the dock and Johnny laughs. "Careful Dad, it's been a long time since you've driven the boat."

"Quiet kid. Unless you want to get whacked beside your head."

Jody giggles. "First it was Mom, then Gina and now you—everyone wants to whack Johnny."

The boat lifted, Jonathan suggests that the kids either watch a movie or go to bed. They don't say what their choice is but they are off.

Jonathan checks out his liquor stash in the storeroom and comes up with scotch and merlot. We sit next to each other without the barrier that has kept us apart for over three weeks. It feels good without the tension. He takes my hand. He feels good without the tension.

Where do we go from here? Do we hang out here and slowly let the fires increase or do we dive headfirst into bed and stoke the fire there?

He speaks quietly. "Have you ever in your whole life been naked in a hot tub with a man you've never had sex with?"

"No, can't say that I have"

"Me neither. Want to do that sometime?"

"No. Not sometime? Now would be nice."

"Yours or mine?"

"Yours or mine what?"

"Hot tub."

"Probably mine since no one is home and we won't be disturbed."

"Let's do it."

"I have a problem."

"What's that?"

"I've never had sex before."

"Oh, only that. I'll be gentle with you."

"Never mind."

"Never mind? Now what?"

"I don't want gentle. I want rough and tumble, no holds barred sex. Take no prisoners sex. Nail me to the wall sex."

"Wow you're making it hard."

"I hope so."

"Have we had this conversation before?"

"No, but we should have twenty years ago."

427

"Maybe we should forget the hot tub and go straight to bed."

"We can't."

"Why?"

"Because we've already had the hot tub discussion and it will be wasted if we don't end up in the hot tub."

"I've got a great idea."

"And that would be?"

"Let's do it."

"I knew we would get around to that sooner or later."

He stands and refills our drinks, then takes me by the hand and we walk silently to my patio and the hot tub. I switch it on and we silently help each other get undressed—not a fancy sexy romantic undress but a medium to heavy urgent undress.

We wade in together and sit in front of his and hers water jets while holding hands and sipping our drinks. Until I have had enough. I get on my knees and take his drink. I place both drinks on the ledge of the tub.

I swing my leg over him and sit on his lap taking care to come in contact with but not injure any of his vital parts that I'm interested in.

He puts his hands on the back of my shoulders and slides them down to grasp my hips. My lips gently nibble his and my tongue forces his mouth open and quickly we are in a feeding frenzy. Our tongues do a dance together as my hands find his cheeks and work down to the beard I've always wanted to touch.

I withdraw my tongue from his mouth and trail kisses to his beard, then his neck and chest. I feel I'm about explode from desire as little volcanos are erupting all over my body. Why isn't the hot tub steaming from my heat?

I gasp and he grins.

"Having fun are you? You might take time to breathe."

"Something like that. You feel fantastic and the hot tub is wonderful, but I want you in bed where we can lay each other without drowning. Come on."

He follows me out of the tub. We collect our clothes and head for the bedroom. I throw my clothes on a chair and head to the bathroom to get towels. I pitch him one and we towel each other down, paying particular attention to the important sensitive parts.

Then the bed. Side by side we commence to devour each other. Our hands try to outdo each other as they search and explore—pinching, rubbing, stroking, kneading. Then our hands discover thighs, pubic hair and, in concert, his hands find my fantasy place as my hands explore his welcome hardness.

The urgency builds but I'm not going there. At least not yet. He suddenly draws away from me and gently pushes me on my back. He parts my legs and bends my knees. His mouth and tongue are instantly playing that sucking, twirling dance with my clit and it is exquisite. I'm boiling inside and I know I can't last much longer. He lifts my hips for a better angle and continues his heavenly assault.

I pull his head away as I sit up and push him on his back. I have no desire to work my way toward the goal so I dive right in. On my knees I take his full measure in my mouth, and he groans in pleasure. His smell is intoxicating. I can't get enough as I push on—out, in, out, in.

"Oh, Gina, you're killing me," he moans. "Please don't stop."

I am flying higher and higher and loving every second of it. Suddenly his fingers are circling my clit and I'm completely losing it.

I release him from my mouth and cry out as I go over the edge. Damn I wasn't ready for that, but I bet I have more.

I lay quietly as my breathing slowly calms. I sit and push him back on his back, swing a leg over him and swiftly mount him, driving him hard and deep into me. We moan our pleasure together. He feels so big inside of me, but I'm not complaining. I want more. I want a lot more.

I lift my hips slightly and fall back on him to his groan. "More Gina," he pleads. "Go hard."

I oblige. I place my feet flat on the bed as I squat over him. I lift my hips again, higher, and fall back. Then again. I pick up my pace and his breathing is becoming more labored as is mine. Up and drop, up and plunge him back into me.

With a groan he lifts his hips and turns, laying me on my back while we are still joined. Now he is in the driver's seat and drive he does. He slips a hand under my behind and as he thrusts he pulls my hips toward him creating an erotic collision.

He repeats and I feel him tensing up for that final big bang. Gladly I'm also gearing up for another uncontrollable point of no return.

He withdraws slightly and crashes back into me as I thrust at the same instant.

"Harder, John, give it to me. Please hurry. Fuck me hard."

He obliges and we are now in a race for that final rapture. "Oh, yes. More. Aggh . . . yes." Together we have one last spasm and crash into each other.

"Damn. What the hell was that?" he whispers.

I giggle. "Just think what we could do with a little practice."

"Umm . . . you're right. And we will be getting a lot of practice. Thanks, Link. Good planning."

Well, it's eleven o'clock and there's been no sighting of Patricia and Chris. They have probably worn each other out as Jonathan and I did. We woke up once in the night and got it on and then had a long leisurely fuck this morning.

I'm happy and Jonathan is doing pretty well as far as I can tell. He has a long way to go but I can already tell an occasional romp in the sack will help him along. It'll certainly help me along. Thanks, Link. Your crazy idea appears to be working.

Jonathan sets my second Bloody Mary in front of me and sits down. We spy the couple in question walking toward us holding hands.

They sit without comment and we all stare at each other. Suddenly we break out laughing and Jonathan heads to the kitchen for their Marys.

He returns and they sip. "There's something different about this drink," Patricia comments and Chris agrees. "What did you change?"

I reply, "We noticed also. We've come to the conclusion that the attitude of the bartender changed and that affected the drink. It's kind of a mental thing."

We drink silently for a moment before Jonathan comments: "I got a call from the local FEMA people of Homeland Security a little while ago. They recorded some strange seismic activity on our two properties all night long. They wanted to know if we felt any unusual shaking."

We laugh.

"Funny, John," Chris says. "Patricia and I will take our share of the blame, but I don't think we are alone in creating this mini earthquake."

Jonathan studies the young couple and says, "I assume everything went well for you two. I know we had quite a, shall I say, mutually comforting visit ourselves."

Patricia wears her usual sexy smile. "You don't need to tell us, John. It's written all over your faces. Congratulations. You both deserve it."

She pauses and studies me with amusement in her eyes. "Gina, you are a conniving little shit. After you said you wouldn't interfere in my love life, Chris tells me the Adele tickets were not only your idea, but you bought them."

I chuckle and touch her on the arm. "I had already bought the tickets when I made that promise so I'm clean. Now, what about you? Last night you stomped down to give John what for after you promised me the same. You'll have to admit, both endings turned out pretty damn good. Thanks for your help."

She smiles and salutes me with her drink. "Thank you, ma'am. It was a perfect plan. I am grateful to you for what you have done for Chris and me.

"There's more." She presents a hesitant smile. "I'm moving in with Chris today."

I'm not surprised but this is really quick. I stand and walk around behind Patricia and wrap my arms around her. "Good choice, woman. I'm behind you one hundred percent."

She grasps my hands and I see tears shining in her eyes. She doesn't comment as I return to my chair.

Jonathan does as he counts on his fingers. "Let's see, just nine days ago you were the great man–killer woman. There wasn't a male on this planet that you wouldn't devour if they crossed you.

"Now, suddenly you've decided that you have to live with one." He nods at Chris. "A very special one at that. He must have pushed all the right buttons for you to completely reverse course."

"He pushed a couple for sure. What's that you said the other day? Something about right time, right place." She covers Chris' hand with hers as he smiles. "That's where Chris and I are—right time, right place. And we thank you two for your part in this. It certainly wouldn't have happened without you."

"We're definitely happy for you. Okay, some news on our side. Tomorrow, Gina is getting her divorce finalized and I will be standing in for her at Bales. In fact, she has asked to be demoted to her old position. I declined. I have fired her."

Chris and Patricia don't react because they know there has to be more. They wait.

"Her column is doing so well that she has decided to hire a staff and expand it as well as make some needed changes.

"She is going to make her column more magazine friendly, meaning each magazine will have a column that serves the people that rag serves. In other words, *Gym Rat's* column will deal specifically with people that go to the gym. This will require eleven different columns each week or month depending on the rag."

I have to get involved. "Yeah, now for the first time in years I'll have to put in a full week's work."

Jonathan chuckles. "Maybe fifty hours a week."

Chris asks, "Are you going to be at BP?"

"For a while until we need more room."

432

Jonathan waits. When there is no additional comment he continues: "Now you, Chris. Gina tells me she feels the purchase of *Hunter's Almanac* is eminent. I may be asking you to take a temporary demotion in your job with Bales if the deal flies.

"I want you to immediately take over the head job over there for a few months until we can hire a permanent manager. Your mission is to get *Hunter's* back on its feet. Then you will return to BP with a sizable raise."

Chris nods. "Whatever you need. I'm for it."

"Good. Alright."

Jonathan stands to go for another round of Marys but is distracted. He points to my patio where a man in a gray uniform is knocking on my back door.

"What's this?" I cross the lawn and approach the man. "Yes sir, can I help you?"

"Yes ma'am. I am delivering a rather large item for uh—" He looks at his shipping order. "That would be Gina Wabbit."

"I'm Gina. Isn't it unusual to be making a delivery on Sunday?"

"The sender specifically asked that it be delivered on Sunday morning before eleven–thirty. Sorry, I'm a little bit late."

"I don't . . . are you a local company?"

"Yes, ma'am, Seguin Parcel Delivery. I can bring the particle here to your patio if you like."

I shake my head in confusion. "Uh, yes, that will be fine."

"Yes, ma'am. I'll be right back." He disappears around the house.

I notice Patricia, Chris and Jonathan watching and motion for them to join me. They arrive just as the deliveryman comes around the house with a rather large flat box on a hand truck. He stands the package up against the wall.

"Where was this shipped from?" I ask as he presents me with the paperwork to sign.

He answers while I sign. "It was dropped off at our location on Court Street sometime Wednesday or Thursday I believe.

I check the shipping order after I sign it to see who sent it. "There's no sender listed here."

"No, ma'am. It's also not on the package shipping label. That's unusual to have only an addressee."

I hand him the order and he says, "You people have a good day now." He grabs the handle of his truck and trails it behind him around the house.

I frown and spread my arms. "Anyone want to hazard a guess as to what this strange box contains?"

Jonathan goes into the kitchen and returns with a knife. "I guess we're going to find out."

He slits the packing tape along three sides and slips off the carton. Next he removes a thick layer of bubble wrap to reveal a large framed painting that he leans against the patio wall.

I gasp and cover my mouth with both hands in surprise as I recognize the painting:

"Oh, my God, John. It's *Carnival*. The painting that I wanted from Link."

John gazes at me confused, then examines the painting closer. He looks at me in complete surprise. "Shit, I don't believe this. What's happening here? This is totally crazy." He points at Link's signature in the lower right hand corner. "Damn."

I see Chris and Patricia watching, wondering what is going on.

I fill them in: "This is one of the paintings that was sold in Link's show two days after she died. I had expressed an interest in it when we were loading it."

"Totally weird," Patricia says as she takes a closer look at the painting. "More than weird."

Jonathan leans the painting out from the wall and checks the back. He reaches behind it and removes a small envelope taped to the back. He checks it front and back, then hands it to me.

I nervously open it. Inside is a small greeting card with a picture of a rabbit waving one paw. Under the rabbit is a handwritten note that says:

Enjoy,
LKB

Patricia looks over my shoulder and asks, "LKB?"
I answer softly with tears, "Link King Bales."

To put it mildly, we are totally shocked. As we should be. This is something we are going to have to think about and talk about. We know the answer but we don't know the question. Or perhaps that is backwards: we know the question but don't know the answer. One thing is for sure, Link is involved. In some way Link is involved.

We eventually head back to Jonathan's patio for one more Mary before we head out to lunch. I must say we are awfully quiet as we focus our thoughts on the mystery surrounding the painting.

John finally brings us back to the present. "Folks, it's time to celebrate this terrific weekend. The boat is now boarding for the great Lake McQueeney Country Club Sunday buffet."

He opens the patio door and yells for the kids before assisting me in standing. We walk down toward the dock arm in arm. It's a great feeling.

Patricia and her new roommate follow holding hands.

Johnny and Jody come out of the backdoor and run to catch up. Johnny runs down to the dock to lower the boat. Jody takes the drink out of my hand and folds her other hand into mine. Along with her, Jonathan and I smile. I'm happy.

THE END

Gina De Georgio